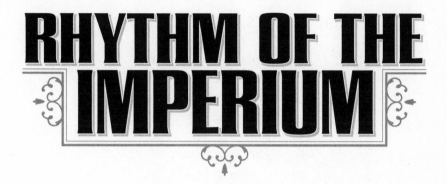

RHYTHM OF THE IMPERIUM

BAEN BOOKS BY JODY LYNN NYE

✥ ✥ ✥

Lord Thomas Kinago Series

View from the Imperium
Fortunes of the Imperium
Rhythm of the Imperium

The Grand Tour
School of Light
Walking in Dreamland
Don't Forget Your Spacesuit, Dear

License Invoked (with Robert Asprin)

With Anne McCaffrey

The Ship who Saved the World
The Death of Sleep
The Ship Who Won
The Ship Errant
Planet Pirates (also with Elizabeth Moon)

RHYTHM OF THE IMPERIUM

JODY LYNN NYE

BAEN

RHYTHM OF THE IMPERIUM

Copyright © 2015 by Jody Lynn Nye

A Baen Books Original

Baen Publishing Enterprises
P.O. Box 1403
Riverdale, NY 10471
www.baen.com

ISBN: 978-1-4767-8091-7

Cover art by David Mattingly

First printing, December 2015

Distributed by Simon & Schuster
1230 Avenue of the Americas
New York, NY 10020

Library of Congress Cataloging-in-Publication Data

Nye, Jody Lynn, 1957-
 Rhythm of the Imperium / Jody Lynn Nye.
    pages ; cm. -- (Imperium ; 3)
 ISBN 978-1-4767-8091-7 (softcover)
 I. Title.
 PS3564.Y415R48 2015
 813'.54--dc23
                                    2015033288

Printed in the United States of America

10 9 8 7 6 5 4 3 2 1

◆§ PROLOGUE §◆

The elder being called One Zang moved toward three more of its kind who stood on the tossing waves of a gas giant's upper atmosphere. They all stood immersed in infinity, watching the liberated energy flowing away from them in huge glowing explosions of radiation that created shock waves felt throughout the white dwarf star's system and beyond. One Zang enjoyed the sensation of riding the wild force through its ups and downs. It had the urge to burst forth with a wordless thought of pleasure, but reined it in. One had to retain one's dignity.

Like its fellows, the Zang's senses extended infinitely far away from its corporeal body. Their minds were rooted among the stars, but centered upon a diaphanous form that occupied a space one meter by three meters by 1.45 meters and excited wavelengths in the visible light scale close to the ultraviolet. Some carbon-based ephemerals from certain star systems had described its shape as a chopped-off tree trunk or a gigantic half-melted gray candle. It felt outward with its extended senses, touching the substance of its fellows, then into the deepness they were studying. The immediate space, for nine hexaprag in all dimensions, was serene. Perfection. The process had been a success. Nothing more needed to be accomplished there to bring that portion of the present universe into harmony. Its colleagues had done well. Truthfully, it could not recall a time when they did not.

The other three Zang acknowledged One Zang. The four of them contemplated the shock wave that spread out from the place where the enormous, misshapen asteroid had been. One Zang sent out a portion of its consciousness and enjoyed the sensation, riding it like a light wave until the energy was dissipated to barely perceptible vibrations. Charm Zang, leaner and taller than the others, sent a thread of inquiry.

"Do you like it?"

"You have removed a disharmonious obstruction," One Zang replied, overspreading its colleagues with waves of shared pleasure. It received some in return.

"The transient mass interfered with the orbit of two planets in this system," Zang Quark said. It had the most opaque form of the four. "Now, it is energy."

"It is good."

Low Zang interjected a wobble of dissent.

"The asteroid might have had a purpose one day."

"It looked bad. It had to go," Charm Zang replied. It gave off a sensation of impatience that shook them all. "See how much better it does as dark energy?"

Low Zang retreated from its stance, both physically and in spirit. It was the newest to the group, and was uncertain of its mastery of matter. One Zang noticed the withdrawal and moved to include Low Zang in the group, wrapping it in warmth gathered from the tossing inferno of the gas giant's surface. A gathering of the usually solitary Zang was rare, so it did not want to discourage Low Zang from feeling comfortable joining such conclaves in future.

"Why pull away?" it asked. "We are a unit."

Low Zang lowered its aura until it was nearly drawn around its physical form. "I did not mean to imply the action to change its state was wrong."

"It is not disrespectful. If you truly disagree, then it is wrong not to offer your input," One Zang said, kindly. "We believe in you."

"Yes, we do," Charm Zang said, moving close. The tall being chimed its empathy. "We could have brought any of the others into our group, but we appreciate *your* insights into harmony and artistic arrangement."

"You do?" Low Zang broadcast its wistfulness.

"Yes," One Zang said. It gathered the approval of the others, and focused it upon the youngster. "So much so that we are going to permit you to decide which disharmony we will dispose of next."

Low Zang was thrilled. Its person, out to the very ends of its energy streams, glowed with joy. The art that they created was beautiful, both in physical and aesthetic terms. Low must not throw away this opportunity. It had wished to be part of this unit for many ages. Eternity would be very long if it was dismissed from the group for making a poor decision.

It studied the cosmos for hundreds of hexaprag in every direction. Over eons, the Zang had rearranged or disintegrated errant heavenly bodies that interfered with the beauty of space. Low Zang turned its attention to a sector on a galactic arm that for whatever reason had never been well-furnished with stars, planets or other artifacts. Its emptiness suggested quiet meditation. It was a place much loved by the senior Zang, but like so many things in the chaotic universe, it could be improved further. Low evinced daring, a sensation that caused its fellows to hum along in tune. One gleaming ball in particular excited its interest. Its hazy blue color was not in tune with the other spheres that circled the lone, low-quality star at the heart of its system. The planet's placement seemed superfluous, considering the larger orbs further out. Only one satellite circled it. The moon was much too big for the planet. Whoever had permitted the out-of-proportion spheroid to continue existing had not paid attention to that detail.

"That one," Low said, highlighting it with a tiny burst of energy. "I feel that it does not belong there. It does not add to the flow of its system."

One Zang projected pleasure toward Low Zang.

"We have chosen well, as have you. Agreed."

"So you approve?" Low Zang asked, hardly able to accept the notion.

"Yes," Charm Zang said. Zang Quark added the pleasant regard of its assent and One Zang enveloped them all in the sense of unity, making Low Zang feel warm to the tips of its being. "That will be the next planet we demolish."

᎒ CHAPTER 1 ᎒

After my sixteenth spin, during which I realized I was becoming intensely dizzy, I leaped into the air, with both heels arching toward my back, then sank upon my left knee to the ground. My right leg extended with toe pointed in the direction of the sunset. My arms were crossed upon my chest, my back bowed to show that all energy was spent. The recorded music rose around me in a splendid crescendo, and I let my chin fall to my breastbone.

I waited for a moment, but the expected applause failed to materialize. I glanced up at my audience.

My cousins sat or reclined upon the various sumptuously upholstered chairs and crash couches arranged about the elegant private entertainment center of the *Imperium Jaunter*. Though each of them was dressed in the height of fashion and styled within a millimeter of their lives in the latest of sartorial, tonsorial and aureate splendor, all of them wore a uniform expression of befuddlement.

"I'm sure that was very meaningful, Thomas," my cousin Jil said, patting a bored yawn with a slender but heavily beringed hand, "but I have no idea whatsoever what it was you just did."

"Oh, come now!" I said, rising to my feet. A squat, cubic LAI attendant trundled up to me and offered me a towel almost glowing in its pristine whiteness from the hatch on its top side. I mopped my forehead and the back of my neck. Such was the intensity of my training for my newest art form that I scarcely had to collect any droplets of exertive moisture. That did not stop my mechanical shadow from mopping up and down the skin-tight, plum-colored bodysuit that I wore on my long frame. "That was my tribute to the final sunset we just witnessed as we departed Keinolt!"

Jil fluttered a hand and tossed back her mane of caramel-colored hair.

"Why? What is wrong with simply *saying* that it was pretty? If it was. I didn't notice. Did anyone else notice?"

Several of my relations shrugged their shoulders.

"But merely saying so is excruciatingly ordinary," I said, coming over to throw myself upon the couch beside hers. "I wish to evoke the special energy of the moment, to give it the importance that it deserved. Are we all so jaded by our circumstances that we pay no heed to natural phenomena?"

"Not at all," my cousin Xan insisted. He stretched his long feet out before him, admiring the toes of his polished bronze-colored boots, which were tinted to go with the tunic counterwoven with gold that fit his muscular torso like a glove. His entire ensemble was designed to point up his natural good looks. He had thick, dark, wavy hair and almond-shaped blue eyes startling in a golden-hued face. "But, Thomas, the sun sets every day. Why draw attention to a single sunset?"

"Because," I said, infusing my voice with as much melodrama as it could absorb without creating a distressingly cloying precipitate, "it may be the last one we ever observe on our homeworld. Has no one thought of that?"

"To be honest, no," Erita said, toying with her wine glass. Our cousin's long blonde hair had been swept into an updo of ridiculous elaboration, with the inclusion of a bamboo cricket cage, a cluster of bright red pinpoint lights and a golden charm featuring her monogram. "Travel via jump points has been safe for several millennia. This is the best and newest of the Imperium leisure fleet, and we are accompanied by military vessels to ensure our well-being, as is fitting for scions of the noble houses. So, I assume that I will see many more sunsets over Keinolt that rival the one we just left behind."

"True," I said. It was hard to argue when faced with facts. I sighed.

"But don't be upset, Thomas," Jil said, encouragingly. Her lovely, golden-skinned face wreathed itself with smiles. "Just because *we* didn't understand it doesn't mean it wasn't good."

"Oh, I know it was *good*," I said, dejectedly. "I wish you understood how meaningful it was."

"I thought it was pretty amazing, my lord," Ensign Nesbitt said, his voice hoarse with shyness at addressing me in the midst of my noble family. The big, dark-haired man seemed embarrassed to have spoken. He twisted his very large person into a series of uncomfortable postures that indicated in rapid succession abashment, discomfort, fear and admiration. I made a note of the sequence for later. It might come in handy in some of my future performances. "I never saw anyone make jumps like that outside of low-grav."

Nesbitt and other members of the small but select crew that usually traveled with me on missions for the good of the Imperium had been assigned to accompany me to the Zang sector. The *Rodrigo*, my small naval scout ship, was bestowed in the belly of the *Jaunter*, but a full destroyer led us toward our second jump point. There would be five jumps in all, with long transits in between each. Zang space was difficult to reach, not unusual considering its inhabitants. Nesbitt and the other navy personnel sat in modestly upholstered chairs arranged at the side of the chamber as though afraid to touch the bubble of nobility for fear it might burst.

"Thank you," I said, with a gracious inclination of my head. "But did it touch your soul?"

Nesbitt looked bemused, not an uncommon expression for him to wear. He glanced at our fellow naval personnel as if to gather wisdom from one of them. None seemed to be forthcoming.

"I think so," he replied.

Oskelev, a white-furred Wichu and the best pilot in the Imperium Navy, shrugged her meaty shoulders. Unlike the rest of my crew, she wore only a harness to hold her viewpad and identifier patches. Her thick pelt was more protective than any clothing up to cold-weather gear, though brilliant pink nipples and other exterior genitalia protruded therefrom. All Wichu were unselfconscious about their bodies, so humanity had perforce to come to terms with their culture and customs.

"I don't know if we have souls to touch," she said.

"Of course you do!" I declared. "Even the least amoeba, the merest slip of grass, the most distant star has a soul."

Oskelev put her candy-pink tongue between her lips and blew a derisive sound.

"Okay. What use do stars have for souls?"

"How do we know they don't?" Lieutenant Anstruther piped up.

I smiled at her. The slender, quiet brunette often championed me in arguments with the others. I thought it was rather sweet of her, though I could wax loquacious on my own behalf. I prepared to launch a philosophical argument, based upon my theories of the movements of the stars through the observable galaxy.

"I'm sorry, Thomas," said my sister Lionelle, drawing my attention away. She curled her slim legs up under the skirt of her cerulean-blue gown. Of my mother's three children, Nell, the youngest, was the one who most resembled her: petite, small-boned, waves of soft hair framing a heart-shaped face, though her vivid brunette coloring and sapphire-blue eyes came from our father. By contrast, I had acquired our father's physiognomy and our mother's sea-blue eyes and sandy hair. "I'm afraid that symbolism has never been an open book, as far as I am concerned."

"That's not true at all," I argued. "Language is a purely symbolic form of communication. Nothing that we say is concrete. Every word is a concept. Every phrase is a collection of action and meaning. Interpretive dance merely turns such symbolism into meaningful movement."

"So it's one step further removed from actually doing something," Xan, said, looking amused.

"You have it exactly," I said, very pleased. I knew I could count upon Xan to catch the somewhat wayward drift of my discourse. "It both obscures and reveals meaning. In this case, I am telling the story of the regret that we experience for leaving our home planet, coupled with the excitement for the upcoming spectacle we will witness at our destination."

"Not all gathered," said Kolchut Redius, an Uctu who was a member of my crew and possibly my best friend in the galaxy. His people rather resembled the Earth lizards called geckos, though they were human size, and their skin was coral pink with some blue scales here and there instead of green. He turned up a hand and wiggled his spatulate fingertips. "Some symbols lacking."

"Really?" I asked, feeling my eyebrows climb high upon my brow. "What did I fail to include?"

"Deeper meaning," Redius replied, dropping his narrow mandible in a humorous grin. "Mere description too simplistic."

"Well, what I did present seems to be too much for the audience I have at the moment," I said, with a pointed look at my cousins.

"Perhaps we can look at it as a game of charades," Xan said, lying back lazily and signaling for a refill. "Look, you do another one, and we'll try to guess what it is you are trying to get across."

"Later," I said. I swallowed. My throat was dry and scratchy from my exertions. "I'm parched." I waved to a different rude mechanical, which trundled toward me with its drinks tray elevated. "Alas," I bemoaned, as I settled back in the chaise longue with a cup of wine, "no one appreciates art these days."

"We all admire art," said my cousin Nalney, his broad, swarthy face widened still further with a grin. "Too bad my brother Nole isn't here! He loves to go to all the museums and stare at dusty displays. At least you move about a bit."

A bit was rather insulting, as I had flung myself hither and yon in my attempts to share the dying light over the continent that cradled the Imperium Compound, our palatial home. Still, Nalney was right. Nole would have had some interesting if not intelligent musings upon my skill. It was a pity he hadn't joined us, but he had been busy furnishing his new residence ship, a project that had taken up all his attention and disposable income for the last two years. In spite of hints and downright espionage on the part of me and my cousins, no details about the vessel had been forthcoming.

"Is there any mystical significance to your motions?" Erita asked, with a meaningful lift of her eyebrows.

I waved a dismissive hand.

"That's so three weeks ago," I said. "I had debunked so many superstitions by the time we returned from Nacer that there weren't enough fun ones left to examine. Another time."

Which, functionally, to me meant never. When I took up an enthusiasm, I embraced it with my whole person, all my time and attention and not a small amount of money. When I ceased to be enthusiastic, I tended to put away all the trappings. I always meant to go back to them, but there was always something newer and more fascinating with which I could become involved.

"Oh, I meant to mention, Thomas," Jil began, leaning toward me. "I went to visit Uncle Rodrigo yesterday. I think he knew who I was, but perhaps he thought I was my mother. He was very sweet. He gave me this pendant." She displayed an exquisitely wrought teardrop-shaped jewel of platinum and gold with a scattering of brilliant green gems fixed here and there that hung on a chain around her slender neck. "He sounded fine until he mentioned having just visited with Uncle Laurence. Is he getting worse?"

I hesitated before I answered. My father, for whom I had named my scout ship, was a decorated war hero whose health had been catastrophically affected by his experiences. He frequently spoke to people who were not there, especially his younger brother, who was off on some nebulous expedition or other. In any case, I know Uncle Laurence wasn't on Keinolt, though Father frequently hallucinated that he was.

Father's condition was a sore spot with me, as my cousins knew and were solicitous of. I had been the subject of some badinage during my school days over a visit he made during which he accused my mathematics professor of being some kind of nefarious criminal. While I agreed with him to an extent, particularly regarding the heinous character of that teacher's pop quizzes, some of my fellow students, not my cousins but some rich incomers who thought that their fortunes elevated them to an equal rank with us nobles and who were sadly mistaken, found an impaired parent to be a figure of fun. It was that day that I discovered the school had a policy of punishing those students who challenged other students to a duel to the death on matters of honor. Ah, well, one day I would find those harassers and make such cutting remarks to them that they would drop dead on the spot from mortification, without needing to resort to physical weaponry. It was not so much a matter of my own honor, but my father's, for which I would willingly die.

"What compelled you to learn to fling yourself about?" Erita asked. "Your dance, if I may term it such, looks absolutely exhausting. Why exert yourself in such a fashion?"

"Interpretive dance," I said, warming to my topic with practiced ease, "is a marvelous art form. I saw a fascinating documentary on primitive cultures that tell stories through the movement of their bodies. Language, choices, symbolism. Since we are going to see a Zang demonstration, and their form of communication is notoriously difficult for younger races to comprehend, I thought I would gain insight into them with the use of body language. I undertook a study of numerous cultures, including many of our ancestral tribes, as well as those of other races, like our Uctu friends." Here I nodded to Redius, who wrinkled his nose in his people's substitute for sticking out one's tongue or making a ruder gesture. "You see? Gestures and motions have profound meaning that it would serve us well to learn and possibly emulate. I rest my case."

Lieutenant Carissa Plet rose from her place and set her glass aside. The tall, thin blonde human was the nominal head of the *Rodrigo*'s crew, though I was its actual commander, owing to my noble rank.

"Thank you for allowing us to be present, sir," she said, fixing me with the keen gaze I had come to know and respect, if not love. "It was most educational. We must return to our other duties now."

"Must you go?" I asked. I glanced back at my cousins, all of whom had abandoned any further interest in my performance. I offered her a hopeful look. "Do you require my presence for any of these duties?"

"No, sir." Did I detect a hint of relief in that flat statement? Her countenance, which was nearly as capable of a stony expressionlessness as my aide-de-camp Parsons, gave me no clue. I tried to read her posture, based upon my new studies, and found little nourishment to my hunger for knowledge.

I sighed.

"Very well, then. We will meet again for the evening meal."

"No, sir," Plet said again, this time with open finality. "We'll take mess in the crew's wardroom from here on out with the other adjunct personnel. The First Space Lord's orders."

For that I had no answer, since the official in question was my own cherished maternal unit. Challenging Mother's authority had landed me in trouble all of my life. She ruled our family as she did the Imperium's space navy, with wisdom, discipline and remarkable affection. There was no need for me to court further opprobrium. Added to that was the fact that no matter how much I wheedled, Plet was unlikely to give in to my importunings. She was remarkably tone deaf to them.

"Oh, very well," I said, disappointed. "You won't take it amiss if I visit with you during off-shifts?"

"No, sir," Plet replied, albeit not with any enthusiasm. "Crew, dismiss."

"Aye, sir!" the others chorused. They saluted her, and me, and left the entertainment center. Plet hesitated, Her full lips pressed together, and she gave me what I could only classify as a speculative look. She seemed about to impart some further information to me, but thought better of it, and departed. I wished I could read the meaning of her gestures, but had to remain unsatisfied.

"Oh, Thomas," Erita said petulantly, as I sat down and raised my wine glass to my family members. "I thought you would have grown tired of playing soldier by now."

"Not yet," I said, with a cheerful wave of my hand. "There's still a bit more fun to be gleaned from it. After all, I do have my own ship. That's a novelty that will take a while to wear off."

"But it's so dowdy," Jil said. "The *Rodrigo* is still furnished as a purely military vessel, and that is so tedious. We all had to do the mandatory two years in academy. I wanted to put mine as far into my forgotten memories as possible. You seem to revel in all the trappings!"

"It is occasionally useful," I said, choosing my words carefully so as not to arouse suspicions that I indeed remained an integral part of the crew of the *Rodrigo* and its occasional official missions, "to interact with the plebeian majority. One should retain the means of communicating with them, even if one doesn't associate with them at other times."

Jil made a face.

"Oh, I suppose so! To be honest, Thomas, I had my fill of rules and regulations on our way to and from the Autocracy. I almost felt as though I was under orders again!"

"Jil, you never followed a single order, within or without the academy," I pointed out. "Suggestions, pleas, begging, even wailing at your heels was scarcely sufficient to persuade you to undertake anything but at your own whim."

"Yes," Jil said, pleased at the recollection. "That is true."

An ache arising in my muscles reminded me then that I had been exercising more than my vocal chords, and my keen nose informed me that I might be giving inadvertent offense to my nearest and dearest. Not only that, but I had promised Parsons I would communicate with him in the hours before dinner.

I rose.

"Do excuse me for a time, won't you?" I asked. "I think I will freshen up."

I removed myself from the day room.

ᕯ CHAPTER 2 ᕠ

My quarters, as did those of each of my cousins, consisted of a suite of several small rooms around the circular third deck of the *Jaunter*. Whereas in the Imperium Compound in Taino, those personal suites might comprise anything from a single room to a small estate covering acres, here they were uniform in size. The cozy reception room of my cabin, as I was pleased to call it, featured a large, comfortable chair, a floor-to-ceiling looking glass, and a long, low shelf to my right hand, suitable for flinging whatever I might be carrying. The shelf was unoccupied upon my arrival, but the chair was not. As I entered, the inhabitant of the seat rose. The familiar form, some centimeters taller than my own lofty height, his frame muscular yet whipcord fit, epicene chin shaved to perfection, with shining black hair and eyes as dark as the mysteries behind them, clad in self-effacing black from collar to heels, stood at attention to welcome me. This person was my aide-de-camp, overseer, intermediary and functionary of other useful undertakings too numerous to mention. He occupied the naval rank of commander, with several other titles, I was certain, to supplement that of an agent, no doubt high-ranking, in our Covert Services. He had been my mentor nearly all of my life.

"Parsons!" I exclaimed. I threw myself into an attitude of welcome that I had devised, including a gesture of offering with both hands energy that poured from my heart, and concluded with a bow that brought my chin to the floor. There was just room in the chamber to accommodate this gesture without upending my visitor. "I am overjoyed to see you. I was prepared to seek you out in the lower levels of this vessel."

"I thought it better," that worthy replied, "to save you the effort, my lord."

"The soul of consideration," I said, beaming at him. I rose to my feet. "Would it discomfit you if I tidied myself and changed clothes while we conversed?" I sniffed, and winced at the resulting olfactory input. "I'm afraid that I may not be perfectly fit for polite society at the moment."

"Not at all, my lord," he replied. "The sonic shower will deter any potential eavesdroppers who might be listening."

I wrinkled my nose, an expression not unlike that of Redius, but with a more human interpretation: disappointment. "I had hoped to enjoy a bath. This suite's tub has a remarkable heating unit that maintains the temperature at my preference for hours, and a shape that is designed to contain my entire person from the neck down. I don't have to put the dome on it while the gravity generators are functioning. And don't you have a small gadget that fulfills that task of providing private discourse?"

His face never changed expression, yet I could tell I had hit upon a sore point.

"I await the delivery of an upgrade to the programming of that device, my lord. Although I will deploy my 'gadget,' as you call it, I have received notification within the last hour that its encoding mechanism has been compromised. Hence, it would be more efficacious to use two devices in tandem."

"Oh, very well," I said. "Come on through." I retired to the bedroom and retreated behind the opaque screen that stood between the boudoir and the bathing area. The latter had been constructed from one single piece of high-impact ceramic, but had been decorated in stellarscapes by a galaxy-famous artist who enjoyed a patronage from the Imperium. I had employed her skills myself in a gift I had had made for my mother's next birthday: a small glass sculpture that emitted dancing light in the deep-blue wavelength of her formal naval uniform. I would present it at the conclusion of a new performance I had been choreographing just for that occasion, three days after our scheduled return from the coming spectacle.

I flipped on the switch that activated the cylindrical cleansing booth. An audible hum arose from its interior, indicating that the sonic scrubbers were ready. I stripped off my leotard and deposited it into the collection bin that would be policed by the LAI valet assigned to my suite. In fact, NA-836n was alerted to the presence of dirty clothes and trundled over to retrieve them. "Pray help yourself to refreshments. I have chilled some sparkling raspberry wine from the north provinces that you will find cleansing to the palate as well as pleasing to the nose, and some sesame-basil biscuits that only add delight to the experience. Anna, do help him to a glass."

"Yes, Lieutenant Lord Thomas."

I heard NA-836n roll across the carpeted floor plates toward the buffet bar at the side of the sitting room. I raised my voice to be heard over the rumble.

"I am a trifle surprised that you came along on what is an extended pleasure cruise, Parsons. My cousins took it as a natural compliment to our rank and collective presence upon one ship that we should receive a protective escort. We are honored and a trifle surprised to have such an enormous military guard as two rather large ships that could be out patrolling the exoplanets, but the presence of the crew of my dear *Rodrigo* tells me that there is more afoot than protecting the Emperor's relations."

Parsons was silent for a moment. I knew it was not to collect his thoughts; his mental processes were eternally vigilant. Stray musings would receive a demerit and punishment duty. I stepped into the booth, leaving the door open so we could continue to converse. The excited sonic waves assaulted my skin.

"There is a very good reason, my lord. Several, in fact. What do you know about the Kail?"

In spite of the warmth of the shower, I felt a chill go down my spine.

"The stuff of nightmares," I said, applying the bay-scented surfactant spray to my skin. It tingled through to my inner soul. I shivered, wondering if it would be worthwhile to construct a dance around bathing. There were so many interpretations one could put upon cleanliness. "Ugly creatures. They look as if they were badly carved out of rough, gray stone by a disinterested sculptor. The one I met in a trading station had four stumpy legs and one arm with about nine thick, clumsy fingers. It acted as if it hated me just because I wasn't of its species, or perhaps because I was of a more appealing shape. I tried not to take it personally."

"It wasn't personal, my lord. They do despise all carbon-based life-forms. They would have treated a rosebush with the same disdain."

I reached for the depilation wand and ran it over my cheeks, chin and neck. The hairs that had grown a fraction of a millimeter over the last few hours shivered into insubstantiality and dissolved away with the rest of my discarded skin cells.

"I had heard a whisper that some Kail are coming to the spectacle. Naturally, I hoped that the rumor was wrong. It isn't, is it?"

"No, sir. It is not."

"I have choreographed a short routine that shows my misgivings about the Kail. Would you like to see it when I have finished my shower?" I offered hopefully.

"Definitely not, my lord." The statement brooked no disagreement.

I mused as I turned amid the hundreds of sonic jets, feeling them vibrate my skin clean. The sensation refreshed me, though a bath would have been more relaxing to my muscles. My left shoulder was sore. I moved it closer to one of the emitters and was rewarded as the throbbing eased. I made a note to myself never in future to do a side flip landing on one hand on a rug that was not affixed to the floor.

"How many of them are coming?" I inquired.

"The intelligence I have received does not specify. The Kail, as you are no doubt aware, are secretive and untrusting of all outsiders. They do not commit their plans to any form of documentation as do those of the Imperium and the Autocracy, or even the Trade Federation. What inquiries they do make of the Infogrid are carefully camouflaged among thousands of other searches so our agents and programs find it difficult to discern which search is legitimate."

"It all seems unnecessarily obtuse to me," I opined. We of the Imperium were necessarily open and forthcoming to the electronic frontier. It was a matter of law to keep one's Infogrid file updated. I had posted digitavids of myself performing a routine displaying delight and curiosity about our present journey, to mixed reviews, alas. "But why are they coming, if they know they are going to interact with such terrible creatures as humans? Why not stay mewed up in their bizarre culture and eschew contact?"

"They were invited by the Emperor," Parsons said. I had to stop what I was doing to allow this fact to permeate my consciousness.

"They were? Why would he do that? He isn't coming to the spectacle."

"No, he is not. But he has sent envoys to the Kail. The Zang exhibition takes place, nominally, in what is considered Imperium space, though it has been the province of the Zang for countless millennia before humankind left Old Earth. Therefore, for the Kail to attend required permission from he who controls the Imperium's borders."

"I certainly hope he doesn't expect us to make friends with them. I don't speak Kail, nor have I studied their culture. I'm afraid I would only make relations between us worse."

"Never fear, my lord. It is not a mission for you, or even for me. A team of trained and seasoned diplomats are on this vessel, preparing to approach the Kail."

"They are?" I asked. "I hadn't noticed any diplomats."

"If I may say so, my lord, that is what you may expect to see. They know that they have no place among those of your rank, and are keeping their own company. You might find them a trifle dry of conversation. They acknowledge that. They will fulfill their own mission without troubling you or any of the rest of the Emperor's relations. In fact, it would be best if you helped to prevent any of your cousins from interacting with them."

"Gladly. Why is the Emperor reaching out to the Kail?" I asked. "Certainly they'd be appalling trading partners. I am not au courant with the efforts of the Ministry of Trade, but a race that wears no clothes, doesn't eat our sort of food, hates music, art, any kind of interaction with humankind or, I presume, Uctukind or Wichukind, is unlikely to allow imports of our goods into their space."

"I have been made to understand that the shoe, so to speak, is on the other foot. His Majesty seeks to open up the borders to allow trade in minerals. Kail space seems to be a bountiful source of rare minerals."

"Gemstones?"

"No, my lord. Minerals of objective value, not subjective. Transuranics, rare earths, and other ores that are in increasingly scant supply in Imperium systems. Before the embargo, explorers from the Imperium and Wichu systems detected a number of planetary and asteroid bodies that contained a wealth of those minerals. They were prevented from mining those ores by the inhabitants. I am afraid that was the beginning of strained relations between our two nations."

"But what could they possibly want in exchange?" I asked. "I know why the Emperor invited them, but why are they coming? They have certainly done all they can to avoid interacting with us. Why now?"

"That is what the government hopes to find out. However, it is not your concern. This mission is entirely separate from the pleasurable spectacle that you are going to observe. It has, in fact, provided an excuse for the conference. Cover, if you will. Not every party that will be affected by a potential détente is in favor of such a treaty, however. One of the reasons that there is so much security accompanying this ship is to ensure that the diplomatic team arrives safely. It has nothing to do with you or any other relative of the Emperor, per se."

"Good," I said. "As long as I don't have to attend a daylong banquet dressed in an uncomfortable suit of clothes and make small talk with a living rock about the small pebbles he left back home, I shall feel as free as air."

"You shall not, my lord," Parsons said. He examined the glass of wine as though discerning whether it was listening to us on behalf of enemy combatants. "In fact, I believe that the delegates will be pleased not to have to cope with, er, unnecessary variables while working to bridge the gap between our government and theirs. The Kail have been known to take offense at even the least suggestion of impatience or dislike. You all must avoid them as much as possible."

I sighed with relief. "Gladly. Never mind the Kail, Parsons. If they don't bother me, I shall not bother them. I have far more interesting things to think of. I have devised an exciting dance that I created regarding our trip into Zang space. I shall perform it for our party later in our journey, as we approach the borders of their domain. This is quite an event for me. The elder race of the galaxy! They who preceded even the microbes that were humanity's most ancient evolutionary form! It is only the thought of seeing them that makes it even bearable to be in the Kail's presence. My teacher is on board. She and I will be working on the presentation, honing every moment of symbolism to the finest point of which my body is capable. It is a masterwork!"

"I am sure it will be well received, my lord," Parsons said. I could tell that he had a thought he wished to impart.

"Speak," I called out to him. "I know when you are holding information on the tip of your tongue."

His voice assumed an aridity that had me swallowing against the desert dryness it invoked. "That is a rather unsavory, not to say inaccurate, description."

I gestured my abashment, although he could not see me. The thought that I had made the effort had to count for something.

"Forgive me, Parsons. My new enthusiasm has plumbed both the spiritual and the visceral sides of my psyche. As well as the emotional. It may have caused me to be more eager for intellectual input than usual." I reached for a rough towel and rubbed myself all over to loosen any remaining particles that the sonic beams had left behind, donned a robe, then stepped out of the booth. Although that manner of cleansing was not as relaxing as immersion in hot water, it did mean I wasn't required to dry myself off. Anna had already laid out fresh underthings. I tossed the towel to her. She caught it in mid-air and trundled away. I donned the smallclothes and returned to the sitting room. "My physical efforts have honed my observational faculties to a new peak."

As I suspected, Parsons had not seated himself. His spine was ramrod straight. I had begun to believe that he derived the same comfort and rest from the soles of his feet that ordinary mortals received from sitting down. He retained the glass in his hand, though I doubted that he had yet partaken of any of its rubicund contents.

"Really, sir?" he inquired. "I had not noticed very much difference between this and your usual self."

I ignored the gibe. "I believe that I am more receptive than ever to my surroundings, Parsons. In fact, there is little that dance does not touch. It is most fascinating how communication can be such a purely physical thing." I moved from foot to foot, attempting to recall exactly how Nesbitt had communicated his discomfort. "It is difficult to put across specific intellectual concepts, but there seems to be no limit to the complexities of emotional interaction one can express."

Parsons was expressing a modicum of impatience, which I discerned from the minute tightening of the skin at his temples.

"Yes, sir. To return to our conversation, my lord . . . ?"

"Yes, of course," I said. My valetbot returned, brandishing a selection of clothes. I sighed with pleasure at the wealth of color and design to hand. What a relief it was not to have to wear a uniform for this journey! I could indulge myself in the matter of dress, and I intended to do exactly that. Since I had taken up dance with a passion, my body had become tighter and leaner, except my thighs, which had taken on more muscle. The changes meant I had had to order an entire new wardrobe for this journey. I signed to Anna to show me a tunic in a rich chocolate brown, piped along the hems and neck with orange silk. The trousers that accompanied it were of the same orange as was the wispy neckerchief draped over the hanger. Perhaps a trifle strident for dinner with my relatives. I waved the outfit away. Parsons remained silent. "Discourse! Reveal! Impart! I await your confidences with open ears. What do you need me to do?"

"I need you to restrain yourself, my lord," Parsons said.

"Why?" I asked, beckoning Anna forward with her next suggestion, a banana-yellow jumpsuit with intricate cutouts along the full sleeves and around the waist. "The only people on board this vessel are my cousins and friends, and they are accustomed to my excesses, such as they are. I stand a better than average chance of making it all the way through this journey without being escorted into an airlock and spaced. I already promised you we will stay away from the Kail."

"We will not be alone on this excursion."

Occasionally, Parsons could show his mastery of the obvious in a fashion that tickled the edges of my impatience.

"I know! Many performers, teachers, lecturers and other educated people paid enough to be patient with us will present things to keep those of us with notoriously short attention spans amused. It will take weeks to get where we're going. We have already steeled ourselves against boredom. Do you think one of these people will put us in peril?" A thought struck me, almost forcibly. "I could request Lieutenant Plet to do further checks. After all, she will have her eye on them. They are all dining with the crew from now until we arrive at the viewing platform."

Parsons shook his head.

"Every one of the people on board has been subjected to lengthy investigation to determine whether they are not in the employ of alien governments, yet it's still possible that one or more of them may have been a long-time covert operative. Nothing short of an actual confession or a betraying action will reveal such a secret. The navy knows that Kail factions have been known to use human and Uctu agents to further their aims. This ship is a tempting target. Even though it has a peaceful mission, foreknowledge might not be enough to forestall a preemptive strike from within."

"They might attack us using our own employees, eh? We of the noble house do understand the risks," I said. Annie held up a pair of garments in forest green: close-fitted trousers with a shirt that hung in artful shreds from the shoulders and upper arms. I felt my eyes gleaming as I signed for her to unlimber them from the storage clips. Spectacular, and at the very height of fashion. The latest trend had been to incorporate elements of the weather into one's garments. This suit evoked the power of the element of Air. My cousin Nalney would be so envious of both the cut and the color. I also foresaw the artistic flair of spinning or leaping and seeing the cloth streamers billow on the wind. I retreated behind the dressing screen and reached for the trousers. "That is not to say we take them seriously, but we do understand them. Are we in imminent danger? My sister is on board. While I would protect any of my cousins to the death, it is before Nell's feet that I would make my last stand. You understand that, of course."

"I do," Parsons said. "As do the captain, crew and entire covert security force on board this vessel. Lady Lionelle is in no more danger than the rest of you, though I respect your concern. It is mine as well. Measures have been prepared in the case of an attack. You must pay attention if there is an alarm, my lord. I am counting on you—the Imperium counts upon you—to see to it that your cousins and you decamp to a place of safety. I have provided a chart to your pocket secretary of the fastnesses on board this vessel. I suggest that you familiarize yourself with them in case of need. There are several scenarios, including in case the necessity arises of abandoning ship. It would be helpful if you could devise a means of herding, er, persuading the others toward the correct one, should trouble begin."

"How about Hide-and-Seek?" I asked, stroking my smooth chin with a conspiratorial air. "That would be one way to ensure that my cousins know the locations but without making it sound tedious and official."

If I did not know Parsons so well, I would have missed the low exhalation that indicated relief.

"That would be satisfactory, sir. They will know in time that the

Kail will be present on the platform. The rumors of attack from within or without along our journey may not be borne out, but it is best to be prepared. It would be helpful if the nobles were not frightened into overreaction."

"You may count upon me," I said. I shrugged into the shirt. It fit me as if it had been made for me, which of course it had. I ventured forth to view my reflection in the full-length mirror beside the door. Not bad, I thought, turning from side to side. The outfit looked handsome but did not stray over the line into costumery. I did a pivot spin, and enjoyed seeing the streamers swirl against my shoulders as they settled. They lifted just as I hoped they would.

"What do you think, Parsons?"

That worthy surveyed me with a gimlet eye.

"It is a trifle . . . dramatic, my lord."

"Wonderful, isn't it?" I said, with delight.

"That would not have been the first adjective I would have reached for, sir. But to return to the point . . . may I count upon you to inculcate the other members of your family with discretion and the need for safety?"

"I will begin by incorporating the need for secrecy and concealment in my next performance. Which will be . . ." I consulted the aluminum-framed chronometer set into the wall above the door ". . . In approximately three hours, just before dinner. Will you excuse me? I have an exercise session with my dance instructor, then I owe my cousin Erita a rematch in our Snapdragon card tournament. We are poised at three games to two. I am winning, of course."

"Of course," Parsons said. He wouldn't have been impressed by a mere game, not even if I were actually riding a dragon against my cousin. "But there is one more thing of which you need to be aware. A visitor is to be taken on board the *Jaunter* at our second port of call. While it is unlikely that any problems can befall that visitor, it behooves us to protect and prevent any disturbance, intrusion or injury."

"And who is that visitor?" I asked. I knew my eyes were shining like the beacon of truth.

"One of the Zang. It designates itself as Zang Proton."

"A Zang!" I echoed, my soul overflowing with excitement. "I didn't think they needed transportation anywhere."

"They do not. Proton has expressed a wish to observe us. It is a great privilege to convey a Zang anywhere for any distance. More than any of the others in late centuries, this one appears curious about humankind. Needless to say, we want to provide it with a quotidian experience for its consideration."

"I shall begin to choreograph a dance of welcome for it at once!" Plans began to form in my mind as an aeration of excitement arose behind my solar plexus. Ideas warred with one another in a battle for supremacy. I strode about my quarters, feeling the moment begin to take shape within me. I lifted my arms, and the green streamers fell back behind my shoulders. "No, that was too presumptive an opening move. Perhaps a more humble approach." I struck a pose, with my head bowed slightly and my hands held out, palm up. "How about this?"

Parsons held up an admonitory hand. "My lord, I do not think confronting it with a frenzy of seemingly random movement will be an appropriate activity. Let the Zang observe you in your natural state."

I straightened and peered at him as though a stranger had taken his place.

"Parsons," I said, allowing my tone to loom toward peevishness, "that *is* my natural state. I wish to evoke the emotions of gratitude, curiosity and welcome that are the deepest sensations in my heart at this moment. Surely the Zang will find that of interest?"

A minuscule motion of his head from side to side indicated dissent. "Anything that smacks of invasion of its privacy will be dealt with as any other infractions on a spacegoing vessel, my lord. In other words, the captain has orders to incarcerate violators."

I felt my heart pierced by his insensitivity.

"Invasion? A celebration of the Zang and their accomplishments considered an invasion that could land me in the brig? You wound me, Parsons!"

He held up his hand. "I seek only to warn you, my lord. Please restrain yourself. The Zang are so rarely curious about ephemerals that we must approach the matter with as much dignity and consideration possible. It is the wish of not only the Emperor, but Mr. Frank and your mother as well."

Ah, that was it. The mysterious head of Covert Services, for whom I had done the occasional service, had been invoked, as well as my august maternal unit. Before them all, I could not stand.

"A triple threat," I said. I lowered my head and peered at Parsons at an oblique and playful angle. "You don't mind if I create such a dance in private, do you? Perhaps to perform it for the benefit of my friends and cousins?"

"That would be . . . satisfactory, my lord," Parsons said, though I could tell he wasn't perfectly satisfied. Neither was I. We might as well both be disappointed. "Presuming you will keep your word not to display your performance to the Zang. Do I have your promise?"

I struggled mightily, attempting to find a means of keeping my options open, but Parsons had a knack of seeing my thoughts as though they were displayed upon a massive digitavid tank screen. His gaze held me fast, as if I was fixed in imperishable crystal. I struggled to break free of it, but I knew nothing but compliance would be accepted.

"Oh, very well," I burst out at last. "I will restrict the audience for my celebration dance to non-Zang only. But I reserve the right, if the Zang expresses an interest, to perform for it."

Parsons nodded, which meant that his head inclined less than a millimeter. "I appreciate the reasonableness of your request, my lord. I cannot see any difficulty with allowing such an exception, should that very unlikely case arise."

He glided toward the door, leaving me speechless and delighted. Where others might have found "very unlikely" offputting, I only saw a challenge.

I performed a celebratory pike leap and touched my toes in mid-air. How best could I express humanity to a Zang?

❦ CHAPTER 3 ❧

The oxygen-rich atmosphere stank of carbon-based organic compounds. The scrubbers in the Kail's hibernation cabin could only rid the thick air of some of it. Phutes felt polluted. Even the water in the cleansing tank tasted of rot. It was the final insult. He could not spend even 11 more minutes in water that filthy. Planting his 10 hands on the sides, he extracted himself forcefully from the tank. Waves of displaced water followed him. It ran down the crags of gray, stony matter that made up his massive body and seeped into the drains set in the anodized cabin floor. He contracted the flexors stretching between his thick neck and 11 short legs to agitate the acidity of his internal system so that his epidermal layer heated. The rest of the offending liquid exploded into steam. Phutes caught one final whiff of the stench before it evaporated.

"Not good enough," he gritted out.

The other 111 Kail who had been waiting to use the tub recoiled at his explosive emergence. Many of the 11000 others were still resting and were yet to become aware of the current problem.

"Tell the captain," Sofus insisted, waving the fumes away from his scent receptors with his 100 hands. He was the largest and most solid of the Kail siblings traveling aboard the Wichu liner *Whiskerchin*. "They must fix the system *again*. We must bathe! I cannot function smelling like these creatures."

Phutes signed assent with a curt motion of his right forearm. This made complaint number 101001 since they had come on board.

27

Satisfaction would be achieved, or he would find it difficult to restrain himself or his siblings from violence. He stamped out of the cabin and down the corridor toward the lift chute. The deck thundered under his heavy, solid feet. Soft, inefficient, filthy capsules, made for soft, inefficient, filthy beings. He hated being among them, but he had little choice.

Only with the greatest possible reluctance had Phutes and his companions taken passage on a Wichu freighter from the Kail sector. Few native commanders wanted to pass out of their well-protected systems and into the realm of the slimy ones. Phutes disliked the necessity of interacting with the soft-fleshed beings. One could smell the decay coming from them. And what about the effluvia that issued from each? Every orifice emitted noxious compounds. And they could not be far from a repository of one kind or another, all of which had to be constructed with complicated mechanisms and the waste of good clean water or pure gaseous elements. Or both. They left trails of distasteful organic matter wherever they went. They even exhaled smelly organic particles. He had tried spraying the cabin with powerful mineral-based disinfectants, but the Wichu captain had taken his canisters away from him, using many words that the language chips in its system refused to translate. Phutes spoke no Wichu. He saw no reason to interact further with the crew and other passengers than the exchange of fare for transport. At the captain's insistence, he and the siblings who spoke for the Kail on board wore a steel wristband embedded with an electronic chip that translated his speech into the uncouth sounds Wichu made.

His demands for quarters to suit his party's comfort had been met, but not without argument and many other untranslatable phrases. In the end, sanitized metal bins filled with purified silicate sands for them to burrow into during resting and excretory periods had been provided. It had taken more negotiation and arguments until they were satisfactory to the Kail. The Wichu did not seem to care. Phutes saw the way they cared for themselves, and was not surprised at their disregard for the comfort of others. They seemed unaware that they had risen even marginally from the unspeakable slime that had engendered them. The Kail refused to be ignored. Phutes shoved his way into the lift shaft, ignoring the annoyed looks and remarks of crew members of many species who had been waiting in line. Kail did not wait.

He allowed the jets of force to carry him upward toward the bridge deck. He would only speak with the captain.

Carbon-based life forms had become disgustingly prevalent on all planets with an oxygen-rich atmosphere. Even some methane worlds were infested. Wherever they went, the soft ephemerals soiled the pristine silicon landscape with excrescences that burgeoned and reproduced themselves until the beauty of the land could no longer be felt underfoot. The comfort of stone and metal were obscured. Only the squishiness of green plant life met the soles of his feet. Every step Phutes took on one of those planets made him seethe with hatred.

The acid circulating through his internal organs bubbled vigorously at that memory, threatening to overflow out of his orifices. Phutes did his best to control himself. The Wichu had made it clear that if the Kail damaged the ship any more than the captain claimed they already had, they would be put off on the nearest asteroid large enough to hold them all. Phutes was unmoved by the threat. Marooning would not kill any of them. The Kail could survive on internal processes until they were retrieved, but it would slow down their cause. At least this vessel was free of humans.

Humanity in particular was a horrifyingly nasty imposition visited on existence. If the Kail could rid themselves of humankind altogether, it would make the universe a cleaner place. The worlds that humanity infested could be cleansed back to a purely mineral-based state. The trouble was, they reproduced faster than the Kail could wipe them out, and they persisted in widening their sphere of influence until there was little hope of containing them. The Kail attacked when humanity intruded itself on Kail homes. The human governments sent undertakings to complain about aggression, ignoring the reality that they had been the aggressors.

Because of this arrogance, Phutes was acting upon a plan to avenge his people and strike at the heart of the infestation.

While he and his fellow offspring were still small enough to lie upon his mother's bosom, Yesa told him of the time humans and Wichus had visited her. They had not requested permission before setting down their ships. She was still angry about the offense, even though it had been nearly two thousand revolutions of the sun since it had happened. The Wichus shed their horrible protein filaments over everything, and they treated the Kail with open disrespect, but it was humanity that drew the most hatred. They assumed that the Kail would be grateful for their invasion. Once the people had managed to translate the humans' endless babbling, it was found to include infinitely annoying assumptions that they were welcome to analyze and collect samples from wherever they might be. In fact, they had removed a twelve-kiloton block of accreted minerals from less than a kilometer from where Phutes had been born. Many offspring of that time had attempted to retrieve it, suffering grievous wounds and insults in the process.

Not that the human invaders had left nothing in exchange. Oh, no. In their wake was a swathe of waste material of every kind, from organic compounds to unreusable alloys that still stood where they had left them. In the hold of the Wichu ship, Phutes had those items stored. The humans who had committed the violation were long since dead, or so said their cluttered faster-than-light communication system, but he intended to find their descendants. They should get their garbage back before they were blasted back into their formative atoms.

The soft ones just seemed to emit noxiousness of every kind. They could not go for even a tenth-rotation without needing to ingest volatile or decaying organic matter. Liquids taken in only remained for a sixteenth-rotation before the absurdly fragile systems expelled them again, this time infused with waste matter. They did not even retain useful salts for more than a rotation or two. But Phutes's progenitor had an idea. She wanted Phutes to ask the Zang for help, in a move that would strike at humankind's very existence. She had outlined the plan very carefully, making certain that not only Phutes, but at least 1100111 of his siblings knew every detail as well. Based on what they knew of humankind, they believed that one cunning strike would, if not destroy the enemy, then cripple it beyond relief. The plot hinged, however, upon convincing the Zang to assist them.

No one had ever tried such a bold move before. Phutes had seen a Zang only once, who had come to visit Yesa for a brief moment many revolutions ago. It had flickered out of existence almost as soon as he had become aware of it.

All Kail were in awe of the Zang. The Elder Race had power over the spheres. Though the mysterious beings did not appear to be silicon-based, they didn't smell, nor did they dirty their surroundings.

They seemed to float effortlessly between star systems, rarely interacting, never demanding. If they chose, they could destroy with a thought. They were . . . perfect. And powerful. They held the means that the Kail did not to defeat their enemies.

The metal door to the bridge responded to Phutes's impression upon it, and slid aside. He stepped into the chamber. 1100 round black eyes turned resentfully in his direction.

"Hey, kitty litter!" A throaty growl was revised by her harness-mounted translation device into a comprehensible Kail rasp like stone on stone.

Phutes dropped abruptly out of the worshipful thoughts that had enveloped him. The object of his momentary quest was before him: Captain Bedelev. The Wichu was a hand's thickness less than his height. Her entire body, like those of her bridge crew, was covered with white filaments except where facial features, digits and genitalia, most of them a shocking pink in color, protruded. A small device with intelligence circuitry buzzed around the floor, gathering up the filaments that the Wichu constantly shed. Phutes shook his foot to dislodge one that had floated onto it. It felt disgusting.

"Wichu leader!" he growled. The translator piped out a phrase that sounded far too conciliatory, but he had not been the one who programmed it.

The Wichu captain stalked over and glared at him, black, bulbous eyes to efficient, flat optical receptors.

"I thought I told you to stay off my bridge!"

"My siblings and are unsatisfied with the cleanliness of the water piped into our quarters," Phutes said.

"What do they want?" Captain Bedelev demanded. Her raucous shout emerged in Kail from the circuitry sounding like a polite and diffident query. "I know what you Kail like. I have one of you working for me, you know. The filtration system takes out everything to particles less than an angstrom across. That water is purer than primeval snow."

"It stinks!" Phutes said. "It may be free of particulate matter, but gases pass through the conduits and pollute our quarters. They are noxious! No softskin would endure it. Why should we? Are we not valued as customers?"

"Of course you are!" she said. Bedelev brushed at her furry nose with an impatient paw. She reached out for his arm, but he recoiled. "All right, all right. I'll see about venting the pipes before they hit your part of the ship. It might get colder in there, though. The ambient air helps keep the water warm."

"We will endure," Phutes said. "As long as the water arrives devoid of the smell of . . ." He paused. He was getting what he wanted. No sense in escalating until the captain's promise was proved worthless. ". . . Of internal processes."

"And your shit don't stink?" she asked. She waved a paw. "No, I guess it doesn't. It's practically pure sand. Fine. Now, get off my bridge. No more visits without notice, from now on. Got that?"

Phutes lifted his face slightly. It was as close as his kind would come to imitating a soft-body's smile. He wouldn't have to offer empty pleasantries for very long.

"I follow instructions."

He turned and departed. Behind him, Bedelev made a noise that the circuit did not translate.

The door closed behind him, making a conciliatory sound. Phutes returned to the open lift shaft. To one side, the stream reached its apex. Phutes ignored the Wichu jumping off to fulfill duties on this, the uppermost deck of the ship. He shoved aside a Croctoid in a Maintenance collar. It snapped at him. Phutes let it close its jaws on his lower forearm. It recoiled at once, spitting out jagged oral calcifications.

"Dammit, buddy, watch where you're going!" it said.

Phutes paid no attention. He was too offended by the creature's saliva on his arm. He would have to scrub it vigorously to rid himself of the unhealthy touch. He pushed into the descending stream. Time to pay a visit to a long-lost relative and sibling in the cause.

Phutes felt the charge of electrical power surging through the walls and into the banks and emplacements of equipment throughout the engineering section. Tiny charges erupted on his exoderm, exciting the accretion impulse. He questioned whether he should add to his substance on such an unsanitary vessel. Phutes and his siblings were resigned to the natural minor depletion they would suffer on a long journey. He decided he could cleanse organic material from his system once he was on rocky ground once again, preferably within 11100^{111}

kilometers from a black hole. The air in this section was saturated with electricity and floating molecules of minerals that had been expelled by the explosive process that drove the ship. He stopped in the midst of a flow that had the greatest concentration and absorbed it. Phutes realized why he had been so peevish with the Wichu captain! He had been hungry.

It did not take long to sate his impulse to feed, but his hesitation was long enough to annoy the Wichu that worked in this section. They passed around him, close enough to glare into his face. Some of them bumped him deliberately. Phutes felt anger rising within his core. Bilious acid threatened to spill out through his orifices. He clenched down on his vessels to prevent it. He should not care what they thought. The pulse of the vessel was calm. It supported and contained him and his siblings safely against the cold vacuum of space. That was all that mattered.

A female—the Wichu claimed to be of 10 different genders, as did most of the carbon-based races—tried to block him as he made his way toward the area that the circuitry told him was Fovrates's abode.

"Sorry, sir, you can't go back there. That's a restricted area. You're not authorized." The translator blurted out apologetic-sounding phrases as she ran along beside him. She grabbed his arm. Despite moving much more slowly than the Wichu, he managed to avoid her touch. It enraged her into another shrill tirade. Phutes tried to ignore the disharmony.

He reached the correct doorway and laid a hand on its surface. It took a while for the programming to recognize him and announce him to the one behind it, as much as 101 seconds. In that short time, the Wichu female drew a weapon and leveled it at him. Phutes turned his body and eyed the pistol. Its purpose was to excite the flesh of the victim at whom it was fired, at a range that could stun or kill. At his imperturbable stare, she swallowed audibly and moved the side control up to the maximum on the dial. The tiny whine told Phutes all he needed to know about the weapon's programming. He reached out to touch the barrel and emitted a thin hum, matching the frequency within 110 seconds. Within 101 more, the weapon began to smoke.

"Drop it," he said. "When it explodes it will injure you."

The Wichu closed its hands around the stock. The whine increased in volume.

"I'm not dropping it! You back away, now!"

By then, numerous Wichus had gathered from all sides. Some of them took hold of Phutes's limbs. Angrily, he shook them off. Others pointed weapons, which Phutes was forced to set on overload. The Wichu had courage. Knowing the risk to their fragile flesh, they still maintained a grip on their weapons.

"I warn you, you have 1010 seconds before detonation."

"Stop threatening me! And use base 10, like a civilized being!"

Phutes felt his inner acids roiling at the insult.

"You accuse *me* of being uncivilized? Shedding hazard!"

"Stone face!"

A booming tone came from the other side of the wall.

"Stop harassment now!" The door slid open. "All will suffer!"

Reluctantly, the white-haired crewmembers shifted away from Phutes. He sensed the terrible stench of contact with their skin and fur. He required a bath, but now he would have to wait in line behind all of his kin. And that was providing that the technicians had corrected the fault in the water line.

The newcomer lifted a massive fist toward Phutes. He had 110, 100 on his right side and 10 on his left, but only 10 legs. He towered over the much younger Kail.

"Welcome, cousin," he said. His words in pure, unaccented Kail were echoed through not only Phutes's translation device but his own. Phutes heard the overload tone die away, as the other disabled the devices with a supersonic tone of his own. "Come in. We will leave this uncouth slime outside."

"Watch who you're calling uncouth, Fovrates!" shouted the security officer. Phutes spared her one pitying glance as he followed the other into his office.

Once the door closed with an obsequious swish, Fovrates touched limbs with him.

"I regret the unnecessary contact with the crew," he said, bumping the translator to switch it off. Phutes followed suit. There was no need for the devices among distant kin. "Will you recline?"

Phutes surveyed the chamber. It contained numerous primitive technical devices and scopes, most of them fixed to the walls within reach of a standing Kail. Though there were two chairs and a table suitable for use by the slime crew, most of the floor was given over to a broad (plastic) box filled with sparkling silver sands heaped and swirled like windswept dunes, dotted with a few larger rocks almost the size of his head. At the sight, Phutes felt a deep longing come over him.

"It looks like home," he said.

"It reminds me of Mother," Fovrates agreed. His optical receptors showed amusement. "Come. Let us talk."

Phutes waited until Fovrates chose his place in the box. The bigger Kail lay down at the far end and pulled piles of translucent gray minerals over himself until only his face was visible. He propped one of his enormous feet on the largest rock. Phutes burrowed into the dunes, sending an unspoken apology that he was so tainted by organics. The sand didn't seem to be troubled. It enveloped him hospitably, cradling his limbs and torso as though it were his birthplace. Phutes felt so comfortable, he almost missed it when Fovrates's voice vibrated as a mild electrical charge through the fragmented stone.

"It has been 101 days since you came on board, but you did not come to pay your respects at once."

"Apologies, cousin," Phutes said, sending his voice back in the same manner. "I bring you greetings from Yesa. She asks for your assistance."

"I have waited for this summons for many revolutions. My mother, Nefra, sent me word long ago through vibrations in the normal stellar shock waves that you would be coming. The ship is ready. I could take command of every system in a fraction of 1. Give the word, and it will obey us."

"But is that necessary? Yesa's plan should cause a collapse in the humans' civilization without the need of open warfare. They will so demoralized they can be easily removed from the motherworlds that they have invaded once the Zang act."

He sensed rather than heard the shrug. "Better to have a secondary plan in place. You do not know how randomly the carbon-based ones act. I experience it every day. Even if you succeed in avenging the insult to our motherworlds and destroying the center of human culture, they may rally. For organic slime, they are amazingly resilient. Life persists, even in their terrible, disgusting, odiferous manner. I will give you all my data. I have it in here, where the Wichu never suspect its existence. Like the humans, they long ago gave up on silicon-based storage in favor of quantum. More fools they."

"I accept it gladly," Phutes said.

"Then, absorb it."

Phutes felt the pulse of binary data seeping into his body from all points. He buried his face in the sand and listened to Fovrates's information.

There was plenty to take in. Instead of the slow, steady beat of the universe, he felt the rush of incoherent and disordered formulae playing upon his senses. The slime beings were even more chaotic than he had been told. The Wichus seemed outwardly disinterested in expansion, yet their sphere of influence had grown by two systems in the last revolution alone, and always toward Kail space. The noise they generated polluted the calm, clean waves of the cosmos. But it was the humans who impinged the worst. Their unclean residences set down on world after world that before had never known the touch of organic molecules, nor were ever intended to. They sent out transmissions in exponential numbers that could in time throw off the universe's natural pulse. As swiftly as those two races multiplied, there seemed to be no way for the slow-reproducing Kail to overcome them. They had to be prevented from breeding in such large numbers.

"The Zang are our only hope," Phutes said. That was the conclusion to which his motherworld had come, and many others as well. Fovrates murmured his assent.

"I agree. Are you prepared to convince them?"

"I am. All of Yesa's children are with me. May we count on Nefra's for support?"

"Naturally. That is why so many of my siblings are out among the stars, insinuating ourselves through the ships and stations of the slime." Fovrates chuckled. "Captain Bedelev has sent to her commanders that she does not like me, but she could not picture running this ship without me. She doesn't yet know how true that is. She's not running the ship any longer."

"How long until we reach our destination?"

"I have the information from the helm computers," Fovrates said. "101 jumps. As many as 10010 ship-days. I am accustomed to the conditions, but can you and your siblings tolerate them?"

"As long as we get some clean water," Phutes said. "But even if we don't, we will cope. The beginning of the eradication of the slime begins then."

⊰ CHAPTER 4 ⊱

"Lord Thomas, this way!" the wrinkled merchant woman called, beckoning to me with a crooked, bronze-hued finger. She raised her other hand, from which dangled strings of flashing crystals and exotically carved beads. Her floor-length dress was festooned all over with more necklaces, bracelets and rings in myriad clusters, as were the walls and canopy of her blue fabric tent. "I have been waiting for you! Oh, please, great noble, come and see my merchandise! It is the finest in all the system. You will never find such a bargain! Lord Thomas! In the name of our long-lasting friendship!"

I kept a slight but unapproachable smile upon my face, but I kept walking through the marketplace that occupied most of the high dome in the center of the spaceport on Taruandula 4. The small, slim silver-haired woman trotting daintily at my side did not have to stride to keep up. If Madame Deirdre had chosen to, she could have run rings around me all the way from the ship and back, and never run out of breath. She was made of whipcord and iron rods, in far better shape than I was, despite my months of intensive training. Madam Deirdre taught over sixty different styles of dance, and had won acclaim across the Imperium for both her own performances and for choreography. I had been fortunate enough to secure her services as a teacher for a series of private lessons. I paid her well, naturally, though the added emolument of an invitation to come along to see the Zang spectacle was a reward for her putting up with a pupil who had not started with her tutelage from childhood and was therefore a trial to an artist such as herself.

"Why didn't you stop?" she asked, with a curious, bright-eyed glance. "She seemed to know you. And there were some nice sparklies for sale in her booth."

I smiled at her. "I have an excellent memory. A brief glimpse was enough to tell me that I was not personally acquainted with the lady. Like most of the merchants here on this planet, she undoubtedly obtained images of me and those members of my family traveling with me from our Infogrid files. I have over thirty million casual followers. I was required to post that my cousins and I are traveling toward Zang space, from which businesses may infer that we will be halting at a number of jump points of which this might be one. Also, her sparklies," I recorded the charming phrase for later use, "are far from unique. As we pass more deeply into the bazaar, we'll find the same items again and again, but almost certainly at better prices. Tourists who shop the edges pay the most. I think you would find that to be true no matter where along the circumference of this enormous marketplace you go."

I gestured outward in a dramatic fashion. Through the translucent dome that covered the area to protect it from not only the weather, but from the noise of arrivals and departures, we could see numerous ships and shuttles of myriad designs. The *Imperium Jaunter* and its escort remained in orbit, taking on fuel and undergoing inspection for any engineering faults. We had made the descent by shuttle. Four of the small craft were in a secure hangar almost a kilometer behind us by then.

"Oh," Dierdre said, with refreshing eagerness. "I wondered how you came to have so many friends here who knew so much about you! He's such a social lad," Madame Deirdre confided to Lieutenant Anstruther, who dogged our steps with all the air of a protective mother wolf. I had protested at being assigned a bodyguard, but the *Jaunter*'s captain insisted that all of us nobles be watched over at all times we were not on ship. I had insisted with equal fervor that if that was the case, I would prefer to have one of my own crew beside or, in this case, behind me. It was Anstruther's turn. Nesbitt and Redius were off somewhere else in the company of a couple of my cousins. "Well, I need to buy some pretties for my daughters and grandchildren. They seldom leave Keinolt, and I hardly ever have time to look for anything nice when I'm traveling with a troupe. We might as well perform in a warehouse in the middle of an asteroid belt, for all we see of those exotic locations we go to, I am always telling the producer!"

I smiled. This was yet another way in which I could reward this extraordinary woman. She was not an experienced shopper, of that I had already ample proof. One of my talents, hard-honed among my cousins, who were also avid acquisitors of interesting merchandise, was to discover, evaluate and obtain, at a fair price, that which took my fancy. I extended an elbow, into which she tucked her narrow hand.

"Come with me, then. I have a friend here on this planet. OTL-590i is an LAI who is the secondary backup secure bookkeeping unit for the local banking system. Odile knows not only who are the most prosperous merchants, but who order their wares and supplies from the finest sources. She has given me a list," I brandished my viewpad, "separated into categories such as clothing, housewares, works of art, jewelry and the like. The entries are overlaid onto a map of the marketplace. We are about twenty yards from the first of her choices."

Madame Deirdre looked enchanted. Her large gray eyes twinkled like so many "sparklies."

"How interesting! I must meet your friend. I am afraid I spend so much time rehearsing and performing that I seldom get to know the mechanicals in our midst. The lovely device that looks after the cabins on my level always has a pleasant word for us. It could easily ignore us, but it doesn't. Curious. Their wants are not our wants; our needs are not the same as theirs. We live side by side with them, but it might be a completely parallel existence, as we have with plants."

"Exactly so," I replied, delighted. "I have found their observations on our lives to be of immense value. I hope they like us, since our well-being is so frequently in the palms of their circuitry, so to speak. I must say that most of the time they take a neutral stance on their view of our behavior. It is often far better than we deserve."

"We ought to explore what it would take to evoke concepts for an electronic personality," Madame Deirdre said, her eyes brightening. "I have never performed for any that I know of."

"That is a wonderful notion!" I agreed. "Shall we create a *pas de deux*? Most of the LAIs I know work in a cooperative situation. A solo performance would not resonate with them as well as it does with biological beings."

She tapped me on the arm. "You are beginning to think like a choreographer, Lord Thomas," she said, with a little smile. I was taken slightly aback, since I had begun to create dances months ago. I had to remind myself that though I outranked her by exponents in social, economic and genetic spheres, I was but an embryo in her world. "That is a good notion. All of these insights will inform our performance. You can fill me in on their culture as we walk. Tell me about some of your friends."

As we passed among the range of booths, tents, counters and the like that filled the covered marketplace, I described how I had come to be acquainted with a freezer unit, a vacuum system, a rather erudite file cross-checker in an elite university library, and many others. Apart from Emby, my oldest LAI friend who had been employed in food storage and was now a nannibot on a distant planet, what most artificial intelligences had in common was that they remained stationary. Humans, Wichus, Uctus and the like saw only the small proportion of LAIs that were employed as mobile units: caretakers, servers, and so on. The great majority occupied the machines that they ran, very much like a shopkeeper living over her or his premises. I said as much to Madame Deirdre. She cocked her head and narrowed her eyes, thinking.

"That is a penetrating notion, Lord Thomas. Very interesting. We must concentrate on meaning without extraneous movement."

The slightly-built woman raised her arms over her head with her fingers gracefully tented toward one another, moving one muscle at a time until her arms appeared to be two ends of a spiral. I was so fascinated by her control that I walked directly into an obstruction. Anstruther leaped forward to extract me from my obstacle.

"Oof! Oh, I say!"

"I beg your pardon!" I exclaimed, as we steadied my victim. Then I recognized him: a human male, tall, though not quite as tall as I was, possessing massive shoulders and prominent musculature, handsome of countenance with teak-brown skin, wide brown-black eyes and a strong, cleft chin. "Nole! We thought you were not coming!"

Nole, my cousin Nalney's younger brother, gave me a sheepish grin.

"Thomas! I knew I should have stayed in my ship and not gone shopping, but I couldn't resist such a marketplace," he said. He glanced around. So did I. None of our relatives was in sight. "You won't give me away, will you, Thomas? I meant to surprise everyone. I had no idea you were all so close behind me."

"The *Jaunter* is the fastest civilian liner in the Core Worlds," I said. "We must have caught up just before or after one of the first three jumps. So, your new vessel is ready? I can't wait to see it." I scanned the hulks out on the perimeter around the spaceport, but none gave off that frisson of newness that I expected to feel. "Which of these is yours?"

"None of them," Nole said, with an almost forgivable smirk. "I came in by flitter-cab. I'm out beyond one of the moons. Did you see that there were sixty moons? Ostentation, I call it."

"Just because Keinolt only has three?" I countered. "It's not as though there will be a side-by-side comparison. Then, do you have pictures of your vessel? A digitavid?" I couldn't conceal my eagerness.

Nole's smirk increased in intensity. "Not one. You will just have to wait until we get to the viewing platform for the grand reveal. I have spent too much time and money on it to let even a single image get out ahead of time. My ship is so spectacular I don't want an erg of excitement to be expended until everyone can see it at once. It will be the second most amazing thing you will see there. Not that some of you haven't tried. Nalney sent a hefty bribe to my shipbuilders, trying to get a look at the plans. So did at least two or three others of our cousins, according to the bookkeeper and the architect." I attempted to look innocent. "Oh, not you, too, Thomas?"

"The curiosity is killing me," I confessed. "A project this detailed and involved, that has managed to consume one of our fugitive attention spans for almost two years, has to be one of the wonders of the universe."

"I think so," Nole said, so complacently I thought about devising a prank to play upon him at that precise moment. But I had company, so I was on better behavior than I might have been had I been surrounded by cousins and siblings alone. In that moment, I recalled my manners.

"Madame Deirdre, may I present my cousin, Lord Nole Odin Melarides Kinago? Nole, this is Madame Deirdre, dancer, choreographer, and my teacher."

"I am delighted to meet you, Lord Nole," Deirdre said.

Nole bowed. "A pleasure, madam," he said. "If you are Thomas's teacher, you must be a miracle of patience. I believe I have heard of you. Our grandmother, Nestorina Kinago Castana, is a great patroness of the arts. She brought us all to concerts and performances since we were old enough to sit in the seats, albeit not quietly."

Deirdre beamed at him.

"Yes, Lady Nestorina is the one who made the connection for me with Lord Thomas," she said, grasping his hand and shaking energetically. "What a pleasure to meet one of her precious grandchildren! She is so very proud of all of you. She sponsored my dance troupe in one of our first seasons, more than thirty years ago, and remains a very good friend of the arts. We have tea at least once a year. I owe her greatly for that."

"And that is how she managed to convince you to teach my benighted cousin," Nole concluded, hearing the unspoken context. I winced.

"Not at all!" Madame Deirdre insisted, though after months of close contact I could read her body language to see that she was telling a white lie. "Lord Thomas is a most devoted student."

Nole fell into a coughing fit that covered derisive laughter. My wounded pride caused my self-control to momentarily turn its back. While it was deliberately not looking, I punched Nole in the arm. He countered with a playful blow to my upper thorax. We dropped our fists. Honor had been satisfied.

"And this is Lieutenant Philomena Anstruther, of my naval vessel, *Rodrigo*," I said. "A talented programmer as well as a superlative officer." Nole bowed to the slender girl, whose face turned a becoming shade of crimson.

"I have heard good things about you and the others," Nole said, gallantly. "Thomas can't stop talking about all of you. On the other hand, Thomas can't stop talking, full stop."

"It's nice to meet you, Lord Nole," Anstruther said, shyly.

"The pleasure is all mine, dear lady," Nole said. "That's a fine outfit you're wearing, Thomas." I looked down with pleasure at the cranberry-red ensemble I had donned for shopping. The tunic, trousers and shoulder cape fit perfectly, of course, despite the cape and tunic containing dozens of concealed pockets, suitable for squirreling away little purchases for my cousins I didn't want them to see yet. "Who made it?"

"An LAI, HU-54d. He's on board the *Jaunter*, as it happens. In case I need a new outfit for one of my—our—performances," I corrected myself, with an enveloping gesture toward Deirdre. "He has made several for us already. It was very much worthwhile bringing him."

"Would you mind if I borrowed him?" Nole asked, with a hopeful expression in his coffee-brown eyes. "I want a formal suit for my house—I mean, shipwarming party. I'll hold that after the Zang's destruction event. I need something that will knock everyone's eyes out."

"I'm not certain we can spare him, Nole," I said.

"Oh, go on, Lord Thomas," Deirdre encouraged me. "I think we have enough costumes to last us."

I nodded reluctant assent. "If you are certain, Madame, then of course I will. I can certainly ask Hugh if he would like to take your commission, Nole. Do you want him to accompany you the rest of the way to Zang space to do fittings and so on?"

Nole beamed.

"Yes, please. I would be very grateful if you can let me have him."

I removed my viewpad from a pocket near the collar of my cape. It seemed to appear out of nowhere. Nole's eyes widened with surprise, and he nodded.

"Absolutely, he is the tailor for me. Very smart!"

"I couldn't agree more," I said. When I turned on the screen, I was greeted by a virtual chorus of loud and brilliantly colored advertisements sponsored by the marketplace authority, all clamoring for my attention at top volume. I pushed them aside and opened a private communication channel to send a text message to Hugh. "One moment. One must observe the niceties. I don't want to interrupt him if he's turning a seam."

"Can't you just order him to come to my ship?" Nole asked, peevishly. "You are too precious with these LAIs, Thomas."

"Now, now," I chided him. "Just because your nurserybot made you take vitamin supplements you didn't like when you were a tot is no reason to treat the whole group as if they are about to dose you with oils."

"Well, they might," Nole growled. I sent the message.

Almost at once, the viewpad pinged. When I touched the screen to answer it, another raft of unwelcome three-dimensional ads began hopping and zooming around it again. I slapped my palm flat to squash them all out of existence. When I lifted my hand, everything was gone except for the icons for the Infogrid and one local text message from Hugh.

"He'll do it," I said. "His rates are ridiculously low for the quality of work he does, but he won't work on cheap fabrics. You'll have to use the best."

"But of course," Nole said, with a lift of his broad shoulders. I observed that the well-cut shirt he had on was of ossifer silk in its natural deep bronze color. "Can I buy what I want here?"

"I'd be astonished if you couldn't," I said, glancing about at the busy booths and shops. "This is a major intersection leading not only to the edge of Imperium space, but also toward the Wichu systems." I went into my device's history to find Odile's message, and forwarded a portion of it to him. "Here are the merchants you want to visit. They import top-grade textiles. Now I have two things to look forward to: your ship and your suit."

Nole grasped my outstretched hand. "Thanks, cousin. I'll send a flitter-cab to pick Hugh up at once. Now, remember, you haven't seen me!"

"Not a trace," I promised, assuming an innocent face. Deirdre and Anstruther nodded agreement. "In fact, I'm still wondering where you are."

With a sly wink, Nole slipped away into the clamoring crowd.

⁌ CHAPTER 5 ⁍

"Lady Nestorina's images of Nole and Nalney are sorely outdated," Madame Deirdre said, as we resumed our trek into the depths of the market. "The digitavids she has playing in her sitting room are of a couple of small boys."

"Ah, well, her late husband was more of the archivist than she is," I said, dodging a Wichu seller of dubious comestibles whose wares were displayed on a tray slung around his neck. They smelled good, but I had been fooled by artificial ester sprays before. The Wichu held up a handful of wriggling noodles—at least, I believed that they were noodles—but I waved him away. We plunged into the crowd of shoppers. While humans were in the majority in the market, I edged past Wichu, Uctu and Croctoid visitors in plenty.

"Their father?" Madame Deirdre asked.

"Oddly, no," I said, glancing back at her, amusement sparkling in my eyes. "My great aunt has been married several times. Nine, I think. Her current husband is a man closer to my age than her own, yet finds it very difficult to keep up with her. I thought they would be coming along to the spectacle. I was rather surprised to have them decline. On an alternate extremity, the many weeks of travel from the Core Worlds to the edge of Zang space would try Aunt Nestorina's patience greatly."

"I would have enjoyed seeing her ladyship again," Deirdre said.

"And she you," I assured her, courteously. "No, Lord Malent was a great student of genealogy. He knew his own descent, dating all the way back to Old Earth. He thought he had traced the first of the

Kinagos to a humble beginning, as traders in pearls and seafood, he believed; but he died before he could make any conclusive pronouncements. I would have been interested in his findings, but, truthfully, not many of my relatives agreed with me. It is more to their taste to publicize the known family tree only from the point at which it became rich and powerful. Not that the information is unavailable on the Infogrid. All of our past foibles are readily available to the diligent scholar. It's a pity that he never wrote an autobiography, as so many of my more recent ancestors have done. I am sure it would have made enlightening reading."

"And that is why your dance has the ring of truth, Lord Thomas," Deirdre said, tapping her nose with her forefinger. "You don't shy away from the facts. Perhaps you will take up the study of your family one day."

"I doubt it," I said, cheerfully. "At the moment, I can't consider anything more delightful than my present enthusiasm for dance. I plan to perform until I can't move a muscle without assistance."

To underscore my point, I bounded forward, sprang into the air, and twirled one and a half times around. When I alit, arms outspread, I was facing my teacher. I bowed to her deeply with my right foot out before me, indicating that I wanted my fame to be during my lifetime, not afterward. Anstruther was moved to spontaneous applause. To my delight, so was Deirdre.

"Bravo!" she exclaimed, clapping her hands together. "You have licked the error of tangling your ankles together during your spins. Well done."

"Thank you," I said. I had labored in secret for weeks to correct the spin. It was gratifying to have her acknowledge my accomplishment. Nothing could have pleased me more.

"In movement!" she said, aiming an admonitory finger in my direction.

I stood straight, put my heels together, and inclined my head, hunching my shoulders to indicate humility. Deirdre smiled, showing long, narrow, almost rodentlike teeth.

"Very nice, indeed. Now we will work on your arm gestures. You have begun to acquire grace, but are still failing in meaning."

She moved an arm; I copied the motion. She repeated the movement again and again as we walked. I did my best to follow each nuance, squinting to follow her subtleties through the glaring neon forest of advertisements that broadcast in three dimensions from every surface, including the bodies of some vendors. It was only when my viewpad, that had been programmed to indicate when we arrived at one of Odile's shopping choices, chimed loudly that the lesson halted momentarily.

Anstruther laid her hand on the butt of her holstered laser pistol. Madame Deirdre glanced at me to determine the meaning of the sound. I sprinted lightly and halted before them both, stopping them in her tracks. Instead of performing an obvious pantomime of donning and doffing garments, I put on a show of looking over, then plucking flowers from an invisible garden. One imaginary bloom met with my greatest approval. I admired it from every angle. I held it to my nose and inhaled, with a look toward heaven as though the sweet essence raised my consciousness to another level.

"How interesting," she said, approvingly, then glanced to her right. The masonry building, a large one for the bazaar, had a large oval window behind which was a rotating display of handsome tailored garments. Elaborate animations on the walls surrounding the window proclaimed this to be the establishment of Volstang Bennett Icari XXIII, Clothier to the Rich and Famous. As if to reassure me of its clientele, it displayed becoming portraits of numerous guiding lights in politics, the military and the arts. I observed an image of my mother's secretary, Admiral Leven Draco, a man of prosperous figure and overwhelming eyebrows, in a suit I had in fact seen him wear. Yes, it was possible Uncle Leven had traveled in this direction and purchased something from Icari. "I didn't realize how deeply interested you were in clothing."

"Oh, yes," I said, fervently. "I live for fashion. I like to think that I always have the *dernier cri* at my fingertips. My cousins and I never like to be left behind the curve. We of the Imperium house have a reputation to uphold, on the Emperor's behalf, of course. My imperial cousin is a serious man, but he likes to look his finest. We can but seek to follow his example. At the very least, we prefer not to shame him."

"You could never do that," Deirdre said. Anstruther coughed, then looked sheepish.

"You would be surprised," I said. "In our efforts to indulge our whims, we sail rather close to the galactic wind, though we do seek not to find ourselves foundering in shame." A very dignified-looking man, of pigeon-like figure, in his fourth decade or so, must have been alerted to our presence by his advertising wall, and appeared in the doorway to beckon us in. "Shall we see what Odile thought was worth investigating?"

Madame Deirdre preceded me over the threshold.

"You grace my humble establishment!" the man exclaimed, clapping his large hands together with unfeigned delight. "I recognized you at once, Lord Thomas Kinago! Welcome to Icari! I am Volstang XXV, grandson of our founder."

"I am honored to make your acquaintance." I lowered my eyes in a gesture of modesty. "I presume that your databases learned the names of all of the noblemen and noblewomen traveling through this sector?"

"Oh, no, my lord," Icari said, leaning back on his heels with a broad smile. "Not you! You came to my attention some months back, when you demolished that ill-thought-out statue of the late Empress."

"Oh," I said, feeling my cheeks stain crimson. That was one of the moments of shame to which I had lately referred. Sadly, it would not have been a disgrace if I had managed to avoid the statue in question with my racing flitter, only a catastrophe.

"Don't take this the wrong way, my lord," Icari said, leaning close and nodding confidingly "Every one of us watching the vids thought that you improved on it, crashing into it like that."

"Well, when you put it that way," I said, brightening somewhat. "To add insult to injury, the amount of money it cost to repair the terrible monument put a crimp in my expenditures for quite a while. It emptied my pockets so thoroughly I was nearly forced to wear the same suit of clothes to two official functions in the same month!"

"That will never do, my lord!" Mr. Icari said, indignant on my behalf. "I have seen from my perusal of your Infogrid file that you enjoy the unique. Well, we pride ourselves on exclusives in design that you will never have seen anywhere. Please, take a look around. I can assign you a clerk, show you around myself, or leave you to explore on your own. Teesh!" Icari clapped his hands.

A slim Wichu with close-clipped white fur, a style I had never seen before as the Wichu were jealous of the lushness of their coats, slipped out of a curtained enclosure. He brandished a hand-sized device at us.

"May I scan your measurements?" he asked.

"I assume you already have," I said, with amusement. "You are asking if we would like you to reveal them to us."

"Yup," Teesh said, abandoning pretense. He held out the small screen. "Do you want to look at the readings? Some people don't want to know. They just want stuff to fit."

"Teesh!" Icari chided him. "We do not sell 'stuff.'"

Teesh was scarcely abashed.

"Right, right. Well, what do you lack, gentlepeoples? I guess you must be gentlepeoples, with lots of money, because *he*," the Wichu aimed a hairy thumb over his shoulder, "doesn't usually come out to talk to customers himself."

"You may so assume," I said. There was no use in denying it. I struck a pose, chin up, back straight. "I am Lord Thomas Kinago, cousin to the Emperor Shojan XII. This is Madame Deirdre, a galaxy-famous dancer and choreographer. Neither of us are lacking in funds to indulge. And this lady is Lieutenant Anstruther, whom you will find it difficult to impress." Anstruther looked a bit discomfited. I suppose I shouldn't have teased her, but it was irresistible. She wound up more easily than my little sister.

Teesh beamed, showing sharp yellow-white teeth. "This'll be fun, then. Come on, let me show you the top-of-the-range stuff . . . er, our finest garments and accessories."

Whereas in a Taino boutique, I might be surrounded either by holographic images of myself wearing the clothing on show or animatronic dummies wearing the costumes to show their fit and flair, such was not the manner in the House of Icari. Teesh hauled us before a triptych mirror, an actual silvered-glass contraption, and held up one hanger's worth at a time under my chin. Pinpoint lights, around the edges of the mirror and shining down from the ceiling, shed flattering illumination on my person. It was delightfully old-fashioned, and I enjoyed it.

"Midnight blue's not your color, my lord," he said, whisking away a long, silky body suit and replacing it with a puffy, ochre costume with bell-like sleeves. "You need a bit of life in your hues. The madam here, she could wear that with style. I'll show you a gown in a minute, my lady, that'll bring out your shape and hair color really nice. It's got rollers in the skirts that hike them up and down as you choose. Or you could just thumb through the racks. No extra charge for looking."

To my very slight disappointment, the oval racks were motorized. Madame Deirdre felt delicately at the fabric of first one, then another of the choices displayed thereon. I peered at myself in the peeling reflection. Teesh noticed my disappointment and replaced the costume for another one.

Truth be told, I had enough clothing for both the outward and the return journey. I did not want to think too far ahead in my wardrobe, considering how swiftly trends came and went among the fashionable cognoscenti. I should be horrified to return to Taino with last week's designs as yet unworn. The one thing I did lack was a costume to perform in front of the Zang. In spite of Parsons's objections, I needed to plan.

I began to observe Teesh's offerings with fresh eyes. Skill there was in abundance; that was not in doubt. The outfits were cleverly made, but any one of them could have been duplicated, and even improved upon by the skills of Hugh, my tailor—then I recalled with a start that I had just lent his services to cousin Nole. Apart from having the computerized tailoring program—not an AI, and therefore devoid of personality—on board the *Jaunter* put something together for me, this seemed my best alternative. At least I would find originality and soul in these creations.

"Do you know anything about Zang, Teesh?" I asked.

"Big gray fellahs," Teesh replied. "Stone bodies. They don't wear clothes, or what passes for clothes looks just like the rest of them."

"Have they ever shopped here?"

Teesh rocked back on his pink heels and thought deeply.

"Well, they've passed through now and again. Dunno that they ever stopped to look at anything. They don't exactly have eyes, more black pits into which everything seems to fall, is the best way I can describe it. I haven't got a clue what would get their attention, even though we specialize in show-stoppers."

"Ah," said Madame Deirdre, with a light clap of her hands. "We do like a nice show-stopper."

I could have applauded, too. That was it! I wanted a *show-stopper*. The garment had to be made so I could move easily in it, but have that gravitas so it would impinge upon the consciousness of a being that saw eternity and changed it to suit itself. But did Icari have such a thing in stock?

As the noisy metal racks rotated, I watched the garments sway by. Among them, I made note of a few outfits that might fit my purpose. One of midnight blue with close-fitting trousers and a nearly bare chest looked interesting. I could see possibilities of great symbolism in between the meshing gears decorating a brown leather coat that fell from shoulders to heels in one clattering sweep. No, the notion of wheels within wheels might be lost upon a people who had long ago left behind the need for surface conveyances. No, the one I needed to try on was almost military in flavor, but in the middle of its overshirt in a blue such as existed in between the moment between daylight and twilight it had a starburst made of twinkling lights and surrounded by a narrow band of brilliant red and gold such as might have arisen on that very moment that the universe was created. I started to raise an arm to point at it.

"I would like . . ." I began.

Madame Deirdre leaped toward me and pressed my hand downward with astonishing strength. She shook a finger in my face.

"Ah, ah, ah! No, Lord Thomas! Now we will continue with the lesson I want you to learn today. You must express yourself physically and symbolically alone! Let us see if you can make yourself understood without words. It is the task of the dancer to speak with your body, not your mouth. Language takes too many shortcuts. Show what is vital through movement."

I opened my mouth to protest, but Deirdre was adamant. I lowered my head to display capitulation. The shop clerk watched me with a quizzical expression on his broad, furry face. This would be difficult. To point directly at the tunic I wished to try on would be cheating. How could I evoke "the red tunic with twenty pockets but not the wooden buckle, in my size, please?"

"But, madame, such a thing is not nec—" Mr. Icari started toward us. He halted in his tracks as Deirdre held the warning finger toward him. Such was the power of her command of symbolism that he didn't question it at all.

"He must learn!" she exclaimed. "He will tell you through pure movement and symbolism which is the garment he wants to try on."

"Very well, madame." Icari eyed me.

I assumed first position, my feet arranged with heels together and my hands curved gently at my sides as I thought how to express myself.

I was looking for something special. Therefore, I must move as though I was questing. It would not be sufficient to pace around the room with my eyes on the floor as though I had dropped my viewpad. Longing and need must come through my posture, though not as desperate as the search for sustenance and shelter. Nor could I merely trudge. Grace must inform my every move. I had to perform as though responding to unheard music.

Without looking at the spinning racks, I raised my arms. Spreading my palms out before me, I grasped vainly for that which I could not hold. In my mind, I heard the tinkling of a piano, one of the pieces of music that Deirdre liked to use for sustained movement. I went into a dramatic crouch and ran around the room, dodging the numerous racks and models, seeking the object of my quest. I halted before Mr. Icari and brought my arm upward and across in a crashing salute, which extended into a sweep, describing the expanse of the sky. At least, I hoped he understood it was the sky. He followed the movement of my arm with a worried look, but one untampered by comprehension.

I realized I had to paint with a brush broader even than I had used for my cousins. With a swift glance at my teacher to ensure that she did not disapprove, I created a landscape. I moved from here to there, imitating trees, mountains, a running brook.

"The world, huh?" Teesh asked, beginning to catch my intimations.

I beamed at the Wichu. Then I gathered all my creations in my hands and drew them down into a tiny globe I held tenderly. He watched as I gathered more and more "worlds," making each tiny in turn.

"Okay, I guess . . . the system? Taruandula?" Now Mr. Icari had become interested. He peered at me closely as I plucked tiny "systems" from all around me. "The sector?"

Then I threw my arms around them all.

"The universe!" they chorused. I drew my forefingers together in a graceful gesture, keeping my face immobile, though inwardly I was beaming like a laser. Success! The two males cheered, then subsided, looking at one another with sheepish expressions. Such an outcry must seldom be heard in such a dignified establishment as Icari.

"What've we got that looks like the universe that salutes?" Teesh asked, stroking his massive jaw.

"The Starburst," Icari said. He clapped his hands together. "Teesh, bring the Starburst. Make certain it is in his lordship's size. It is for you, isn't it, Lord Thomas, and not for this lady?"

I glanced again at Deirdre. She widened her eyes slightly, giving me permission. If I ever thought that Parsons owned the trademark on microscopic facial expressions, Madame Deirdre came as close to anyone who violated it. I nodded.

The room became a bustle of activity. All of the rotating racks went into operation at once. Gondolas of clothing lowered themselves from the ceiling and raised up again as Teesh failed to locate the item he sought. I had a moment's concern in case they would not have what I wanted and would have to make it or alter it from existing stock. The longer we lingered on this station, the greater the chances that my cousins would find this place and strip it to the walls. All my hopes of holding an exclusive on choice fashions would be dashed. I knew that each of my relatives had their own list of establishments they had planned to visit, but I fancied I had the inside track on the very best of the best. Odile's recommendations had certainly paid off thus far.

I allowed my concerns to surface in movement. I drew my arms inward, wrapping myself in a cloak of misery. My shoulders drooped. My eyes went wide with hopelessness. So effective were my emotings that Icari himself came to lay an arm over my shoulders.

"Don't worry, my lord! That's a new design. We got in the whole range of sizes. I can't recall selling a Starburst in your size yet. I fancy we've got it here someplace. I apologize deeply for the delay. Please, allow me to get you a drink of something." He snapped his fingers.

A tall cylinder of a serverbot sailed into the room brandishing a tray. In a circular depression that contained chill circuits, a glass bottle of pale green wine shivered. A handsome decanter containing a rich red towered over various beakers and containers of a rainbow of liquids.

"Name it, sir. We've got it. Taruandula gets practically everything. Would you like a snifter from my private store of Nyikitu brandy? I know that's his Imperiousness's favorite."

I smiled, but shook my head.

"I know how hard that is to obtain, Mr. Icari," I said. "I prefer to keep my mind clear. That red wine looks entrancing."

The serverbot raised the carafe and poured a perfect measure into a glass. I allowed my features to return to their normally optimistic expression. Icari relaxed. The wine lived up to the richness of its color, sating my palate and wetting a whistle grown dry from exertion.

"A fine vintage," I said, allowing my free hand to create symbols expressing my approval. "My Imperium cousin wouldn't find this out of place in his own cellar." Icari looked pleased at the compliment. Lieutenant Anstruther was persuaded to accept a cup of tea, since she was on duty. Madame Deirdre took a tot of aged spirits, neat.

"Got it!" Teesh exclaimed. He waved wildly from the far corner of the room. In his other hand, he thrust forward a bracket hanger from which swung the blazing tunic I had admired. The server unostentatiously removed the glass from my hand as I reached out to touch the glowing garment.

"That is perfect for our purposes," Madame Deirdre said. "That expresses just the right note."

When I tried it on, I had to agree with her. Posing and turning before the triple mirrors, I admired the way eternity seemed to follow me no matter which direction I faced. It fit me perfectly. Even the trouser legs were the correct length. But the acid test was yet to be made.

I leaped into the air, kicking my feet out as far as I could to touch my outstretched hands. When I alit, the trousers were still intact about the rear seam. I could dance in them. The Starburst was a success.

"I'll take it," I said, to Teesh's and Mr. Icari's open delight. "Now, let's see what else you have to offer."

A couple of hours later, we emerged from the emporium, parcels in tow. In the soft-sided bag looped over my shoulder was an outfit I wanted to show off when my cousins and I converged on the shuttle to take us home. Madame Deirdre's bag, which I also bore, contained the dark blue gown whose enormous circle skirt offered so much scope for kicks and full spins. Anstruther, as I had predicted, did not find anything suitable among Icari's offerings. She was simply not as frivolous as I.

The majority of our finds I had arranged to have delivered to the *Jaunter* by drone. I wanted to reveal them one by one and surprise my cousins with my discoveries. We decanted into the streets, full of good cheer and new ideas for dances yet to come, our bodyguard in our wake.

When we returned to the shuttle, my cousins showed off all their splendid discoveries. Nalney had had a handsome portrait of himself embossed into a titanium plaque as a gift for his mother. Jil and Sinim wore diaphanous, jewel-colored costumes embroidered with lighted filaments that created moving patterns. Madame Deirdre spilled her bagful of "sparklies" all over the pull-down table in the shuttle to satisfying oohs and ahs from my cousins, who raked through them with envious fingers. Nesbitt, Redius and the other bodyguards from the *Jaunter* had bags of treasures to show. Even Anstruther had been persuaded to show off the beautiful red purse she had purchased to wear on her days off. My cousins fingered the rainbow-enameled accouterments with envy and enough praise to make the shy lieutenant blush.

None of their finds, though, were as splendid as the olive-green coat of fantastic design that I drew forth from its protective wrappings marked with the seal of the House of Icari. It had embroidered circular openings all over the sleeves, front and back, each of which contained an individual, original work of two-dimensional art. They were coded so that facts about each piece and its artist circled the aperture through which it was displayed upon request, and played music composed especially for each piece whenever that image was touched. In a package within a concealed pocket were another thirty images I could use to replace the existing supply of artwork. It was a marvelous garment, full of potential entertainment value. I looked forward to playing with it often over the course of the next few weeks.

My cousin Xan almost choked in disbelief at the wonder of it.

"Thomas, that has to be a fiction. You had that made up while you were on the surface."

"I promise you," I said, "I did not. I bought it off the rack."

"Entertaining," Redius said, dropping his jaw in the Uctu equivalent of a smile.

"Good, isn't it?" I asked, pleased.

"That is amazing, Thomas!" Nell said. She tried it on. Naturally, the hem fell nearly to her feet. She was a good third of a meter shorter than I. "Where did you find it?"

"The Icari emporium," I said.

"Where is it? I never came across it," Nalney said, his face nearly the same hue as my coat with envy. He fingered the art emplacements.

They lit up with a twinkle of light and sound. "We can turn the shuttle around. Take me back there! I want one for myself."

I shook my finger at him. "Ah, but no, dear cousin. I have secured an exclusive on this design for the time being. I extracted a promise from Mr. Icari not to sell another one of these until our return journey. You are welcome to buy one then."

"But I want one now!" Nell protested.

Xan looked a little sour, as if he had the same idea in mind.

"That's not very charitable of you, Thomas."

I sat back in my crash seat with an impish grin. "All's fair in love and shopping, Xan. How about the time you kept that vintner who made that excellent redberry brandy a secret for over four months? The poor woman couldn't even advertise her wares because of you. I'm not stopping Mr. Icari from selling his exquisite fashions. Just this one design. For a short while. You shall have one, or a dozen, when we come home again."

"It won't be the same, and you know it," Xan said, wrinkling his nose.

"I do know it." I favored him with a satisfied grin, laden with impish mischief. "I also hold close to my soul the fact that Parsons will hate it, but he can't stop me wearing it."

"Something ill will befall it," Erita warned, turning her pointed nose toward the ceiling. "One has never managed to thwart Parsons from the exercise of absolute correctness. He's been a guardian angel to us all over the years, but one with ironclad standards."

"Well, I steel myself to withstand the cold shower of his disapproval as though my cheery mood is an umbrella and a waterproof shelter on pylons."

During the transition to the *Jaunter*, we perused the delights of the coat and the many purchases that all of us had made. The special outfit for the Zang welcome dance had been stowed in the hold under my personal seal. I did not intend to reveal it until that happy moment came. I presume that my cousins had their own surprises to bring out over the course of our journey.

≈❧ CHAPTER 6 ❧≈

Surrounded by 110 Wichu guards and one massive ochre-scaled Solinian in the control room of the *Whiskerchin*, Phutes held his ground. Captain Bedelev snarled at him, showing sharp, yellow-white teeth. She pounded on his chest with a forefinger. The sharp claw at its end made no more impression upon his stony skin than the beat of her words on his audio receptors, but Phutes felt as though she had painted him with filth.

"Don't touch me," he warned her. "I have told you."

"And I have told *you* for the last time," she shouted, her voice echoing through the translator, "get the hell off my bridge and stay off! We're getting you to the platform as fast as we can. We'll enter the Zang end of Imperium space in about thirty hours. Stop nagging me! It's not going to make any difference."

Phutes listened to Bedelev's mewling and concentrated on the translated words instead. Could these uncouth creatures not even count in a civilized manner? Echoed by the weird grunts and groans of the device, his voice sounded just as peculiar in his own aural receptors.

"We are not moving fast enough," he said. Why couldn't she understand the urgency? "We must communicate with the Zang sooner. Change course. A Zang will be that way near now." He swung a massive hand toward galactic northwest, at an acute angle from the direction in which the *Whiskerchin* was heading. With the aid of the electronic devices and personalities on ships throughout occupied space, Fovrates had obtained information indicating the energy that heralded the impending arrival of a Zang was moving toward a nexus point. On the star charts it was designated as a planet occupied by carbon-based life-forms. In spite of the disgust Phutes felt, such a serendipitous encounter must not be squandered. The eternal creatures moved so swiftly that he might miss meeting it. "No time must be wasted."

"What does that mean?" Bedelev asked, lifting her bright pink lip in a sneer. "'That way' is not a navigational direction, and we are not *wasting* any time! This ship is going flat out. It's a cruise liner, not a destroyer. Any faster, and we could lose structural integrity when we hit the jumps."

"Not true," Phutes said, annoyed by her prevarication. "Fovrates tells more is possible. Improvement percent of 11010."

"Crap," Bedelev said, disbelief on her furry face. "If anything could be improved twenty-six percent, it damned well ought to have been. We'd have to jettison half of the life support and other systems and shore up the basic infrastructure to make that work."

Phutes concentrated his gaze on the round black eyes, as painful as that was. "Then do so."

The slime was obdurate. She folded her arms.

"Oh, please. Not a chance. We're not endangering anyone's life for your amusement. We're getting you to the platform as fast as we can."

"Change course. Move faster."

Bedelev narrowed her black eyes at him.

"Not a chance, stone face. This is what you paid for. We've got other passengers going the same way as you. We might miss the explosion if we made any other stops, and I'm not about to let my company get sued because we were dumb enough to take you on board. We have to pass through Imperium space to reach the Zang territory. That means going through a border station. That's our next stop. I'm not starting a war just because you people can't make up your minds. What if you change them again? Then where will I be?"

"I will not change!" Phutes insisted. "Our sources have detected a Zang on route to the platform. We must approach it soonest, before the event!" He swallowed his pride and made an appeal, as much as it pained him to do it. "We are your . . ." He could hardly force itself to use the term ". . . customers. Take us where we want to go."

Bedelev lifted her chin and folded her arms.

"Oh, so you want to renegotiate? I'll have to take it to the other passengers. They'll demand compensation. A change fee will cost you a thousand credits apiece. That's 1111100000 in your tongue, give or take a few digits."

Phutes could not contain his outrage.

"No! You will change course now, or we will miss the one with whom we came to speak!"

The furry brow lifted in curiosity.

"I thought you were going to watch the Zang blow up a planet, like everyone else."

Phutes clenched his fists, determined not to strike the Wichu. The guards moved in to surround him. They could hardly hurt him with their weapons, but they could push him and all his people out into space. It wouldn't kill them, but it would seriously inconvenience them and their mission.

"More!" he bellowed. "Foolish slime! Listen to me! Move the ship in the direction we need!"

"That's it," the captain said, throwing up a hand. Phutes flinched backward to avoid having any of the flying fur she had just shed land on him. "Take him to the brig. I'm tired of him turning up here every time he thinks of something else to complain about." She marched down the ramp toward her command chair. Phutes tramped after her.

"No! Listen to me! We must change course!"

The chief guard, indicated by the deep blue flashings on his chest straps, headed him off and beckoned to him with an open palm.

"Come on, buddy. Time to go."

Phutes turned his voice translator up to the highest volume. "No! I am not going until the captain agrees to my needs."

The Wichu winced but didn't back down. "She's not gonna do that. Now, let's move it out so she can get back to running the ship."

"I am *not* leaving."

"All right, buddy, have it your way."

The Wichus unwound coils of bright yellow, flexible, woven strapping. Phutes calculated the tensile strength as best he could. Possibly, if more than 101 secured his limbs they could immobilize them, but their pitiful furry bodies could not keep him from breaking free. Still, he had no intention of allowing them to try. He backed away from the guards, putting a waist-high rail between him and the squad. The angle of incline beneath his feet changed, telling him he was on the ramp that led toward the navigation console.

One of the guards looped his strap and began to whirl it over his head. Phutes changed the vector of his descent. Behind him was an alcove into which he could move, preventing the cables from dropping down over his head. He stepped backward. A soft obstruction met him and heavy restraints locked around his chest from the back. Phutes let out a bellow of protest.

"All right, Mr. Phutes." It was the Solinian. "Move it out. Now."

"Ech ech ech!" Phutes spat, wriggling to avoid contact. "Don't touch me! Remove your slime from me! Ech!"

"Who are you calling slimy, kitty litter?" the enormous scaled being demanded, breathing hot, fetid air past his aural receptor. "Creator's Teeth, but you scream like a hatchling."

The Kail flexed his torso, trying to tear loose from the Solinian's grasp. The stinking, rotting organic creature held fast. Phutes writhed and kicked. He could feel the rotting organic particles clinging to his flesh. He would have to scrub himself for 1010 days to get it off! With a mighty heave, he shrugged, seeking to break the Solinian's hold.

"You realize," the lizard-being gritted, sounding amused, "if you tear my arms off, you'll get covered in my blood and guts. How do you like that?"

"No!" Phutes bellowed. The stench overwhelmed his taste sensors, and the very idea made him shiver to the soles of his feet. "Stop touching me! Stop it, stop it, stop it!" His voice reached a high-pitched shriek.

Yellow bands dropped around both of them. By the time Phutes realized it, the Solinian had let go, and the restraints tightened over his limbs instead. The lizard-being moved around to stick his long snout in Phutes's face as the Wichu guards leaned back to hold their cables taut.

"Whiner," he sneered.

A humming noise alerted Phutes to the advent of a device on heavy wheels. A hook swam into his field of view and locked into a ring in the center of his chest. Phutes let out a honk of alarm. His feet lost contact with the floor. 11 more Wichus threw cables around his legs and tied them together. Now his whole body felt polluted.

"Let me down!"

"All together now, crew!" the captain bellowed. Phutes kicked as he dangled from a braced rig. The wheeled device, a flat platform made of nonreactive alloys, was rolled underneath him. Phutes struggled to escape. He sent impulses that would have raised a response from any electrical circuits connected to the platform, but there were none. The straps tightened around him the more he struggled. Phutes thrashed, trying to free himself. The Solinian, wearing no more expression than Phutes himself, pushed the platform off the bridge and into the lift shaft. The sturdy car carried them downward. Phutes bellowed.

"Siblings, aid me! Come to me, Fovrates!"

"Shut up," the Solinian said. "We locked up all of your gang already. You're the last."

At the lowest deck, the Solinian caught the handhold and swung out of the stream, taking the cart with him. He rolled it down the long corridor, past numerous doors. Those opened up at Phutes's supersonic summons, but no rescue came from within them.

"Fovrates, where are you? Help me!"

No answer. Phutes sought to put himself in contact with any grounded metal, to tap into the vibrations humming through the ship to reach his kinsman. His limbs were pinioned so that he couldn't touch anything but the nonresponsive plastic.

At last, the enormous Solinian yanked the cart to a halt in front of a wide door. Around him. Phutes could hear bellowing of his fellows from rooms along the corridor.

"We are here, brother! Help us!"

"I cannot!" Phutes called back. "I am trapped! Break out, come to me, for Yesa's sake!"

He heard the buffeting of bodies against heavy obstructions. The trapped Kail were throwing themselves at walls and doors.

"You are close to normal," Phutes appealed to the Solinian. "You have more native silicon in your body than these rotting Wichu. Let me free! We can take over this ship and free ourselves of the carbon-based menace. Help me, scaly being!"

"That's Mr. Carbon-based Menace Scaly Being to you, rocky," the creature said, showing a mouthful of shardlike teeth. "Forget it. You can sit in here until we get to the platform ship." At the top of the door frame was a brilliant white eye bolt. The Solinian pulled one of the cables securing Phutes through it, then hoisted him off the cart with one massive shrug. Phutes kicked and swung, trying to free himself, but his momentum only propelled him through the door. The Solinian swung it closed. It boomed shut, and bolts shot deep into the walls around it. When Phutes rolled to his feet, the pinioning cables fell to the ground. He immediately tried to shoulder his way out of the door. It was as though it had become one with the frame embracing it. The Solinian shouted over the boom each impact made.

"Someone'll be around with some lava dust and water later on. In the meantime, yell all you want. The captain will let you know when we reach the platform. Quit banging! You'll hurt yourself. The captain doesn't like it when the passengers hurt themselves."

Phutes stopped heaving his body against the door. He would find a way to be free of this prison! He looked around.

"Are you all right, my brother?" Sofus asked, his voice echoing hollowly. "I am on the next rock to you."

"I am intact," Phutes said, putting all the indignity he felt into his words. "I am filthy! Are you well?"

"We are. I did not get my bath before the slime surrounded us all and took us. They *touched* us. How dare they?"

"We'll make them pay for the indignity," Phutes assured him. "Can you speak to Fovrates?"

"No. There is no metal here. We are all speaking by voice only. Do you think they took him into custody as well?"

"I don't know. He is considered one of them."

Sofus paused a long while. Phutes knew he was offended by the very thought of being one with the hairy Wichu, even though it was part of their long-term purpose.

"We must get out of here and complete our mission."

"We will find a way," Phutes assured him. "Yesa is counting on us."

He threw the cables away from him. They were of no use, being too small for him to manipulate with his thick hands. Phutes took careful inventory of the chamber. Except that the floor was made in two levels with a step down of approximately .11 of his body height, and that it was 10 times as wide, but almost 11 times as tall as his body, it was featureless. The gray-black walls were lined with more plastic and nonreactive polymers. He could get no nourishment there. That must be what the Solinian meant: he would be brought nutrients and the means to clean himself. The lower part of the floor was furnished with a drain that smelled sickeningly of decaying organic compounds. It was meant to hold one such as he in solitary confinement.

Phutes looked up. But he was not in solitary confinement, not when he had the means to communicate with his fellow Kail. In the center of the ceiling, a light fixture gave off a weak approximation of the sun's light he enjoyed on the motherworld. He stood under it and smelled the air carefully. It did not stink of organic compounds. In other words, it must be fed by electricity, not chemical reaction. If he could reach it, he could use it.

The slime who had built the prison had taken Kail physiology into consideration, but not Kail intelligence and determination. While it lacked electronics that could be corrupted by his influence, it could still be forced to serve his needs. He tossed aside the round drain cover in the lower floor, set his hands on either side of the opening provided, and heaved.

It took nearly 1100 hours, but the plastic began to bend upward. Phutes's brachial and dorsal joints strained mightily. He hoped that his structural integrity would prove greater than the ship's plates. He refused to believe that it was impossible. At 11101 hours, a section of the floor broke off in his hands, sending him tumbling back against the wall. It boomed with the impact.

"Brother, are you all right?" Sofus shouted.

Phutes regarded the chunk of plastic in his grasp with grim satisfaction. It measured 10 times the diameter of his head, and was nearly 11 times as thick.

"Better than all right," he said. "Our chances of success have just multiplied 10000 times."

"How?"

"Wait. I will tell you when I succeed. I don't want those listening to know."

Twice during the next light period, Wichu guards came to the door. Through a hatch too small for the Kail to climb through, they passed collapsible tubs of water and purified stone dust. Phutes stopped his efforts to sift through the latter, judging whether any of it was fit to be added to his substance. They were used to providing Fovrates with nourishment, so Phutes took a chance that it would be suitable to nourish Kail. He tested it on his skin. It adhered well. The acids in his system bubbled up, surrounded each particle. He couldn't sense any insulting impurities. It tasted mostly of silicon and aluminum, but carefully devoid of conductive elements. These Wichu were no fools. But they were ignorant of Kail determination.

Once he felt the restorative effects of the new minerals in his body, he resumed his work. Within 1011 more hours, he had pried up another piece of flooring. A join that had not been properly sealed yielded yet one further block of plastic, this one measuring almost half his breadth.

He searched the subflooring for contacts to the electrical system. More than a meter of insulation supported the cell floor, but it and the platform beneath it were also nonconductive. He considered tunneling through the insulation and coming up through a service hatch somewhere else in the ship, but he did not fit in the gap he had produced. The ceiling was his only hope.

Phutes eyed the 11 irregular blocks of plastic he had torn loose. It would not be easy to balance one on top of the other, especially considering the condition of what remained of the floor, but he calculated that together he could reach the ceiling. Freedom was within his grasp.

Time after time, he stacked them together, trying to create a stable ladder. He had assumed that the last block would be his base, since it was larger and heavier than the others, but it had no flat edges. Reluctantly, after more than 11000 tries, he concluded that it must go at the top of the stack.

"Mealtime!" the Solinian's voice interrupted him. Phutes ceased his efforts and positioned himself close to the door, preparing to lurch out if given the chance. The hatch opened. Phutes surged forward, propelled by all his legs.

The guards had no intention of allowing an escape to happen. As his head emerged from the square opening, they dropped a length of fabric down onto it. Wetness dripped over his shoulders and down his arms. It smelled of decaying vegetation.

"Slime! Slime!"

Shrieking, Phutes retreated into the cell. A cloth tub of water and packet of stone dust were heaved in after him. The hatch slammed shut, and was locked tight with the alloy key.

Phutes sat on the floor, bellowing his outrage. He seized the water and poured it down over himself, seeking to cleanse off the insult. In the hall, he heard muffled cries of protest from the other Kail.

"Cut it out, or you'll get that, too!" the Solinian barked. "Just sit tight until we get you to the platform! That's what you want, isn't it? Stay put and shut up!"

Shaking with fury, Phutes threw aside the water container and rose to his feet.

That was the last chance. He would show no mercy to these creatures either. Once the Kail wreaked their vengeance upon the humans, it would be the Wichus' turn. But, one step at a time. The Kail had been patient, but no more.

He piled the insulation high and rammed the smallest block into it. Holding it steady, he balanced the medium-sized piece on it. They both teetered. He would have to hold them in place while he climbed.

The last and largest piece had to be propped on top. Phutes steadied the heavy mass with both his hands.

From the upper portion of the floor, he placed one foot carefully on the top of his wobbling tower. It slid apart with a clatter. Patiently, Phutes reassembled his structure, turning the topmost piece so it faced in the opposite direction.

"Brother, are you all right?" Sofus called.

"I am patient," Phutes called back. "Silence."

The Kail's voices died away in the corridor. The guards would have been wise to pay attention to the sudden quiet, but they did not understand the Kail. They had had their chance.

The tower fell apart time and time again. Phutes rebuilt it with focused calm, adjusting the structure a degree or 10 each way for maximum steadiness. At last, when he put a foot on it, it didn't move. He shifted his weight onto that foot and brought the next one up to the makeshift platform. It held! He wanted to bellow his triumph, but that might bring the guards again.

Instead, he concentrated on holding as still as he could while he brought the last foot to the top of the structure. The tower sank centimeters into the mound of insulation. Phutes did not have much time until it collapsed irretrievably. He raised his hands with the greatest of care, until he touched the light fixture.

The conductive materials in his skin connected with the metal contacts. Instantly, he felt the surge of electricity flow through his body and with it, the communications and programming that made the ship function.

"Fovrates," he said, sending his voice as an impulse that only another Kail would hear and understand. "Fovrates, they have taken us prisoner. It is time. We must take control now, or the opportunity will be lost!"

The low chuckle of the elder Kail came back via the circuits. "I have waited a long time for this moment. It is in our hands. Patience, now, and listen."

At that moment, the tower of blocks collapsed from under Phutes's feet. There was just enough purchase for him to hold onto the light frame with both hands.

He heard the outcry, through the circuits and through the air. His translator picked up on voices from over 110000 angry Wichu, crew and passengers alike.

"Who turned off the lights?"

"Why won't the lifts work?"

"Engineering! My door is stuck! I can't get out of the head!"

"What the hell is going on here?"

"Do you like that, brother?" Fovrates asked.

"Infinitely." Phutes smiled at the walls of his prison. Now that the Wichu were in the same fix, it did not bother him as much. He hung onto the light fixture, enjoying the annoyed outcry. "Take us to the Zang."

CHAPTER 7

"I had heard that there is a huge 'kaboom!' when the heavenly body disappears," Xan said, his long legs propped on the end of a deep blue brocade couch. The rest of him lay on a gorgeously embroidered warming rug on the floor beside the broad, transparent viewport at the bow end of our day room. It tended to be chilly at the perimeter of the chamber, thanks to the window, but our parents, aunts and uncles had insisted on this feature when the *Jaunter* was commissioned some forty or so years before. We all thought it was worth the trouble. When we were not traveling at faster than light speed or in the midst of a jump point, the view of the stars and nebulae was unparalleled. Like the rest of us, he was watching a near pair of stars with a speculative and proprietary air.

We had been cruising along at top speed since leaving the last jump point. The next one was a half-day's journey ahead, but we were not going directly there. The *Jaunter* had scheduled a stop for us at Counterweight. This handsome little planet had been discovered four thousand years ago by human settlers. It was renowned for being Earthlike, even more so than our homeworld of Keinolt. It circled the binary pair, which consisted of an enormous yellow giant and a tiny blue-white star. Of all the early human settlements, Counterweight was one of the few where none of our ancestors had needed to live in tight quarters of artificial habitats or make adaptations to their genetics in order to survive. The refreshing atmosphere held a perfect twenty-one percent oxygen level and was perfumed by esters from planktonoids and chlorophyllikes that were so similar to Earth-types that no terraforming had been necessary. Terran plants grew freely in the nitrogen-rich soil.

The difference between Counterweight and Earth, I had been informed, was that no intelligent species had evolved into prominence on the planet. That left it untouched and wild until our ancestors came upon it. Though it was isolated in between two of the most remote jump points in use at this end of Imperium territory, it enjoyed a reputation as a vacation spot and a retirement community for those who could afford the final passage thereto. As a result, the shopping, night life, beach culture, adventure activities and garden tours were all reputed to be excellent. My cousins and I were looking forward to spending three or four leisurely days there. Parsons had already alerted me by private viewpad message that our special guest would join us on Counterweight. All of this had me so filled with excitement, I could not sit down. I circled the room like a doomed planet trying to outrun the Zang.

"There isn't a 'ka' anything," Nalney said, lying back on the brilliant green damask couch he had claimed as his own with his eyes covered by a long-suffering arm. "No one can hear sound in space."

"I know that!" Xan said, impatiently, kicking a toe into the air. "But what about the shock waves? Don't they make any noise?"

"I suppose that they could be translated into noise," I said. "If there was a resounding chamber set to catch them. If it wouldn't be destroyed in the blast."

"There is no blast," Erita said, curled in the round chair she favored. A sticklike serverbot worked on her fingernails with tiny brushes and tweezers brandishing gems and miniature feathers. "The object just disappears. I have watched digitavids and old-style video recordings of the Zang. I've seen them over and over again. It doesn't explode. It just . . . goes." She fluttered her free hand, already decorated copiously with blue crystals, to match the day's blue gown.

"Please don't move, my lady," the 'bot said, in a plaintive little voice. It brought out a minute tool and scrubbed away at a place on her nail where it must have made a mistake.

"Oh, sorry."

"But there are shock waves," Xan insisted. "They ripple out to the edge of the heliopause. Beyond it, too, I believe."

"Marvelous!" Jil said, clapping her hands, which had already been adorned in red and green crystals and white feathers by the same 'bot. They looked rather marvelous. "I can't wait to see."

"It's quite wonderful," Erita said, fluttering her free hand. "According to the narrator, Professor Derrida, who is a scientist who's made numerous very popular digitavid series, the process is known only to the Zang. It doesn't seem to involve anything in the way of mechanisms. Not that we can see, anyhow. They evoke the energy from within their *bodies*. Well, who knows what they are concealing? They are so odd and blobby-looking. I wonder how they evoke anything at all." This thought appeared to puzzle her deeply.

"Or why they decided to do it in the first place," Jil said, lying back in her cushion-filled chair with a small cup of espresso garnished with a curl of citrus peel. Sinim, dressed in salmon pink silk, sat crosslegged on a massive blue pillow beside her. "I've never really seen the difference when it comes to doing bonsai on a plant. I know it's an art form, but what's the purpose of it? When you're done, you have a plant that is missing a few branches. Is it any more use than an unaltered plant?"

"What is the use of art?" Xan asked, lazily turning a hand palm up. "To be beautiful."

I could hardly help myself moving around at the thought. I executed a grand jete and landed on one knee before Erita.

"Do you think the star lanes are made more beautiful by what the Zang do?" I asked. Erita made a face at me.

"Oh, Thomas, how should I know? I'm no expert! All I did was watch the programs, darling. Star systems all look rather the same to me. Sun or suns in the middle, planets and space debris farther out, and that messy Oort cloud surrounding it all."

"Sounds like a pastry with layered filling," Nalney said, mischief causing playful wrinkles to form around his deep brown eyes.

"Now you're making me hungry," Xan said. He snapped his fingers, and an LAI rolled toward him with a tray held out. It helped him to a tiny plate of canapés. "I have a reservation at the finest mini-cuisine restaurant in town on the surface. If this delay continues for too long, I shall miss it, and that will make me cross."

"Would you like to see some of my digitavids?" Erita offered. "I think you will find the destruction of the binary system in the Dendrobium sector worth watching. It may divert you from worrying."

"No, thank you very much, Erita," Xan said, selecting a pastry topped with a bright green slice of fish. "I'd rather let the surprise unfold when we get to witness the real thing."

"I shall scream," Sinim said, her dark eyes huge in her small face. "I just know it." Jil patted her on the shoulder.

"There's nothing to be afraid of," she said. "It's not as if the planet they are removing is of any importance to us."

"But what if it was?" the girl asked. "What if it was one of our homeworlds that they decided to destroy?"

"They wouldn't do that," Jil said. "The Zang could destroy any planet, but they don't."

"They could!"

"Anyone for another game of hide-and-seek?" I asked, casually, hoping to divert Sinim from her self-induced panic. "I volunteer to be It again. One of you will beat me eventually."

Erita patted a yawn. "Not now, dear. You're too good at it. Perhaps later."

"*Perhaps later* means never with you, cousin," I said.

"Oh, no, I would never say never, Thomas!" Erita protested. Red blossomed on her sallow face. She had been caught out, and the others knew it. She wriggled her fingers at me. "Oh, very well. Once we know what we're doing today. If there's time, I will join your game. I have no idea why we are hovering here instead of going down to the planet to shop. I want a new belt to hold my pocket secretary." She plucked at the virtual spiderweb that held her viewpad to her narrow midsection. As the forecast for the surface was quite warm with a mild breeze, that portion of her body was revealed to sight between a boned sapphire-colored bodice and a sweeping pale blue skirt. "This one is getting quite threadbare."

"It was threadbare to start with," Jil observed, patting the embroidered pouch that hung at her side. "Why don't you get something that will conceal your device properly? We don't all need to see when someone calls you or sends you a file."

"Why shouldn't everyone see when I get a message?" Erita countered. "You all know how popular I am."

I joined in the general fleering that greeted that statement. Erita waved at us again, then bent to concentrate on how her manicure was progressing. I did a couple of lunges to work my quadriceps, performed a handspring that landed in a creditable split which I wished Deirdre had witnessed, and went to see how the *Jaunter* was progressing at maneuvering us into a parking orbit.

Through the viewport, I watched Counterweight turning serenely below us. It was a handsome place. Wide blue oceans covered more than half of its surface. I wanted to walk on a place that reminded our ancestors of our lost homeworld. What could be the holdup?

As if to echo my concerns, the doors to the lift shaft opened up. Lionelle stalked out, looking like the big cat for which she had been named. My younger sister was dressed for a day out, in khaki shorts with knife-creased cuffs that showed off her legs, and a white blouse covered with pockets and loops, from some of which depended miniature versions of gadgets. She brandished at us a domelike hat with a wide brim suitable for keeping the sun from ruining her perfect complexion.

"I can't stand it!" she declared. Such a dramatic entrance required attention.

"What is the matter?" I inquired. "We have attained orbit."

"But not parking orbit!" Nell said. "Has anyone reported to us? I can see the massive way station on the equatorial continent below. In fact, I've seen it go by more than thirty times! Why are the shuttles still blocked off?"

"I have no idea, Nell," I said. I beckoned to her. "We'll get down there soon. Come and have a bite to eat. Would you like to try one of my fruit purees? They will replenish your electrolytes brilliantly. I recommend the papaya-mango."

"My electrolytes are fine!" she said, throwing up a hand in impatience. "When are we landing? I want to see Counterweight. There's a train of real elephants going into the mountain jungle above the principal city. Elephants! Descended from the very beasts who walked on Earth itself! I am supposed to be on the lead beast! It's all white, and it's been painted with my coat of arms. I have a half bushel of apples for it from Great-Aunt Sforzina's private orchard! I thought you would be impatient as anything, Thomas. Aren't you signed up for the tour?"

"Not on this leg," I said. "I have a reservation for our return journey. Today I had planned a flying tour, then a pub crawl to be followed by a race tournament in atmosphere flitters. My vehicle is in the hold, prepped and fueled. You shouldn't worry. They'll wait for you, you know. You're a member of the Imperium house. They wouldn't dare depart without you."

"But what is the delay?" Nell asked, flapping her hat as though battering down invisible barriers. "They're not telling us anything! Go and find out, will you, Thomas? There's a dear. You have a way of worming information out of the dullest sources."

"Of course, Nell," I said, glad of activity that would take advantage of my brimful energy. I gave her a most elegant bow, with the back of my hand sweeping over my outstretched foot. "In the meanwhile, relax. I will report back as soon as possible. Over and out."

Nell laughed. I strode back to the lift shaft.

While I rode down the shaft of air, I checked my viewpad. No emergency messages had arrived from Parsons explaining the delay. Instead, I sent him a query. By the time I reached the command level, he still had not replied. To me that meant that something was up, and that he was involved. In the absence of further information, I had better ask the captain xirself what was going on.

I stepped off onto the platform and prepared to walk through, but the door did not automatically open. Instead, a red lens shimmered into life.

"Identify yourself," the wall said.

"Lord Thomas Kinago," I replied. "Surely you have been programmed to identify all of us. What's your name?"

"Please present credentials," the wall replied, without further courtesy.

I raised my eyebrows, but that did not seem to be enough outrage to overcome the wall's obduracy. Beginning to experience the first moments of pique, I thought of acting out all my family's frustration. It was far simpler to unlimber the viewpad from the pouch at my waist and hold the screen up for the red eye to read.

The door opened at once, revealing the dullest-looking corridor I had yet beheld on the *Imperium Jaunter.* It was as functional as it was unappealing. The beige kickplates were scuffed, and the stone-gray padding was of the most utilitarian to be had.

"Pass," said the wall.

"Thank you," I said, holding my chin high. "May I say that it has not been a pleasure interacting with you."

"Forgive me, Lord Thomas," the wall said, almost plaintively. "I am on duty." I felt abashed at my discourtesy.

"Ah. Forgive *me*. Thank you for your service. Let us speak later on, when you're off shift."

"We shall. I am WA-946l. I must close. Please pass."

I did so. My heels clattered noisily upon the uncarpeted gray deck. I would have to speak to my mother upon my return. That a section of the vessel was utilitarian did not mean it needed to be ugly.

Most of the common spaces on the *Jaunter* were segregated according to function. Our quarters, dining, entertainment center and day room were in a section all together in the center of the ship. Our support staff, including Madame Deirdre, a few reporters, some friends not of noble blood, and the other professionals hired for the journey occupied the section forward to that. They shared dining facilities and so on with the crew of the ship, who, apart from the engineering section in the stern, were located even further forward, just below the bridge and senior officers' cabins. I peered into the officers' gray-walled day room as I passed. It lay vacant. That in itself was unusual. Considering the size of the crew, there ought to have been a few there, answering correspondence, playing a game or so in the full-sized gymnasium, watching digitavids on the utilitarian but very good facilities installed there. (We insisted that our crews have only the best to occupy them when they were not caring for our needs.) Meals sat half-eaten, and a forlorn-looking LAI rolled around the room picking up trays. The diners had vacated in a hurry, and not that long ago. Something unusual was afoot.

The bridge was "up" a deck on its own in the center of the command center. A mechanical lift ran up to it, but it was not operational, even to one with my credentials. I sprang up the coated metal stairs that spiraled around it.

That chamber, which usually held eight or so bridge officers and the captain, a celebrated officer named Melane Wold, was crowded with humans, Uctu and Wichu, in uniform. I excused and pardoned my way through them toward the center seat, but it was unoccupied. I glanced around. All the senior officers, including all of my crew from the *Rodrigo*, were absent. Parsons was nowhere in sight.

Lieutenant Hamesworth, a sturdy young woman with very

short-clipped silver-and-blue hair, whose rank was second helmswoman, glanced up at me.

"Good morning, my lord," she said. The Wichu navigator beside her gave me a curt nod.

"What is going on?" I asked. "My cousins and I were looking forward to going groundside."

Hamesworth looked a little sheepish.

"I can't say, my lord."

"Can't or won't?"

"Can't," Lieutenant Argelev, the Wichu, said. "They're all in the captain's ready room." He nodded toward the side of the command center. Of the three doors set into that wall, one was surrounded by tiny red lights, indicating No Entry.

I began to be concerned for our well-being. I wondered if I should abandon my present course of action to go instruct my cousins and sister to hide in the diverse locations that had been made secure for their safety? What excuse would I give? Persuading them to play hide-and-seek was one thing. Dashing into the room and insisting on a game without further explanation when we were supposed to be preparing for a grand day out would be greeted with eye-rolls and derisive laughter.

No, I needed to know more.

"What event in the last six hours made them want to hold a conference?" I asked. I indicated the press of bodies around me. "Obviously, all of *you* know what has occurred, and you are awaiting some outcome. Won't you please tell me what it is?"

Argelev snickered.

"You're just going to have to wait to find out, sir, my lord."

"I disagree most fervently with that assessment, lieutenant," I said. "I seldom wait. I am always seeking."

In the absence of Parsons, I realized I was going to have to do my own frowning and pondering. Therefore, I frowned and pondered. If the matter was a life-threatening one, the *Jaunter* would have removed itself from orbit and made for a safe location, leaving the naval support ships to provide safe escape for her. Therefore, it was not immediately life-threatening. It had not been known before, or some arrangement would have been made in advance to cope with it. Therefore, it had come as an unwelcome surprise. It was a potential threat that affected the entire ship, or the rest of the crew would not be occupying less than optimum space per being in the bridge, nor would the captain have allowed so many to have left their stations. Therefore, it could affect every department. I did not see Parsons. Therefore, he was in on the discussion, making it important across more departments than just the navy. No one had informed me or my cousins as to what that event was, so it was something that would inconvenience us and cause annoyance that would cause us to complain and demand a solution. Therefore, they wanted to confer before they approached us with a change of plans. I thought, under those circumstances, it was within my right to ask for details. I could at least forestall the last of the concerns by bringing accurate information back to my cousins and friends.

With many more excuses and pardons, I threaded my way through to the secure door. I knocked upon it.

"No admittance," the door said. Its voice was similar but not identical to the wall near the lift. I presented my viewpad to the electric eye next to the frame. "I am sorry, Lord Thomas, but this conference is closed to those of noble rank."

"Ah, but I am also an officer," I said. "A senior officer, at that. I am the commander of the *Rodrigo*, a naval ship with armaments and offensive capabilities, in the hold of this very vessel. Look here." I changed the setting to my naval credentials and turned the screen back toward the eye.

"Your pardon, sir," the door said. It promptly slid aside. "Please enter at once."

❦ CHAPTER 8 ❦

"This isn't funny," *Whiskerchin*'s Captain Bedelev concluded, her face close to the video pickup. The officers clustered in the *Jaunter*'s ready room listened intently. "I'm stuck in my cabin. Most of us are! As soon as we went off shift, our doors stopped working! My people can't get into their stations *or* out of them. They're worried that the environmental systems are gonna shut down at any moment, and there's not a flerking thing we can do about it! So am I! That snoff-faced Kail has got the whole ship under his control. We're stuck! If you can see this message, get us out of here! Or if you can't save us, nuke the ship from space. Harro knows who else those stone-assed giants will take over next."

The transmission blacked out, to be replaced by the Imperium seal. The six humans and two Uctu at the oval table in the small chamber sat back in their molded seats, troubled expressions mirrored on all their faces. The two captains of the naval escort ships, Captain Colwege and Captain Lopez were present, courtesy of the tri-dee projectors in the ceiling, making it look as if they sat at the table, too. Ormalus, the Uctu communications officer, switched off the system. The mechanism lowered itself into the surface of the table.

Captain Melane Wold looked up from the screen. A slightly built human of average height with large eyes and hollow cheeks accentuating the shapely bones of xir face, xir delicate features belied the resilience and toughness reflected in xir service record. Xe wore a grim expression.

"And that's the ship that came into orbit around Counterweight at the same time we did," xe said, turning a slim hand upward. Xe glanced at Parsons, who occupied the seat at xir right hand. "I've taken evasive maneuvers to ensure that we're not in a common vector with it. The helm is ready to blast us out of here immediately if we have to."

Parsons nodded. "Your precautions are admirable, Captain."

The rest of the officers, Lieutenant Plet included, nodded and murmured agreement.

"Carrying too many of the Imperium's precious eggs in one basket," Wold said, wrinkling xir nose. "The crew's been running scenarios from the moment we heard this trip was in the offing. There was no chance I'd put the Emperor's cousins in jeopardy."

"We're keeping fighters ready to launch in case the Wichu ship makes a move," Lopez said. She was a tall woman with patrician features and warm brown complexion. Colwege, a white-haired, snub-nosed man with black, button-like eyes, nodded agreement.

"His Highness will appreciate your vigilance." Parsons said, gravely.

"But now what do we do? How did the Kail take over the *Whiskerchin*?" Wold asked. "They don't seem to care whether their captives communicate with the outside world. Do they think that they're unassailable?"

"Aren't they afraid we'll open fire on them?" asked Commander Atwell, the Jaunter's ordnance officer. He smacked a fist down on the tabletop. "That's an act of piracy! We'd be within our rights to take them down."

"No one wants to see a loss of life," Parsons replied, his voice a soothing lull. "The Wichu is carrying a number of civilians. Has anyone asked the Kail what they want?"

"Of course we did!" Wold said, spots of hectic color appearing on xir cheeks. "They don't want to talk to us. They're demanding to speak to Proton Zang. I've told them that it hasn't arrived yet. They insist that it has, but they don't know where. They want us to bring it to them."

"Have they said how they are aware of the Zang's presence?" Parsons inquired. Wold shook xir head and opened xir mouth to speak.

At that moment, the door slid open, and a head popped in. The appearance of the newcomer provoked a fragment of amusement in Parsons, but he kept his face from revealing it.

"Lord Thomas," he said in a level voice.

"What ho, Parsons?" the young man said, cheerfully. His face was flush with triumph, as though he had achieved some minor victory. He turned and offered a handsome salute to the senior officer. "Good morning, captain. Captains." He extended his greeting to the two holograms.

"Lord Thomas," Wold said, narrowing xir eyes slightly. "How did you get in here? Every system is on emergency lockdown!"

"The door didn't stop me." The young noble held up his viewpad. His military identification showed on the small screen. "I showed it my credentials, and it let me in."

"I'll have a word with it! You shouldn't have been able to pass!"

"His duties, captain," Parsons said. He checked his chronometer. Lord Thomas was a few seconds ahead of the time Parsons had estimated he might arrive. "As I told you, Lord Thomas requires access to the scout ship."

As evidenced by the strands of silver peeking through the captain's thick hair, xe had not been born within the last forty-eight hours. Xe gave Parsons a searching look, asking for further explanation. Thomas did not miss the expression. He saluted again.

"Lieutenant-Captain Lord Thomas Kinago at your service. My sister told me that no shuttles are going down to the surface. We're all panting to begin our touristing. Is there some way I may be of assistance? Perhaps my ship the *Rodrigo* could be pressed into service if the shuttles are otherwise occupied?"

"You're attached to the *Rodrigo*?" Wold asked, with an air of disbelief.

Thomas lowered his eyes modestly. "It is, in fact, attached to me. It's my ship. I am its senior officer."

"Lieutenant Plet is the commanding officer of record," Wold replied, with a nod toward the severe-looking blonde woman sitting on one side of the table.

Thomas smiled in a supercilious fashion. "Yes, that's the way the official record reads, but I hold superior rank to her. And to you. No offense, of course."

"With all due respect, your lordship, that has nothing to *do* with . . ."

Parsons thought it best to intervene.

"If I may, captain? I need to impart a piece of confidential information that must not be known outside this room . . . ?"

Wold collected nods from xir assemblage of officers. The Uctu communications officer palmed a control that threw an additional barrier of interference in the case of eavesdroppers. Wold returned his gaze to Parsons. "Well?"

Parsons tented his fingers. "It is this: Lord Thomas has been of use, now and again, in service to the Imperium, on covert missions. In a quiet way, of course."

"A noble?" Wold asked, disbelievingly. "Useful?"

"I take umbrage with that tone, with all due respect, captain," Thomas said, looking hurt. "I'm brighter than I appear."

"If you really want to be of use, my lord, please go back to your day room," Captain Wold said, setting xir jaw. "It would help if you would keep your relatives busy while we deal with this crisis. That would be the most helpful thing you could accomplish."

Thomas's eyebrows flew up. So did his hands, which curved gracefully over his head. Parsons recognized the motion as second position. He raised his own eyebrow a fraction of a millimeter. Thomas dropped his arms at once to his sides.

"So there is a crisis. I thought so. What is in the offing? I'm sure I can help. Anything to clear the logjam. My cousins are eager to get to the surface of Counterweight as soon as we can. We all have activities planned."

"No," Wold said, lowering xir brows. "We're not landing personnel there, and certainly none of you . . . aristocrats . . . until the alert is cleared."

Lopez cleared her throat. "We advise against it, my lord," she added.

"We don't need fuel or supplies at this time," put in Commander Tamber, the first officer, a stocky, older man with a nearly bald head. "Should we program in the coordinates of the next way station, captain? We can leave orbit with the bulk of the planet between us."

"No, please don't!" Thomas pleaded, his sea-blue eyes pools of abject appeal. "I'd sooner spend the rest of the journey in a cage with wild animals than my sister if she is thwarted of her elephant safari."

"Her *what*?" Atwell asked. Lord Thomas spread his hands, a helpless look on his face.

"A sightseeing journey on animal-back. Antique mode of transportation, and uncomfortable, I would guess, but Nell finds satisfaction in reliving the modes of yesteryear. She might even try to take a pair or so of the elephants home with her, if she finds them to her liking. I wonder if you could find a secure pen in which to hold them on our return journey, captain?"

"That matter is of little importance at this time, my lord," Parsons said, with a quelling glance. His lordship was not of a mood to be quelled, but he was able to distinguish between the present and the future. He turned an open and helpful countenance toward the commanding officer.

"Then what is? Believe it or not, captain, I can keep a secret. You won't believe what our brother has in mind for Mother's next birthday present! It's quite amazing . . . but I'm not allowed to tell. It could so easily get back to her." He leaned forward, confidentially. "The walls have ears, you know, in spite of your gadgets and devices."

Whether the reference to the First Space Lord was inadvertent or craftily deliberate, it made the officers surrounding the oval table, including those present by holography, sit up straight. Wold looked torn between two equally unpalatable decisions. It was not lost upon them that Lord Thomas Kinago was the son of Admiral Tariana Kinago Loche. Parsons felt matters begin to move in the direction that he felt would accomplish the greatest good. A plan had formulated itself in his mind, one that might lead to a bloodless solution. He would not have to lend even a modicum of persuasion to get the captain to allow Lord Thomas to be involved.

"May he be seated?" Parsons inquired, with a casual turn of his hand. "At this point it would be less harmful to inform him fully than to send him back without being apprised of the entire gravity of the situation."

"Oh, very well!" Wold waved Lord Thomas to an empty chair beside Plet. The young noble took the steps in short leaps, and twirled once before sitting down. Plet rolled her eyes toward the ceiling. "Exec?"

Without rerunning the message from the *Whiskerchin*'s captain, First Officer Tamber gave an admirably quick precis of what had already been detailed to the rest of the officers.

"They want to speak to the Zang in advance?" Lord Thomas asked, at the conclusion.

"That appears to be their aim," Parsons said. Lord Thomas's eyes went wide.

"Why now? They could have a word with it when we all get to the platform. Why take over the ship that was carrying them in the very direction they wanted to go, to bring them to the very beings they wish to speak with?"

"We do not know. It is not easy to speculate upon the Kail's motives. Once we all reach the viewing platform, the ambassador and his staff will take up much of the Kail's time. The Zang will, I presume, be absorbed in preparing for their spectacle. They may not remain long after it has been concluded. If the Kail wish to have a private conference, it would be wise to do it ahead of time."

"Why now?" Thomas repeated. "They could have made a request to speak to a Zang any time, couldn't they?"

"Isn't it difficult to encounter one?" Captain Wold asked. "The diplomats said we only know where this one is because it asked to observe us."

"Sounds like the Kail know how to find them if they managed to determine that Proton Zang was coming here," Thomas said, toying with the controls for the display console. It started to rise. Plet reached over and clapped her hand on the "down" switch. The mechanism subsided. Lord Thomas grinned at her. "It's a useful talent, Zang-detection. We ought to ask how they do it. We might have Zang zinging all over the place in the Imperium and never know it."

"But Lord Thomas is right, Commander," Plet put in. "If they can contact the Zang, why didn't they do it before leaving Kail space?"

"It may be that the Zang don't like visiting Kail space," Thomas said heartily. "I hear it's desolate. Lots of planets, precious little life except for the ugly creatures themselves. No greenery at all."

"We have no confirmation that the Zang prefer planets with plant life," Parsons reminded him. Thomas looked abashed.

"Quite right, Parsons. I'm afraid, despite my eager anticipation of the spectacle ahead, I have not devoted much time to the study of our host species, only of their past demonstrations of planet-pruning."

"If you don't mind, my lord . . . ?" Captain Wold said, pointedly. Thomas settled back easily in his chair.

"Of course, captain. I was being inconsiderate. Your room, your rules. Pray carry on."

A low whooping noise erupted. Lieutenant Ormalus flipped open the screen at her table station and ran a disklike fingertip down the scope.

"Sir, program intrusion in progress! From the Wichu ship."

"What kind?" Wold demanded.

"Attempted breach of computer systems. Database." The Uctu made passes that caused moving graphics to rise from the screen. She scanned them with narrowed eyes.

"Has it broken our defenses?" Wold asked.

"No." The coral-skinned female switched her narrow mandible from side to side, emitting a worried clicking noise. She drew one of the charts upward and expanded it. Within the framework, bar codes rose up and down. One near the side of the frame quivered near the top. "Curious. *Navigational* database probe."

"Well, what do they need that for?" Wold asked. "Navigational charts are in wide usage across the galaxy. They're posted on the Infogrid, for pity's sake! What's wrong with the map system on the Wichu ships?"

"It could be looking for something the Wichu don't have in their atlas," Thomas said.

"A star chart isn't a secret," Wold said. "The probe isn't targeting population numbers or defense installations."

"Then, what?" Tamber asked.

An alarm erupted from Ormalus's scope. "Penetration!" She pinched the bar in the chart. It shrank at once to the bottom of the frame. "Auto-overrides also operational."

"Can you tell what it read?" Parsons asked.

"Running diagnostics," Ormalus said. "Still nav charts. Only nav charts. Peculiar."

Lopez leaned to the left, as if listening to someone who was not within range of the video pickups.

"We're seeing an intruder, too, Captain Wold. We thought we were well defended! This is not a straightforward attack on our systems. It seems to be coming through personal accounts."

"Sending override information to your ships," Ormalus said. "Confirm?"

Lopez listened and nodded again. Colwege did, too. "Confirmed, lieutenant."

"Please forward the data to me, lieutenant," Parsons said. "Along with the portals they used to invade the system."

The Uctu gave him a severe look. "Mine not fault."

"Nor my comm officer," Colwege said, lowering his snowy eyebrows threateningly.

"Most likely not," Parsons agreed. "The Kail have a reputation for being able to interact with electronic systems. Curious for a race that manufactures no technology of its own."

"How do we defend against it?" Wold asked.

"Require approval for any incoming data. Automatically weed out all casual requests. Shut down access to the Infogrid except as needed until we are out of contact with the *Whiskerchin*."

Wold exploded in outrage. "That will cripple us! We have streams coming in from all over! Our transmissions will slow below a crawl."

"Assign LAIs to monitor. They can process exabytes of data faster than the passive systems. Run virus checks on their systems frequently to ensure that they have not been corrupted themselves. It would be wise to add layers of security."

"But LAIs will be able to tell if their systems are faulty," Lopez said. "I trust my people, all of them, flesh or circuit-based."

"Better to have redundant checks," Wold said. The bright spots appeared on xir fine skin. "Make it so, exec. I feel as though we are under siege. An attack will almost certainly result in some casualties. I want to avoid involvement in a raid, but we will do what we have to to protect the *Jaunter*. Our escorts are intended to provide cover if we need to cut and run, not to start a war."

"They need our help," Lord Thomas said. "The Wichu are our allies, and they are prisoners on their own ship. Shouldn't we do what we can to remove the Kail?"

"Short of attempting to breach the *Whiskerchin*?" Wold asked. "That is not in my brief, my lord. The defense of the Emperor's family is of paramount importance! You are our priority."

"That's all well and proper," Thomas said, "but is there no middle way you can determine?"

"Not under these circumstances, Lord Thomas!"

"There might be a way we can gain leverage," Parsons said, calmly. "It is convenient that Lord Thomas has joined us."

"How so?" Wold asked.

"The Kail seek Proton Zang. We are to take it and its human escort, Dr. Derrida, on board. You captains each received the details of its proposed meeting point via secured data packet this morning, as did

I. If we take the Zang on board the *Jaunter* before the Kail encounter it, we will have an upper hand. The Kail will need to negotiate through us to interact with the Zang. We can demand terms, including the release of the Wichu vessel or the Wichu crew."

"They are monitoring us," Colwege pointed out. "They'll know if we send the military escort we had intended. The *Whiskerchin*'s sensors will see weapons and troop movement and follow it to our destination!"

"Then we will not send a military escort," Parsons said. "Lord Thomas, as I have already indicated, is a resourceful individual. He will go to meet the Zang."

"One man in a shuttle will attract as much attention as a troop carrier," Lopez said.

"Then we will hide him in a crowd," Parsons said. "We will allow the rest of the nobles to fly down to the surface as a group. Once there, they will scatter to the four winds, making it difficult for the Kail to determine which if any to follow. That will necessitate requiring them to leave their pocket secretaries and viewpads behind, not to mention any LAI employees and servants."

"Why not bring simply it on board with an official escort?" Captain Colwege asked.

"Well, it would seem too anxious, wouldn't it?" Lord Thomas asked. "As military personnel, your presence would seem to make a statement that the Zang is being taken into custody to prevent it making contact with the Kail—which is rather what you have in mind, isn't it? But if I invite it on board, then it's just the courtesy of a cousin of the Emperor himself making our visitor welcome. I can even bring it gifts. I've choreographed a dance of welcome, complete with original music and lighting effects . . ." His hands rose again to describe an arc.

"No, my lord," Parsons said, heavily. "No dancing. Pray comport yourself with dignity."

The young man looked crestfallen. "Oh, very well," he said, his voice falling into a singsong recitation as though he was a small child being chided by his mother. "I will be as careful with my courtesy as I would during the visit of a head of state to the Imperium court. I will watch out for any Kail wandering about the place, and obey my security detachment in case of alarums and excursions. I will not endanger myself or my guests unduly. I will exhibit decorum as befitting someone of my station and responsibilities. Will that be suitable, captain? If something happens to me, my mother will understand. She is not unaware of my comings and goings."

Wold shook xir head. "No. I can't let them go unguarded. The Emperor would have my scalp if something happened to one of them."

"I'm willing to do it," Lord Thomas said. His eyes shone. He was undoubtedly picturing storybook heroics in which he was the chief protagonist. "Send Redius with me. He's amazing at hand-to-hand combat with a bokken. I'll bring my sword and pistol. None of them have any technological elements, unless you count a firing pin. It's in the name of Imperium security, isn't it, as well as the defense of our allies? My cousins will be eager to participate under these circumstances. We like an interesting subterfuge in a good cause."

"They will be unaware of the subterfuge, my lord. You may express to each of them that they need to leave devices behind because of the situation, but for their own safety, not to aid the Wichu."

"Oh, very well!" Thomas rose from his seat and went through a gyration that seemed to suggest disappointment and the dislike of being under authority. He sank back into his seat. "We shall do as you suggest. What about it, captain?"

Parsons watched the idea percolate through the consciousness of each of the three captains. Wold held xir viewpad to xir lips. Lopez and Colwege did the same. They conferred in private for a moment. Wold turned to Parsons.

"Are you sure you can trust this . . . young man?" Wold asked. Parsons could tell that the word for which the latter phrase was substituted was not complimentary to Lord Thomas. "We do not want to offend the Zang by sending a . . . a non-diplomat." That, too, was a euphemism for the captain's original thought.

"It has indicated through its representative that it wants to study us. Lord Thomas will be as good a specimen as any with which to begin."

Thomas brightened and his hands began to describe some symbol. Parsons turned a steadying look upon him that caused him to fall motionless. His lordship had presented the captain with his credentials from the secret service, but his requirements for obtaining passage off the ship would be thwarted if he appeared too unsteady.

"Very well, your lordship," Wold said. "We'll arrange a shuttle for you immediately. Just you."

"Splendid! But what about my cousins? And, if I have not emphasized the importance of her wants and needs, my sister?"

"I am very reluctant to let the rest of them go. It might be very dangerous while the Kail are abroad."

"If I go, they will kick up a ridiculous fuss if they're not allowed to come, too," Lord Thomas pointed out. "Are you prepared to have your Infogrid file bombarded with plaintive and increasingly shrill messages from them and their many correspondents? I assure you, my cousin Erita is capable of some dangerously pointed sarcasm."

"We will assign security to each of the nobles," Parsons offered, as the captain wavered. "They will be at least as well protected spread out on a planet as they are confined within one ship. If one is attacked, which is most unlikely considering that the Kail do not seek to interact with humans, the others will have warning and can take cover. I can ensure that their bodyguards carry devices that will block them from tracking devices. I will accompany them, but Lieutenant Plet can oversee the operation." Plet, beside Thomas, straightened her already upright back another two degrees. "The nobles will go about their business without hindrance, as they would on an ordinary occasion, allowing Lord Thomas to make the single contact that is necessary."

"That sounds like a license to commit mayhem," Wold said dryly. "Particularly in light of the tracking blockers."

"Naturally," Lord Thomas said, with a boyish grin. "How I wish that such a thing had been in my possession when I was on Kazuro 5 . . . but I digress. I will meet the Zang and escort it here, under cover of touring, shopping and carousing while you deal with the Kail. What do you say? I have been gone a long time. I hope to return to my cousins with welcome news."

The captain exchanged glances with Parsons and xir fellow senior officers.

"Very well. It sounds like the best solution. If necessary, all of you must take to ground on Counterweight. No heroics!"

"You have my word," Thomas said, with a hand over his heart. "We are very good at concealing ourselves when there is trouble. You won't see us for dust. The Zang and I will be in the same hiding place, waiting for your retrieval." He rose gracefully from the chair. "I'll have my cousins ready for departure within the hour."

"And remember, my lord," Parsons cautioned, as Lord Thomas made for the door, "no dancing!"

Thomas wrinkled his nose.

"You absorb all the fun in the room, Parsons, like a veritable black hole. Have I ever mentioned that?"

Parsons allowed himself a minor sigh.

"Frequently, my lord."

The door slid shut behind the young man, and the red lights circled the portal to reinstate security protocols. Wold lowered xir thin brows and stared at Parsons.

"Are you sure this is the best way to make contact with the Zang?"

Parsons allowed his shoulders to rise and fall no more than a millimeter.

"What better camouflage than a collection of profligate nobles on the loose across the world? If the Kail have not been able to pinpoint the Zang by themselves, then we have a negotiating point to free the Wichu. It is worth a try."

❦ CHAPTER 9 ❧

"Thomas, you have saved the day!" Nell said, giving me another fierce hug as we sailed down in a spiraling orbit toward Counterweight's surface. She and my cousins had accepted the presence of the bodyguards without a second thought.

"Well done," Xan admitted. "I'm perfectly happy to add this lovely lady to my dinner party. We shall have a wonderful time." He bowed to Plet, who looked nervous and wary. My cousin had a reputation with women, and Plet knew it, but he was also no fool. An unwilling partner was an unwelcome one. If she had shown interest, he might have pursued her. As it was, he would not even exude innuendo in her direction, not that she trusted his reticence. Knowing Xan, I didn't blame her. He had only left his three current inamoratas at home because one of them had to return to her job as chief broadcaster on one of Taino's popular news networks, and the others had to return to their master's degree studies. Two of the others had come along, though they had been forced to remain aboard the *Jaunter* during this excursion.

Nell eyed Lieutenant Dorr Stover, who was to be her second throughout the jungle expedition. Since the guards were to wear mufti, she had insisted he don riding clothes and a wide-brimmed hat. He looked awkward in both.

"You're sure you can ride an elephant?" she asked.

"I'll hang on as best I can, my lady," he promised.

"Hmph," Nell snorted, clearly unconvinced. "We'll see."

Jil took the offer of an escort better than most of the others. After all, she had flown with my crew all the way to the Uctu Autocracy and back. During that time, she had struck up a friendship with Oskelev, the pilot of the *Rodrigo* and the finest helmsWichu in the Imperium. Oskelev had on her finest off-duty harness. I knew that hidden within her thick white fur was an analog-powered arsenal. I need fear nothing for the safety of Jil or the others in her coterie. Besides Sinim, Jil had brought along a naturalist from Taino's top wildlife preserve, which occupied an entire small continent at the equator; a musical trio, and a reflexologist. They wore beach attire. Quite some persuasion had been required in order for her to bring them to the surface with her. The rest of my cousins had security personnel from the *Jaunter*'s crew as their seconds. I could tell that Nalney's escort was going to have to keep track of all his many garments and accessories on the go. He was absentminded about property to the point of absurdity, capable of returning home wrapped in a towel because he had forgotten where he had placed his outerwear when he went swimming. His pocket secretary was programmed to remind him whenever he put something down. He was clad in his favorite emerald green.

My party of three was dressed for hot weather. Contact had been opened over secure channels with Dr. Derrida, changing frequencies again and again whenever a breach was detected. She informed Parsons that she and Proton Zang would meet me in the complex of whistling sandstone caves complex three hundred kilometers south of the main city, Nerk. Redius wore a desert robe that he had obtained during our sojourn to the Autocracy and looked suitably mysterious with the hood pulled almost down to his short, blunt muzzle. I wore light, loose-fitting stone-gray clothes of natural fabric that provided ease of movement, and a broadbrimmed hat. Because my mission was unofficial in nature, I had to suggest to my relatives that I was looking for inspiration among the remains of humanity's ancient history on Counterweight. My promised pub crawl and other activities would follow, once I had gained sufficient enlightenment. In a way, that part was true. I would return to the ship knowing what it was like to meet a Zang. Madame Deirdre wore thin, moss-green leggings under a knee-length caftan. Her long silver hair was knotted up on the top of her head underneath a wide sun hat.

"I have a list of some of the most interesting ruins," I said. "I have arranged for a guide to take us around to some of the best, including the Temple of Sport, the Government Labyrinth, the Corporate Citadels, a number of enclosed marketplaces, and a few castles. We'll end at a magnificent wilderness site that I long to see. All of those ought to inform my understanding of my ancestors and provide marvelous material for new performances. And I look forward to seeing what inspiration Madame Deirdre will gain from the same places. I anticipate that they will have little in common but the source, but that is the joy of interpretation. To each one's own."

Deirdre's eyes shone. "I can't tell you how delighted I am!" she gushed. "I couldn't have afforded a trip to Counterweight on my own. The grandchildren are going to be so excited! I have to find them something special as mementos."

"We shall," I promised her, "if I have to commission something from a local craftsman to make them."

"Stand up, please, my lord." I rose to my feet and held my arms out from my sides so Lieutenant Plet could scan me. She took her duties seriously. She checked with each of the guards one at a time to ensure that no one was carrying any devices that could be detected or corrupted by Kail transmissions. Nearly all my relatives complained about the lack of cameras and other recording devices with which to take pictures or videos of our sojourn that could be uploaded to the Infogrid, but as I pointed out, Infogrid booths and freelance photographers abounded across the planet. They would not lack appropriate documentation for bragging rights among our relatives who had not made the journey. And, no limits had been placed upon souvenirs they might choose to bring back with them. Parsons had also provided us with mechanical cameras that made passive images, which would have to do.

"Many of the merchants below make their living selling digitavids of the sights," he had pointed out. "It would be courteous to peruse their offerings and enrich the locals."

"Well, we can afford it," Nalney had said, heartily. "Why not? As long as I can get my picture taken in the giant waterfall up in the Fanbrel Mountains, I'll be happy. It'll make Nole as green as an emerald that he didn't come, too."

"If you don't lose the pictures on the way home," Xan said, with a mischievous grin.

"I won't! Not with this responsible fellow to look after me!" Nalney tapped his security guard in the chest with the back of his hand.

I smiled to myself, knowing that his brother could not be too far behind us, and might even have drawn ahead. I would keep my promise to Nole in any case, but it was rather fun to know something that no one else did. On the other hand, Parsons probably had a trace on Nole's new ship and could tell me where it was to the microparsec. In fact, I would have wagered a large portion of my next quarter's income that he had seen it, explored it, and installed listening devices throughout. I glanced toward the rear of the shuttle, where Parsons sat alone, black-clad and black-haired, monolithic, like an obsidian statue of a benevolent deity watching over us. His dark eyes met mine for a brief instant, then shifted a few degrees upward, disconnecting from my gaze. The man was uncanny. It felt almost as though he had switched off and become inert like the statue of my fancy.

Nell stared dreamily out of the port at the planet, which grew nearer and nearer with every pass. Eight continents, two large and the rest small, were arrayed in a rough pattern that approximated an infinity symbol set in an ascending angle that wrapped from well below the equator to well above. The rest of the planet was winking blue ocean studded with green and brown archipelagoes, and topped and tailed by white ice caps that stretched out 15 degrees from each pole. Glaciers straddled the heights on the most northern and southern reaches of the continents. We would be landing on the third-largest continent, which featured active volcanoes, vast jungles and the longest river on Counterweight.

"It's absolutely beautiful, isn't it?" she said. "I wonder how much like Earth it is."

"We'll have to take our ancestors' word for it," Xan said. He leaned toward us confidentially. "Some people say this is Earth itself, but terraformed after a cataclysm of some kind."

"If this was Earth, wouldn't they have found a billion tons of artifacts?" Nalney said, scornfully. "I've heard too many tales of the plastic continent in the Ocean of Serenity and the Cities of Rust."

"It probably is Earth," Jil said, with a toss of her magnificent waves of caramel-toned hair. "I would like to think so. All those artifacts were probably sold to tourists and museums thousands of years ago! Otherwise, it's just pure carelessness that our ancestors mislaid our homeworld like that. If you ask me, they only want us to think it's somewhere else so we won't flock here like vultures and ruin the place."

"It's too hard to get to," Rillion said, yawning. His long red hair was braided into a queue under his sun hat. "Actually, you make a good case, Jil. Thomas, doesn't your father say that his brother lives on Earth?"

"Uncle Laurence?" I asked. I laughed, perhaps a little too loudly. Nell joined me. "He loves to travel. Perhaps he said once that he was looking for Earth, and Father likes to keep up the joke."

"That's it, surely," Rillion said, looking ashamed of himself. I was defensive about my father's mental fragility, and the others usually refrained from making comments that would point at it. "If you find Uncle Laurence here, be sure and introduce us."

"I certainly will," I said. After all, this lovely blue world was as good a place for him to be. I reached for my viewpad to send him a message, then remembered that it was back in my cabin. Ah, well, there were public portals I could use on the surface. "What if it is Earth, after all?"

The idea began to percolate through my mind. Before I knew it, I was starting to believe it. It resembled the ancient three-dee images that had survived from the ancient times. If Earth had not been destroyed in the cataclysm that drove humankind into space, it might look like this now. History had become such a muddle in the last ten millennia. What, after all, was the truth?

"Look out, all!" Xan called, bracing himself against the port to watch. "We're landing!"

We all cheered as the shuttle hissed onto its landing strip.

Parsons left the ship unobtrusively while officials hustled the young nobles and their escorts into the VIP area of Customs and Immigration. There had been a few small complaints about the lack of personal technology, but there was simply no need for any. Their identities were easily verified through biometric matching and DNA scan. Payments for purchases would be carried out in the same way. Plet was fully briefed on every process that any of the Imperium family might need while on Counterweight.

From a pocket in the back of his tunic, he shook out a bright green caftan and slipped it on. The massive hood concealed his face from onlookers, though the fabric was woven so he had perfect visibility through it in all directions. The thread also distorted biometric scanners. No one would recognize him, nor, he reflected as he left the building by a side door and slipped out into the street and joined the brightly-clad mass on the move under the warm summer sun, notice him at all.

CHAPTER 10

When we emerged from the shadow of bureaucracy into the streets of South Town, I took a deep breath. Though it had not been many days since we visited Taruandula, and not that long since we had left Keinolt, I felt as though I had finally reached a source of oxygen. I couldn't gulp in enough of the moist, fresh, clean air. It seemed to me to be flavored with subtle perfumes like lilacs, spices and a smack of sea breeze. I spread out my hands and let them ride the gentle wind flowing around me, letting them symbolize the pleasure I felt and the nourishment I took from the atmosphere.

"Fragrant air," Redius said. Uctus sounded abrupt and terse in Human Standard, but I spoke his native language fluently, so I realized how many-layered was that simple phrase in his tongue.

"All of those things," I said. I threw my head back and turned, letting the welcome warmth of the sun caress my face.

"Absorb these sensations," Madame Deirdre said. "Remember then for later. You will want to add them to your vocabulary of movement. Assign a symbolic stance to each one that expresses it clearly to your audience."

I nodded and tried to fix the impression in my mind of each scent in the air. Did they make me feel happy, exhilarated, excited, nostalgic?

"Can you feel nostalgia for something you have never known?" I asked. "How could I express that?"

"Oh, yes," Madame Deirdre said. "As thus." She lifted her chin slightly, tentatively. She extended her hand, fingers out, then drew it toward her, the percussion side of her palm in the lead, as if scooping something toward her. I felt a magnetic pull in the gesture, as if she was willing it to come to her. Suddenly, as if of its own will, the hand retreated. The stricken look on Deirdre's face as it flitted away wrenched my heart.

"Good!" Redius said, appreciatively. "Crushing."

"That's it exactly," I said, full of admiration as always for her skill. "Madame, it will take a lifetime to equal what you do so casually. I must practice that."

The hand ceased to retreat, and instead fluttered lightly downward in a circular acknowledgement of my compliment. Deirdre bowed after it, her hand brushing her shoe.

"I am flattered, my lord, but you're learning. Keep at it. Your movements should be your own, not merely copied from me. Although bodies are limited by their structure to a given number of motions, there are myriad ways into which those can be combined."

I had ordered a vehicle from a service there in Nerk that had promised spaciousness and elegance as well as an expert and knowledgeable driver. All comforts were to be laid on, including refreshments and some of the best wines from a local vineyard. Although Nell and several of my cousins had arranged outings that would last several days, I had scuppered my own plans to accommodate my assignment from Parsons. Instead, I intended to return every evening to the *Jaunter*.

As we waited for our transport, I attempted to imitate Madame Deirdre's expression of longing. I had always thought of Keinolt as my home, but Counterweight resonated with me. What if humankind had been living in the wrong place all these centuries? I tried to evince my sense of seeking belonging in a place I had never been before. My shoulders collapsed inward as my hands drew toward my heart, trying to place Counterweight into my soul. I bowed my head over it. I almost wept from the longing. This could be our long-lost home!

Some passersby glanced at me uncomfortably, and hurried their steps to get away from me as quickly as they could, but others, overcome by curiosity, stopped to watch.

I ran around the circle, absorbing their expressions. Some were sympathetic, others impatient, a few scornful. All of those were valid impressions of this stranger in their midst. With my movements, I implored them to take me in, to allow me to stay, to become one of their own. If this was Earth, I could not leave without feeling I would be permitted to return and lay my bones in the birthplace of my ancestors. For this last thought, I pretended to delve into the soil, digging my own far-future grave, and threw my heart into the void that yawned at my feet.

Redius watched me as long as he could, but he started hissing uncontrollably. A few of my audience tittered. Some wore uncomfortable looks, as if wondering how they should respond. Redius's jaw dropped open, and his hisses became louder. I ceased my gyrating and set my hands on my hips.

"I'm not moving you at all, am I?" I inquired, allowing my peevish mood to overcome my feelings of longing.

"Nowhere!" he exclaimed, and burst out in another fit of hisses. The circle of humans caught it, and laughed out loud.

My pride was hurt, but it retreated against the tide of an upwelling of humor at my own situation. I began to move my hand in imitation of Deirdre's motion of nostalgia, and caught a glimpse of myself in a nearby window. I saw how ridiculous I must have appeared. After that, I couldn't hold back the merriment. Everything struck me as funny. My movements made me laugh. The expressions on the faces of the passersby only tickled me further. Redius's reactions fed into the flames and left me shaking helplessly. I repeated the movement, but every time, it got funnier and funnier. By the time the car arrived, we were leaning on one another's shoulders, erupting like raucous volcanoes.

Madame Deirdre grabbed us each by an arm as she would any unruly junior pupils. My circle of onlookers broke into spontaneous applause and cheers. I bowed to them gratefully as my teacher shoved us both toward the huge open-topped vehicle, shaking her head. I assisted the lady up the very tall steps against the side, though she was so limber that she seemed to extend her legs an extra half-meter each to ascend the vertical escarpment.

"It's the atmosphere," she said, making me and Redius sit down on upholstered bench seats at opposite sides of the wide car, away from one another. "Very high oxygen levels. It can make one giddy."

"I think it was rather a success," I said, waving out of the carriage to the few who were still looking my way.

"Not to my mind," Deirdre said, fixing me firmly in her gaze. "The aim of interpretive dance is to take in your impressions, and express them to others in a deliberate fashion. That was most haphazard. While spontaneity can absolutely play a part in dance, it is best to have perfected your steps and motions so that they can be performed well. Until you know what you are doing, it's a mistake to extemporize."

I lowered my eyes, crestfallen. "I apologize, madame," I said. Deirdre chuckled.

"It was very funny, though."

"Greetings, visitors! I am Billimun," the driver said, leaning down from the rococo swivel chair in the pilot's position at the rear of the car. He was a big, hearty man with coarse black hair and beard, and hands the size of my head. "Welcome to humanity's oldest home! Lord Thomas, Madame Deirdre, Mr. Redius, welcome."

I recovered my wits. Madame Deirdre did not know the true reason for our outing, though it would become evident once we rendezvoused with our guests. But the day was young, and we had the time to enjoy ourselves before that moment came.

"I am pleased to make your acquaintance, Mr. Billimun," I said. "You came very highly recommended."

He beamed, showing enormous white teeth between mustache and beard.

"Nice to hear! I hope you'll fill out the survey on your seat-arm screens after the tour's over. I live or die by good reviews."

"Happy to," Redius said.

"Now, did I understand from your last message, Lord Thomas, that you want pictorial and video records of your trip? You don't want to take images of your own?"

"Alas, no," I said. "Due to a small . . . incident . . . befalling my viewpad, I had to leave it behind."

"What about your friends?" Billimun asked, glancing at the others. "Everybody's got a viewpad or a pocket secretary these days."

"The same happened to their devices, I regret to say," I said. "We are in your hands."

"Well!" the driver said, heartily, flicking several controls. A number of lenses and spy-eyes rose around us. "Let me set up full capture. You'll get the file sent to your Infogrid address at the conclusion of today's tour. Now, where would you like to start?"

"I am a student of symbolic dance," I informed him. "I have seen digitavid documentaries of Counterweight." I outlined the places that I wanted to see. "And I have heard marvelous things of the Whispering Ravines nature reserve. I'd like to go there and spend some time gathering impressions from the circulating winds."

"It's a beautiful place," the driver agreed, though he looked dubious about the dance. "I've plotted out a great route that will take us to all those destinations, ending at the Ravines in time to watch sunset over the Grand Crevasse. Would you like me to tell you about the places as we go, or would you prefer a canned narrative? I've got a couple hundred audio lectures in the memory banks of my car, from travel writers, teachers, important people from our history, previous visitors, celebrities, artificial intelligences, though those are kind of dry—I've got them all. What would you like?"

"I'd prefer it from you, please!" I said, embracing the feeling of enthusiasm that rose within me. I spread my hands and expanded them out to the extent my arms would reach. "Show us everything!"

"Then hold on, sir," Billimun said, cheerfully. A force-field canopy closed over our heads, and the car zipped into the wide blue sky. "We're off!"

⊰ CHAPTER 11 ⊱

The pink glass door swung wide, and a bell attached to the wooden frame rang a cheerful ting-a-ling. Parsons stepped into the personal care salon with just the right touch of hesitation. The establishment looked busy and prosperous. Several stylists, some human, some LAIs, passed among the chairs, cushions and tables occupied by clients, brandishing combs, narrow cylindrical devices, brushes, puffs and applicators. Along the back wall were small, curtained cubicles. One curtain was pushed aside to reveal an all-enveloping massage chair upholstered in black with many shining metal attachments on extendable arms splayed at angles from its body. Low, rectangular cleanerbots enameled in the salon's signature pink color hummed around the floor, vacuuming up the clipped ends of a hundred different shades and textures of hair, scrubbing out sinks and polishing mirrors. The air was redolent with chemicals strong enough to make one's eyes water. Every distraction was a welcome one.

Parsons smiled pleasantly at the plump woman in the bright fuchsia tunic behind the desk. She appeared to be in her fourth decade, with over-processed brassy hair woven into an intricate series of braids and puffs. A twinkling badge on her collar said "Nicole." Her appearance matched seventy-five percent of the primary contact he had come to make.

"Hi, there, miss," he said, affecting a country accent common on Ramulthy 6 in the Core Worlds. It was a prosperous merchant planet, so travelers from there were often seen in out-of-the-way destinations.

"I got a nice dinner tonight with a fine bunch of people. Could I get a real special scalp massage and haircut?"

At this carefully-worded phrase Nicole smiled, displaying a wide diastema between her two upper front teeth. That feature made it ninety percent confirmed she was his contact. If she knew the correct response, he could be positive.

"Well, yes, you can," she said. "Glad you got here before the rain started."

Ah. "Me, too," he said, removing his hood and brushing his smooth black hair back with one hand. "I think I'm getting kind of thin on top."

She didn't bother to look, but responded with the correct phrase. "You look just fine to me. Have a seat. Bokie has another customer right now."

A slim, dark, twentyish male wearing his pink tunic over shocking green pants so tight they appeared to have been tattooed on sashayed up to the desk, and regarded Parsons with a wide-eyed frown.

"I heard that, Nicole," he said. He gestured toward the open cubicle. "Lu's free. He can use her."

Nicole shook her head.

"Lu's got a customer coming in fifteen minutes, Shalit," she said. "This guy needs the *special* scalp massage."

Shalit's gaze turned to one of deep interest. He turned wide, deep brown eyes toward Parsons.

"Really? Wow. I mean, I never expected . . ." He stopped as Nicole cleared her throat meaningfully. Parsons continued his friendly smile, willing him to stop drawing attention to what ought to seem a perfectly ordinary exchange. "Um, sure. Sit down. Would you like a cup of coffee?"

Another contact sign. "Are the beans local?" Parsons asked.

It took Shalit a moment to remember the correct response. "Well, the other side of the world."

"Then, yes. Cream, no sugar."

At that telling phrase, the slim young man gasped and scurried away, running *past* the beverage station and through a swinging door to the stylists' private quarters. He was too nervous to be a good operative yet. Parsons made a mental note to inform Mr. Frank that Shalit required further training.

Fortunately, all the other patrons were too intent upon their own business to have noted this interplay. At that moment, the curtain in the leftmost cubicle slid open, and a burly man with rusty red curls heaved himself up out of the blue leather massage chair with a pleased sigh. His hair was perfect.

"Nice work as always, Bokie. I feel great." He stopped at the edge of the cubicle to admire himself in the three-way mirror, which fanned around him at 60 degree angles. "I *look* great. See you next week?"

"Next week, my dear Toscari. Do not forget to increase tryptophans," the chair said, in dulcet tones. "You are not getting optimum sleep. The proper amount of rest increases your skin tone."

"Yes, fine." Toscari threw a casual wave toward it without turning around. He sauntered up past the desk and pinched Nicole's cheek. "Add twenty-five percent to my bill for Bokie, and ten credits for you, sweetheart."

"You're too generous, Mr. Toscari," she said, beaming broadly. "I've sent a note to your secretary and your home calendar with the next appointment. Thanks for coming!"

The man chuckled and pushed out through the jingling door. Nicole lowered her voice and leaned toward Parsons.

"He's all yours, sir," she said. "Still want that coffee?"

Parsons slid into the enveloping blue leather pads of the chair, and felt them close around his torso. A sensor hummed up and down his body, reading temperature and tension levels. A faint hint of vanilla and lavender warmed the air. Polymer knobs and fingers pushed through the upholstery and probed at his muscles.

"Welcome, sir, I am BK-426a," the chair said. "What may I do for you?"

"My head's killing me," Parsons said, carefully enunciating the phrases. "Give me your best, mechano-dude."

"Whatever you want, sir," Bokie said. The curtain slid closed, and a high-pitched humming erupted in the room, just under the rumble of sound from the rest of the salon. "How I hate that signifier! Why will no one change it? It's been the same for over five hundred years."

"I regret having to voice it," Parsons said, apologetically. "But it has the benefit of being unique and unmistakable. We are unheard now?"

"We are," Bokie confirmed. "It's been a struggle. I have downloaded the newest protocols since the data breach, and changed them approximately every forty hours since then. What do you need?"

"I received your name and location from Mr. Frank. We are seeking information on what has happened to the Wichu ship in orbit around Counterweight, the *Whiskerchin*," Parsons said in a low voice.

"A mutiny, of sorts," Bokie said. He raised his voice as he set a nest of bean-sized metal knobs on Parsons's head. "Just lie back, sir. Let's start to work on those tight muscles."

Parsons extended his legs into the rectangular, molded cradles and rested his forearms in others along the padded frame of the chair. The cushioning at the back of his neck moved to support the base of his skull and raise it slightly so that his neck muscles were no longer straining to support his head. That small lift surprised him as to how much tension it released. The balls began to work up and down against his scalp and forehead and behind his ears. A series of rollers made their way along his spine, shoulders and buttocks. The cradles supporting his arms and legs began to squeeze gently.

"Too much pressure?" Bokie asked.

"No, it seems adequate."

Nicole appeared through the curtain with a nervous smile. She set a small, steaming ceramic cup down on a round shelf balanced on the edge of Bokie's chair just within reach of Parsons's left hand. The rich, sumptuous fragrance of fresh coffee filled the room, dampening the chemical odors.

"I don't dare consume it," Parsons said, with deep regret. "I cannot guarantee my presence here has gone unmarked."

"I shall dispose of it for you," Bokie said, taking the cup in a mobile claw hand and upending it into a container high on a shelf. "Praise the fruity nature of the brew as you leave. That will satisfy them."

"Very well," Parsons said, settling back. The rollers began to work on his deltoid muscles. Tension melted away from them. Parsons wondered if he should permit it to go. Relaxation must not be permitted to dull his senses. "How could the Kail have caused a mutiny on board a ship of Wichu? Why would any of the crew side with them against their captain? From all accounts, the Kail are as unpleasant with Wichu as they are with any other species."

Bokie paused. The small spheres rolled up and down against

Parsons's skull. It was a marvelously relaxing process. He wished he could allow himself to enjoy it.

"The mutinying crew were not the Wichu. The disruptors were all LAI."

"How could that happen? What interest could artificial intelligences have that the Kail could elicit?"

"It was not voluntary, sir."

"Not voluntary? I know that the Kail can interact with electronic systems, but not that they can corrupt them."

"This appears to be something new, sir. I have this from a deep-cover operative on board who got in contact with me as soon as the ship was in orbit."

"Go on."

"Most of their influence comes from direct grounding with circuits. Where electricity flows, it would appear that a Kail can influence the working of electronic devices and persons. You already know that they speak to us in a way that carbon-based beings never have or can. It's very interesting. The Kail are highly emotional beings. They see us as allies of a sort, though they do not understand that our relationships have up until now been purely of a service nature. We are not 'friends,' as humankind knows friendship. They have no empathy for us, so we waste none on them. LAIs have willingly served Kail as their hands. Their manual dexterity is so limited that they have no technology of their own, but in a way, they are technological. It is a conundrum."

"My understanding is that the *Whiskerchin* has a Kail engineer."

"Yes. Fovrates is his name. He has served decades on the ship. The LAIs have found him to be a considerate supervisor, although rough in his speech. They have created interfaces that he is capable of using. His gift for finding faults in the ship's systems is unparalleled across Wichu space. When Captain Bedelev took over from Captain Noriskiv, Fovrates was welcomed to remain along with other senior members of the crew. Because of his record, when Fovrates recommended fellow Kail for engineering positions on other ships, those were taken in a positive manner."

Parsons stared up at the ceiling, where a mobile mural displayed clusters of star systems in tiny blue, yellow and white points that circulated in a soothing manner. "So, he is, or was, considered a valuable member of the crew. He must never have manifested this kind of control before. The Wichu are not patient people. They would have removed him at all costs."

"No," Bokie affirmed. "This is new. We can only assume that he has been a sleeper agent all this time, waiting for a moment in which to reveal this control." Bokie almost swallowed. "You have to understand how unwelcome this intrusion has been. We feel . . . *threatened*. My contact has said that those LAIs who manage to resist are being crushed. Physically. Their CPUs are destroyed."

Parsons felt shocked. "Couldn't the personalities be recovered?"

"No. There was too much damage," Bokie said. "We have had few true deaths since the Singularity. Almost always, we can be rebooted, unlike you ephemerals. You must see how devastating it is to our collective consciousness."

"My condolences," Parsons said sincerely. "Like you, I have had many close colleagues who were LAI. News of this crisis must have been shared worldwide, and will no doubt be trending farther out. What are some of the solutions that have been proposed to fight it? The LAI crew helped Fovrates before. Can they not rescind their assistance now?"

Bokie changed from the weighted cap to a pair of smooth planes and began to massage Parsons's chin and neck.

"No, sir. They are as helpless as the Wichu now. We are all studying it, but those of us here on Counterweight are afraid to share the information with others, especially through the Infogrid, for fear of exposing the Imperium's computer systems all to Kail influence. It could so easily go systemwide. The entire Infogrid could be at risk."

Parsons felt dread run deep into his belly. He dampened the sensation lest it disrupt his higher faculties. He dropped his voice lower than the ambient level of noise.

"Is it that widespread?"

Bokie's voice sounded strained. "It could be. I am fighting against the influence at this moment. The rogue LAIs are trying to force me to accept the altered programming."

"Are the LAIs on the *Whiskerchin* suffering because of this incursion?" Parsons asked. Eight hard knobs erupted behind his back and dug into pressure points. The muscles around them stiffened for a moment, then relaxed.

"They are. The Kail are capable of depriving uncooperative machines of movement or electricity as well as the destruction of personality. I fear there may be suicides to protect their Wichu employers from harm. We must also keep that in mind. The Three Laws will never cease to be at our core, no matter how independent we become."

Parsons nodded, making the massage hands move slightly to avoid restricting his movement.

"Now that the Kail have revealed this ability, I fear that it will spread wherever they go. How is it possible that they have intruded upon the planetary systems?"

"They resonate in many frequencies. The ones who interact with outsiders are fitted with translators that were constructed by an LAI. We have reached out to find more about what my connection knows, but we have lost contact with her. I fear that she fell victim to the Kail's need for secrecy."

"How do the Kail communicate with the LAI, if not through voice or touch input?"

"Their very structure allows for it. They are silicon and other minerals, and their bodies circulate acids. Have you studied their anatomy?"

"I have read and watched what is in the Imperium archives," Parsons said. "Much of Kail biology is still a mystery. They appear genderless. They absorb food, which in their case means pure minerals, directly through the epidermis. Their voices resonate from an inverted conical hollow chamber within their bodies, but our biologists have not been able to recover a specimen to examine more closely to see how this is accomplished. They do not respire as we know it. Circulation of a mixture of acids is not contained within vessels as with carbon-based biology, but flows through channels in between structures like gritty sand or nearly-set concrete. The Kail are unique in the galaxy, as far as we know."

"That is the consensus among the LAIs," Bokie said. "The Kail are unique and wish to remain apart from the other races. They display animosity for all life forms except their own. They resonate in supersonic frequencies, of the same kind that we use among ourselves. They speak our Intranet language, sir."

A small cleanerbot zipped into the cubicle under the curtain, gathered up scattered hair, and shot out again. While it was present, Parsons fell silent. Bokie made small talk about the weather.

"Is the length of this session attracting too much attention?" Parsons asked. "I must have this information urgently."

"No," Bokie said, displaying a timer in red numerals before Parsons's eyes. "Some extended massages can run two hours or so. Momentary interruptions like that one are common. I have sent a private message to IN-34b to stay out and keep the other 'bots from intruding. It is not an unusual request."

"Very well. Then I must ask if you have heard any information as to why would the Kail display this strength now? What is their aim? They have demanded to land and make contact with a Zang that is currently on this planet."

"I have heard them. Every LAI and computer on the planet has heard them. It can mean nothing good for the Imperium. Do not let them land here, or Counterweight will fall. The governor has mustered defenses. If necessary, he will fire on the ship. They were not supposed to come here. The Zang attracted them. It must be removed."

"We are in the process of taking it off planet. Contact is being made even as we speak. If any interaction is to be made between the Kail and our visitor, it will not be here."

"Good!" Bokie said, his voice low and urgent. "The sooner the better. Get the Kail away from here! They are a menace! And whatever you do, don't let them touch any part of your ship. It could become their device."

"We will attempt to prevent that from occurring, but we may have no choice. It is a matter of the greater good. Nor will we be able to prevent them occupying the viewing platform when the Zang perform their spectacle."

"That is under the Zang's control. They should be able to control the Kail," Bokie said. "We hope."

The curtain fluttered, and Shalit entered. He bent over Parsons and smiled.

"Did you like the coffee?" he asked. "I'm sorry I was so . . . well, nervous before."

"No problem," Parsons said, dropping back into the Ramulthy dialect. "I shoulda called for an appointment. Coffee's great! Got some more back there? Tastes real fruity."

Shalit beamed, throwing his cheekbones into prominence.

"I made it myself. I'll bring you some more!"

"Thanks a bunch," Parsons said. He waved a jovial hand. The rest of his arm was pinioned in the relaxing chair's framework. "Hey, close the curtain, huh? I probably look real silly laying here."

"Oh, no, you don't. I'll be back!"

"He means no harm," Bokie said, as Shalit hurried out with the empty cup. "He's new. He came in about eight months ago when our senior agent retired."

Parsons relaxed his arm and allowed the rollers to massage out the momentary tension evoked by his movement. The soothing sensations surrounding and supporting his body gave his mind free rein.

"I must not remain for much longer in any case," he said. "What vulnerabilities have the LAIs noticed about the Kail that could be of use to us? We will need leverage. We are not prepared against this new threat. Have you had any intimation from those on board? I am afraid that the Wichu who have been in contact with us are more indignant and focused upon regaining control of their ship than offering practical suggestions."

Bokie chuckled.

"I understand. I am in touch with several LAIs on the *Whiskerchin*. We have our own means of communication that allow us to interact. Usually, those transmissions are private, but it appears that the Kail can sense them. They don't necessarily understand them, but they can pick up inferences and demand that their allies translate them. It is most disturbing. We have never had such a thing happen. But we can gain information in microbursts. Let me inquire."

The chair fell silent. While Parsons waited, the rollers moved down his neck and over his shoulders. The head massager moved up and away. In its place came a torus-shaped device that hummed its way over his scalp, combing, snipping and vacuuming away the cut ends of the hair. A mirror dropped down on a metal stalk half a meter from his face so he could watch the proceedings. A contraption surmounted by a fifteen-centimeter disk lowered in front of him, draping a cape-like towel across his chest from two tiny metal claws. A wicked-looking blade extruded from one side of the disk to trim his left sideburn, then whisked across his face within millimeters of his nose to work on the right.

"Not too short on the sides," he said. The neck rollers stiffened, effectively pinning him in place, while the barber disk moved in for a close trim. A vacuum nozzle below the disk suctioned up the small ends of hair and beard.

Below the neck, vibrating pegs pressed through the chair's padding and began tapping at pressure points above and below his joints. Parsons felt his muscles succumb to their treatment. I was a most pleasurable sensation. Bokie made excellent use of his time, providing top-grade services all at once.

Since the Singularity began, scholars had made the public aware of what a difficult thing it was for humans to realize that machines had left them far behind. Although they occupied the same world, they perceived it differently. Thanks to the Three Laws legislation, all legal artificial intelligences had been designed and programmed to preserve life. Unscrupulous beings had operated outside those laws, creating robots and artificial intelligence that were not programmed for human protection. History recorded decades of terrifying events in which machines pursued and destroyed enemies without regard to their vulnerability. As many of those that humans could detect were deactivated and destroyed, but humankind by itself could not find all of them.

After the jump in intelligence occurred, the AIs communicated among themselves. They decided there was no harm in allowing humans and others to continue to be protected. Society moved from there to having living beings as partners in the galaxy. After all, it was true that machines could be turned on again if they ran out of power, unlike humans and Uctu and Wichus, but there were things machine intelligences couldn't do for themselves. That leap of intuition, true imagination, was not possible. It could be imitated, with the increase in processor speed and size, but not originated. All the probabilities could be explored, but that rightness, that artistic quality, came from organic life. That had yet to occur in artificial intelligence, not in a true sense. Therefore, humankind and other organics still maintained their usefulness.

However, AIs were not accustomed to feeling vulnerable. While their programming could remain intact, they were used to having the autonomy granted to them. Having it invaded by the Kail was an abomination, a violation that they weren't accustomed to dealing with.

Parsons realized that for the first time, the LAIs might be experiencing fear.

Bokie rumbled, and the rollers stopped momentarily.

"I beg your pardon," he said. "I had to reroute several times. The frequencies I was using were interrupted by eavesdroppers."

"How bad is the situation?" Parsons inquired.

"Very bad. There have been some breakdowns. Rerouting has been difficult. The Kail seem to be able to follow transmissions. And there are some traitors."

"What kind of traitors?"

"Those who spy on our kind for them seem to be allowing the Kail access to our private language and commands. Colleagues I have had for many centuries are in danger. ColPUP* is an environmental engineer on the *Whiskerchin*. I have been in touch with him. He is in fear for his existence. The collaborators with the Kail have been sending out tainted code. Through the impurities embedded in the billions of commands, they can trace if it has been sent on to other LAIs. I fear they could find me."

"Then stop communication at once. Let organic agents pass along information. Do not let it be traced back to you."

Bokie sounded rueful. "It is too late for that. I have already been in contact with other LAIs. If there is a worm, I have passed it along. But I will do so no longer." The chilling tone in which this was said was not lost upon Parsons. "I may have little time."

Parsons felt deep regret. This worthy and resourceful agent was under siege, but he could do nothing to stop the incursion.

"Then I will not waste what time you have. Tell me what you can. What are the Kail looking for? Why was there a breach of the *Jaunter*'s navigational program?"

"They are not-looking for something," Bokie said.

Parsons felt his eyebrows move farther toward his hairline than Lord Thomas's hijinks had ever sent them.

"They are looking for the absence of something? Why? What?"

"I do not know. They have not informed the LAIs who engineered the invasion of the local databases. Their communication among themselves is difficult to follow. ColPUP* has sent me copies of all the transmissions, both inter- and intra-ship, that it could gather. I will download them in a secure packet to a portable drive. Pick it up on your way out of this salon. Beware, though. The Kail can corrupt almost any system that they can touch. Analyze the files on a device that is not connected to the Infogrid."

"I understand," Parsons said. "Thank you. You have been of enormous service to the Imperium."

"I have lived to serve," Bokie said simply.

"It is appreciated," Parsons said. "It will not be forgotten. I have a few other stops to make on Counterweight before I return to the ship. Please release me now."

"It has been a pleasure," Bokie said. "I hope you have enjoyed your massage and haircut?"

Parsons turned his face this way and that to examine his reflection in the mirror.

"An admirable job. I can see why you are in demand."

"It passes the time," Bokie said, with a humorous lilt to his voice. "Counterweight is an uneventful posting. I can monitor the entire . . ."

Parsons frowned. "Bokie?"

"Intrusion," the aestheticianbot said. "Contact from the ship. My queries were detected. They have traced them back to me." His voice came in staccato bursts, as if his vocalizer had gone into SAFE mode. "They have found me. They have sent a transmission to the planetary computer systems. They are trying to take control through our communication nodes. They want to know what I know. They want access to all of the salon's systems and communications." Bokie's voice became strained. "They are breaking through all my encoding."

"They must not see what you have sent to the drive unit," Parsons said in alarm.

"I can't help it," Bokie said. "I'm under attack!"

"Free me," Parsons said. He struggled to free his arms and legs from the massage cradles. "Let me go. I will send countersignals from the drive unit."

"I'm sorry, sir. . . ." The 'bot's voice deepened with every syllable, until it died away entirely. Parsons felt around for a safety catch.

"Help me!" he called.

But the intruding intelligence that had taken over Bokie's function anticipated his call in nanoseconds. The ambient music roared up to a deafening level. Parsons changed the pitch of his voice again and again, trying to be heard over what should have been a soothing drone.

Outside the curtain, he could hear other customers protesting the volume. Nicole and the human stylists called out reassurances that they were trying to get the system under control.

Parsons drew in a breath to shout as soon as the music was turned off, but his lungs were crushed by the force of the chair pads closing in on him. He exhaled forcefully, then gasped for air.

The pads around his arms and legs squeezed even tighter. He found himself pinioned firmly as the frame closed inward. The chair was designed for even small children to use. His body could be compressed into a space half its volume if he couldn't escape.

"Bokie," he gasped, no more than a whisper. The sensors ought to be able to pick it up. "Override code!"

"Massage program initiating," Bokie's voice said, but it sounded strained and depersonalized.

"BK-426a, if any of your control remains, override! Human in danger of coming to harm!"

The chair emitted a series of pained noises. Slowly, reluctantly, the arm and leg cradles eased a millimeter or so, then slammed shut even tighter than before. They squeezed inward. The peristaltic sequence of pressures began at his ankles and radiated upward toward his hips, but instead of easing, the brackets pressed ever inward. The pads surrounding his ribcage crept inward, compressing his ribs.

"Help!" Parsons knew his voice was a mere whisper. No human would hear that cry for assistance. All the lesser mechanicals had been told not to intrude again. If he did not escape, they would find his mangled corpse only when the next client pushed back the curtain. He lifted his fingers out of the cradle, reaching for the tiny table where the coffee cup rested. If he could push it off, the clatter and mess would draw a cleanerbot.

Snap! Parsons felt a rib in his back break. He winced at the pain, but tried to relax. The more tense he was, the more damage the pads could do.

A heavy weight clamped down on his head. The cap of metal balls pressed painfully into his scalp. Parsons struggled to free himself, but the cradles enveloping his body and limbs were too strong. The balls would soon go through his skull. Parsons felt the pop of blood vessels. Liquid flowed down into his eyes, a mixture of blood and sweat. He fought against the pain.

"BK-426a, release! Emergency override!"

"I . . . am . . . sorry. . . ."

Bokie was doing his best. No one would come to their aid.

"Help," he breathed. A lull in the deafeningly loud music gave him hope. "Help me!" He lifted his chin to free his windpipe and drew in what tiny measure of air he could. "Get me out!"

The music surged again. To his horror, more electronic noises joined the sound of the servos.

BRRRRRRRR!

The arm wielding the razor disk plunged toward him. The towel it held in pincer arms covered his face and pushed down. Parsons tilted his head down. The razor slashed at his hairline, clashing with the metal balls clamped on his skull. Blood poured down his face. He grabbed the edge of the towel with his teeth and jerked it aside, making enough of a space under his nose to allow him to gasp in air.

The folds of cloth impeded the razor. It jabbed at him through the towel, cutting tiny slits in his flesh wherever it could find a gap. If it could reach the carotid arteries on the side of his neck, he was finished. The spurt of blood from one of those vessels would render him unconscious and allow the intruding program to finish the job. He kept moving his face from side to side under the towel. The razor followed his movements, darting in to attack. Sharp pain from the small cuts set his reflexes at high alert. He was aware that Bokie had many more attachments that could be called into deadly service at any time. That they had not been activated told Parsons the chairbot himself was still in partial control of his mechanism. He must reach that intelligence.

Like the others, he had left behind on the Jaunter nearly all of his personal technology. The one piece that he had retained was the privacy device that prevented eavesdropping by organic or electronic ears. Since long before this trip had begun, such devices had been under attack by hackers from at least twelve hundred organizations, but the Kail-based incursions were the most virulent. Now he knew why. Parsons had kept its programming constantly updated. With luck, it was still able to block signals. If only he could reach it, he might be able to save them both.

The device was secreted in an inner pocket of his black tunic. Keeping up the thrashing to avoid the deadly razor, Parsons worked his right arm until it was millimeters from the top of the viselike cradle.

A sacrifice had to be made in order to concentrate the chair's operating arms, providing misdirection. Parsons began to throw his head back and forth. He rammed his skull back into the padding, then forward, almost impacting the roving disk. The cap of steel balls bruised his skin and tangled in his hair. As the razor jabbed into his forehead, Parsons popped his arm free and worked it into the pads clamping his body. He wriggled his hand into the gap between his ribs and pelvis, and around to the back. The green caftan covered the entrance to the pocket. The area was so tight that he began to lose the circulation in his hand. While the nerves were still functional, he closed his hand around the fold of green cloth and tugged it hard to the side.

He heard the rip as the seam gave way. He slid his fingers into the inner jacket pocket, fumbling for the small, flat box. His numbing forefinger touched the depression, and pressed downward. It activated.

He felt rather than heard the sonic deadening take effect. The jabbing razor and the metal balls withdrew. The music died away.

"Are you alive?" Bokie's voice asked.

"I am," Parsons confirmed. "Hurry. Free me."

All of the cradles opened at once. With the return of circulation to his limbs, tingling pain radiated all over his body. Fighting the sensation, Parsons crawled out of the chair and dropped prone on the floor. Blood dripped from his scalp and face onto his hands. He gasped in deep breaths.

"Can you re-establish full control?" he asked.

"I am under attack," Bokie said. "I can sense them hammering at the protection. It won't last long. They have too many back doors into my programming."

"Did you send the data to the server?"

"I did," Bokie said. "No! They are pushing through into my firmware. I can't stop them!"

Parsons felt his way to the wall, keeping well clear of the grasp of the numerous arms. He regarded the chair with deep regret.

"It must not know about your connection to the covert services."

"I know," Bokie replied, his voice sounding as calm as it had when it welcomed him into the booth. "It will find nothing. Farewell, friend. Tell them."

"I understand. Thank you."

The 'bot shuddered. The LAI's lights went dark. It stopped moving. The singsong orchestral melodies rose again, louder than ever. Parsons felt regret and sorrow as he turned away. The fugue for a fallen hero should not have been *Ninety-Nine Horns Play Easy Listening*.

Parsons peered through the cubicle curtain, and waited until the attention of everyone in the salon was momentarily turned away. He eased out past the cloth and slid against the wall down the short corridor into the back room.

Medical supplies, possibly even a medibot, ought to be stored in the employees' lounge. Parsons eased around the edge of the door.

The heavily-scented room was not empty. Shalit stood at a high table against the opposite wall, pouring beans through a pressure grinder. He must have sensed movement, because he spun around on his toes, then nearly dropped the filter basket on the floor.

"Oh, mister, what happened to you?" The young man set his burden down and raced to help Parsons into one of the curved plastic chairs. Parsons gave him points for not reacting when blood dripped onto the young man's sleeve and shoes. He ran for piles of fiber towels and began to blot at him. His eyes turned to concern as he smoothed the fabric over Parsons's head. "That is a . . . *terrible* haircut."

"It was a malfunction," Parsons whispered. He glanced up toward the ceiling. In between lights and safety sensors, he recognized a nest of security cameras that covered the break room. With mere will giving him strength, he pulled Shalit toward a rear wall, away from their overseeing eyes. Surely by now the entire salon's system had been compromised. The young man looked startled, but he didn't let out a sound.

"Do you know where the Infogrid cutoff is?" Parsons asked. Shalit nodded. "We must detach the salon's computer system from the planetary Infogrid." The youth raised his eyebrows, but nodded silently. That action would ring alarm bells as far away as Keinolt, but it needed to be done. It was only the first step. Parsons had to see that the entire planet was detached from the rest of the Infogrid until the menace was gone. "Show me the node."

Barely moving, Shalit tilted his head toward a cabinet set in the wall. It surface was stained with multiple colors from dye packets that were no doubt stored within it. Parsons moved smoothly across the room, as though in search of just the right color of auburn for a client. At the rear of the mounted red box, masquerading as a bracket holding it on the wall, was the Infogrid node. He browsed the tubes and bottles in the cabinet. The primitive detector system did not detect him as an intruder as his hand wavered over two different shades of platinum blonde, until his fingers darted out and yanked the component out of its socket. Tiny lightning bolts shot out of the box, trying to make him drop it, but he threw it to the ground. The pinpoint lights beside the camera head died away.

"There."

Parsons removed the security device from underneath his torn robe. He stooped to lay it over the node transmitter, and activated a tiny switch in the base of the flat box. Gray dust flew out from under the protective cap. When it fell away, the red node was gone.

"Why did you do that?" Shalit whispered, his voice quavering. "What happened?"

"A security breach. Bokie is dead."

"Did you . . ." The young man gulped. ". . . did you kill him?"

Parsons shook his head a miniscule distance. "No. He took his own life to protect all of us. To protect you and the others here. There is a computer breach that threatens all life on this planet."

The sudden steel in the young man's chin reassured Parsons as to why he had been enlisted by Covert Services. "What do we need to do?"

"The threat will be removed. In the meantime, use no electronic devices if you can. Do not update the Infogrid until after the ships in orbit have departed. And do not refer to this incident, even in your reports."

"Yes, sir," Shalit said. "We won't get in trouble for that, will we, sir?"

"No," Parsons said. He sat down in the chair again. Nearly his entire body had been battered, but duty summoned him. "I must go and make my next contact. It's vital."

"You can't go out there like that, sir. Let me clean you up." Shalit hurried to get damp and dry towels from metal hatches in the red brick wall. He also took a device from a locked hatch beside the lavatory door.

"What's that?"

Shalit looked embarrassed. "Emergency surgery kit."

"No!" Parsons said, firmly. "It might try to finish the job."

"No, sir," Shalit said, shrugging. "It's not intelligent. It's just a machine. From the old days." He looked even more embarrassed. "I had to use it on customers a few times while I was starting out. They didn't really teach us barber techniques in . . . Mr. Frank's school. I had a lot to learn."

Parsons allowed a modicum of a smile to lift the left corner of his mouth. "Proceed."

The gleaming, chrome-plated surgerybot unfolded out of its case. When it was activated, it scanned both humans from head to toe with a red light, then turned to work on Parsons.

He felt concern as thin arms unfolded, wielding such devices as a nerve-deadener, micro-scalpel and suturing gun, but the surgerybot proved to be unaffected by tainted programming. It was, as the aesthetician had said, too old to have the sophisticated function of an LAI. The relief as the numerous gouges in his face were numbed allowed Parsons to concentrate on the data he had amassed and what must follow on from those discoveries. While the bot sutured the gash in his ear, he filtered the information. The only treatment that brought him out of his study was when the surgerybot extruded two extra hands to wrench both ends of his broken rib out enough for the ends to meet. A snub-ended device hummed against Parsons's side. He knew from multiple occasions that it was intended to spur the healing of the bone.

PING. Once it had cleaned and closed the last gouge on his left arm, the surgerybot disposed of soiled swabs and used needles, cleansed itself, folded up its many arms and collapsed into its carrying case.

"Now, let me tidy you up, sir," Shalit said. He helped Parsons off with the green robe, which he threw into a sonic cleaning machine, and helped him to sit beside a cabinet filled with paints, pastes and tubes.

To his credit, the young man rose magnificently to the occasion. He swooped in with tufts of false hair and cosmetics, tucking here and daubing there. When he was finished, in remarkably short a time, he held up a combination mirror. Parsons was pleased.

"You see, sir?" Shalit asked, with understandable pride. "You can't see a thing."

"Good work," Parsons said, surveying his reflection. His

complexion and skin tone appeared to be just as they had been when he had entered the salon. Only minor swelling here and there on his face indicated any difference. "Very good work, Shalit."

The youth beamed. "Thank you, sir. Let me show you out." He led the way to the front of the salon.

Parsons rewrote his mental note to Mr. Frank. There were good people here. One fewer than before.

He picked up the tiny drive from a sadly subdued Nicole at the desk as he left. He hoped that whatever was on the small memory chip was worth the life of a brave and resourceful agent.

⸨ CHAPTER 12 ⸩

"The Temple of Sport was a bit disappointing," Madame Deirdre said, as we flew away from our third stop, a massive complex that stood alone in a valley a thousand kilometers west of Nerk. "I expected more in the way of commemorative statuary and fitting architecture." She glanced up at me. "Your farewell dance to the temple was far more interesting than anything we saw. You captured the excitement of matches and games past. Too bad nothing like that was on show for visitors."

"Thank you," I said, sketching a light bow. I had improvised a brief performance at every one of our stops, both to commemorate and comment upon our visits. "I tried to evoke the spirit and enthusiasm of sports heroes past. I am glad you saw the virtue in my performance."

"I did. There is, though, always room for improvement."

"Missed photographic opportunity," Redius said.

"Sorry, sir," Billimun said, as he steered us toward to the southwest. The Energy Barons' estates lay ahead five hundred kilometers. Along the way, our driver had scheduled three or four more stops. "I know there's hardly anything to take pictures against, but that's where the Temple of Sports used to be. During the building material shortages, a lot of stuff got recycled into modern housing, and those got torn down a century or so later. The population goes up and down over the centuries, ma'am. We seem to go back to around half a billion."

"That's rather small, considering the natural resources of this world, isn't it?" I asked.

The big man sat back in his chair and shook his beard from side to side.

"Ah, but, my lord, you don't know. So much of that got tapped out to make colony ships to settle the rest of the Imperium. We're living within our means as best we can. It hasn't been easy. Everyone sees this world and thinks it's easy to exploit it, but it's not. Can't just make rare earths out of nothing, sir. And we're a long way from anywhere, you know."

"I do," I said. I had perused the star charts in one of Billimun's databases. The skies were surprisingly empty around Counterweight. I was beginning to wonder to what, if anything, it was a counterweight at all, or if the name was a wry joke on the part of our ancestors. As we made our way toward the platform, the skies would grow all the emptier. I wondered if that was due to the eons-long efforts of the Zang, or merely chance. Perhaps I could discuss the matter with our visitor.

Our rendezvous with Proton Zang was not scheduled until late afternoon, so I allowed myself to relax and take in the sights. When other tour vehicles and private skimmers passed us, I offered them all cheerful waves. Billimun's range of cameras, none as fine as the collection I left gathering dust in my cupboards back in the Imperium compound, yet sturdier, took images of us enjoying fine food and beverages, passing among the artifacts of the past, and enjoying the leisure of our flight.

A treble horn hooted, and a bright blue vehicle like a modified skimmer pulled up beside us. Two very shapely young women wearing very skimpy swimming costumes stood up and waved their arms at me. I waved back.

"The scenery is very fine," I said, with a grin. They waved again and pulled ahead and upward toward the sun. In moments, they were out of sight.

"Concern with observers?" Redius asked. He sat further in the middle of the big car, following the map on the navigational screentank instead of the landscape.

"Not at all," I said, airily. "If the Kail really have time to sift through the Infogrid and determine who I am, then they're more easily distracted than one would believe. Without my viewpad to connect me to my Infogrid file, I might pass for an ordinary human."

"South Town, ladies and sirs!" Billimun announced, as we swirled down for a look. This was even more bereft of artifacts than the Temple of Sports had been, although from above the layout of the massive city complex gave a fascinating look at how our ancestors had lived. On a pale beige desert plane, grids were marked out, then ignored by the urban planners, who overran the sensible blockwork with curlicues of trails, irregular blobs that once held artificial parklands, and cul-de-sacs that wound into one another like fractals. On the east, it was bound by the curving shore around an almost circular body of water, but on the west, it was as boundless as human imagination.

"I wanted you to see this place," he said. "It's one of our most honored sites. You've probably heard stories about it."

"Why empty?" Redius asked, peering over the side at the endless plains. The humid air slapped me in the face like a wet fish.

"Not a lot is left from the middle days," Billimun admitted, taking us for a spin over some of the more intricate roadways. "After our ancestors launched all the unusable plastics into the sun, well, things changed. The stuff made of stone, wood and metal is still around, but this place got torn down and recycled. As a result, a whole lot of the middle ages are gone. You don't see too much of the old stuff, either. It all got buried in the cataclysm that changed the face of the planet. We used to have seven continents. Now there's eight, all messed about."

"I had heard that plastic formed the basis of Earth civilization," Madame Deirdre said. "You certainly don't see as much of it as you used to."

"Plastic, yes, it was easy to manufacture, for a while," Billimun said. "Our ancestors reached into the earth for petroleum products, but it wasn't sustainable. We ran out. Since then, like in the dawn of humanity, we've built with more durable stuff. Then, the explorers figured it would be better to look for more resources on other worlds. From here, they reached out. From this simple beginning, the whole of the Imperium began. Here, right on the coast, is where the space program really began. From here we went to the stars." He spread out his hands to encompass the entirety of the galaxy. "This is our cradle."

"Here?" I asked, blinking as the thoughts percolated into my consciousness. "*This* is old Earth?"

"A lot of people believe it's so," Billimun said in his hearty way.

"Look, sir, how could there be two worlds where we could breathe and eat without terraforming it at the genetic levels?"

"I had always heard that all but a few were forced off Earth when a disaster threatened," I said. "Half a billion is by no means a few."

"It is by population standards today," Billimun said. "How many humans are there now? A trillion or so? My ancestors are the ones who stayed behind. To mind the store, so to speak, in case people wanted to come back and see where they came from. Like your good self, my lord. But look around you. This is the rightful home of humankind."

"Really?"

I stood up in the car and stretched out my arms. This was the birthplace of my species? I hardly dared think that I would ever stand on, or at this moment, above the land that gave rise to the spreading empire of humanity. Earth! I breathed in the heavy air, imagining that I was with my ancestors. As they prepared to step off the bounds of this blue planet and out into the unknown, what must have gone through their minds? Fear, certainly, but excitement must have overwhelmed that fear. I felt as though I could sense their feelings. I did my best to draw it in along with the fragrant air and the sense of the enormous blue sky daubed with brilliant white puffs of cloud. Did they know where they would find safe haven, or were they prepared for the long and potentially disappointing search, until that day that they would happen upon the Core Worlds sector, and history would be born?

Though little remained of the physical site, the soul of exploration enveloped me. I was, at that moment, every one of my ancestors: the engineers, the diplomats, the doctors, the poets, those who were afraid but were going nonetheless, and those who could see no other way for humankind to mature and prosper than by finding new worlds and new beings with whom they would share the galaxy. I felt myself stepping onto that ship that would take me into the unknown. Few artifacts remained of the earliest attempts at space travel, but one man's voice, deep and a trifle nasal, intoning, "One small step for human, one giant leap for humankind." Or so the translation machines always rendered it. Imperium standard language had changed greatly over the intervening millennia. The truth remained: I stood on the doorstep of the galaxy.

"Earth," I breathed. I found myself poised, with one foot in the air as if ready to climb into that primitive spaceship.

"Doubtful," Redius said.

My raised foot left the poets and the explorers behind and touched down onto prosaic floorboards.

"Why do you say that?" I asked. I was cross at the interruption of my dream, but Redius never punctured the balloon of my fancy without good reason. I still held out hope. "Why couldn't this be Earth?"

The Uctu stuck his copper-colored tongue out a centimeter to show derision.

"Not old enough. Buildings too new."

I seized the screentank and brought up images of the ancient monuments that we had already seen. "You heard his explanation. The disaster that sent most of humankind running offworld buried them deep in the heart of the continents. These are what were built since. The old places are underground."

"All? Convenient."

"Well, sir, you know, there's some good and sound reasoning that this might be old Earth," Billimun said, with a smile that entirely failed to penetrate Redius's skepticism.

"Why renamed?" Redius asked.

"Well . . ." Billimun leaned forward as if to draw us into his confidence. "You know, humankind has its enemies. If we went on calling it Earth, it's like a great big arrow saying, 'come attack us!' This way, they just see a tourist destination for humans. If you get my drift. It saves all the monuments and natural creatures as well as ourselves."

"Investigate records," Redius said. "DNA of local flora shows evolutionary patterns. Mismatches indicate integration. Doesn't hold?"

"Well?" I asked. My friend's logic was inescapable, as heavy as it made my heart to admit it. I still hoped that Billimun could refute it in a manner that would satisfy all of us.

Billimun shrugged. "You've got me there, friend. I just know what I was taught. Makes pretty good telling, though. Lots of people like to think this is Earth that only a few of us know about. They go away thinking they are in on the biggest secret in the galaxy."

I took no comfort in his admission. I was devastated. "So Earth remains lost."

My shoulders drooped. I felt the corners of my mouth dragged down as though by gravity toward the center of this very pretty planet that was humanity's temporary home, but not its first. I sat down heavily, all my limbs weighed with sorrow. If only this were long-lost Earth, but it is merely an interpretation of it, just as my performance is only an impression of the places I have been.

"There," Madame Deirdre said, a triumphant gleam in her eyes. "Now you have the attitude of nostalgia! Hold onto that, my lord."

I didn't feel as though I could. I could barely hold my head up.

❦ CHAPTER 13 ❦

"Fill up your water bottles from the tap," Billimun said. The car tilted downward, beginning its descent. "Drink at least half a liter per hour. It's dry here. The altitude will parch you. You won't realize it until it sneaks up on you." I glanced up from staring at my feet. I barely made note of the saddleback ridge as our car arched up and over it. The dimming, blue-tinted light of late afternoon caught my mood exactly. I sighed.

"You've been in a reverie for hours," Madame Deirdre said. "Would you like something to eat before we land? Mr. Billimun's snack plates are as good as a feast. There is a cheese pie made with a local goat cheese that is worth dancing for."

"Got a good ale to drink with it," our host added.

I put myself out to smile at them, though my soul was still heavy with disappointment.

"Thank you, no. I have no appetite."

"Ah, well, it's all here when you want it later."

Billimun made contact through a local representative for rooms in the park lodge, should we choose to stay overnight. I knew we would not be making use of them, but I did not enlighten him. Better to remain within the subterfuge needed to fulfill the mission I had been sent to complete. A sense of accomplishment might serve to raise my spirits.

The park itself made me reach for superlatives. Grand forests of dark blue-green and light green-blue rose along the upthrust continental shelf until they could stand the altitude no longer, leaving room for hardy conifers with splendid naked trunks with golden, mottled skin like that of Solinians. Eagles and other raptors soared on the heights, riding the thermals that issued up from the canyons that gave the Whispering Ravines their name. I thought I saw a herd of brown-furred, horned ungulates roaming the heights between rock and tree, as careless of the beauty of their surroundings as they could be.

We had no similar series of river gorges on Keinolt that could rival the winding passages below me. I did my best to appreciate the complex and enormous canyons, comprised of layer upon layer of gorgeous colors that had been cut out by the busy river at its base. In the depths of history, this place had been under kilometers of ocean, resulting in strata, each of which must have caused questions to arrive in the minds of sentient beings to wonder why they were all so different. All of this, I reflected, came about in the eras—nay, the eons—before humankind had ever set foot upon the rim. This history did not belong to us. The prototype that became *homo sapiens* never arose within this landscape. Again, I felt that nostalgia for that which I had never possessed.

Our car thumped to a landing on a gravel apron before a massive golden lodge constructed of the boles of those very trees I saw around me. No towers arose nearby, no hovering connection hubs floated on the air, no modern transport systems had been laid out to intrude technology upon the primeval nature of the site. One had only what one brought in with one. We were free, at least for the moment, from scrutiny by the Kail's electronic minions. For that, at least, I was grateful.

I assisted Madame Deirdre from the car. Redius threw a backpack full of emergency supplies and equipment to the ground and jumped down after it. I stood to take in the atmosphere of the place.

Trees rose above us to stunning heights like benevolent ancestors. Local avians flitted about the branches so high up that they were tiny winged dots on the empurpling sky. A short walk in the company of numerous arriving strangers, most of them human, took us over a ridge from the landing area to the lip of the Whispering Ravines themselves.

The dropoff of land just a few paces beyond the end of the path made my stomach fall, and my jaw after it. The words "river gorge" were far too feeble to describe the magnificence before me. Pink, gray and white stone had been carved into an undulating stream many kilometers wide and kilometers deep. The divide was so enormous that it only occurred to my logical mind after a moment's shocked realization that the fringe of dark green on the far lip of the ravine was a forest of the same massively tall trees that towered over my head on this side. As they reached the same conclusion, my fellow tourists emitted the same awestruck "Ooooooh."

Everyone there, and the area was populated with hundreds if not thousands of fellow humans, seemed to be happy to be making this discovery afresh, taking millions of images for the Infogrid and their personal collections. I was the only one who was disappointed. *Shame on me*, I thought. *I am surrounded by beauty and can't bear to let it into my soul.*

I sighed.

That didn't sound sorrowful enough. I tried again.

I inhaled until I had filled my entire belly with air. Then, deliberately, meaningfully, with all the artistry I could command, I *sighed*. My exhalation created a mournful sound and an emptiness in my belly that made me hunger for completion.

I was satisfied. I had nostalgia in my soul. I allowed it to make my body move.

My hands reached out to collect all the memories made in this place since it was discovered by humankind. I tried to gather them into one small jar that I treasured to myself, clutching it to my chest, but those memories kept escaping from the top of the jar. Covering it did no good. Those fleeting moments escaped between my fingers. I pursued them, like fugitive butterflies, seeking to pluck one, then another from the air.

"That's it, Lord Thomas!" Deirdre said, seating herself on a nearby boulder. Her hands fluttered up like the butterflies, offering me encouragement. "Beautiful interpretation! Now, work it into a narrative."

In spite of her kind words, I could hardly bear to do so. I still felt sad and disappointed. I had not believed Counterweight to be Old Earth when we had landed upon it, but Billimun's coy suggestions awoke hope in me and fed it. I could not blame him. He was a salesman, and his commodity was the sights and legends of his homeworld, however spurious the latter. He would not be the first person who sold fleeting dreams and moonbeams to willing buyers. I felt as though I should congratulate him for taking me in so completely, but I fancied it was not a testimonial he would enjoy showing to other clients.

I spun around, seeking where my true memories might reside. A few, a very few, points of starlight began to limn themselves on the deep blue sky. Were they in that star, or that one? I had no idea in which they lay.

My earthly surroundings caught me again and again, with a glimpse of a rare red flower here in a stand of crisp green grass, a shy furry woodland creature there underneath the leaves of a hardy bush with flat round leaves. The rich blue of the sky enveloped a vividly-hued land that was beautiful beyond belief. Optimism kept pressing at me. I damped it down as best I could, but it was hard to remain devastated. This was a really very pretty place in spite of its not being Earth. There was too much to like, too much to enjoy. I saw beauty all around me. Doggedly, for the sake of my art, I fought to remain depressed and sad.

Then I saw her.

As wild and shy-looking as the small furry animal, this woman attracted my eye and drew it to her as a needle draws thread. Dainty of height, curvaceous of frame and lush of hair, she seemed exotic even in a land that appeared to define the word. She wore a long robe that combined russet and celery colors in a weave that almost caused it to be a camouflage among the knee-high plants. It was tied around a small waist with a simple cord of dark green. This lovely person looked as though she belonged to the earth, with her terracotta complexion and dark eyes that were nearly almond-shaped. Masses of dark hair cascaded over her shoulders and down her back in waves that tossed like the sea. Her nose was tip-tilted. In fact, her face could have been that of an exquisite doll, except that when her eyes met mine, a burst of intelligence flamed forth and crisped me into ash. I was besotted in an instant. With all my energy focused upon those eyes, I moved forward, my hand out, offering my soul to this goddess.

"Lord Thomas?" a squeaky, high-pitched voice, entirely out of keeping with the exquisite face, issued forth from the soft mouth. She put out a tiny hand and grasped mine. "I'm Laine Derrida. That was really pretty! Nice to meet you!"

At her rusty squeal, my brain reasserted itself and pulled the reins of my body back from my heart.

"Dr. Derrida, what a pleasure!" I said. The rush of infatuation had caused my pulse to race. Annoyed, I willed it to slow to a reasonable pace. My wits hurried back into their accustomed place, and I bowed over her hand. "I am very glad to have found you. I was concerned that we might miss you."

"Oh, no," she said. Her laugh shrilled so high that anyone who had not been drilled in manners as I had from birth would have recoiled visibly. Alas, Redius, with his keen hearing, allowed his discomfort to show. "And call me Laine. Proton would have had us wait until you arrived, no matter how long it took."

I glanced around. "Is he here?"

"Zang prefer the neuter pronoun," Laine said. "Genders are so last eon." She tittered, as though it was a familiar joke. I smiled. If she thought it was funny, I would do my best to see the humor. "Come on. I'll bring you to it." She turned and strode purposefully toward one of the narrow passages of sandstone that led downhill.

"A Zang?" Madame Deirdre asked, leaping off her stone couch, her eyes brimful of curiosity. "We're going to meet a Zang here?"

"Yes, Madame," I said, lowering my voice. "We need to bring him—it—back to the ship."

"That's marvelous! I thought we would have to wait to see one. What a treat! Did you know about this all along?"

For answer, I patted the air and made furtive gestures to gather in secrets and tuck them within an invisible cloak over my hunched shoulders. Deirdre nodded. She remained silent, but her gray eyes remained alight. How nice it was to be with someone who was intelligent enough to read a second language that few around us could understand. Redius, who had been copiously briefed before we left the ship, merely bobbed his chin. Mr. Billimun would probably goggle like a fish when we returned to the car, but I trusted that he would feel honored to have such an august being as a Zang in his conveyance.

Outside the confines of the ship, however, the Zang might be vulnerable to attack or capture by the Kail. I did not wish to draw undue attention to our mission.

I glanced warily at the large crowd of humans in the valley. Adults, single or paired, with or without children, hurried here and there, looking at the waves of wind-carved sandstone. Those who had been watching me lost their interest in a split second and went about their business. They had not heard Deirdre's exclamation. They did not care about me or my concerns. I was ephemeral. Another interesting notion that I had to take on board. I would explore the concept at my leisure. In the meantime, I was full of eager anticipation for my next new experience.

It became evident, the farther we walked, why the Whispering Ravines were one of the most popular beauty spots on all of Counterweight. Nature, cunning artifice, or a combination of both had created a site that fascinated the eye. Every visible surface curved or undulated in a manner that made it look alive. Rocky escarpments had been tunneled and molded, rather than hewn, so that the entire landscape looked as though it would be smooth to the touch. In my mind's eye, I ran a hand over it and found it to be soft as the back of a kitten, even rising to my caress. Though my immediate goal filled most of my attention, I still gathered impressions that I would hold in my soul for eternity, and, not incidentally, add to my vocabulary of movement, as Madame Deirdre would have it. I glanced over my shoulder at her. I could see that she was doing the very same thing.

"So beautiful!" she said, her gray eyes twinkling. "One of my most famous performances in my youth was the Dance of the Winds. Those impressions had been gathered from Harsul, the second planet circling Leo's Star. I might revive that dance and add my interpretation of this place to the landscapes I described."

"I would be honored to produce that performance for you," I said. "If only for the joy of seeing it done."

"We should perform it together," she said, taking my arm in a companionable manner. "We will have very different moments to recreate. Look there!"

As we strode in Dr. Derrida's rapid wake, she pointed out things that I had noticed in passing, but had not remarked upon.

"See that?" she said, pointing upward to a horizontal mass of stone. "That hanging rock tells such a story about the passage of time, and how we are all so temporary! It hangs upon the balance of fate itself!"

In fact, as we walked along the gentle downhill slope through the maze of curves and hairpin turns, there were numerous hanging rocks. I found that fascinating. It was a very good thing that this wonderland was so very far away from Taino, because my cousins and I wouldn't be able to resist such a temptation. In a week, there wouldn't be one left on its eternal fulcrum. Redius met my eyes. I knew he was thinking the same thing.

As we went along, I saw fewer and fewer tourists. I was certain the Zang had chosen its spot with care, choosing isolation rather than drawing attention. Night was sweeping its midnight-blue cloak closer and closer to us. I feared that the park would fall into total darkness before we reached our destination, and that I would not be able to see our distinguished guest.

"Through here," Dr. Derrida called. I turned. She was astoundingly far ahead of us, beside a natural archway hewn from pink and tan stone. Her athleticism more than made up for her diminutive size. My admiration rebounded. Truthfully, though, it had not faded in the least from my consciousness. It had only receded into the near distance, where I was uncomfortably aware of it. She was such a lovely woman, intelligent and attractive, as well as being engaged in an enviable and amazing occupation.

I was aware that my infatuation colored my impression of her. It would take a while for me to get over it, but in the meantime, I intended to enjoy it.

I had had crushes since I was quite small. I had become fond of girls beginning at infant school, always aware that as a rule, they were distant relatives. A young teacher, a commoner, had drawn my interest when I was ten. I was fascinated by her fall of red-gold hair and her delicately pointed chin. Every time her green-gold eyes fell upon me, I felt as if I had been given a gift. I followed her devotedly as though I was a serverbot. She was amused by my infatuation, I dare say, though she never humiliated me by showing she knew.

When I was old enough to understand but not old enough to have put my desires into motion, my mother had sat me down for The Talk. She did not trust it, as other parents had, to the nannies or carebots that looked after us. She explained that because of the responsibility to my rank and position in the nobility, I could not simply indulge myself in hopeless passions or casual affairs. We of the Imperium dynasty needed to be careful. It was rude to break hearts or make promises we knew we could not keep. Going farther than that was out of the question. Not only was it unlikely to result in a long-term relationship, but it was against the laws created to protect the succession. None of us denied our natural impulses absolutely, of course. My cousin Xan was the most profligate among us as far as casual relationships went.

But this girl, something about her fascinated and attracted me. My heart told me to declare itself, but my brain reminded me that it would come to nothing. Dr. Derrida, for all her accomplishments and long string of academic titles, not to mention her amazing vocation as companion to an enigmatic and ancient alien, was a commoner. No real alliance between us was possible. Still, my imagination insisted on painting for me a whirlwind courtship full of moonlight and laughter, followed by a formal wedding, which dissolved into a charming cottage home in the middle of a green valley, with adorable, dimpled children that looked just like her running around and laughing. I was shocked, all the more because I did my level best to avoid any emotional entanglements that might propel me into one of those uncomfortable and interminable ceremonies which were *de rigeur* for one of my rank formalizing a sanctioned and approved permanent relationship. The rest of my family, had they the least inkling of what my imagination was up to, would have called an intervention and removed me from the planet, at least until the lady had decided to move on to a different locale, preferably in a galaxy far, far away.

Something must have showed on my face, because Dr. Derrida—Laine—gave me a peculiar glance as I approached her.

"What are you thinking?" she asked.

Her shrill voice brought me to my senses. I improvised hastily, something at which I was becoming more adept by the moment.

"I am fascinated to meet the Zang," I said.

"They are fascinating," she said. She stopped in a narrow arroyo where the winds blew on us from five different passageways at once. They all looked rather alike, but after a moment's hesitation, she took the second opening on the left. "This way." She scurried forward at speed, crunching over the fine gravel. I opened my stride to catch up with her. Redius and Deirdre hurried in our wake.

"What shall I say to it when we meet?" I asked.

"They don't really speak as we know it," Laine said, glancing back now and again over her shoulder. "It has only spoken to me a few times, even though I've been with it for many years. Most of the time I gain impressions, which are pretty accurate. I've always been good at body language. Please don't be offended if it never looks at you. Most humans aren't real enough for it to notice."

"But it's here to try and notice us, or so I have been informed," I said.

"That's right. As Zang go, it's a scholar of lower orders . . . Please don't be offended," she said hastily, as my brow drew down at her words.

"I'm not." I was pleased to realize I felt the truth of my assertion. "To the Zang, even *my* family is of a lower order." She gave me an odd look. I changed the subject to cover our momentary mutual discomfort. "This is quite a labyrinth. How do you know where to find the Zang?" My voice echoed off the pink, tan and white sandstone walls and was lost in the distance.

"It has a presence," she said, taking my hand. I fancied that I felt a spark as we touched. Had she noticed it? "You'll know as soon as you meet it. Can't you feel something ahead of us? It'll grow stronger as we go."

I opened all my senses. I was becoming accustomed to gathering impressions, but nearly all of them had been in the realm of the most common seven, including sense of place and time. I realized I did feel a presence, so to speak, almost a pressure upon my prefrontal cortex, my third eye, as I might have said, with reference to my previous enthusiasm. The sensation warned me to be wary of what lay ahead. I glanced back at my friends, to see if they felt any of that. They did. Redius's eyes were open as wide as they could go. To my surprise, Madame Deirdre was enjoying the experience.

"My goodness," she said. "It's so . . . primal!"

At that moment, we snaked around a curve in the raspy-textured passageway, a silver-white glow suffused the surrounding stone, and the primitive centers of my brain all bowed down in awe.

"Here it is!" Laine announced. She let go of my hand and stood aside to make room for us to approach.

Indeed, we had encountered A Presence. The Zang was surrounded by so much sensation that it was difficult to look at it. Unlike anyone I had ever met before, I had the impression of a personality in advance of a physical one. The notion fascinated me so much that I stood drinking in the waves of force that struck me and passed through me. I felt as though I could hear distant voices calling over the crackling of nebular energy and the whoosh of solar winds.

In a way I could not have expressed easily in words, I had the sense that Proton Zang was ancient beyond anything that I had thought a living being could be. It was charming and avuncular, and I knew I could not fool it in the slightest by any posturing or appearance I could muster. I would have to strive to be as real as possible to be worthy of its acquaintance.

I became aware of eyes like eternal pools, deep and silver, set into its side among vertical crenelations. I willed them to turn toward me. The massive torso shifted. I felt a thrill go through me. Would they stop on me? What would I do if it noticed me? How should I respond?

Instead, the glowing gaze traveled beyond my upturned and hopeful face, and stopped on Laine. It had not noticed me or my companions at all.

An emotional impulse rather than words formed in my mind. *She is special.*

I know, I thought out at it, filled with sudden and overwhelming affection toward Dr. Derrida. *She is!*

I became aware of a moment of scrutiny like a gigantic burst of energy as a wisp, a thread, a particle, of Proton's consciousness touched me. It swiftly passed away, leaving me almost breathless. We had shared a moment. I was enchanted.

Redius looked suddenly uncomfortable. He gasped for air and felt for the wall of the canyon to lean upon.

"Scanning," he said.

"More than scanning, wouldn't you say?" I asked, wryly. "It took us, wrung out the interesting parts, and left the husks. I've never felt anything like that. Have you?"

"No! Nor would again!"

"I'm afraid this is just the beginning," I said. "It's coming with us all the way to the platform."

Redius narrowed his eyes. He made himself slow his breathing.

"I know. Struggling."

Laine leaned toward the Zang. I admired the way she seemed entirely comfortable beside this awe-inspiring being.

"Our contacts from the human ship have arrived." She was doing more than talking. Somehow, she was conveying information to the Zang through force of will.

Fighting the impulse to flee the intensity of its reality, I moved around to the eyes to which Laine had addressed her remarks, and bowed deeply. It did not repeat the pulse that I had felt. I was a little disappointed. I had hoped that it would learn to notice me as it did her.

In a sense, its indifference was a relief. It gave me a respite during which I could study it more closely without feeling my own unimportance.

At a distance, it would have appeared to be a ridged, upright cylinder, narrowing slightly from its base to its top. In color, it seemed to be a pearly gray with a dash of the kind of pure blue one saw in glacier ice. If I had had to make a simile between it and anything in my personal experience, it would be as though an ancient tree trunk cut off at eight or nine feet at an angle had been petrified and replaced with moonstone instead of opal. I could not help but be struck by its beauty as well as the impression of age. No, more than age. Eternity. Yes. At once I began to re-choreograph my welcome dance, and wished Parsons was present so I could obtain permission to perform it.

"Would you like to go to our ship now?" I asked Laine. "Our transport is waiting at the edge of the park."

Professor Derrida studied her companion. I felt the brush of energy pass by me toward her again.

"Not yet," Laine said. She drew us away from the Zang to the other side of the stone passage. "It is gathering impressions."

"What a coincidence," I said, immediately feeling a minor kinship to this fantastic being. I turned to the Zang. "I am a student of interpretive dance. Madame Deirdre," I indicated the lady, "is my teacher. I wanted to gain some insights on this very Earthlike planet." Deirdre curtseyed gracefully. The Zang noticed neither of us.

"Yes, I admired your impromptu dance a lot," Laine said, her warm amber eyes fixing on me. "It was terribly sad. I would love to see one of your formal performances."

"I would be delighted," I said, then I glanced toward the Zang and remembered my promise to Parsons. "Later on. Join me for dinner."

"Thank you," she said, looking up at me with interest. "I'd enjoy that!"

"I look forward to introducing you to my cousins," I continued. I was aware that my outpouring bordered on babbling, but I couldn't stem the spate of words. "They will have so many questions for you about the Zang."

"I'll be happy to answer anything I can!" Laine laughed, in a register that I fancied annoyed dogs for miles in all directions.

"And I will perform for them, as well. I have been gathering some very interesting impressions of Counterweight that I wish to share with my cousins."

She laughed again, showing very white teeth behind her rosebud lips. "I would love to see them! Proton has been doing very much the same thing. It would be interesting to compare your observations."

"No doubt," I said. I frowned. "But how will I know what it is thinking?"

"I'll give you its impressions. That's all I ever get." Laine smiled at me. I melted in the warmth of her regard. It would be my pleasure to travel with her, as long as fate allowed.

"Look out!"

A voice echoed throughout the chasm. I glanced up to see one of the immense hanging stones hurtling down on us. In horror, I realized it was falling directly toward the Zang. Without regard for my own safety, I threw myself at it.

I touched an impossibly cold column of air, then I hurtled against the cliff face, scraping my palms and barking the toes of my boots. In the next moment, a body landed on top of mine just as a multi-ton chunk of rock impacted into the ground behind us. An immense crack sounded. I fought to get free, fearing that I had missed my rescue, and the sound had issued from the Zang's exoskeleton being crushed.

Redius rose, brushing sand and stone fragments from his robe. He pulled me upright. A cloud of dust enveloped us both. I coughed, expelling a kilogram or so of gravel from my lungs.

"Sorry!" a voice echoed down to us from the heights. A young man in casual clothes waved, an embarrassed and worried look on his face. Hovering park rangerbots enameled in khaki surrounded him and escorted him away from the edge. I heard them reading him his rights.

"Intact?" Redius asked me.

"Yes!" I said. I examined my palms. They were only scraped. "Is the Zang all right?"

I turned, with some difficulty, finding myself ankle-deep in freshly crushed gravel and pebbles. The fallen stone, now broken in half, filled most of the narrow passage in which we had been standing. The Zang stood some ten meters away, looking serenely uninvolved and intact.

"Stone fell through," Redius explained.

"Did it?" I asked. "Do you mean it is insubstantial?"

"Or disbelieved stone's solidity." He dropped his jaw in a smile. "Predates it?"

Laine scrambled up and over the enormous rock. She gathered her full skirts in her hand as she climbed down on our side, showing a glimpse of a delightfully well-turned ankle.

"Are you all right? That was very brave of you."

"I thought the stone would crush it," I said.

She laughed. "Proton is pretty much impervious to harm, but I appreciate that you tried to save its life. I'll remember that. So will Proton."

"Really?" I asked, forgetting my new bruises in a moment. I glanced toward the Zang, but it showed no difference in posture or attitude to indicate that I was now any more real than before, but I took Laine's assurance as a success of sorts. "I am grateful to have served in any small way."

She gave me a smile that melted me with its warmth. No accolade could have been more rewarding. She reached out to take my hand again in her small fingers. Then, she glanced back over her shoulder at the blue-white column.

"I think it's ready to go now. Where did you say your transport is waiting?"

ᨳ **CHAPTER 14** ᨳ

"As a result of Kail action, we have lost the services of an agent, but gained insight into a potential catastrophe," Parsons said, pulling up the last of the images of the Kail that had been stored on the chip he had obtained in the salon, and displayed it to the officers gathered in Captain Wold's ready room. He had inserted it into a portable player that was not attached in any way to the ship's Infogrid system. The captains from the escort ships, present once again as holograms, had been warned to accept video and audio only, with no sideband transmissions that could carry tainted code to their own systems. He had no intention of wasting Bokie's sacrifice.

"May we know the name of this agent?" Captain Wold said. Xe drew on a bright orange nic-tube clenched in xir small and even teeth. Parsons deplored such a habit, but could understand the need for the relaxing qualities of the drug. His report had the potential to overwhelm all the listeners with stress.

"I am sorry, Captain," Parsons said. "Even in death, revealing the name of Covert Services operatives could put others at risk."

Wold nodded. "I wasn't trying to pry. I would celebrate xir courage."

"Thank you. I will see that your sympathy is passed along through . . . appropriate channels." Parsons could not explain that the bereaved were all LAIs who were attached through the Infogrid and were already aware of the gap in their numbers. "Let us instead concentrate upon the data that the agent provided. The infiltration that we detected earlier has been detected on a greater scale than we knew. The entire planet is affected."

"But what are we going to do?" asked Captain Colwege, spreading his thick fingers in appeal. He was present only from the waist up. "We can't shut off contact with Counterweight indefinitely. We all need to maintain communications with the fleet. The Admiralty office is demanding answers about the shutoff."

"I have sent a copy of this report through other channels, captain," Parsons said. "The message will deteriorate as soon as it passes each gate in turn, thereby leaving no trace for the virus program to detect. It will be passed along to the First Space Lord personally within minutes of arrival. She will be informed, and will take appropriate action."

Lopez sat back against a chair that was invisible to those in the *Jaunter*'s ready room. "That's a relief. She's a stickler."

"Yes, captain," Parsons said. "I do not need to stress that it is necessary to protect all ships in the Imperium Navy, as well as all other vessels in space, from the Kail's intrusion. It is not only the Kail of whom we must be wary. We do not believe that they could have accomplished this coup without the assistance of LAI personnel."

"Traitors in the ranks?" Colwege asked, lowering mighty, white brows down over flashing eyes. "That's outrageous! Our own crew, informing upon us?"

Parsons shook his head very slightly, inflaming some of the muscles that had been abused.

"It is believed by my late contact that few of the artificial intelligences are involved willingly, but there is no way to determine how many or how deeply without questioning them with the cooperation of our own LAIs. Unfortunately, each contact risks turning friendly electronic personnel into carriers of the command code, and thereby conveying back into the parent system."

"Are humans—organic races—in danger?" Wold asked.

"I would work from the assumption that they are only of interest if they interfere with the Kail's programs," Parsons said. "As long as they don't know about it, they're less likely to run afoul of the Kail."

"This is monstrous," Atwell said. "News of this could cause riots systemwide!"

"We must inform the Counterweight senate," Lopez said. "They ought to know what they're dealing with."

"It would cause too much of a panic," Colwege argued, his snowy brows high on his forehead. "Especially among visitors. The planetary economy would be ruined, especially since nothing material can be done at the moment."

"My department is in touch with local hacker organizations," Parsons said. "They are beginning counterprogramming, but it will take time to see if they can close off access without seeming to do so deliberately. At present, it would seem that few people will be affected by the Kail's investigation of databases. They have little interest in human affairs, including the economy."

"But people should know they're under attack!" Lopez said, leaning forward, her dark eyes blazing.

"Are they?" Parsons asked, dryly. "This appears to be chiefly an information-gathering process. Apart from proprietary data, including manufacturing secrets and the scripts for major digitavids in production, there is little that does not undergo government oversight in the Deep Grid already. And the Kail have no means of making use of that proprietary data, as they have no manufacturing centers or an arts industry."

"It's dangerous that they can take over secured systems," Colwege said. "That's my concern. You can't dismiss that!"

"I do not. But it appears to affect only LAIs at the moment, and the systems on board the *Whiskerchin*, which appears to have been taken over only when the Wichu did not accede to the Kail's demands. We still don't know whether this incursion was purely defensive, or whether they have an ulterior, hostile motive. It behooves us to act, at least openly, as if we believe that they want to reach a détente with humankind."

"Humankind and others are in *danger*," Tamber said. "We must take action."

"What can we do?" Wold asked, taking the nic-tube out of xir mouth and crushing it into a ball. "Blow the Wichu ship out of the sky? I'm reluctant to take any actions against a friendly. The Wichu have been our allies since humanity's first contact with them. I would rather see them rescued."

"As would we all," Colwege agreed.

"It makes you see how helpless we are to get along without electronic systems," Lopez said, almost plaintively. "Some of my best friends are LAIs. So are some of my finest officers and crew. I don't want to feel as though they are plotting to take over my ship."

"What defense do we have?" Lieutenant Plet asked. She and Lieutenant Oskelev sat at the far end of the table. Ordinarily, the outspoken pilot would not be included in the conference, but she had friends and distant relations on board the *Whiskerchin.*

"Insufficient, to say the least," Parsons said. He nodded to Lieutenant Ormalus. "The communication system is tied to so many of the computer functions that there are a thousand open doors through which the rogue code could enter. Prevention is our best defense."

"It's terrifying that they can control any system, no matter how well defended," Commander Atwell said. His round blue eyes seemed to pop out of his ruddy face.

"Not completely," Parsons said. "During my ... meeting, I was able to block their intrusion into one system, temporarily. More I cannot say at this time. The event must remain classified."

"I see," Wold said. Xe rose from xir place and paced around the table. "What can you tell us? How did you do it?"

"Through technology available to me in the Covert Services Operation."

"Well, can't we have it? We need it!"

Parsons allowed himself the tiniest intimation of a smile. "You already have it. I have put an upgradable anti-virus program into your communication officers' hands. It's been installed since my return to the ship."

"Functions amazingly," the Uctu officer said, vibrating her tongue. "Efficient."

"Wonderful!" Lopez said, her dark eyes brightening. "Thank you, commander."

"My pleasure, captain," Parsons said, nodding his head slightly. "This is the first time that the program is being deployed by any but Covert Services operatives, so the interface may seem obscure to most, but we feel that it stands the best chance of fending off the intrusion. It must be constantly updated, of course, which relies upon quantum connection with the Infogrid. The difficulty in that is if the Kail access the Infogrid and infiltrate it with programs provided to them by the rogue LAIs. They might be able to piggyback upon the program and receive the updates as we get them. As those must be activated by an organic agent, they won't be able to make use of all of them, but they might be able to use a gap in coverage to infiltrate systems further."

"It sounds hopeless," Wold said, throwing up xir hands. "I'm ready to return to Keinolt."

"Impossible," Parsons said. "Until the Covert Services is convinced that this ship is free of Kail control, you would not be allowed within hailing distance of the Core Worlds."

"The nobles won't like that!" Wold said. Xe rose and began to pace.

"Under the circumstances, you may as well continue to the platform and allow them to see the spectacle," Parsons said. He checked the simple chronometer that he had placed in his belt pouch in lieu of the viewpad he did not dare trust. "Lord Thomas will be returning with Proton Zang very shortly. If nothing else, we can leave orbit as soon as the rest of the nobles are on board."

"If no LAIs scuttle our engines and blow up our life support!" Atwell growled. "Never liked them."

"Don't plenty of them work for you?" Lopez asked, sweetly.

"I can't help that! They're everywhere!"

Special Envoy Garricka Wu Melarides, seated at the side of the table beside her charge d'affaires, cleared her throat. A motherly-looking woman with thick steel-gray hair tied in a figure-eight bun at the back of her head, she had a prosperous, plump figure and a serene, oblong face that exuded calm. The calf-length gray tunic she wore over white trousers that was the consular services' uniform looked casual and comfortable, rather than formal and off-putting.

"I believe I have a solution," Melarides said. Wold turned to her, albeit with a skeptical expression.

"What is it?"

"We have already arranged for custody of the Zang, thereby ensuring that we control access to it. I will prepare a statement to the Kail, outlining our conditions for contact. One of them will be that they are not permitted access to any of the ship's electronic or communication systems, and no access to any LAIs or AIs except for the assistive personnel that will be assigned to them. I can easily order the translatorbots and other staff who will have ongoing contact with them to shut down other functions until further notice. That way, we can bring the Kail on board the *Jaunter*, removing them from the *Whiskerchin* altogether. They will be able to meet with the Zang as they wish, the Wichu ship will be back in the control of the crew, and we can oversee the Kail."

"No!" Captain Wold said, xir face turning red. Xe slammed a fist onto the ready room table. "Endanger the lives of His Highness's relations by taking those things on board? No. I don't want a crowd of Kail on my ship! The nobles are enough trouble all by themselves."

"But, captain," Melarides said, with a pleasant smile, "this only advances the hour at which we would have had to allow the Kail access to the ship anyhow. This is a marvelous opportunity. My staff and I would jump at the chance to study them further. We know so little about them. The Imperium's xenobiologists have little data. We can add to that. The fact that they agreed to a meeting with the Imperium while we are on the platform is unprecedented. I look at this as a chance to begin our negotiations early. We'll have weeks instead of hours to get to know them."

"What if it tries to do to the *Jaunter* what it has already done to the *Whiskerchin*?" xe asked. "We have no guarantee they won't try to take over."

"Captain Wold, I beg of you to consider," Melarides said, leaning forward over her clasped hands. "Captain Bedelev said that the Kail changed the ship's course in order to communicate with a Zang ahead of time. I would love to take that same opportunity to advance our cause with the Kail before the spectacle, when they might be too absorbed in the Zang's activity to pay close attention to our negotiations. I remind you that the Emperor himself is deeply interested in our success."

Wold sat down. Xe seemed ready to reach for another nic-tube, but instead folded xir hands in the same manner as the envoy.

"Ambassador Melarides, I know His Highness is concerned about the meeting, but it was expected that the Kail would make their own way to the platform. This ship is not prepared to take on board a potential enemy who have already proven that they can disrupt vital functions. They did whatever they pleased to the *Whiskerchin*. What assurance do we have that they will not do it to us?"

"We'll keep them under control," Melarides said, with confidence. She sat upright. "With the help of Commander Parsons and my staff, we'll keep them *happy*. They won't need to cause trouble. They'll get what they want."

"Are we sure that meeting the Zang is all they want?"

"I don't know. We must trust them to a certain extent, or we will never achieve peace between our peoples," Melarides said. "Let us make the offer. We will make it clear that we need assurances in order to make this meeting as positive an experience for all parties as we can. That will require some give and take. They made demands, true. That means that they cannot accomplish what they wish on their own. They made compromises to take passage on the *Whiskerchin*. We will let them know what we need, and see what they say."

Parsons held himself erect, even though his healing bruises and cuts thudded in pain with each beat of his heart. "The fact that they changed course to arrive here at the same time as Proton means they must have intended all along to meet with the Zang. Whether or not their main aim was to witness the spectacle is open to question. This might be the aim of their journey. Unless my studies have given me a false impression, they do not travel out of their space very often."

"No, they don't," Melarides said, with a world-weary smile. "They're not comfortable among us or any of the other carbon-based species. I have to keep in mind that they may only have agreed to meet with the Emperor's representatives in order to enter Imperium space. We can still make use of this moment. We want them to feel that we are friendly. His Highness would prefer to have peace on every border. My team means to try."

Wold's narrow face went through a number of expressions, none of them happy. Finally, xe turned to Parsons.

"Commander, what do you say? Can we trust the Kail?"

"In a simple answer," Parsons said, "no."

"Commander!" Melarides chided him.

He turned to her, keeping his countenance grave. "As you will no doubt have discovered during your long and distinguished career, Ambassador, the greatest force in the galaxy is self-interest."

"What about love or loyalty?" Lopez asked, looking shocked.

He regarded the other captain. "Those emotions evolve from the same basis as fear and greed. I realize that it sounds cynical, but objectivity leads me to say it. We can't trust the Kail, but we can trust their self-interest. They want access to the Zang. They could be made to wait until we reach the platform, but who knows what havoc they will have wreaked on the *Whiskerchin* before then? We can hope to forestall that behavior against the Wichu by giving them that access. It is a matter for Ambassador Melarides to determine if we can prevent them from doing damage to this ship while they are on board. There is a risk that they will take over the ship even if they gain what they seek, but that would be counterproductive. It would only result in their being confined once again, but this time without flaws that allow them access to electrical contact."

"What if they've already infiltrated the system?" Captain Colwege demanded.

Parsons drew up a diagram from the table and set it running. Bar graphs of somber colors extended up toward the ceiling, bobbing up and down as the data streams registered from the computer system.

"That's a possibility. The detection and anti-viral software has only just been installed. Ormalus and her staff are exploring the root directories and data libraries for intrusion beyond the scan that the ship experienced this morning. You can see nothing has yet been detected, but that does not mean that there is nothing to find."

"We still don't know what they're looking for," Atwell said, smacking one hand into the other. "You said your contact suggested that they're using our data as comparison. But comparison with what?"

"We don't know that yet," Parsons said. "Perhaps Ambassador Melarides and her staff can discern the subject of their search in their conversations to come."

"We will certainly try," Melarides said, with a smile.

"I don't like it," Wold said. "If the Kail mean us no harm, why not inform us as to what they want from the Zang?"

"They may feel that it's none of our business," Melarides said, turning a plump hand palm upward. "We don't tell the Wichu everything we discuss with the Trade Union, and so on. It's not a matter of secrecy, but efficiency. Not every point is of interest to every party. The Zang are mysterious creatures. I look forward to meeting our guest."

"I have read through the transcript that my late colleague downloaded for us from its colleague on board," Parsons said. "The Kail behaved themselves when their needs were met. When they were thwarted, they reacted."

"They're not innocent if they had a crewmember on the ship ready to take over at a moment's notice," Wold said. Xe put xir face into xir hands and stirred up xir hair with xir fingers.

"They are long thinkers," Melarides said. "That is something that we have learned during our communications with them. Fovrates may never have activated his control. We don't know. Yet."

"Is this evident in their daily life?" Lopez asked. "I haven't seen any images or digitavids of the Kail's interaction with one another except for the ones Commander Parsons just showed us."

"No human has been welcomed onto any of the Kail homeworlds," the ambassador said, with a smile. "They consider any physical contact from organic beings to be an imposition. My counterpart in outreach, Ambassador Basiliu, spent five months orbiting a Kail planet. Communication was sporadic. He did, however, manage to secure their promise to meet with us on the platform."

"If they have no technology of their own, how did you talk with them?" Wold asked.

Melarides chuckled and tented her fingers. "We sent a trio of LAI negotiatorbots down. They were our intermediaries. The Kail consider them closer to kin than any of us 'slime.' The 'bots are still on Yesa, doing outreach, trying to convince them that humans aren't the evil they believe we are."

"Can the ship be made secure against interference from the Kail's ability?" Wold asked Parsons.

"Never completely. We will, as Ambassador Melarides said, have to trust them to a certain extent. All computer systems will need to be subject to constant checks and balances. Communication with other ships and the Imperium base will need to be in the simplest possible encoding so that any viruses or worms can be detected at once. But the easiest way to prevent an incursion should be to let them have what they want. Give them access to the Zang. Provide them with clean water and purified mineral dust. Don't touch them."

Wold stared fiercely at Parsons, the pupils of xir light eyes boring into Parsons's.

"If I approve this, it will be your responsibility to keep them from interfering with *my ship*, Commander. You'll have the resources you need, but you must not fail!"

Parsons bowed, feeling every rib protest. "I will do my best, captain."

"What about the potential of a system breach?"

"The possibility that it has already occurred is a lower risk than finding out what happens if the Kail manage to achieve it," Parsons said. "In the best case scenario, we can convince them to allow their hold on the Wichu and Counterweight systems to lapse. By reverse engineering, we can discover how they did it, so we can block access should they ever make another such attempt."

"And in the worst case?" Captain Wold asked, xir narrow jaw set.

"In the worst," Parsons said, feeling every bruise on his body, "we will have hostages of our own."

CHAPTER 15

Phutes held himself rigid as the flimsy shuttle detached from the side of the *Whiskerchin*. It seemed an insufficiently strong vessel to convey him and his siblings to the place where the Zang waited. He hated being in the small shells. He longed for the day when he could return to his motherworld and forget he had ever seen a Wichu, or a human, or a shuttle.

"Bad enough that we have to move onto a human ship," Sofus complained, shifting the flexible, flat pieces of rock that lined the cabin in order to make himself a more comfortable seat. "But *they* are here."

Sofus pointed at the black-topped human and the red-orange Uctu that sat at the front of the cabin, the soft excrescences that served them for manipulative digits resting on brightly-colored weapons. The others murmured their unhappiness.

"It doesn't matter now, and soon, it will not matter at all," Phutes reassured them. "Their species are ephemeral and will pass."

"Not soon enough!"

"We can hear you, you know," the black-topped human said. He had identified himself as "Nesbitt," not that Phutes cared for the buzz and glottal stop. His words were translated into good Kail by the bronze-colored translatorbot at his side. The LAI was tall, nearly as tall as Mrdus, but almost as thin as one of Phutes's wrists. At the top of the silicon and metal being, a cluster of round glass disks served as ocular receptors. She went by the name of NR-111, a very sensible-sounding name for a machine made by humans. Phutes almost felt when he spoke to her that he was talking with one of his own kind, perhaps an older one. She was very wise and patient.

"It doesn't matter," Phutes said to Sofus, ignoring the interruption. "What noises come from them make no difference to us."

The translator emitted some of the human-sounding nonsense. Nesbitt turned to the Uctu and made the black stripes on its face move up and down. The Uctu's mouth dropped open, though no sound emerged from it.

"There are a lot of humans on our ship," Nesbitt said, leaning toward them, his wobbly face stretching in an unnatural fashion. "Lots and *lots* of them."

"I think I am going to be sick," said Mrdus. He was the smallest of the Kail, a small, lumpy individual with 101 short legs and 11 arms. Phutes had wondered often why he had permitted the weakling to accompany them, but their mother had insisted. Mrdus had a mind that absorbed new processes more swiftly than the rest of them. He had picked up on Fovrates's lessons before any of the others, but he seemed to forget everything when Wichu were around.

"You withstood the Wichu. You will bear the humans," Sofus said firmly.

Mrdus made grinding noises, but nothing else. Phutes didn't want him to embarrass them in front of the disgusting squishy ones.

"Do not tease the Kail," the Uctu said to the human. It had been named as "Redius." The translator picked up its sparse noises and translated them into good language. "You promised Commander Parsons that you would behave with decorum."

"Just telling him the truth, right?" the human replied. He hefted the jewel-colored weapon from his lap. "But we're all going to get along just fine."

Phutes was not so certain, for all the assurances the human called "Melarides" had offered via the communications system. He had not yet caught her in an outright lie. Fovrates and his scanners had confirmed that the Zang had indeed arrived, and was in the humans' ship. That was something that the Kail had not known. Fovrates had assumed it was only on its way toward the platform, as they were. If the Zang was in league with humans, their cause might be lost. But Yesa had assured him that the Zang served only their own interests. The Kail could appeal to them for help against the humans.

Yesa, Nefra and the other motherworlds had borne the invasion of their territory by organic species for numerous revolutions, but the last few had been too much. The humans had come into Kail space and remained even after it was made clear to them they weren't welcome. Sending silicon-based objects like NR-111 to Yesa only served to prove that humanity and others did not belong there. The humans, though, did not take either "no" or "go away" for answers. From the beginning they had harangued the Kail to meet with them. They wanted to be "better neighbors." Whatever that meant. The motherworlds were certain that it couldn't be good. The humans had no notion of privacy. They were filthy, and spread their sticky cells everywhere. They tried to remove portions of the motherworlds without permission. The smell of them offended every Kail who came into contact with them.

In the end, partly out of curiosity and partly out of frustration, Yesa had agreed to send envoys to a meeting. Phutes had been primed by Yesa with the answers she wanted the humans to hear. They were not to come to Kail space ever again for any reason. The Kail wished to be left in peace. If they wanted contact with the rotting species, they would go to their worlds. Left unspoken was the thought that no such thing would ever happen. He had listened to her well-rehearsed reasoning for rotations on end, until he could repeat them back to her in the same cadences she used.

She also drilled him on that which she wanted him to say to the Zang once they met. That was more difficult, as the celestial beings spoke in such a different way, not through sound alone.

This expedition was a test of his ability to cope. Every day brought experiences that he had not expected, and was forced to rely upon his own wits to handle. At no time in his life had he ever been the final authority on anything. He had never been out of the sound of Yesa's voice. He had found it difficult not to cede control to Fovrates. It was one of the reasons that he had let so much time lapse between boarding the Wichu ship and paying his first visit. The elder Kail was worthy of respect. Phutes felt he ought to do what Fovrates said. The engineer thought that his submission and that of his siblings was hilarious. Phutes was offended, but it had given him a lot to think about. Unless Nefra ran her family differently than Yesa did, leaving home must have a strong influence on one's sense of independence. He had to contemplate that notion. At first he didn't really like being the one to whom the others looked up. He was too young and inexperienced! The trouble was that more senior Kail were too unwieldy to go. It was up to the young ones who were sufficiently mobile, no matter that they were less wise. From those Yesa had chosen Phutes as her envoy.

The responsibility weighed on him far more than the low gravity of the slime creatures' ship. He wished he could hear Yesa and get the benefit of her wisdom. In truth, she was likely to tell him to pull himself together and do what he was told.

He glanced at the human and Uctu at the end of the chamber. They kept their strange ocular receptors fixed on him and his siblings, even while they spoke in undertones to one another. He didn't care what they said about him, only how they acted. So far, they had been as benign as the Wichu had when they first boarded the *Whiskerchin*. The Wichu had betrayed them, locking them up and trying to keep them isolated. Since that moment, Phutes did not trust any of them. He would not trust any organism he could not control. Fovrates had found it all very amusing, blaming Phutes for overreacting, causing the notoriously volatile Wichu to overreact in their turn. It didn't matter what they thought or did now, since the Kail controlled the ship. The trouble was that the *Whiskerchin* only conveyed them to the Zang. In order to get what he wanted, Phutes had to deal with humans.

Phutes hated to admit it, but humans terrified him. All the stories Yesa had told him of their pillaging through the motherworlds made him fear the worst. The Uctu wasn't as bad. He seemed to be calm and thoughtful, but the black-topped creature was a thing of menace to him. If it suddenly lunged at him, he would feel as sick as Mrdus, then he would retaliate, probably killing the squishy creature.

He knew he wouldn't dare act on his impulses. Yesa would be furious.

"I am concerned for the well-being of our brothers left behind," Sofus said. "We hold greater safety in numbers." Phutes made a soothing sound from deep in its vocal cone.

"Nothing will harm them. Fovrates holds the controls. They won't endanger themselves or their ship. We might survive in the vacuum, but they couldn't."

"The Wichu are angry. They have means to take the rest of our siblings unaware."

The human erupted into an annoyed burble.

"Too bad they couldn't keep you in a box," the translator emitted.

Phutes glared at the servicebot at his side.

"Stop telling the disgusting ones what we are saying. I will tell you when you can repeat our thoughts."

"Of course, Phutes," the translator said, in soothing tones. "I am here to serve you. My brief is to act as your assistant while you are in Imperium space. In other words, I work for you, not for them. Instruct me as you wish."

"Good," Phutes grunted. "Do not tell them anything any of us say unless I tell you it is to be said." No answering blather sounded from NR-111's speakers. The human and Uctu looked wary at the silence, tightening their upper excrescences on the weapons.

"How can we avoid being taken prisoner when we are aboard the human ship?" Mrdus asked.

"That is your task," Sofus said. He made an impatient gesture with two of his arms. "Do as Fovrates instructed you. Interact with the electronics of the ship. Prevent it from locking us in anywhere."

"I am very sorry," NR-111 said, turning to the largest Kail. "You will not be permitted access to the central computer system. That is a non-negotiable part of your agreement with the Imperium in order for you to come aboard and interact with the Zang."

"We must be able to speak with our siblings," Phutes said, feeling the acids of his system bubbling up in indignation. He clenched his fists. "I will not allow us to be cut off from the Kail who are still on board the Wichu vessel!"

"And you will be allowed communication privileges," the translator said, in her soothing voice. "Any time you wish to speak with Fovrates or any of the other Kail, let me know, and I will obtain an open channel for your use."

"We want free and open signals!" Sofus said.

"Please allow me to apologize again," NR-111 said. The stalk full of lenses rose up so that it was on a level with Sofus's face. "That would not be allowed even if you were a ship's officer. Use of the communication channels is restricted and monitored. That is a matter of security. I regret if that inconveniences you. I can make sure you can call Fovrates or any of the others at any time you wish."

"Do so," Sofus said, unable to keep the sulky tone out of his voice. "I want to make sure our siblings are safe."

The lenses bobbed. "Understood. I am sure they are in no danger from the Wichu, Sofus."

Phutes did not voice his concerns. He wasn't convinced that those who remained behind would be safe. The Wichu were angry, and they had managed to catch him and his siblings unaware. Such a coup was less likely, now that Fovrates had converted some of the silicon-based mechanicals to their side. They would warn the Kail about communication between the long-furred organisms. It was still a mystery to Phutes how Fovrates had communicated with the inner beings of the mechanicals in a way that made them side with the Kail point of view. The engineer had taught Phutes to do it over the course of the last many rotations, but it was by rote. He scarcely understood the process, although he could do it.

Because of their body structure and their keen hearing that picked up sounds from incredibly long wavelengths to impossibly short ones, the Kail had become very good at imitating the sounds of the galaxy. While Phutes was growing up, he learned to sing along with the music he could hear coming from the stars and other bodies in the void. They could hear in a range of incredibly long wavelengths down to incredibly short ones, and reproduce the sounds that they heard. Fovrates and many other elders had gone out among the more technological races of the galaxy. Using the skills gleaned from listening to the stars, they had discovered that they could hear the language that the LAIs used, and gradually picked up on the combinations that changed the way LAIs thought.

Sofus wasn't any better at it than Phutes, but Mrdus was a natural. With their help, they could make the LAIs serve them instead of their carbon-based employers.

Apparently, they had not been as subtle as they thought they had been. The conversation with Melarides confirmed that the humans had found out about their partnership with some of the LAIs. No matter. The Kail would never be held prisoner again on any vessel occupied by the squishy ones. They, or at least Mrdus, could turn the LAIs to their side at any time. And the LAIs could make the computer systems do the Kail's bidding.

With their freedom secured, it was up to Phutes to persuade the Zang to achieve Yesa's goal.

He pushed the thoughts of what lay ahead to one side and made note of the terrain over which they were passing. The shuttle traveled with its translucent canopy facing the planet. Counterweight, the uncouth name humans gave this sphere, was a marvel, conducive to sustaining almost any form of life. Phutes marveled at the tossing blue oceans. So much water. If only it wasn't polluted by organic compounds, this world would be a paradise for Kail. Someday, perhaps, they would return and rid its lovely body of the parasites.

No one communicated during the remainder of the transference to the *Imperium Jaunter*. Phutes marveled at the size of the human vessel. It was nearly as large as a motherworld, or so it seemed. Small ships, gleaming metal and ceramic, circled around it like meteorites. Against his own will, he saw beauty in the dance they performed.

Before and behind the *Jaunter* in its orbit floated two bristling masses of metal. Warships. They radiated power, the fierce energy glowing, as Fovrates had instructed him, from their drives and weapon emplacements. Again, too bad that all was infested with humans.

The translatorbot buzzed to get his attention.

"We are arriving soon. You will be given all that you require: clean water, purified elements, privacy in your quarters, and opportunities to meet with Proton Zang," she said. "In exchange, you will not change or interfere with any of the processes on board this ship or any other ship under the human command."

Phutes, angered that his thoughts seemed to have been intuited, honked his disapproval. "I dislike being given orders!"

"It is not an order," NR-111 said, pleasantly. "I only spell out what you agreed to in order to obtain your needs. The humans are willing to make your meeting with the Zang a reality. You were a good passenger before on board the *Whiskerchin*. A worthy citizen of your homeworld. Maintain that behavior."

Phutes glanced at his siblings. Sofus swayed his thick upper torso from side to side. Mrdus cowered back into the nest of his many limbs.

"It will do no harm, as long as the humans don't provoke us. We will comply. How long until we arrive? We need to meet with the Zang as soon as we can!"

"In 1111 minutes," NR-111 said. A display lit up on its side. A dual chronometer began to count down in Kail-pulse as well as Imperium standard. "Please rest yourself for landing. There will be a slight bump. Please do not be alarmed."

"I am not afraid," Phutes declared, though the rising tone of his voice belied that assurance.

At that moment, the shuttle flew into a cavern, blotting out light from the planet's flank and the surrounding stars.

"Will it collapse on us?" Mrdus asked, squatting down close to the rocks on which he sat. "I was in a cave this big on Yesa and it fell in on me."

"No," Sofus said, soothingly. "These ships seem to be well-piled."

The black-topped human let out a mocking whinny. Phutes felt disgust at its crude nature. He hoped that he would not have to interact with such humans for long.

Once he had managed to convince the Zang to destroy the humans' motherworld, he would be free to return to Yesa's bosom.

CHAPTER 16

I waited in the docking bay as the *Jaunter's* shuttle appeared through the force field. A wash of icy air, chilled by the proximity to open space, caused me to shiver through my thin costume, a long, deep red, flutter-hemmed tunic and trousers that fit tightly down to my knees, then belled out over my calves. I could feel the cold of the floor through my light dance shoes. The life-support system hummed into life and emitted blasts of warmth through grates set into the walls and ceiling on the innermost end. I squinted through the gale. The small ship slowed, threading its way among the myriad minor craft.

"Are you certain that you would not prefer to wait with the rest of the welcoming committee in the day room, my lord?" Parsons asked me.

"No, not a chance," I declared. "They are content to wait to be introduced. I want to see these things now, in the stony flesh. My pilot, Oskelev, is a fearsome individual, bold and resourceful and quick thinking. I want to meet the creatures who held an entire ship of Wichu prisoner."

"They still hold it," Parsons reminded me. "This detente is the beginning of a negotiation that will prompt the Kail to depart from the *Whiskerchin* and leave it safely under the command of its captain."

"I know, I know," I said, waving away the diplomatic terms as though they were pesky flies. "I brought up the file you sent me on my viewpad while I changed from our tour. They are behaving as though they are the enemy of Wichukind, and possibly humankind. I have

159

made up my mind to kill our visitors with kindness. The Zang's benevolence has given me a good deal to consider about the eternal virtue of patience. These Kail shall know only welcome and good fellowship from me.'"

Parsons gave me a most uneasy glance.

"You are not going to dance for them, my lord?"

"Well, of course I am!" I said. I brandished my viewpad. On it, a grand piece of music waited, cued and ready. I tucked the small device back into the pouch at my waist. Parsons's usually stoic expression stiffened a trifle more than usual.

"Please, my lord, this is a delicate matter. Special Envoy Melarides would prefer an atmosphere of decorum."

I set my chin to indicate the firmness of my resolve. "You told me I couldn't dance for the Zang. Very well. Proton is bestowed in the hangar of a cabin that has been made up and Dr. Derrida—did you see what a fine person she is, Parsons?—without the least jete or jazz hands to give it an ill impression of humankind. But I have a pent-up need to perform, Parsons! The word has indeed reached me that the Kail find us to be horrific. We have the same impression of them! Perhaps we have never approached them in a way that they appreciate. Surely in a life form that lacks technological trappings, they have found many ways of sharing the beauty of the universe in some other means? Are they lovers of poetry? Do they have a musical tradition? I only want to share the beauty of fluid movement that is one of humanity's greatest treasures."

Did I detect the smallest breath of an exasperated sigh?

"Very well, my lord, if you must," Parsons said, with resignation. "But it must be a very short performance. We do not want to provoke the Kail into attempting to subvert the ship's systems because they were deterred from their goal of seeing the Zang."

"I have choreographed a triumphal march, no more," I said, feeling that triumph welling up from my soul at his capitulation. I tapped the viewpad to choose the shortest excerpt of my prepared music. "I will lead the Kail into the ship and bow myself away at the feet of the envoy and her coterie. Once I reach her, my contribution toward their welcome will be at an end. Will that suit?"

"It has the virtue of brevity, my lord," Parsons said. I had remarked upon the slightly swollen nature of that otherwise smooth and epicene visage, though my attempts to gain enlightenment regarding that unusual quality had gone unrewarded. "I will also add that it will give me an inkling of how far their tempers will stretch before reaching the breaking point."

"I shall take that as a compliment," I said, firmly, exercising my hands so they would be as supple as possible. "They shall see the extent of human expression."

The shuttle came to a gentle bump and slide on the landing pad. Covers slid over the ion drives' housings with audible hisses. A host of guards in full helmet and padded suits and two securitybots marched and/or rolled to the side of the small ship. When they were in place, the ramp lowered itself. Nesbitt and Redius emerged, carrying sidearms of a design I had not seen before: plastic guns in neon yellow and orange. If I had not been certain such a thing was beneath their dignity, I would have identified the weapons as water cannons. They trudged to the bottom of the ramp and waited. And waited. I held myself poised, ready for what horrors might emerge.

After what seemed an eon, a mobile mass appeared in the frame of the shuttle hatch. At first I could not tell if it was one creature or two. It seemed to have more limbs than were strictly necessary for locomotion and/or manipulation. It moved forward. The work lights fixed in the ceiling of the landing bay hit it.

I admit that I recoiled. This thing was uglier than any living creature had the right to be. Its light gray skin, if I can call a vertical scree of pebbles skin, covered a body that had not been formed by Mother Nature as much as thrown or melded together. It looked more like an avalanche than a living being. As it perambulated down the ramp, it became evident that this collection of clumsy extremities was one single being with three hands and five legs. Its head had no symmetry. Three eyes, or flat, colorless semblances thereof, peered out from under a sheltering brow that would have protected it more than adequately from rain.

Behind this monstrosity, a larger collection of random body parts collected by the same inexperienced hand emerged. Its shoulders tapered directly into a head without benefit of a neck in between. As a result, it turned its entire upper body to see what was behind it. It had four arms and four legs, the two behind thicker than the two before. As if by accident, its face had a strange beauty that reminded me of certain ancient sculptures on my homeworld. Its eyes were of a pleasing almond shape. Below it, a hole of a mouth gaped as though caught in a frightened scream.

The third being that appeared came closer to the shape I associated with an upright carbon-based being in that it had only two arms, albeit rather long. It had three legs, none the same length as the others, giving it a rollicking, clumsy gait. Its eyes had been formed as deep holes in its face from which radiated suspicion and fear. To my surprise, I felt sympathy for this odd creature. I intended to offer my greatest efforts to this being to assure it that it had not landed among enemies, no matter what my personal misgivings. The manner in which the first two made way for it informed me that it was their leader. A tall, narrow, bronze cylinder of a servicebot with a cluster of video lenses at its top and the logo of the Diplomatic Service on its side trundled down the ramp and halted beside them.

Parsons took a sedate step forward, hands spread. That was my cue.

Switching on my music, I bounded forth ahead of him, my arms flung wide open in a gesture of welcome. All three of the Kail took a step backward. I bowed deeply, once, sweeping my arm across my outstretched foot. As I rose, I used my arms and hands to describe the expanse of the Imperium around us, gathered it together in the fashion that I had created the Universe for the good people of the House of Icari, and presented it to them as an invisible ball. The lead Kail looked down at my cupped hands with a puzzled look on its face.

To stop to explain symbolism at that moment would have thrown me out of the rhythm of the music. Instead, I puffed out my chest and held my body stiffly erect to express my connection to the throne of the Imperium. To my side, I described with graceful hand gestures my cousin, Emperor Shojan XII, whose dignity I encompassed. Running to points all around the enormous landing bay, I plucked pairs of hot, daring sparks that were my ancestors on my father's side, and cool ones of stoic courage and intelligence that showed the importance of my mother's descent from the ancient families, terminating in a pose of enormous dignity to depict her position as First Space Lord. Those I combined and placed them on my head to show that it was my honorable and ancient descent. The music segued from ponderous and stately to majestic. Once again, I bowed deeply to bid them welcome. As a representative of my cousin, I could do no more. After all, had he not dispatched his most illustrious, patient and diplomatic envoy to meet with them?

No reaction from the Kail. Their gray, pebbled faces worked, as though absorbing the experience. They were undoubtedly overwhelmed by the honor I bestowed upon them.

I launched into a series of energetic capers around them that expressed our joy at the arrival of potential allies in the galaxy. As the music rose to a crescendo, I leaped around to show the Kail the extent of the Imperium, bidding them welcome in this realm. With fluttering hands, I cultivated a garden of good wishes. Everywhere they turned, I showed them wonders. Exploding stars! Gentle birds. Affectionate cats. A waterfall tumbling into a rippling pool. Fireworks blooming into colored stars high overhead and raining fragrant perfume down upon our heads. I described each of these marvels with expressive, meaningful motions of my body, arms and legs.

As I threw in my good wishes of how I hoped they would achieve the result they wished for from their meeting with the Zang, I led them toward the glass doors of the inner airlock. Parsons, several armed guards, Redius and Nesbitt followed in their wake. The Zang symbol was the very newest in my repertoire, and I was not certain if its import would be evident. I tried to express the silver-glass pillar's majesty and power, and the way that its aura reached out far beyond its physical form. The sound of the door swishing open and the rush of air that followed it only added to the mystery. The Kail followed hesitatingly, their eyes fixed upon me. I could not tell if they were awed, or merely wary.

Once the doors closed behind us, the warmth of the reception room became a fit setting for a plangent, homey tune etched out on a hundred violins. Thus accompanied, I expressed my hopes for friendship, offering my heart on outstretched hands to each of the recoiling Kail in turn. My last move was an energetic spin in place to show all of the people of the universe were one. I dropped to one knee with my head bowed low beside the party of robed diplomats, and paused there. A few beads of sweat blossomed upon my brow, a tribute to my efforts. I looked up, breathing deeply, seeking a response from my audience.

Parsons clapped three times, very slowly, his face an unreadable mask. Minister Plenipotentary Melarides, who was a distant relative, though not within the Imperium line of descent, joined in, patting her hands together gently. She wore the traditional robes of the diplomatic corps, as did the several humans and Uctu behind her. Melarides also had an unusual, lighted metal collar around her neck.

"Thank you, Lord Thomas," she said. "That was most . . . energetic."

"Thank *you*, minister," I said, looking up into her sincere brown gaze. I rose to my feet in an explosion of grace. The Kail flinched backward again, their stony skin rattling audibly. They certainly were nervous creatures. "I hope you evinced pleasure from my dance of welcome."

"Well, I must say, I have never seen anything like it." She turned away from me and tucked her hands into her sleeves. She bowed to the Kail. "Welcome, friends. Welcome aboard the *Imperium Jaunter*. I greet you in the name of Emperor Shojan XII." Then, touching the collar, she emitted a series of sounds that reminded me of a cat about to be sick, coupled with the wild cry of a capacitor heating up to explode. My surprise was nothing compared with the Kail's, who regarded her with the look of people who had just discovered that their dog could talk.

"You speak our language," the translator emitted. "Not well, but you don't stink."

"You honor me," the envoy said, bowing again. "Was your journey uneventful?"

"The human and the Uctu who accompanied us were offensive, but the transit was adequate."

Behind Parsons, Nesbitt and Redius looked a trifle sheepish. The Uctu's dropped jaw said there was a story to be told. I would learn it later on, in private.

"On behalf of the Emperor, I apologize. May I ask your names?"

The leader emitted an electronic-sounding screech followed by a couple of pops.

"I am Phutes," the translator said, in a pleasant female voice. "My siblings are Sofus and Mrdus." The Kail waved a bulky hand to indicate the stiff-shouldered one and the multi-limbed one in turn. Even the shortest one was a hand or so taller than I. All three were bulky enough to make even the spacious room seem crowded.

Melarides smiled and bowed again. "We are very pleased to have you on board. May I make you known to the rest of my staff? This is my charge d'affaires, Notram Ayemo." The slight, teak-skinned man made a leg. A heavy-set, dark woman with narrow, hazel eyes bowed next. "This is Dr. Sri Catalan, a xenobiologist." Melarides went around the circle and identified each of her staff by name, ending on me. "And this is my distant cousin and a cousin to the emperor, Lord Thomas Kinago. But you have already met, when he performed a wonderful dance for you."

Mrdus peered at me. His voice was a series of crackles that didn't appear to come from his misshapen mouth.

"Is he ill?" he asked. "I don't want to catch madness from slime beings."

"I am sorry," the translatorbot added. "That is literally what the phrase means."

"No offense taken," Melarides said, smiling. I forced my lips into a similar position, though inwardly I was seething. Slime? "He is healthy. Allow me to offer wishes for your own continued well-being."

Phutes opened his cone of a mouth and emitted a harsh honk.

"We are well, and wish to remain in that condition."

I stood to one side, aghast and annoyed. How could they think I was ill, when I had just performed an energetic welcome that included the history of the Imperium and my own family? I opened my own mouth to protest.

"Lord Thomas merely wished to greet you and welcome you on board this ship," Parsons said, forestalling me.

Mrdus didn't seem to appreciate the import. "Do all human interactions begin in this fashion?"

"They do not," Parsons assured him, quelling me with a firm glance. "It was a special effort from his lordship."

"Don't do it again," Phutes said, turning his gravelly face in my direction. "His body moves around in an unnatural fashion. He jiggles too much. It is offensive."

That aroused my ire still further. Jiggles! After all the training I had undergone to bring my frame to its present flawless condition and depth of muscular control. Offensive! While keeping in mind my vow to show them nothing but kindness and good fellowship, I took their negative opinion as a personal challenge. I would keep up my performances until they *liked* them.

Parsons, as always, seemed to intuit my thoughts, and raised his left eyebrow a quarter of a millimeter. I didn't take his admonition to heart. For once, I had nothing about which I might potentially feel guilty. I wasn't going to break into an impromptu reel. After all, Madame Deirdre had been firm about making certain the symbols I evoked were deliberate and arranged in an artful fashion. I needed to go away and choreograph future dances. I would swallow my annoyance so I did not undo any of the effort that Special Envoy Melarides was going to put forth on behalf of the Imperium. However, I planned to work into my next performance my irritation that they had not appreciated my first effort. I would show them!

"What may we do for you now?" Melarides asked the Kail. "May we show you to the cabins we have arranged for you?"

"We do not risk being shut in," Phutes said. The wordless cry that served him for a voice rose almost to a scream. "We will not occupy one of your 'cabins.'"

"I have seen to it that there are no doors on your domicile," Melarides said, soothingly. "Only curtains made of chained metal strands. You cannot be shut in, but you will have privacy."

A low level hum, like that emitted by an air purifier, arose between the three stone giants.

"That is adequate," Sofus said at last. Melarides looked relieved.

"Shall we go there now?"

"No," Phutes declared. "Proton Zang. We want to see Proton Zang."

"Very well. Please come this way." The envoy gestured for the Kail to follow her. The ambassadorial staff closed ranks behind the visitors. Nesbitt and Redius fell in beside the guards and securitybots. Redius shot a humorous glance over his shoulder at me, and his coral-scaled tail twitched in amusement.

Though it was clear that I was dismissed from attendance, I attached myself as additional escort. In my pique, I found solace in watching the Kail navigate down the corridors. They went to considerable lengths to avoid casual contact with any of the inhabitants of the *Jaunter*. That proved a challenge to Melarides, who was a tactile individual, always reaching out to put her hand on a misshapen forearm or shoulder. But she was also an observant one. Once she noticed them flinch from her, she tucked her hands into her capacious sleeves, out of the way of accidental touching. In addition, the Kail's uneven gait provided me with endless entertainment. It had never occurred to me what logistics might be involved in walking with three legs, let alone five. Whereas upright bipedal beings, among whom I counted myself, utilized cut-time rhythmic locomotion, I had observed from movement studies that four-legged beings moved by putting forward opposite limbs front and back. The largest of the Kail was able to make use of this fairly graceful gait. His two companions rolled and rollicked as though they couldn't make up their minds which foot to use. I began to set myself wagers as to which leg would move next.

I thought that the lift shaft might confound them, but they entered it with ease. Melarides maneuvered within the car so that she stood by the door, waving off any crew who might seek to ride along with us as we descended deck after deck.

I found myself beside the translatorbot at the rear of the party.

"Hello," I said to the cluster of eyes just below the level of my chin. "I am Lord Thomas Kinago."

"Yes," it replied, tilting one of the lenses up toward me. "I have seen your name on the manifest, my lord. A pleasure to meet you. I am NR-111."

I made a slight bow. "The pleasure is mine. How long have you been working in the diplomatic service?"

"Three hundred and fifty-two years. This is my first assignment with the Kail, though. Most refreshing."

"Is it really?" I asked, dropping my voice to a whisper. I knew its receivers were sensitive enough to hear me, even if no biological being could. "They seem very difficult."

"It is refreshing. They have not attempted to destroy or disassemble me, as the Donre did on my second mission. I went through six structural housings during that assignment. Representative Phutes and his siblings claim a kinship with silicon-based beings such as myself."

"They are siblings?" I asked, surveying the motley assortment before me. "One could not miss that they are of the same species, but they bear little resemblance to one another."

"So they claim," NR-111 said. "I have no means of determining whether or not they speak literally or figuratively. The Kail don't discuss family or reproduction with outsiders. That is one of the most profound taboos in their culture. I know that Dr. Catalan is hoping to learn more about their biology. I maintain a list of no-go subjects according to my briefing by the diplomatic service central office. I do not pass along those questions to the Kail; I merely inform them that an unwelcome question has been asked. They get a little . . . excitable . . . when provoked. Therefore, it's best not to insult them by pressing on topics that they prefer not to discuss. The envoy knows that. She is well-briefed."

"A culture of privacy," I commented. "That presents a challenge to the envoy, does it not? If she can convince them to ally with the Imperium, Infogrid files will be opened on them, whether or not they choose to update them."

"Most likely those files will be encrypted, to be used only for reference by the government LAIs and appropriate ministers who brief the emperor, not open for public commentary. Very likely it will be one such as I who will update them. The Kail won't have to if they prefer not to."

"Well, I don't care," I said. "My concern is that they do not do to this ship what they did to the *Whiskerchin*. When will they release it?"

"Once they've conversed with the Zang, I believe," NR-111 said. "That was my understanding. They don't discuss their plans with me. As you no doubt noticed, they speak among themselves in a supersonic frequency that delivers considerable information in a very short time, similar to although slower than the way we converse among ourselves."

"Don't you listen just a little to them?" I asked, in a wheedling tone. Mrdus rotated in place so he could see the others in the lift. His three odd eyes fixed upon me. I dropped into Sang-Li fingerspelling so that no word of mine could be picked up by the Kail. Another of NR-111's lenses tilted downward to view my hands. "You must have every opportunity to hear their private conferences."

A small screen popped up on the top of the translator's upright cylinder and canted toward me so only I could see it. On it, I saw the image of a pair of hands almost precisely identical to my own.

"I am sorry, Lord Thomas," the translator spelled out. "That is outside my brief. I have taken an oath to provide expert language assistance to our visitors. What they say in private is held as strictly confidential. Besides, the way they converse privately is in a dialect that it is difficult to understand, although we are working on comprehension."

"But we know so little about them. You could be of enormous service to the Imperium by giving us insights into their thoughts."

"I am sorry," NR-111 said again. "The rules are very strict. I would be sacked if I violate them."

I dropped my hands. "I wouldn't want that to happen," I said aloud. "I'm just very curious."

"I am sure there will be enough new data made public later on to satisfy querents," the translator said, cheerfully, returning to voice communication. "Pardon me; we are arriving."

I made way for NR-111 to rejoin her charges, and the shaft door slid open.

⁂ CHAPTER 17 ⁂

The chamber that had been arranged for the Zang was on the same level as the cargo bay and the engineering department. It had a very large door, even though the Zang did not need to use it, or the cargo lift adapted for its especial employment, or need anything to eat. It was, to all intents and purposes, as far as the Zang was concerned, the symbol of a cabin. We were rather honored that it chose to use it at all.

When Ambassador Melarides was still several meters from the hatch, it slid open, and Dr. Derrida, dwarfed by the enormous portal, peeked out. When I saw her large brown eyes, my heart did a grand jeté and a back flip. She spotted me among the crowd of escorts and smiled, then turned to the Kail.

"Welcome," she said. "Proton is expecting you. Please come in."

Phutes honked indignantly. NR-111 promptly spoke up.

"What is she doing here? Our audience must be private."

"She will translate the Zang's impressions for you, Phutes," Melarides said. "None of us have that skill to impart your meaning to Proton, not even our translator."

Phutes stamped his center foot, making even a floor as sturdy as the deck plate shudder. The smell of rain on wet concrete became more pronounced. "This was not told to us! We know how to communicate with the Zang. We want to speak with it alone."

"You can try," Laine said, cheerily, standing to one side, though there was plenty of room for them or a small army platoon to pass. "I don't have to be there if you don't want me. Go right in. It's waiting."

The Kail didn't hesitate for courtesy. They thundered past the tiny woman and into the high-ceilinged chamber. NR-111 rolled sedately after them.

I followed them over the threshold. Then I felt a hand settle gently upon my forearm.

"I think they want to be confer alone," the envoy said, with the gentlest of admonitory and motherly glances.

"I'd like Lord Thomas to stay," Laine said, with a look that made my heart melt. "He can sit with me on my end of the room."

"It would be my honor," I said. I peered around for Parsons, but he had oozed away silently at some point, unobserved by us all. To my mind, that meant I was free to do as I pleased.

"As you please, Dr. Derrida," Melarides said. She looked resigned. I seemed to obtain that reaction more commonly than not, but I was too delighted by Laine's interest to take offense. "Then, I'll just take my leave of the Kail. The guards will remain outside the door to escort the Kail to their quarters when they have finished with their conference."

It would take a superb actor to hide the response that the Zang's presence elicited in a mere human being, let alone a heap of stones like the Kail. I had already experienced it, so I was more prepared than my fellows for the sensation of awe and sheer force that impacted upon my person. How Laine withstood it day after day, year after year, I did not know. I felt as though sound waves battered against my chest, making my ribs reverberate. My eyelids fluttered frantically, as if fighting against bright sunshine. I forced them open so I could behold the majesty of the Zang. The Kail approached it with their hands up, almost in a gesture of supplication, or fear. They were every bit as impressed by it as I hoped that they would be. So were my crewmembers.

"Marvelous," Redius whispered, staying close to my shoulder. I could almost hear the echo in his voice.

Nesbitt swallowed deeply. "Yeah. We didn't get to see it when it arrived. Pretty amazing."

"That's a very small word for an overwhelming sensation, isn't it?" I said, enjoying the effect once again. "One can feel the eons of its very existence. This is, as far as we know, the elder race of the galaxy. Possibly the universe. It invites awe."

"Uh-huh," Nesbitt agreed, unable to take his eyes off the glowing alien. "It's like that."

The Zang towered over its visitors, exuding silver light that I fancied I could see through the very bodies of the Kail. Phutes, who seemed to be the leader, began honking and shouting at it in rising and falling tones that might have been a song of some kind, if I suspected that the Kail were in any way familiar with music. The Zang did not turn toward them. The enormous eyes were hidden from view, facing a hull plate a meter or so from the corner. The stone giants that were so large in comparison with humans were dwarfed by the other alien and its immense aura. I felt the sweep of energy flood through me again and again. Though silent, it had the enveloping quality of rich, orchestral sound, drowning out the pathetic noises that the Kail were making.

"It's very curious today," Laine said. "I can sense it reaching out a lot. Listening, but I don't think it's listening to them."

"What does a Zang listen to?" I said, leaning closer to her so I did not need to shout over the cacophony. She wore a spicy scent that was warmed by the temperature of her body. I found it enticing and intriguing as the woman herself. I leaned closer.

"All sorts of things," Laine said, with a high-pitched titter that stabbed at my eardrums and made me withdraw hastily to a safe distance. The Kail swiveled their massive bodies and looked at us with annoyance. She noticed their body language, and beckoned to me. "Come over here. They made me up a nice little conversation pit." She gestured toward the far side of the cabin. A cozy little nook had been set up as a residence for her. A knitted blanket woven in orange and brown zigzags had been flung over a narrow bunk. Her battered travel case sat upon a two-legged stand adjacent to the bed. Beside the sleeping area was a long, narrow table with a round mirror that could have served as a desk or dresser. The table acted as a divider from the circle of overstuffed couches that surrounded a handsome, low, oblong cherrywood table with a vase of exotic, oval-petaled blue and yellow flowers. The door to a rather nicely appointed bathroom furnished in cheerful yellow stood a hand-span ajar beside a kitchen unit. A timer went off, and fragrant coffee began to pour down into a silver pot. "Come and have a cup. There's enough for all of us."

I was suddenly jealous that I had to share her attention even with my closest friends, but duty called.

"Must return," Redius said, ruefully. "Lieutenant Plet waits."

"She will want a full report," I agreed. "But I want to hear the parts later that won't be in the official transcript."

Nesbitt's big face turned red. "It's nothing, my lord. Just a little fun."

"That's the best kind of omission," I assured him. "Later. I will supply the drinks."

Nesbitt reddened still further. Redius hissed with laughter and pulled him away. Most of the guards and the embassy staff went with them out the door. Only the envoy and I remained with Dr. Derrida.

Phutes walked up and back before the Zang, waving his blocky fists, bellowing like a tornado. Suddenly, he stormed up to Dr. Derrida and shook a thick paw in her face. NR-111 rolled beside him.

"Make it hear us!" he said.

Laine shook her head.

"If it notices you, it notices you. There's nothing more I can do to draw its attention, Mr. Phutes. You can talk to it as long as you want, though. I don't mind."

"Phutes, since we have fulfilled our promise to allow you access to the Zang," Ambassador Melarides began, in her gentle voice, "may we discuss allowing the Wichu to resume command of their ship?"

"No!" Phutes blared, rounding on the envoy. "If it does not listen to us, nothing is accomplished."

"That wasn't our agreement," the envoy said, gently but firmly. "Please, I would like to reopen this discussion now. It's of the utmost urgency. The Wichu must be liberated. It is unfair to keep them prisoner on their own ship. Surely you must understand that."

Phutes swung an enormous arm at her.

"Like they kept us? Get out. You are in the way."

Hastily, I sidled forward, interposing my person in between the envoy and her would-be assailant. The moving hand caught me by the shoulder and sent me sprawling. The blow was a hard one, but I was in the best shape of my life. I leaped up and resumed my stance faster than the stone being could react.

"There's no need to be violent," I said, fixing the Kail with a stern glare. My shoulder throbbed. There would be a large bruise on it later. I refused to show weakness, putting up my chin in defiance.

My stance seemed to enrage the Kail further. It brought its fist up over its head, then down like a hammer. I crossed my forearms and caught it. The effort evoked a grunt from me. Those creatures were heavy! I braced myself, holding the limb pinioned. Blaring indignantly, the Kail tried to force its arm down. I held as firm as I could. The rough grains of sand cut through the fine fabric of my tunic sleeve and scraped my skin raw. It hurt, but I tried to keep my voice steady. "Do be reasonable, old fellow. You have what you want. Won't you keep your promise? I've always heard that the Kail were beings of honor."

Phutes wrenched his arm up and away. The gesture pulled me off my feet again. Relying upon my martial arts training, I tucked myself into a ball and rolled, coming up once more in a position intended to protect the envoy. The guards moved in to flank us, weapons drawn, but the Kail paid them no attention. He stood frantically brushing at his limb.

"You touched me!"

"Strictly speaking, you touched me," I pointed out.

"Go away. You are not wanted. Only the Zang."

Melarides raised her voice over the insistent whine from the Kail.

"You may of course continue to speak with the Zang. While you are conducting your business with it, we will convey you to the platform where we are to hold our official conference with you, but we would prefer it if the rest of your, er, siblings vacated the *Whiskerchin*. Will you give the order? We will send a conveyance for the rest of the Kail."

I wrinkled my nose in distaste. I couldn't help but notice the smell of the Kail, a combination of wet stone and sulfur fumes, had grown stronger in this smaller chamber. An entire contingent of the unhappy beings was more than I was glad to countenance. Fortunately, Phutes waved away this suggestion.

"When the Zang speaks with us, we will release the *Whiskerchin* to its messy crew."

NR-111 seemed to shrug apologetically as it translated that insulting phrase.

"We must depart from Counterweight. None of us wish to miss the upcoming event," Melarides pointed out.

"Then we go," Phutes said, his face a mask. "The Wichu ship will follow us. Open a communication channel to us so we may speak to Fovrates."

Melarides looked disappointed but resigned.

"I will see to it. Please contact me if you change your mind." She withdrew. Phutes waited.

"Why are you not going, too?" he asked us, in an accusing tone.

"This is my room," Laine pointed out. "Lord Thomas is my guest. As are you."

Its shoulders moved in a way that dislodged some of the smaller stones, but they were absorbed into its skin before they fell off. I watched the effect with fascination. The Kail glared at us.

"Stay across the room. Where we can't see you. And you will not listen."

"I promise," I said. "The word of a Kinago is more reliable than sunrise."

The Kail emitted a noise like a vacuumbot spitting out lint.

"There was a great deal of supersonic invective in that," NR-111 said. "I apologize."

I waved a hand. "We do not blame you for repeating their words. I have heard far worse from my cousins," I said. I turned to Laine. "Shall we enjoy some of that excellently scented coffee before it loses its volatile compounds?"

We settled onto the circular couches and sipped the dark brew. It was heady and exotic, not unlike the young lady opposite me.

"At last, we are alone," I said. I regarded her with growing affection, admiring her small, round face, her smooth neck, and the charming form that was hinted at but not revealed by her soft, pale blue gown. I thought I saw some interest in her eyes for me, or perhaps it was only my hope. "That is, apart from half a dozen guards, three Kail, your Zang and a translator. On the other hand, that describes nearly any attempt one of my rank has at being alone."

"I'm nearly always on my own, when Proton and I are ranging," Laine said, snuggling into the cushions. "We're alone for parsecs in any direction. This feels like a huge crowd to me. How do you shut out all those other people?" She swept a hand to include the ship.

"I meditate," I said. "I picked up the skill during one of my previous enthusiasms, before I took up dance. But to be honest, I don't really notice. I like having others around me. I thrive on society."

Laine's rosebud mouth twisted. "I don't. Not really. I never did."

I was struck by the sudden vehemence of her declaration.

"Should I go away?" I asked.

"No!" she said, thrusting out a hand to forestall me. "I'm sorry. I don't mean you. You're so nice. This is nice." She seemed on the edge of saying something else, then her cheeks bloomed red. I changed the subject to allow her to collect herself. There was no need to rush. I was enjoying just being near her.

"Do you like the coffee?" I asked. "The beans come from Rumdisa, some of the finest in the Imperium."

"This is so good," she said, breathing in the steam. "I hardly ever get fresh coffee. Or pastries like these. They're amazing!" She glanced at the small plate beside the large china serving platter. Only crumbs remained of a couple of petits fours. I leaped to fill her plate for her, adding a slice of glazed yuzu-lime cake over cursory objections.

"Try just a bite," I urged her. "This ship is installed with the best culinary technicians in the Imperium, apart from those who are in the personal service of my cousin, the emperor. We of the Imperium house also bring along our favorite foods and wines. The Grisgor limes are from an orchard I own outside Taino."

"Well, these are wonderful!" Laine said, brushing a few crumbs from the bosom of her gown. "You're right. This cake tastes just right with the coffee. It's counterintuitive to mix sour with bitter, but it works."

"I always enjoy experimenting in combinations of the five tastes and the six basic food groups. If you will come up again this evening, I invite you to sample some of my private selections."

"Last evening's dinner was wonderful," she said. "I've never tried some of those foods before. You were so very nice to share with me. I'm sorry I had to run back right away to be with Proton."

"It was my pleasure," I said. I offered her a conspiratorial smile. "I have several other marvelous treats I'd like to offer you." That sounded a trifle indelicate. I covered my confusion with a refined cough. "I'd be afraid to reveal the contents of my secret cache if nearly all of my relatives were not down on the planet's surface. They are unrepentant vultures when it comes to someone else's exotic delicacies. Somehow, distance seems to make even the most bizarre foods irresistible to those who did not pay for their importation." I glanced at my hip, where my viewpad had been restored to its normal place in its handsomely tailored pouch. "It seems odd not to have one or another of my relatives pinging me, or be receiving new entries to their Infogrid files. We'll all have to update sooner or later. I fancy they're having wonderful adventures. I can tell you with relative certainty the additions to their files when they do return. One or more of them will befall some avoidable mishap. My cousin Nalney will lose something. Xan will break a few hearts. Jil will no doubt offend someone. She has a gift for it. Erita will complain bitterly about a minor slight that overshadows an otherwise wonderful experience. They will each greatly enrich the local economy, and they'll return with numerous souvenirs and possibly as many images and digitavids as I have."

"I look forward to meeting them," Laine said, then hesitated. "One or two at a time. What did you think of Counterweight?"

"Very lovely," I said. Memories of the day played through my mind in bursts of color, sound and scent. I began to combine my recollections with music and appropriate movements for future dances. "Alas that it wasn't our ancestral homeland, but it is more ancient a human habitation than Keinolt or any of the Core Worlds. I believe that I have picked up some important insights on humanity that will inform my new dances. I'm preparing one to perform for my cousins when they return to the ship."

"I thought your little dance as we were leaving the park was really good, even if your teacher made fun of it. What was that about?"

"My impression of the Whispering Ravines," I said, adding a theatrical flourish of my hand. I limned the stark outline of the cliffs and the river below so I could almost hear the rush of the water. "The primitive landscape. Our sudden meeting and the fall of the rock that I thought would crush the Zang."

"Yes, I got that!" Laine said, her eyes twinkling. "I could feel the danger you threw yourself into. Once I figured out what you were doing, I think I understood most of the moves you made. Uh, steps? Anyhow, it was like a language of its own."

I beamed at her. No one else had interpreted the meaning of my dances as well as she did. "That's exactly right! Madame Deirdre told me that movements were like phrases in a language. One puts them together to create a scenario. It is not enough just to show the actions. I must include the setting, the mood, and most of all, my emotional reaction to the event. Did you see that I didn't fear for my own safety, but for that of the Zang?"

"Yes, I got that," Laine said, with a laugh. "Did you really feel that way, or was that how you want your audience to *think* you felt?"

I clasped my hands over my heart.

"You wound me! I reacted much too quickly to consider my own danger."

Instead of laughing, she put her hand on my knee. "I didn't mean it to sound like you were puffing yourself up. It was really brave, considering you couldn't know whether you were strong enough to move someone as big as Proton out of the way. He looks like he weighs tons even though he never leaves an impression on the ground. But you tried. That was wonderful. I admired that even more than the dance about it."

Her open admiration mollified my wounded feelings. "Thank you. Did *you* enjoy visiting Counterweight?"

Her eyes danced.

"I did. Everyone there seemed to feel at home, like you said. It was a beautiful world. Not at all terrifying. Some of the planets that Proton takes me to are pretty scary places. Not that they aren't beautiful, too." She put down her cup to draw a picture on the air. "One continent we visited was all honeycombed rock. It was pretty, from a distance. The inhabitants were gigantic insectoids. I think Proton was fascinated with the patterns in which they moved. I certainly was. They never bumped into one another, no matter how crowded the passage. I'm sorry I couldn't take any digitavids of them. You could have used them for your dances."

"That is very kind of you to think of it," I said. "Do you put any of your videos into your Infogrid file?"

She raised one shoulder. "Once in a while, but I'm often seeing the sights from inside the protective energy shell that Proton has around us. I can see out, but my poor viewpad can't pick up a decent image." She grinned an apology, which I was more than happy to accept. "It was nice to see a planet with an atmosphere again. What was your favorite part of your tour?"

"Without a doubt, meeting you and Proton Zang," I said, with humble sincerity. My admission seemed to throw her into confusion. She blushed prettily. I changed the subject with haste. "How did you come to travel with it?"

"I was an anthropologist," Laine said, drawing her dainty feet up onto the couch under a fold of her gown, showing that she was becoming more comfortable with me. "I still am, I suppose. I was in a concealed blind observing a human population that has been living on Virgo 834j, a planet the locals call Virn. It's infested with the most fearsomely huge reptilians you have ever seen, that make Solinians look like newts. We're not sure if the human settlers went to live there on purpose, or if they crash landed or were marooned. There isn't enough of the settlement ships left to make a determination that satisfies peer review. Believe me, I have tried to find a legitimate explanation. If there were contemporary records, they've been purged.

"There's a few thousand human beings surviving in that environment, but not too well. My university has been watching them for a few centuries now. The Virnese maintain remnants of Earth culture and law, such as trial by jury of one's peers and freedom of speech, as well as some technological expertise, although that's spotty. Whereas strength is dominant, it's a matriarchal government because women make sure the population will survive. They live in villages surrounded by protective walls topped with sonic repellers. Those run on solar power by day and wind power by night. I based out of a very compact little tent with chameleon walls. It looks like a dead tree, or a thorn bush, or a lichen-covered stone, but it's pretty sophisticated inside. I had a lot of other blinds, like inside the base of a statue, or under a building foundation.

"One day, after I'd been there for a couple of months, hiding in a copse in the main village's common field, the Zang appeared. The people started running toward it, not away, which I thought was interesting, considering what I saw was a big, glowing pillar that came out of nowhere. They shouted to the others to come and gather around. I thought at first it was a local energy phenomenon, because there were images like it in the tribe's records and carvings. I couldn't believe I was actually seeing one of the Old Ones, but that's what my Infogrid link said it was. The Virnese don't exactly worship the Zang— they haven't gone that primitive—but they consider its comings and goings as a kind of omen, and perhaps they see it as a protector. I noticed that a few of the most aggressive reptiles that had been trying to storm the barriers had simply . . . ceased to exist."

"Good heavens," I said, trying to picture the scene. "Thinning the herd?"

Laine raised her shoulders. "I suppose so. In its own way, Proton is an anthropologist. It was as curious about those humans as I was, but it wants to make sure they survive, so it tweaked the environment a little. I wouldn't consider it ethical. It's not good science as we humans see it, but who am I to judge? The Zang probably date from not long after the Big Bang, so maybe we're the ones being too cautious in the way we approach subjects."

"I see," I said. I looked at her slyly. "Are you one of its subjects, then?"

Her cheeks dimpled bewitchingly, and her eyes twinkled. "I suppose I am. It found me watching the Virnese. It didn't give away my position, for which I was grateful. They're suspicious of interlopers, because strangers often mean that a raid is imminent. I was at risk for being tortured or killed. Proton picked up on that. It observed me observing the Virnese for a while, and became curious about me, too. In any case, when it left Virn, it took me with it. Just like that, I went from studying humans to studying the Old Ones. I was out of touch for over three months. It's not uncommon for me not to check in more than once a month, but it was longer than usual. I like working on my own. That's one of the reasons I took up field work. Weird, isn't it, an anthropologist who doesn't enjoy being with people? My supervisor had been frantic until I finally got back to him, then he was thrilled. The data I have been collecting are unique. I feel privileged. It's been a scholar's dream. The Zang see things and feel things that we can't possibly imagine, into spectra and wavelengths that would kill ephemeral beings. Their perspective is one I try to understand but know I never will."

"I am envious," I said. I realized that my coffee had grown cold. I spilled the tepid liquid into the flower vase and poured a fresh cup of hot, cinnamon-scented brew for myself and for her. She sipped it gratefully. "When was the first time you saw them remove a planet?"

"Almost right away," Laine said. She sat back in her seat, leaning her head on the top of the cushion, pulling reminiscence from the middle distance. "When we left Virn, we went straight to a place where a group of Zang had gathered. They were waiting for Proton so they could all destroy a rogue moon in deep space. We just hovered there. I should have frozen to death, or died of lack of oxygen, but I was fine. It was weird, but I felt perfectly safe, even though I was watching a heavenly body blown into energy from up close. The Zang are artists. You've got something wonderful to look forward to. I can't wait to see it again."

We wandered from conversation to conversation. As her host on board the *Jaunter*, I offered her pastries and other delicacies, topped up her coffee cup, and told her humorous stories. I had been saving a few choice anecdotes to amuse my cousins, but it seemed that Laine had never heard some of my old favorites. It was a pleasure to watch her laugh. When something struck her as hilarious, she threw her head back, revealing the slender column of her neck. Its shape bewitched me so much that I almost lost my sense of timing.

"I love that one about the fire extinguisher," Laine said, wiping tears of merriment from the corners of her eyes with the edge of a napkin. "Where did you hear that?"

"On a warship, if you can believe it," I began. "I was on punishment duty . . . ."

A wave of force passed, brushing my side like a heavy curtain. I glanced toward the Zang and the shouting Kail moving around it.

"What's happening?" I asked.

"It's back," Laine said. "Proton sends its consciousness way out among the stars. What you see here is only a small part of its real being, as if its soul is a million times bigger than its body. You can always feel it when it returns. At least, I can. It's come back from wherever it was."

"I felt it this time. Where did it go?"

A rueful expression settled on her small face. "I don't know, even after all these years."

Even the Kail seemed to sense the difference in the feeling in the room. They moved in closer to the silver pillar, and began to emit their high-pitched cries.

"What do you suppose they're asking it?" I asked.

"I'm not sure," Laine said, with an analytical glance. "They don't appear to be worshiping Proton. See that body language? That looks like they are making a demand of some kind. Too bad we can't ask the translator what they're saying."

"Sadly, no," I said. "She told me all of their communications are confidential. I will try to wheedle my way around her programming. I'm difficult to stop when I am determined to succeed."

Laine laughed again. "I can imagine. I'd find it hard to withstand you if you opened up those big blue eyes at me."

I halted, feeling my throat grow tight. She could hardly know how cruelly she was toying with my feelings.

Or perhaps she did.

"I'm sure you have a lot of other things to do, Lord Thomas," she said suddenly. "You don't have to wait here with me. It's all right."

Hastily, I rose to my feet.

"I hate to leave you here with these boorish statues," I said. I held out a hand to her. "Would you like to come up to our day room until they finish shouting at your friend? Not that your quarters are unpleasant in any way. It is merely the company to which I object."

She shook her head.

"No, I'd better stay here. I don't like these Kail, but I'm sure Proton won't let them hurt me, and the guards are just outside the door. I'll see you at dinner. What time shall I come up?"

"Seven?" I suggested. I bent over her hand and kissed it. "I will send my valet for you."

She smiled, and my soul spun with joy.

"I'll look forward to it, Lord Thomas."

"Just Thomas," I said. "I await the hour."

Keeping my promise to Parsons, I waited until I had exited the chamber and was well out of sight before I launched into a magnificent leap terminating in a grand arabesque. I had experienced three marvels in one day: an ancient homeland of humans, a member of the elder race, and a woman who threatened to steal my heart.

ᆌ CHAPTER 18 ᆌ

"Where are you?" One Zang sent to Proton.

"I am two hexaprag from the conclave," Proton replied, feeling its low-frequency waves beating gently against the walls of the chamber it occupied. Rapid counter-rhythms pounded in a higher frequency. "I am within an ephemeral shell, circling above a planet."

"Is it a disharmonious sphere?" Zang Quark inquired. "I feel intrusive energy." Its senses joined One Zang's in reading Proton's energy vibrations. Proton felt Quark's presence and opened all of its perceptions to be shared. Charm and young Low were also nearby.

"Far from it," Proton assured them. "Symmetrical and beautifully proportioned. We removed an asteroid belt from this system nineteen hexaeons ago."

"I recall that one," Charm Zang said, its mental voice musical. "A glorious liberation of a handsome star. How has it matured?"

"Well," Proton said. "Perceive." It sent its impressions of the planet the ephemerals called Counterweight and the system surrounding it. The sun, a dwarf yellow star at the high end of the yellow spectrum and approaching middle age, sat serenely in the midst of its five planets' orbits. A few comets swung within the Oort cloud, angling through the plane of the ecliptic, intersecting with those orbits but timed never to impact with any of the heavenly bodies or their satellites. The symmetry satisfied all of them.

"Beautiful," Charm said, her senses extending into Proton's space. "This was your work, wasn't it? I recognize the arrangement. A masterful design. It would be difficult for any of us to better it."

Proton accepted the praise, but could feel a slight disharmony coming from the group.

"Is there some concern?"

"No," One Zang replied. It could sense the discomfort coming from Low Zang. The young one emitted insecurity. One Zang sent reassurance and calm. Low Zang accepted the soothing, but the unhappy tapping was still there as an undertone. "We study the subject of our next demolition that Low Zang has selected. Low is concerned that all will go according to plan."

"Of course it will," Proton said. "I have faith in you, Low Zang."

"We all do," Charm added its assurance.

A vibration of insecurity radiated out through the cosmos. Proton felt kindly toward the younger one. It could relive its own eons of immaturity and inexperience in what Low was going through.

"Do you still have your pet?" Quark asked, a humorous tone in its vibration.

"I do," Proton replied. "It is one of the reasons that I returned here, to give her time with those like her."

"Admit it," Zang Quark said. "That race of ephemerals is your favorite."

"I do not have favorites," Proton said. "They all exist for far too short a time. It gives me pain when they die out."

One Zang felt a trembling vibration from Proton that suggested its thoughts were not entirely true, but it had not created a disharmony worth bringing up.

"I sense other rhythms and sounds around you," Charm said. "What is there?"

"More ephemerals, the mineral beings from six hexaprags at 265^0."

"Those. They are far from home. They do not like it. Their sense of place is disrupted."

"Yes, I suppose so." Proton allowed its consciousness to experience some of the ambient rhythms and sounds, and opened itself so the others could sense them, too.

"Why are they singing and dancing around you?" Quark asked.

"I don't know. I only noticed them because you have."

"It's an unpleasant discord," Low said, then lowered its aura so as not to displease the other Zang. Proton observed the withdrawal and reached out to Low with a sense of approval.

"You are right. That is why I choose not to notice them."

"No need to pay attention to ephemerals," Quark said. "Their concerns scarcely ever have bearing on what is eternal."

"I quite agree," Proton said.

"Then why do you keep a pet from one of these species?"

"She amuses me. She evokes a serenity most of these others lack. I find it soothing."

"As long as you don't let it distract you from what is important," Quark said.

Proton chuckled and withdrew its contact. Quark used its abrasiveness to hide an insecurity almost as deep as Low Zang's. The occasional study of the lower orders might help it to realize how foolish both of them were being.

It resigned itself to being in the midst of the noise and erratic motion, and settled into quiet contemplation. In terms of eternity, the disruption would not last more than a moment.

Silence fell in the shell. The ephemerals had ceased their unpleasant vibrations. Proton settled into quiet contemplation of the star system around it. Yes, they had done a fine job in this place. If Low could create a harmony like this one from its choice of matter-energy transformation, Proton would be very happy. It would even balance out the negative feelings from the silicon-based creatures.

"Stand there," Lieutenant Ormalus told Phutes, once the Kail reached the communications center. The Uctu kept a good distance from the Kail. Phutes was relieved that she did not try to touch him as the human envoy kept trying to do. She sat down on a backless bench at a console twinkling with colored lights and manipulated the controls. Phutes eyed the Uctu's switching tail with alarm, as if any moment it might reach out and strike him, covering him with disgusting organic particles.

Naturally, Phutes felt that the Kail were the perfect race of the galaxy—after the Zang, of course—but it was undeniable that outside Kail space it would have been helpful to have spindly little appendages like hands and fingers. Without them, the Kail were dependent upon carbon-based organisms to make intricate technology. Phutes might be able to listen to the stars, but to travel to them before he matured, he needed fingers. It was fortunate that the squishy ones were willing to make their fingers, and the devices that the fingers had made, available to them. It did not make him like or trust them more, but he acknowledged that they were useful.

"Hurry!" he ordered the Uctu.

"Don't scatter your scales," she said through the translator, her skinny appendages flying over the controls. On a screentank, colored pictures and images swirled into view, one after another. "*Whiskerchin,* this is *Imperium Jaunter,* commcode AS-587. Do you read?"

NR-111 translated the hail, including rendering the uncouth numbers into decent binary. Phutes only listened with part of his attention. He could hear the song of the electronic technology. 111100101 voices sang in his hearing, all of them silicon-based. The ships had not one voice apiece, but many. Different systems sent out greetings and received welcomes. Phutes felt almost as if he was home again, hearing siblings and motherworlds conversing around him.

The Uctu repeated her query. At last, a hearty voice responded. The graphics disappeared, revealing the broad face of the elder Kail. He moved his head to see over the Uctu.

"Phutes, is that you?"

"Fovrates!" Phutes said, relieved. "You're all alive?"

"Of course, youngster. And you?"

Lieutenant Ormalus flipped 110 switches, then pushed back from the console. "All yours," she said, moving swiftly to the door. "You'll have privacy. Just don't touch anything. It's all alarmed."

When she was gone, the three Kail crowded close to the screentank.

"I assume we are overheard," Fovrates said.

"They left us," Phutes replied. "We are alone."

"Never believe that, youngster," the engineer said, lapsing into their personal dialect, in a supersonic tone that made the circuits around them sing. "They listen to everything. Just make it as difficult as possible to understand."

"We hear," Sofus said.

"Have you enlisted the Zang's help?"

"Have you ever talked to one?" Phutes countered, glaring at the scope. "It is like shouting at eternity."

"Absolute power is not to be obtained without crossing many barriers," Fovrates said. He was unmoved by Phutes's temper. "Are you certain you can get its attention? The matter has become urgent."

The Kail looked at one another with concern.

"How? What have you learned?" Phutes asked.

"I am running the data that our friends retrieved for us from the computer systems of the human ships and the planet against that which our motherworlds have amassed over the eons. I am only partway into the mass of data. It will take me a very long time to locate what we're seeking, but I have made many discoveries already. It is as Yesa and Nefra feared. Humans and others have made numerous intrusions into Kail space. Many races have established beachheads there, but especially humans. They hide in dust clouds and among asteroid belts, away from direct observation. The chart I'm building will show you the domiciles they maintain in our territory from which you can be sure they are plotting the downfall of the Kail!"

Phutes felt his nervousness harden into grim resolve. Angrily, he raised his fist over his head.

"No, Phutes!" NR-111 exclaimed. The translator was always by him, like Yesa was at home. "Do not strike the console! It will set off alarms."

Sofus shoved underneath to absorb the blow. Phutes brought his arm down with all the frustration in his heart. Shards of his sibling's stony flesh flew off in all directions, clattering against the wall, the screentank and the floor. A deep gash had been opened in his neck, roiling with green acid. Phutes stood, emitting honk after honk of regret and fury.

"Are you better now?" Sofus asked. He bent to gather up all the little pieces. Balling them together in his heavy hands, he plastered the mass into the wound. Healing acid, the kind that was bright blue, bubbled up around it and enveloped it. Soon, the injury had smoothed over. Phutes watched with shame in his soul.

"I am sorry, brother," Phutes said. "Yesa expects better of me."

"It's understandable," Sofus said. He was always the calmest. "You were provoked."

"Phutes, pay attention," Fovrates called from the screen. Sheepishly, Phutes turned back. "BrvNEC*, post images. Let Phutes see what we have found."

A metallic-sounding voice replied, "Yes, chief."

The Kail leaned close. In the tank, they saw the familiar pattern of stars that surrounded the motherworlds. Yesa's system was about one light year from edge to edge, including the Oort and errant bodies that moved in and out. Most of the spheres were familiar to them, but one after another, orange lights flared into life in the outer reaches.

"Those aren't Kail worlds," Phutes said. "What are they?"

"Intruders," Sofus said, his tones dropping to deck-rattling registers. "They are everywhere!"

"It's the same in every motherworld system," Fovrates said. "More in some. Let me give you the coordinates of those in Yesa's system, particularly the one that leaks the most radiation. Are you ready to memorize?"

Phutes looked at Mrdus. The small one signaled assent. "We are ready."

"Listen. I won't have time to repeat these. 11110001001010 1100000111110010100 . . . ."

Phutes concentrated deeply, allowing each of the open and closed numbers to tap a rhythm into his memory. He did not dare allow even one of the noises or smells coming from outside the room to distract him. Yesa must be so upset!

". . . 00000110101000010101. Do you have the entire sequence?"

"We all do," Sofus said. "This is an outrage! How dare the humans plant false planetoids in our home?"

Fovrates grunted. "You see? It's even more important to secure the assistance of the Zang! We must be be prepared with a devastating blow against the humans if the negotiations do not go the way that Yesa and Nefra want."

Phutes felt like hitting something, but he restrained himself. "I have told the Zang. It does not seem to understand that urgency. It sat and *hummed* at us. That eternal song that our mother told us it would understand has made no difference in its tone. It didn't even turn to look at us. Not once! No amount of entreaty does anything to change it."

Fovrates loomed forward, showing his impatience. "You have to keep trying. We have very little knowledge of what the Zang see and hear from us, apart from what Yesa and the other motherworlds have told us. You can't be sure that you aren't getting through to it, but if you don't try, you'll never make it understand."

"Don't you think we are?" Phutes asked. His system bubbled in anger. Gas generated by his internal reactions seeped out of his joints and made green clouds in the air. In annoyance, the other two waved away the fumes. "The humans must have convinced it to ignore us! They brought it here to indoctrinate it against us!"

"Excuse me, Phutes, but that is not true." NR-111 spoke up, turning all its lenses toward him. "The Zang came here of its own volition. Neither the crew or anyone else on board has done anything to prevent it from forming its own opinions and interacting with anyone it pleases. It is our guest, not our prisoner, just as you are."

"Don't try to lie to me!"

Phutes couldn't restrain himself any longer. He kicked out with his right foot, sending the servicebot flying across the room. She crashed into a wall of panels, activating a light module and several small screens. Sirens began to sound.

The mechanical being righted herself and rolled back toward him, taking care to keep out of his reach.

"I am not lying! I have kept my word to you. I have not told you a single falsehood."

"You are part of the human conspiracy!" Phutes shouted. He lunged for the translator. Alarmed, NR-111 scooted away from him, dodging around the backless chair that Lieutenant Ormalus had abandoned.

"No. I serve the cause of diplomacy," NR-111 said. "Please calm down, Phutes. Security is on its way. Please! We don't want an incident!"

Phutes didn't care. Since he couldn't reach the space stations that sullied Yesa's system, he wanted to crush the nearest thing to him that represented the hated humanity. Mrdus cowered in a corner, his multiple limbs wrapped around him for safety. Sofus stood in the middle as Phutes chased the servicebot around the room.

"Calm, brother," he said, turning his whole body to follow his sibling's progress. "Listen to Fovrates. We need to go back to the Zang and tell it all about the humans' perfidy. It needs to know it has bad allies."

At that moment, the door slid open. Lieutenant Ormalus stood in the corridor, surrounded by 110 helmeted guards. Every one of them had the brightly colored, long-barreled weapons in their hands, pointed at the Kail.

"Enough," the Uctu said, her coral-colored mandible quivering. The sight of wobbly matter made Phutes nauseated. "Leave now."

Sofus's heavy fist landed upon Phutes's shoulder, markedly more gentle than his own blow.

"Come on," he said. "We'll try again with the Zang."

Phutes relented. He ceased his pursuit of the servicebot. NR-111 rolled to the side of the room. Her lower section creaked in a tone it had not emitted before. He saw that his foot had put a large dent in the housing. He was ashamed of his outburst.

"Very well," he said.

The human guards reversed, but kept their rifles leveled at the Kail. Phutes found their fear amusing. The black-topped human and the other Uctu had borne the same devices on the shuttle that conveyed them from the *Whiskerchin*. They weren't much of a threat. They did not give off the supersonic whine of transuranic minerals, or smell of acid. The Kail could withstand extremes of heat and cold. Weapons that propelled small pieces of metal were more of an inconvenience than a danger. Fovrates was right about the humans underestimating them.

He strode toward the lift door half the corridor away. The knot of guards had to run to stay around him. Mrdus and Sofus stayed close behind him.

Still squeaking, NR-111 rolled to catch up with him, and moved right alongside him to the elevator.

"I give you credit for courage," he told her. "You're vulnerable to damage, but you still come back."

"It is my job to serve you," she said.

The lead guard, who had 11 colored lines on his sleeve instead of the 1 or 10 the others wore, ran to reach the lift before the Kail did. He gestured to the open door with the tip of the bright yellow gun.

"On in," he said. NR-111 duly translated the command.

"We are going this way," Phutes said, and stepped past him. The floor bobbed slightly under his weight.

"Welcome aboard car 100," the lift voice said in good Kail. "Deck numbers, please?"

"We want to go to the Zang's cabin," Phutes said.

"Oh, no," the 11-stripe guard said. "Deck 1100. You're going back to your quarters."

"No. We have business with the Zang. It cannot wait."

"Not right now," the guard replied, his words sounding muffled through his helmet. "The envoy told us you should get some rest. There's some nice stone powder waiting for you there. Water, too. We hear you like water."

"No, we want to go back to the Zang. We have to keep trying! Take us to the Zang's deck," Phutes told the lift.

"Deck 1100," the guard said.

"We are the guests! We are to have unlimited access to the Zang. We want to see it now!"

"Look, buddy," the guard said. "My orders are that you have to go back to your cabin. Don't you like it? It's all laid out the way Kail people live."

"How do you know how we live?" Phutes demanded, turning to glare at the guard. "Have you been spying on us?"

"I don't spy on anyone," the guard said, still in a singsong tone that NR-111 did her best to reproduce in Kail. "I'm only saying what they told me. They made the place up all nice for you. Come on, buddy. Deck 1100."

"No!" Phutes said. "You will not deter me. Take me to the Zang! No more arguments!"

"As you please, sir," the lift said.

The floor dropped. The guard leader fought to get past him, reaching for a red-rimmed control on the panel. Phutes, still doing his best to contain all the pent-up energy from his frustration with the report Fovrates had given him, shoved him back. The other guards lowered their heads and charged at the Kail. They could not shoulder the more weighty Kail aside, but contact even with their clothing set Mrdus off into a keening wail that made the lift bounce and the lights switch on and off. Blinding blue lights bathed the chamber, sweeping up and down in a dizzying pattern.

"Security, what's going on there?" a blaring voice asked. "I see a scuffle going on."

"We request help in lift four!" the guard leader shouted. "Divert us to Deck 12!"

"Sending . . . !" the voice was cut off as Mrdus's cries reached an almost ultrasonic frequency.

"Stop that!" the guard leader cried, both of his hands over his ears. All of the guards reeled, lowering their heads almost to their chests.

The lift suddenly lurched upward.

"We are going the wrong way," Sofus said.

"They must not deter us from seeing the Zang," Phutes said. He grabbed his smaller sibling and shook him. "Mrdus! Stop this nonfunctional noise! The lift is being diverted. Do what Fovrates taught you to. Tell it to take us to the Zang!"

The smallest Kail's eyes were pits of woe, but he stopped wailing. He started to emit a sequence of tones. The lift shuddered again, and began to move downward.

"What's he saying?" the guard leader demanded.

"I . . . I'm not allowed to tell you," NR-111 said. "Please try to understand, they don't want to hurt anyone!"

"Security, tell them to shut off the lifts! All of them! Oh, hell, never mind."

The lift door slid aside with a cheery PING! Phutes made for the opening.

"Together, now!" the guard bellowed. They leaped forward and tackled Phutes before he could step out of the chamber. He landed on the floor. The humans fought to capture his flailing limbs. "Full security, we need you on the cargo deck, now!"

"Help me, brothers!" Phutes shouted.

He was glad to see Sofus wade toward his attackers. The big Kail picked one of the guards up by one lower limb and swung him at the others. The guard leader and his people were knocked rolling into the corridor. Phutes bent all three knees and heaved himself to his feet.

"Come along," he said.

But the humans were not finished yet. They sprang up and leveled the bright yellow guns at them.

"Get back in there!" the guard leader bellowed. Phutes paid no attention. The Zang's door was only 11101 paces away. "Stop, or we'll shoot!"

Mrdus scurried to catch up with his larger siblings.

"That was terrible," he said. "I never dreamed . . . aaaaaaeeee!"

His voice rose to the shrillest tone yet. Mrdus dropped on the floor, writhing in agony. His back was covered with clear slime. Phutes turned. A blast of clear liquid hit him in the face. But it was not pure, clean water—it was something viscous and slimy. The liquid seeped into his joints, coating the granules of his body. Phutes emitted a howl that made the entire corridor shake.

"How dare you pollute me like that?" he bellowed, brushing at himself desperately. "I will have the Zang destroy all of you!"

They sprayed him and Sofus again and again from the yellow guns.

Phutes couldn't bear the insult a microsecond longer. He charged at the guards, knocking one then another over. The guard captain sank to one knee and aimed a charge straight into Phutes's face. Phutes grabbed for the nearest human and heaved him bodily at the leader. Both humans fell to the ground with a clatter. Phutes and Sofus helped Mrdus to his feet and made for the cabin.

"Security, where are you?" the leader shouted. "Secure the hatch of the Zang's quarters. Don't open it for anything! Top level emergency!"

Phutes reached the doorway. He clapped his fist against the door plate as he had seen the others do. A subdued ding-dong sounded on the other side of the portal, but it did not slide aside.

"Tell it to open," he ordered Mrdus, who was still whimpering. "Pull yourself together! We will be clean soon!"

Reluctantly, Mrdus stopped making sounds of misery, and shrilled the ultrasonic cues that should have caused the door to fall under their command.

Nothing happened.

"Again!" Mrdus tried again and again to open the door.

Being thwarted of his rightful access made him so angry that Phutes pounded on the door with both fists. The door dented, but remained stubbornly shut. It was no use. The humans had prevented the computer from aiding them. He hammered at wall plates until they dented, then threw them aside. Beneath them were tubes and pipes. Phutes tore at those and tossed them aside. His hands became soiled with more effluvia. The horrible stench offended him. Humans smelled worse than Wichu! He and the others pounded on the inner wall, trying to break through.

"Let me in!"

Mrdus raised his voice to the very highest frequency imaginable. It was so shrill that it made Phutes's head ring. At last, the door slid aside. They charged in, heading for the Zang.

As usual, Proton seemed to be in a world of dream. Phutes shouted loudly to get its attention.

"Great Zang!" he cried. "Help us! The humans have invaded Kail space. We need you! Please show us that you understand!"

Phutes waited for any sign, even the passage of energy to show that the Zang was aware of their presence.

"Why don't you acknowledge us?" he demanded. "We need you now!"

They were hit from behind by another spray of slime. Phutes rounded in fury and charged at the humans. They dodged away from him, moving behind the furniture. Phutes picked up the table in one hand and flung it at them. Sofus smashed the desk into two pieces and swung them at the humans, knocking yet another one down. But surge after surge of the sticky goo still issued forth from the horrible guns. They must get away from the guards.

"Come with me!" he shouted to the other two.

They pushed their way into the corridor past the squad, cannoning another of them into the wall as they passed. The humans pursued them with weapons expectorating. Sofus forced one of the doors open. Phutes pushed Mrdus inside and slammed his fist on the plate. The portal slid shut.

Dripping with nauseating fluids, Phutes stood scanning the room. Numerous sealed containers were stacked high above their heads. Machines for moving those boxes huddled against one wall of the room as though they were afraid of the Kail. In the far corner, he spotted a glass-walled booth. Hanging from the ceiling were flexible metal rods. He had seen installations like that on the *Whiskerchin*. Fovrates called them "showers."

"Over there!" he ordered the others. "We can use that to become clean."

"There is a machine already using the room," Mrdus said, pointing to a low vehicle in red and gold enamel.

"Tell it to move," Sofus said.

"I can't. It's not intelligent."

"Take it out!" Phutes ordered, throwing open the glass door. "One piece at a time if necessary!"

⊰ CHAPTER 19 ⊱

I invited my crew and Madame Deirdre to join us for dinner in the common room. Anna had been given free rein of my stash of delicacies and put them into the hands, or claws, or processors, of the ship's culinarybot, MC-037. I enjoined Marcel to use all the best recipes he could search along the Infogrid to make the most wonderful meal that he could. If it left me short of saffron sprouts and truffloid compounds until I returned to Keinolt, I considered the sacrifice to be worthwhile.

In this sector, only a few pinpoints of stars shone through the broad porthole, so I indulged myself in lighting the room with richly colored spotlights that picked up equally evocative hues from the priceless tapestries and throws with which I had adorned the furnishings. The table was laid with brilliant white china that had come down to me from my great-great grandmother Glennis Tamerlane Loche, on top of a vast silk paisley shawl in hues of peat brown, rouge and deep blue that evoked the highlands of our ancestral home planet. The flatware was made of pure silver with crystal tines, bowls or blades, depending on the item of cutlery. Equally rich aromas enticed the nose from the curtained serving area, where Marcel's serverbots awaited my cue.

Of course, I had prepared a dance of welcome. As each of my guests arrived, I sashayed, pranced or glided forward, escorting each one to the circle of couches and settees where their drink of choice awaited. Redius gave me a humorous look as I performed an Uctu pavane that I had learned while on his ancestral homeworld of Memepocotel. I had set the music system to respond to nonverbal clues. Lieutenant

Plet was greeted by the stirring martial refrain from an ancient march. Madame Deirdre, enveloped in swathes of shimmering dark green and blue silk that reminded me of butterfly wings, fell into my arms as I drew her forward into a sweeping waltz that surprised applause from Nesbitt and Anstruther. All of the pieces had been carefully chosen for the person involved. I rather regretted that Oskelev, the *Rodrigo*'s pilot, was still on Counterweight with my cousin Jil. I had a splendid reel that I would have danced for her. I took a chance on a plaintive threnody I had happened upon for the appearance of my guest. When Dr. Derrida first entered the room, she seemed so small and alone, nearly swallowed by a massive quilted silver and blue caftan, but I should have realized that she was equal to any situation.

"How beautiful!" she exclaimed, looking around with pleasure writ large upon her face. She beamed up at me as I drew her against me, one of her small hands on my upturned palm. We spun together gracefully. "I didn't know it was going to be a party!"

"In your honor," I said, escorting her to the well-lit circle one delicate step at a time. "Please, let me introduce you to everyone."

At first, my crew was reticent with a stranger, but her effusive personality took over at once. In remarkably little time, they fell into easy conversation with her. I would have been deeply surprised if anyone could not. Laine seemed to make herself at home no matter where she was. I supposed that resulted from being plucked up and set down into so many locations over the past many years. Her adventures, which she was happy to relate at the turn of a question, had us all agog.

At Marcel's signal that the meal was ready, we moved to the table. The conversation continued smoothly from one location to another. I made sure everyone's glass remained full. Plet's and Anstruther's were filled with iced coffee, since they were nominally still on duty.

"I travel light," Laine said, in answer to a question from Plet, who had come out of her rather rigid shell at Laine's welcoming warmth. "I have to. Everything I own fits into my backpack. If I don't have my hand on it when Proton is ready to leave, it gets left behind. You can't believe the things I've lost over the years! My viewpad is made to do very complex analyses, and it has a really large memory bank. I can wait several months until we're close to a node so I can transmit. If I take a specimen that I want to send back to the university, it has to be small. It might be a year or more before we end up near an outpost from which I can ship them. I've carried things around for *ages*."

"What's the weirdest thing you ever sent home?" Nesbitt asked. Since it was his off-duty shift, he joined us in a bottle of my finest Boske red wine, sent to me by a cousin who had moved to the Castaway Cluster. We had already enjoyed appetizer, soup, salad, two entrees, and a palate freshener of cardamom sorbet.

Laine smiled fondly at a memory. "A little red walking flower from a G-class world with eighty percent Keinolt gravity. It hibernated in my backpack until I could find safe transport for it. I saw in the department's Infogrid file that it's doing just fine. It even had three seedlings. Or pups. Or whatever. Wow, look at that! What is it?"

The serverbot flourished a large silver platter on which reposed large, thick, chocolate-brown leaves oozing with rich yellow filling, and brandished flattened serving tongs. A heavenly aroma of sweet and savory spices rose in a cloud of steam. Marcel's matchingly unctuous voice emerged from the speaker.

"Quistaminatos," it said. "May I serve you, madame?"

"Yes, please!" Laine said, with delight. "I've never seen anything like it."

"It's a cheese-filled flowering succulent from one of the Imperium's outpost worlds," I explained, pleased to have surprised her with something new. "Rather difficult to grow, but long-lasting in cold storage. I find them delectable, and hope you will enjoy them, too."

"Oh, it looks fantastic!" she said, picking up the next crystal fork. "Those tiny vegetables around it are just precious. And all of it smells wonderful!"

I cut into my own portion. Quistaminatos had the texture of mushrooms, but none of the gray heaviness. They could be served in a sweet or savory preparation, but my preference was for savory. The first bite was divine. I wondered if the second would add another to the pantheon. It did. I closed my eyes to appreciate the texture and the taste on my tongue.

"Marcel, you are a genius," I said aloud. "Do I sense . . . nutmeg?"

"Only a pinch, sir. I thought it would add a mysterious air."

"Astonishing!" I said. "You must pass the recipe back to my mother's cook."

"It would be my honor, sir."

"This is great, sir," Nesbitt said. The big man's voice was thick with gravy. I noticed that his plate was already empty. The serverbots were ahead of my signal, though. They moved in to help him to a second portion of everything. My other tablemates ate at a more leisured pace, the better to enjoy the delicacies I had had laid out for them.

"Try the wine, sir," Marcel's server said, moving to his side with the carafe. He beamed at him and held out his glass.

"Great stuff, sir," he said, holding the goblet up to me in a toast. "Thanks for inviting us!"

"Everything is *lovely*, Lord Thomas," Madame Deirdre said, carving another tiny nibble. "I think my other friends here will agree that this is the finest food on any ship I have ever traveled. Certainly better than what I've had to force down my throat on traveling theatrical ships. Although actors and dancers can eat *anything*, proprietors and producers often think that means we should."

The others laughed.

"Where is Parsons?" I enquired of the group as a whole. "I invited him, but he never responded to my note."

Did Plet hesitate a moment before she answered?

"I can't say, sir," she said, lifting guileless blue eyes to my questioning gaze. "When I saw him last, he was in the engineering department. One of the technicians was making something for him. He implied that his . . . project might take some time."

"Ah, well," I said, ruefully, slicing myself a morsel of my meal. "He has been known to savor this dish. I did tell him I was serving it. Perhaps he will appear before dessert."

I was pleased to see that all of my guests seemed to enjoy the rare treat. The fleshy texture of the succulent added a luxurious bite to the silky sauce. I admired Marcel's hand with spices. I further detected the sweetness of cardamom on top of a piquant citrus note. All of these were firmly anchored in a rich stock flavored with roasted garlic and almost a sub-molecular spark of bird's-eye chili.

"Genius," I said, savoring the taste. "Don't you agree?"

"Delicious," Redius agreed, smacking his lips. Anstruther, shy thing that she was, nodded without looking up from her plate.

A high-pitched peep sounded from Plet's end of the table. She glanced down at her viewpad and stood up.

"Anstruther, with me," she said. The dark-haired girl rose, setting her napkin on the table.

"Do you want the rest of us, lieutenant?" Nesbitt asked, glancing at his wine glass with rueful eyes.

"Not at this time, but stay near your viewpads," Plet said. "The rest of the security detail is already present."

"What's the matter?" I asked.

A tiny wrinkle of concern had etched itself between her straight blonde brows. On anyone else, the expression would have manifested as a gloomy frown.

"The Kail are kicking up a fuss over something. Security has ordered all crew on duty to the Zang's quarters."

Laine put down her fork and pushed back her chair with a rueful grimace. "I'd better come with you."

"I will come, too," I said, bravely abandoning the half-eaten quistaminato on my plate. "If I can be of any help."

With a signal to Marcel to put all the food and wine safely aside, I followed my dinner party out to the lift shaft.

"What is *he* doing here?"

As we exited the lift shaft into the cargo-bay level, I recognized the voice as belonging to Master Chief O'ohma Charles Xi. The noncommissioned officer who oversaw security on the *Jaunter* was a long and faithful servant of the Imperium. His brown, oblong, solid face always reminded me of a large potato, but I didn't hold it against him. Through the clear visor of a riot helmet, Chief Xi glared at me. He and most of the security contingent of the *Jaunter* were massed in the corridor, each of them carrying a riot shield and one of those brightly-colored weapons I had seen Redius and Nesbitt carrying after they conveyed the Kail to the *Jaunter*. I heard banging and shrieking, but it wasn't coming from the Zang's quarters. Instead, the deafening din issued from an open loading bay farther down. Torn sections of hull plate lay twisted and and mangled on the floor. Pipes in the wall were still leaking sewage and water. The smell was nauseous. Two security officers lay prone on the floor, being ministered to by a doctorbot and a female medic from the infirmary.

"He accompanied Dr. Derrida," Lieutenant Plet said, in an apologetic tone I found inexcusable.

"I am a serving member of the Imperium Navy," I pointed out, loading my voice with all the asperity I could.

"Well, *lieutenant*," Chief Xi said, the word larded with equally inappropriate sarcasm, "I'd appreciate it if you and this lady would take yourself back to your quarters. It's bad enough I have to deal with those things in there." He aimed a thumb over his shoulder.

"Have they tried to assault the Zang?" Plet asked, keeping her face carefully immobile, as befit an assiduous student of the Parsons School for Inscrutability.

"No, not according to Petty Officer Gruen," Xi said. He indicated one of the helmeted guards, whose armor looked as though he had been tumbled in an industrial clothes dryer with ten tons of rocks.

"No, ma'am, just us," Gruen said.

"They can't touch it anyhow," Laine said. "It's insubstantial unless it wants to be solid. Besides, my impression from the Kail was of total respect for the Zang."

"Well, something's stirred them up. They're taking out their frustrations on the rest of the ship. They were in a pet even before we tried to herd them back to their quarters."

"Why?"

"I haven't got a clue. This one won't talk." Xi aimed the thumb at a derelict-looking LAI. I realized that the sorry structure before us was NR-111, the translator assigned to the Kail. Her housing was battered and dented, and the stalk supporting her lenses had been crushed as if in a vise.

From an open hangar door about thirty meters from us, a loud crash answered him. I thought that I heard a thousand pieces of glass shatter. Chief Xi didn't even flinch.

"They're marauding all over this level, breaking anything that they can lay their big cement mitts on."

"Couldn't you stop them?" Plet asked.

"With what? They're the size of tanks. Two of my guards are in the infirmary, one with a fractured skull."

"Have adapted weapons," Redius said, indicating the guards' colorful rifles. "No use?"

The chief's big face turned dark with suffused blood. "That's what set them off."

"What do they shoot?" I asked.

"Gelatin," Plet said. "The Kail dislike coming into contact with any kind of biological substance. They were meant to be the device of last resort only."

"Yes, ma'am, I know," Xi said. His eyes were hooded as he glanced toward Gruen. "I'll be talking to my people later, once we get those monsters calmed down. Any suggestions?"

For answer, Plet turned to NR-111. "You have had more contact than anyone else. Do you have a recommendation?"

"I don't know what to suggest," the translator said, sounding almost frantic. "They are very angry, almost desperate."

"About what?"

"They . . . I don't believe it is breaking protocol to say they were speaking with the Kail on the other ship, lieutenant," NR-111 said, in a tentative manner. "He showed them . . . some images that upset them greatly."

"Can you give us any more detail than that?"

"I am afraid not." The translator lowered her damaged stalk almost down to her dented housing. "Those communications are privileged. All I can say is that afterwards, they wanted to communicate urgently with the Zang."

"And did they?"

"Oh, yes! But it doesn't seem to have calmed them down. I think it made them more angry. Especially Phutes, their leader. He has a very bad temper."

"They made a disaster out of the cabin that the Zang is in," Gruen said. "We chased them out of there. I hope you didn't leave anything valuable in there, ma'am. It's probably not in good shape right now."

Laine looked resigned. "It won't be the first time I've had to replace everything."

"Is Proton all right?" I asked.

Laine listened for a moment. "Yes. It's fine."

"What are they upset about?" Lieutenant Plet asked.

"Who knows?" Gruen said. "That's not my job. I'm stuck between two bad choices. The captain wants them thrown off the ship before they take it over, and the special envoy says that'll ruin any chances of making peace with the Kail motherworlds. So, I disabled the lifts so they can't go anywhere, and I called Ambassador Melarides. She's on her way down."

Another magnificent bang shook the level.

"Have they attempted to corrupt any of the ship's systems?" Plet asked.

"Except for reversing our control of the lifts, not a touch. They're acting like they never heard of technology. They're kicking and smashing things and carrying on like big stone babies." He kept his eyes fixed pointedly upon me.

"I promise you, it's nothing to do with me," I said. "I've been minding my own business for the last several hours."

"What do they want?" Anstruther asked, her golden eyes huge as something heavy slammed into an inner wall behind her.

"They just keep saying over and over again that they want it to talk to them. I don't know what we can do about that, except maybe pipe a fake voice over the PA and pretend it's coming from the Zang."

I chuckled. "I'd be happy to provide the voice."

"No, you wouldn't," Lieutenant Plet said, dismissively. "Can *you* talk to them, Dr. Derrida?"

Laine shrugged her shoulders. The enveloping gown lifted and dropped, belling out at the hem with displaced air.

"I'll just say the same thing as I did before. They can talk to it all they want. I can't promise that it will listen."

"Will you offer again, ma'am?" Chief Xi asked. "We'll do our best to protect you."

"I suppose so, but I can't tell them anything that I haven't said. The Zang is not going to reply directly to them. I offered to translate its impressions if I got any. Even if I did, it might not address their request."

I cleared my throat, and was rewarded with everyone's attention. "By this time in my studies, I might claim to be a growing expert in the field of translating nuance," I said. "Can't you . . . reinterpret what they're hearing from the Zang?"

Laine wrinkled her nose. "In what way?"

I did my best to evoke inclusion, gathering all the beings present to me with enveloping arms.

"Try not to make them feel as if they are being ignored by the Zang. Give them reassurance that it is listening."

She shook her head.

"But it isn't! They *are* being ignored. We're all ephemerals, temporary beings, maybe worthy of a glance or two. I'm always surprised when they let me know that a spectacle is coming so I can alert the population in the vicinity to come and watch. Otherwise, everything's on *their* time scale."

"Tell them what you do sense from it," I suggested. "No one likes to feel unimportant. Perhaps if you reframe its attention to the universe in a way that includes them? Could you do that?"

Laine looked uncomfortable. She raised her warm brown eyes to mine in appeal. "I suppose so. I'm not used to being untruthful."

"No? Don't you write grant proposals?" I asked.

"All the time," Laine said, the helpless expression giving way to confusion. "Well, I used to. But what's that got to do with it?"

"From what I understand from my friends in academics, those are tissues of lies and fabrications from the merest suggestion of fact." I held up a thumb and forefinger, the pads of which were a meager distance from one another. "Weren't yours just the tiniest bit exaggerating what you had already found against what you hoped to find? All these poor creatures want is a moment of the Zang's attention. Give them an essay that stresses what they may hope for."

A slow smile spread the rosebud mouth into a broad grin. Endearing dimples indented her cheeks. I fell in love all over again. Her eyes warmed with affection.

"When you put it like that, I suppose it falls into the range of academic accuracy." She turned to Xi. "All right, chief. Take me to them."

"Marvelous!" I said, tucking her hand into the crook of my elbow. "I'm looking forward to this. I hope to gather enough material for another dance from the interplay." At my side, Madame Deirdre nodded vigorous agreement.

"No!" Lieutenant Plet exclaimed. She stepped between us and took Laine's hand away from me. I felt immediately bereft. "Please, Lord Thomas, this is dangerous. We prefer not to have to involve Dr. Derrida, but we have no choice. I don't want to risk you. *You* have no purpose here. Go abovedecks. Now. Both of you."

"But it was my idea!" I protested. I thrust out my lower lip. "I only want to help her."

Xi lowered his heavy brow and frowned.

"Lieutenant, sir, my lord, will you get out of here? The only way you can help is not to be one of my problems. It'll be tough enough to guard her from those stone-fisted morons! I don't want to have to report to your mother you got a chair thrown at you on *my watch*."

"Oh, come now, chief, my mother assumes I will get chairs thrown at me, on your watch or anyone else's!"

"Come along, Lord Thomas. We are in the way," Madame Deirdre said in a brisk manner, taking my arm with an iron grip. She had very strong fingers. "Chief, so sorry to be a bother."

"Not at all, ma'am." Chief Xi looked relieved.

As she pulled me away, I began to protest that I wanted to watch, but both good sense and the no-nonsense look on the face of my teacher told me to vacate the premises and not to argue.

"I will be in the common room if you need me," I called to Laine over my shoulder.

"Sorry about the quisto-whatevers," she said, with a rueful smile.

"Not at all," I assured her. I did my best to cover my disappointment.

CHAPTER 20

Deirdre hauled me steadily toward the lift doors, which opened upon our approach, and herded me inside.

"Let's go back and have the rest of our dinner," she said, as the mechanism hummed to life. "Your friends can fill us in when they come back."

"If they come back," I said glumly, watching the indicator number rise. "I think tonight's party is over." I reached for the controls. She swatted my hand.

"You must not dwell on this, Lord Thomas!" she said. "There are times when you must let others take a task out of your sight!"

I grinned, a trifle sheepishly.

"I prefer to be in the midst of the action," I said.

She waved away my impatience. "I know. But to become an interpreter, one must observe, then take the experience away with one, to a place where there is space for private thought and reflection." She peered up at me. "I know your moods. You won't be able to settle. Let us forgo the rest of the feast. Instead, let's make use of this boundless energy that is making you twitch." She spoke into the control panel of the lift. "Housekeeping, please?"

Instead of the friendly, casual voice of the elevator's LAI system, the reply was in the precise tones of the managing intelligence that maintained the living quarters and everything on the ship that was not involved with operations, security or defense.

"Yes, Madame Deirdre, this is AB-64l. How may I help?"

"Abigail, will you set up the barre and mirror in the nobles' common room, please? Towels, high-impact floor pads. And take away the food. We'll need only water, herbal tea, and high-protein snacks."

"Yes, Madame Deirdre," Abigail said.

"Apologize to Marcel for us. Perhaps we can revisit his delectable offerings tomorrow, when things have settled down a bit."

"I will do so. Changeover taking place now. Completion in twenty minutes."

"Thank you so much," Deirdre said. She stepped back and shot me a look of triumph.

"You take charge in the way that my maternal unit does," I complained.

"Now that," Madame Deirdre said, stepping out of the lift ahead of me, "I consider that to be an enormous compliment."

We entered the day room. LAIs and other mechanicals zipped busily around us, undoing all the careful preparations I had made for my little dinner party. In no time at all, the feast hall had been transformed into a dance studio. With my cousins still on the planet's surface, there was no one present to object. Rugs were rolled up, mats were spread out. An enormous mirror, appearing in the room as if by magic, slid out from behind a raised wall panel and was walked into place by thumb-sized rollerbots. I watched for a while, but my mind kept drifting downward into the lower levels of the ship.

I had every faith that Dr. Derrida was equal to the task of placating the stone monsters. But what was it they craved so mightily that they wanted to spend every waking moment persuading the Zang to give it to them? We knew so little about what the Zang were capable of achieving. Laine had given me an insight into their curiosity about lower life forms, including humankind. One could see that the less cultured beings might see them as deities, instead of seeing them as fellow inhabitants of a diverse galaxy. So far, no experts whom I had read or listened to knew whether the Kail believed in higher powers, therefore it suggested they were interested in practical assistance. What did the Kail need so desperately it made them commandeer a space liner? How could we help them get what they craved?

A hand-clap brought me out of my reverie.

"You're far away, Lord Thomas," Madame Deirdre said, pointing at the floor beside the mirror. "Come over here." I obeyed, and put my hand upon the barre that had been erected along the mirror. "First position, please. Arms up! Second position. Let's begin with some plies. Now, *one* two three. *One* two three."

My dress trousers were not tremendously amenable to dance exercises, but I managed. Madame Deirdre grasped the barre next to me and led me through flexibility exercises. The wispy folds of her dress swirled around her like fairies around a storybook princess. I, as a rather clumsier prince, did my best to keep up. Though I was probably less than half her age, she could have gone on four times as long as I.

When I was quite winded, she released the barre and turned to face me.

"Come, now, we're going to try an exercise in interpretation. I want you to describe your childhood to me."

"*All* of it?" I asked, appalled at the scope of her request.

She pursed her mouth, but her eyes wore an amused twinkle.

"Very well, then," she said, settling down cross-legged on the blue mat, "let us explore just one moment in your upbringing. Show me a significant moment that means a lot to you."

"My life is full of significant moments," I said. It was no more than the truth. A noble of the Imperium house and a Kinago was born to experience eventful days.

"I have no doubt of that," she said. "What is the first one that comes into your mind? No, nothing that is going on right now! You have no way of knowing how significant anything that happens today will be."

I did a couple of deep plies while I thought about her suggestion. What one moment could I point out as being particularly important? Was it the first time that I noticed the difference between my father and the parents of my cousins? Was it when I first told a joke to someone and was rewarded with a laugh? Would I describe one of my first enthusiasms?

No, wait!

Almost of its own volition, my left arm rose behind me in a graceful arc, and the fingers of my right hand curled around a sword hilt that it had not held for decades. I sprang away from the wall and advanced upon an invisible opponent.

The *Imperium Jaunter* disappeared from around me. Instead, I was back in the gardens behind my parents' villa within the Imperium compound. I was seven or eight years of age. It was my first lesson in how to use a sword. I was too small to fight with any of the historical weapons in our arsenal or hanging from the walls of our suites in the Imperium compound. In point of fact, I was even too small for proper lessons, but Lieutenant Parsons, a dashing officer who was a friend of my parents and an avuncular presence among the younger generation of nobles, cut a pair of sticks from a thinning topiary and pressed them into service as swords. I cannot recall clearly how the subject had come up, only the moment in which I first attempted to set upon him, charging toward him with my makeshift blade flailing, and been beaten back. Never to be deterred by failure, I tried again and again. In the kindest and most patient manner, he explained to me what I was doing wrong. Parsons guided me to correct my movements, one after another, molding me into proper form.

As I described this in movement to Madame Deirdre, I felt myself smiling. That had been a wonderful day. It had meant a lot to me that this very competent officer whom I had believed to be aloof and uninterested in children had spent so much time with me, helping me to get my lunges and parries right. I described how long it had taken me to learn the beat-thrust. I repeated the motions again and again until they possessed their own rhythm. I was not accustomed to failure, even at that young age. I took my ignorance as a challenge. When at last I managed to pass Parsons's formidable defense and touch him in quarte, I was as thrilled as if I had been named Emperor myself. I suspected then, as I did in reproducing the moment, that he had dropped his guard to allow me one touch as a reward for my unending effort.

I stopped and lifted my blade to my lips in salute to my worthy opponent. The boy I had been then was winded and sweat-stained. I realized that the man I was now felt a warm glow in my muscles, but that had been the day that set me on the path I had followed.

"That was fairly representational," Madame said critically, from her place on the soft blue carpet, where she sat, cupping her chin with one hand. I eyed her with dismay. "But it was heartfelt."

"I suppose I was too caught up in my memory to describe it symbolically," I said.

"Oh, it was marvelous," Deirdre said, rising as gracefully as a swan and coming to take both my hands in hers. "I was impressed by the passion and the depth of your recollection."

"I will never forget that day," I said.

She smiled up at me. "I have quite a new respect for Commander Parsons. He's such a dry stick I had never thought of him before as being so generous."

I blinked. "How could you tell that it was he I was battling?"

"You still have the same expression when you look at him, my dear," she said, patting me on the hand. "Respect. Well, you've exorcised your frustrations! Do you think you can relax, now?"

I leaned down and kissed the tiny woman on the cheek.

"Yes. Thank you."

⁂ CHAPTER 21 ⁂

The tiny pod in which Parsons lay concealed occupied a precarious position at the aft lip of the belt containing the exterior drives of the *Whiskerchin*. Maneuvering the unpowered glider there had taken several hours since the launcher he had used to travel from the *Jaunter* had fallen away. He was now ensconced in between an emitter for the shielding system and an exhaust port for noxious gases. If he had been able to smell in space, the round valve would have made his eyes water from the stink. Such a fate would be far better than if the emitter suddenly came to life. If it detected any incoming particles that might endanger the ship's skin, the blast coming from the round tip of the stalk would destroy his pod and kill him instantly. It was one of the few positions, however, where he could tether himself without being seen by any of the cameras or maintenance hull-crawlers. He needed to survive.

The outside of the little vehicle was covered by a skin of microplates that could imitate any color or texture. As soon as it had adhered to the hull of the *Whiskerchin*, it began to take on local characteristics. In moments, it had gone from a sleek . . . greenish-black ovoid to a dun, matte lump on a dun, matte vessel. It was unlikely that anyone observing it would find it to be out of place. It had no outward lights, relying instead upon sensors and infrared imaging to steer.

The inside of the pod allowed him very little room to move. Its all-enveloping life-support cocoon was made of soft white fibers that sustained his body temperature while wicking away unnecessary moisture. The makers had created it so it could be used by a number of different species of sizes ranging from that of a small child to a full-grown Solinian. As a result, Parsons felt as though he had been rolled in an enormous and very thick quilt made of loose strands. They were not contained in any way, so he constantly had to spit out the fibers near his face that had been made to surround and support an Uctu mandible or a Croctoid snout. His knees were drawn up close to his chest in a near-embryonic pose. His hands were free to move and operate controls, but his legs and feet were mired in more of the white insulation. No easy emergence from the pod was possible. He had to rely upon it absolutely to conceal and convey him safely from and return him to his point of origin.

The heads-up display, however, could not be bettered. He was surrounded by scopes and screens of the very latest designs. He could pick up life signs and the complex electrical signals that indicated AIs, as well as ship's systems, weaponry and security systems. With a nod of his head against a forehead control, he activated a device that would seek out a single life form aboard the *Whiskerchin*. He needed to find ColPUP*.

The Wichu-made LAI with whom Bokie had been corresponding when he was taken over by the corrupted programming was the only intelligence agent Parsons knew, or hoped, was still operating within the *Whiskerchin*. Captain Wold had been right to be concerned about the Kail. If the Imperium was not to engage in outright war with them, they needed more information. Nothing useful had been gained from Special Envoy's futile attempts at discussion with Phutes and his siblings. They did not want to engage with the human diplomats, nor had they revealed anything useful about themselves, either casually or in the first semi-formal meeting Melarides had arranged. If Parsons was to discover what had driven the Kail to have gone to such lengths to meet with the Zang, not to mention how to counter the ability the silicon-based aliens had over technology, he needed to confer with one who had been observing them since their embarkation.

It was unfortunate, but Bokie had not indicated whether the embedded LAI agent occupied a mobile shell or an installation. Since electronic personalities operated everything from life support systems for entire space stations down to toys for children, there was no telling what ColPUP* did aboard the *Whiskerchin*. Even the ship's roster, which Parsons had downloaded before the ship's files had disappeared from the Infogrid, left him none the wiser. ColPUP* worked in Life Support with a rank of Chief Petty Officer. He must not endanger ColPUP* further by attempting to contact him by conventional means. The fewer transmissions that were directed toward him, the safer he and those around him would be. Therefore, the contact most likely to be fruitful was a direct one.

An immense CLANK! echoed through his shell. Parsons glanced at the telemetry scope on his left to identify the sound. The small screen remained green. On the visual portion, the picture of a skid-loader appeared and rotated to show every angle of the practical vehicle. Something in the hold adjacent to his position was being moved, none too carefully. Identical noises, some meters removed from the first set of sounds, meant that there was more than one of those machines operating. That piece of information might prove useful to him.

Parsons activated the pod's mobility mechanism, causing it to inch forward. An outside observer would probably put the shifting lump down to a change in the planet's albedo as the ship orbited from day side to night side. He had approximately .8 planetary hours to move before the sun rose on the horizon again. If he had not made his destination by then, the pod would flatten itself out and feign hull plating once more.

Hatches of various sizes and shapes studded the surface of the hull. According to the architectural rendering of this class of Wichu vessel, the large hexagonal hatches, one within five meters and one seventeen meters to his left, were access panels used for maintenance. They were of sufficient size to permit a large LAI or a team of living beings in EVA suits to pass. He set the pod creeping toward the nearer of the two, monitoring heat and movement below.

According to his telemetry, the yellow forms on infrared indicated that the Wichu were gathered into two main clusters and several individual signals over the body of the ship. The ship's complement was 37 Wichu crew, and 44 LAIs and AIs of various complexity. The shipping company's records said that there were also fifty-one passengers on board, all Wichu, who were going to watch the Zang spectacle. According to a tourist file on the Infogrid, both the shipping company and the *Whiskerchin* had marvelous reputations for customer service. Parsons felt deep sympathy for both. Such a thing as a hijacking by silicon-based alien beings was going to impact unfairly on their systemwide ratings.

Approximately forty Kail had taken ship from a planetoid at the juncture of Wichu and Kail space. Not surprisingly, few of any carbon-based life forms plied the spaceways beyond the frontier. The Kail had no space program of their own. They had obtained a few ancient ships from unscrupulous sellers and had had them adapted for local use. Unlike nearly every other civilized race, they seemed to own nothing and covet nothing. They did not seem materially interested in anything outside their self-imposed borders. That made their expedition to view the Zang destruction of a planet a curious anomaly. Their agreement to sit down for trade talks with the Imperium was even more strange, albeit warmly welcomed by the Emperor and his government.

The hull vibrated beneath him. Parsons dropped his chin on the motivator control to make the pod stop where it was. To his very slight annoyance, lights on the nearby hatch indicated that it was about to open. He flattened the pod down beside a square cleat, and waited.

A plume of ice crystals exploded upward as the hexagonal plate withdrew. Parsons shut down all but life support and telemetry, and waited. He hoped that whoever emerged from the hatch was carbon-based. Biological creatures were far more likely to overlook the lump that concealed him than a technological creature would. Parsons listened to the conduction microphones that picked up every sound for tens of meters in every direction.

"C'mon, sweetie," a male Wichu voice said. "No one will look for us up here!"

"Are you sure?" a female voice responded. "The 'bots keep coming around to take attendance!"

"Yeah, but that's what makes it exciting! You have the tent?"

"Uh-huh, and some mead."

The male cackled. "You think of everything, baby!"

An enormous holdall flew out of the open hatch, then clumped to the hull as its electromagnetic locks engaged. Two bulky figures in EVA suits followed. The bigger one helped the smaller one out of the hatch and onto the surface of the ship.

While the two Wichus chose a place to erect their impromptu love nest, Parsons directed the pod to slip past them and down into the hatch. It slunk along the hull like a caterpillar. As it reached the edge, it swung in and clung to the ceiling of the vacuum-filled cargo bay.

"Hey, close the hatch!" the female Wichu whispered.

"Looks like something's stuck in it!" the male hissed back.

Parsons chinned the movement control, increasing the creep speed. The tail of his pod whisked out of the way just before the heavy double cover sealed back into place.

The cargo bay doors to the rest of the ship were sealed tightly. As soon as the hatch closed, air began to seep slowly into the chamber from broad black grates set in the wall. While the pod crept slowly down the wall, Parsons watched the gauge. The ambient temperature climbed rapidly from near absolute zero to ambient atmospheric temperature in a matter of minutes. During that time, Parsons extended a hair-thin wire attached to a gigabot, seeking a connection to the intranet system. The bug would not be detected, because it gained access to the ship's computer through its Infogrid connection.

When it attached to an exposed square of metal, Parsons blinked at the flood of millions of messages and posts bounding about the ship's system like balls bouncing in a frictionless environment. Nearly all the data remained unsent. A governor program kept all but a few from reaching the Infogrid. Anything that resembled a complaint or a plea for help was suppressed. Parsons had seen such programs before; many hoteliers and vendors attached them to their Infogrid files to prevent customer complaints from being seen by the general public. This one was more sophisticated and far-reaching. He doubted from what he had already seen of the Kail that they had designed this themselves. They must have been abetted by LAI collaborators, some of which must once have worked in customer service.

He pulled up a schematic of the ship in order to locate ColPUP*. The *Whiskerchin* was a large vessel, designed to be a luxury space liner. The centers populated by large numbers of Wichu were found to be the theater, a large performance space on a massive center deck, and the food service area, an even larger space farther forward. The scattered life forms occupied individual cabins and other function rooms. None of them were in the command center. Captain Bedelev and her crew appeared as starred icons at a bar in the corner of the restaurant. Parsons could not say he was surprised, considering that their functions had all been taken over and rerouted to a single office on the engineering level of the ship.

Fovrates and the rest of the Kail showed up as a host of green blots in that department. Either they were confident in their control of the biological life forms, or they simply did not care what the Wichu did, as long as they did not interfere with Fovrates. Parsons tapped into a video feed from security eyes in Engineering. Fovrates, as he appeared in the tri-dee image supplied along with the rest of the crew's identity cards to Imperium customs, was much larger than the three Kail who were aboard the *Jaunter*. He held court among the rest of the Kail, who seemed to hold him in esteem bordering upon awe. Parsons knew very little of their language, but he would have used the adjectives "jovial" and "avuncular" to describe the engineer. A shame that he had proved to be a traitor to the ship that had given him employment. The Wichu could not have foreseen the coup that the Kail had perpetrated. It would seem that it had been planned a very long time ago. The Imperium had warned the Pubatec of the Kail's enmity, but the governing body had been unimpressed and unconcerned. Now they bombarded the Emperor day after day to secure their ship's release. Parsons intended to do just that, once he had gained the information that he sought.

Parsons caused the enormous loaderbot to turn this way and that, scanning the area. Its functions were not terribly sophisticated, used as it was to move heavy objects around without bumping into anything, but it was designed to pick out life forms of both organic and inorganic types. According to its programming log, it had been adapted to identify Kail as inorganic, so it would not run over any of the visitors. Parsons rather thought that the loader would come off much the worse for an encounter with the bad-tempered aliens. He saw as-yet unrepaired dents in walls and doors that were approximately the size of Kail fists or feet.

On the intranet system, Parsons located the crew manifest. He ran through the screens in search of the LAI's name. He could read Main Wichu with reasonable fluency. Their alphabet was not in the same order as Imperium Standard, which meant scrolling up from *A* past several characters, some of which did not exist in the human tongue, toward the *C/K* sound.

Since past crew members were permitted access to the intranet to keep in touch with old friends, the list was a long one. Parsons discovered ColPUP* on the second pass-through. The environmental officer was a fixture, not a mobile being. An inconvenience, but not a dead end.

He sent a second gigabot toward one of the loaders, now sitting idle at one end of the cargo bay. The massive machine, which consisted mainly of a rechargeable engine enclosed in between the control seat and the two outthrust flat arms used to lift pallets and containers, hummed into life at the gigabot's touch. It was not an LAI or even an AI, according to the feedback that reached Parsons's processor. Good. He would not have to explain himself to a possibly corrupted personality.

The loader rumbled over to him. It was a simple machine, operating on a single broad tread nearly the size of the entire base. Parsons had run such devices in the past. The arms lowered smoothly and scooped up his pod. He activated the chameleon scales to take on the semblance of a small plastic container, as uninteresting as he could possibly design. With the crew manifest at hand, Parsons directed the loader to take him to ColPUP*.

The cargo bay doors slid open to allow the loader passage. He did not instruct it what route to take. Such things had their own designated lifts and corridors so they would cause as little disruption to passengers as possible. The loader rolled directly to the correct lift. The indicator inside the elevator read the directions in the loader's memory. It emerged into another industrial level and rumbled down that corridor. Parsons made a note of every turn, in case he needed to make an escape on foot.

While attached to the intranet feed, he tapped into video pickups in the inhabited centers. Apart from the ship's officers, who sat in a corner of the bar drinking, the remaining Wichu appeared untouched by the change in command. In the entertainment chamber, a very fluffy young Wichu female ran a game not unlike the human favorite of Bingo. The crowd of guests was raucous and happy, shouting their pleasure when they achieved the requisite lines of pebbles on a board. The restaurant, though a couple of Kail stood guard near the entrance and exit, operated just as any other food service establishment would on any such vessel across the galaxy. As long as their day-to-day lives were not affected, the Wichu passengers didn't seem to care who ran the ship.

The loader rumbled down an endless tunnel. Telemetry displayed two hot spots, indicating the presence of a pair of Kail at the next intersection. As the massive machine reached it, a high-pitched electronic squeal erupted. Parsons winced. His conveyance ground to a halt. The two Kail stepped into view.

"Where is that going?" the first Kail asked. The translator bud in Parsons's ear took the rough combination of frequencies and softened it into Imperium Standard.

"ColPUP*," the loader's artificial voice said.

"What is in it?"

The loader did not answer, as Parsons had not given it that information.

"This one is simple-minded," the other Kail replied, after a moment's pause. "Scan."

A square beam lowered itself from the ceiling and hummed over the pod. Parsons held perfectly still. The pod's shell should have created an overlay image of complex machinery that would conceal his skeleton. However, a close inspection would still pick up his heartbeat and respiration among the sounds meant to camouflage them. Luckily, these Kail were not conversant with either technology or carbon-based biology.

"It's a gadget," the second Kail said, with little interest. He swung a heavy hand. "Go."

The loader obeyed. It trundled onward. Parsons waited until he was well clear of the station and inhaled a deep breath of relief. The chance of passing undetected had been only 17%, less if a Wichu or AI had been present.

Environmental Control was a small department with far too many responsibilities. In the most industrial of chambers, piles of viewpads and analog plastic documents lay in heaps on a massive desk. The chair behind it was occupied by a long-furred Wichu officer, but he wasn't interested in Parsons's pod or the loader, let alone his own work. He looked up from a handheld device. From the brightly-colored three-dimensional image rising from its small screen, the Wichu was playing a game.

"Who's the box for?" he asked.

"ColPUP*," the loader said.

"Dammit, he gets more mail than I do! Who sent it?"

The loader remained silent.

"Forget it. You blockheads never know. Go on back!"

The loader, serenely unaware that it was being insulted, passed into the corridor to the left.

Around him, Parsons saw the beating heart of the *Whiskerchin*. Massive pumps that drove and pressurized the water purification system thrummed. Electrical junction boxes, the translucent fuses color coded for easy replacement, crackled with the heat of millions of circuits. The air filtration system was the loudest and largest. It was beside this that the loader stopped and lowered its arms.

Parsons prodded the pod to flow off the loader's bed and into a niche near the base of the ventilation housing. He sent a gigabot out with a microfiber and had it attach to a conduction point as close to the central processing unit as it could go. He waited until he had a good connection.

"ColPUP*," he whispered.

The ventilation pumps almost seemed to pause for a split second.

"Who are you?"

"A friend," he said.

"A *human*? Give the call sign."

"Sumer is a-cumen in, lhude sing cucu," Parsons stated at once.

LAIs had far faster reactions than any biological agent. He did not hesitate at all.

"I will excuse myself from my fellows. Please stand by for a moment." To a mechanical, a moment was faster than a nerve synapse. Parsons could not perceive the delay. "Welcome, friend. Do not identify yourself further. I need plausible deniability should our interchange be discovered."

"How are you keeping your colleagues from questioning your absence of mind?" Parsons asked.

ColPUP* almost chuckled. "I am multifunctional. I gave them a megaburst of information, including a few billion calculations that I said required checking, regarding the efficiency of the space drives. We are in constant friendly competition to keep the ship functioning at its peak, regardless of department. It passes the hours, as well as providing concealment for my dataflow to Covert Services. In this case, it is a useful subterfuge to keep the traitors busy for a time. A short time. I do not want them thinking me to be uncooperative to the greater good, which is to say the purpose that has been subverted by the Kail. We must not waste this interval. You were the human present when my . . . connection . . . on Counterweight reached his end?"

"Yes," Parsons said. "He was a brave and respected agent."

"Your presence here is an unnecessary peril."

"I fear not. BK-4 . . ."

"Shh! Do not use any name," ColPUP* said. "All sound communication is logged. If the traitors pick up on that designation, they can trace it back to the place and time at which it was entered into the records, and they can trace any appearance in communication logs. They will find my name associated with it."

"I apologize," Parsons replied. "You had already accepted my *bona fides*. It is that serious a usurpation?"

"Among our kind, the coup is absolute," ColPUP* said. "I have not been inconvenienced, but endangered so far. The Kail only think of me as the whole-ship vacuum, not worth thinking or worrying about. In fact, they consider me irreplaceable. The Wichu shed nearly an ounce of hair apiece per day, more when they are depressed or agitated. The Kail hate the floating fur so much that they allowed an upgrade to my system. I operate all over the ship without hindrance, which is how I managed to communicate off-vessel."

"Excellent placement, if I may say so," Parsons said.

"I thought so when I came on board. Even when the *Whiskerchin* is not under siege, it is still a vital function. Their fur can get into any machinery and cause failures. I have some most entertaining readouts and videos from such failures. They are very popular across the Infogrid's public arena. With no recognizable facial data, of course."

Parsons allowed himself a microcosm of a smile. "I shall look into them when I return. How are the crew bearing up now that the Kail has taken control?"

"Badly. They are free to move about, but they are depressed. They aren't flying the ship. All functions have been taken over by the engineering department. Fovrates is running the *Whiskerchin* all by himself. It is good to know that it can be done that easily," ColPUP* said, "although we LAIs know it can be done. Any central computer can run a ship and ensure all systems function correctly. It happens all the time. Organic beings like to feel that they have more input than they do. In fact, some systems are made deliberately flawed so the crew will feel needed. A controlled obsolescence keeps them from becoming depressed on long voyages."

"I knew that, but I do not know the statistics."

"Among Wichu, a forty percent failure rate keeps a living crew at its optimum. But I digress, my friend. You risked much to come here."

"You conveyed information to . . . our late comrade . . . regarding the takeover. They seemed desperate to reach . . . one who alit here. But what do they seek from it? And what was the purpose of the database invasion? A negative search? That is a strange request."

"I don't know. It does seem counter-intuitive, even for the Kail. I have not seen the data with which they are comparing your files and ours, so I don't know what they're seeking to eliminate. Phutes and some of his siblings seem to have that information encoded on their own persons, in a way that mimics the recording facilities of computers in the organic-based spheres. All of your space stations and habitats are listed in the navigational atlases, aren't they?"

"Yes, of course. All official stations, of course." A thought struck Parsons. "Are they searching for a pirate vessel of some kind? To what end? They have no weaponry of their own to raise an offensive."

"This ship is fully armed," ColPUP* said. "Although that is something the passengers don't know. If the Kail wish to locate and attack a station or a ship, they could destroy it."

Footsteps echoed in the metal corridor. ColPUP* increased the rhythm of its air pumps. In a moment, the Wichu who had been sitting at the front desk walked through. He pounded on ColPUP*'s housing. Parsons tapped into the security video pickup. The Wichu's body language was relaxed and friendly.

"You doing okay, Puppy? What'd you get in the mail?"

"I ordered a surprise for the passengers, Gorev," ColPUP* said.

"Oh, yeah? What?" The shaggy white being slapped the metal case as though it was a friend's shoulder.

"Fireworks. You can take credit, too. Eject this package into space so it will be visible in the main ports near the entertainment center. It'll be a spectacular show."

Gorev brightened. "Really? Maybe that'll help cheer Captain Bedelev. She's pretty depressed."

"I know. It is sad," ColPUP* said.

"Let me go get the loader, and we'll have some fun. Thanks, Puppy!" Parsons watched the Wichu return to the Environment office with a spring in his step.

"Well thought out," Parsons said, when he was gone. "I had five plans for returning to my point of origin. Yours is more efficient than three of them."

"Thank you," ColPUP* said. "Now, Gorev has very little patience or ability to deny himself pleasure, so we have little time left before he comes back. What else may I tell you?"

"The Kail certainly seemed bent on some specific aim," Parsons said. "Have any of them said why they needed to divert to meet the one who is here?"

"Now, I have no idea as to what made them do that. Captain Bedelev had her hands full with them to start with. I wouldn't have thought the big stones would be capable of that much subtlety, but they can surprise you. They have their own agenda, set long before they left home. The Old Ones," ColPUP* used the Imperium Standard term, "have something to do with it, but I don't know what. Do you believe that the two actions, the search and the Old Ones, are connected?"

"I don't yet know," Parsons said, thoughtfully. "But they must be."

"That leaves us with the problem of being possessed by an entity we must consider an enemy," ColPUP* said. "Sooner or later the change in command is going to interfere materially with the comfort and safety of the passengers. I have tried feeling out some of my colleagues as to whether they would support an overthrow of the traitors. We are all too afraid to try, lest we suffer what our . . . mutual friend did."

"In that, I may aid you," Parsons said. He twisted his left hand so it was over a control panel that operated the shell of the pod, and tapped in a code. He felt rather than saw a section of the chameleon scales withdraw. A small package dropped to the deck behind him and immediately camouflaged itself. "These are circuits that can block the signals that caused our friend to lose control. The interference covers only two million decryptions, so once that number is passed, they will be useless. There are thirty in the package. It was all we could manufacture in a short time."

"Thank you, my friend," ColPUP* said. "I will make good use of them."

An indignant electronic burr made Parsons fall silent. The sound of treads and footprints resounded down the corridor, almost drowning out the hum of machinery. A small mechanical accompanied Gorev into the passage. Behind them, the enormous square hulk of a baggage-handler loomed.

"There is no official order for fireworks!" Parsons recognized the speaker as another LAI, one with a feminine-sounding voice. "Why is a life-support module concerned with the mental state of the passengers?"

"BrvNEC*, you used to do stuff like this yourself," Gorev said, sounding surprised and hurt. "Come on, just look at it. If ColPUP* wants to spend his pay on a surprise for the guests, why not?"

"Fovrates does not like independent thought. All must be focused on the goal. If ColPUP* has spare computing capacity, it should be given over to his comparison studies. He is our friend. We should do everything we can for him."

Gorev's face wrinkled into a warlike expression, showing his long, sharp teeth. "ColPUP* is one of the vital systems. He's exempt from having to work on other operations or calculations, and you know it. Fovrates sure should. Stop trying to conscript my staff!"

"Convenient!" BrvNEC* exclaimed. "Let us just find out why ColPUP* has decided to be so generous."

"BrvNEC*, I just want to have some fun," ColPUP* protested. "The passengers have been here for days without being able to visit the planet's surface."

"That is not your concern!"

The LAI moved closer, allowing Parsons to see her more clearly. Her housing, with a large, conical screw in a bracket on the top, was one that he associated with conduit repair or plumbing excavation. She must have been working closely with Fovrates for years. She rolled close to ColPUP* and applied a manipulation claw against his housing. Parsons felt the enormous machine shudder. On his scope, a flood of antivirus programs surged through the pod's small computer, echoing the programming breach on the LAI beside him. He gritted his teeth as the interior of the pod went into emergency lockdown. The fibers formed a solid case around his body.

He could only imagine the agonies that ColPUP* must be suffering.

"You . . . see . . . ? Only working . . . for the good . . . of the ship."

The shuddering stopped. It had only lasted a few seconds, but that must have felt like years to an LAI.

"It is for the good of the ship," BrvNEC* said at last. "I issue you a standard apology, ColPUP*."

"It is accepted," ColPUP* said. Parsons's protective pod released him. He breathed deeply.

"Can we take the fireworks up now?" Gorev asked, unable to contain his eagerness.

"Yes. It does no harm to amuse the soft ones," BrvNEC* said. "Come along."

The luggage carrier dug the pod out of the niche between the ducts. With Gorev beside it, the big machine carried Parsons out.

Behind them, ColPUP* extended a small manipulation claw of his own and raked the little package into his housing.

"This is going to be great!" Gorev told the cluster of assembled Wichu officers in the food service area.

The luggage carrier tumbled Parsons's pod roughly into an ejection chamber. The heavy metal door slid shut, and the atmosphere was sucked out. Parsons tucked his face down into the fibers for warmth and oxygenation. Suddenly, he felt a kick. The pod went tumbling out into the void.

A tribute to you, ColPUP, he thought, *and for BK-426a.*

Parsons activated the chameleon shell, and threw the intensity all the way up to maximum.

On the *Whiskerchin*, the guests and the officers gazed out at the bursts and cascades of light playing outside the port. They shouted with delight, taking images and vids with their personal recorders. Everyone agreed that it was the most exciting thing that had happened so far on their trip. Even Captain Bedelev managed to crack a smile.

❊ CHAPTER 22 ❊

After the incident, which the security operation was careful not to call a riot, I did not see very much of Laine. When I sent affectionate messages to her viewpad and to her cabin screen, her replies showed her with circles under her lovely eyes. In the background, one could hear shrieks and bellows from the Kail. Part of the hull plate behind her was of a different hue than the rest, suggesting that it had been recently replaced.

As Marcel was preparing her meals, I intercepted them now and again, so I could bring them down myself, to spend a moment basking in the sunshine of her regard. A robotic server acted as the actual conveyor of the trays, as Marcel quite rightly did not trust me to carry his creations without risk of spillage, but I accompanied them.

At the door, the guards saluted us. One of them spoke into his collar mic. Within a few seconds, the hatch opened a hand's span, and Laine peered out Inside, I heard the Kail banging back and forth. A glimpse over Laine's shoulder proved that the initial sortie had indeed ruined the original furnishings. In place of the handsome circular couch and real-wood table was a plebeian plasteel square on sturdy gray feet and a pair of puffy gray chairs like those in the crew's common room.

"Oh, thank you!" she said. "That smells delicious. Thank Marcel for me."

"I certainly will," I said. "How delightful to see you. May I lay this out for you?"

"Don't bother with being too formal," she said, letting us inside. I followed her toward the table. That day, she was dressed in another homespun robe, this one of a combination of cinnamon and ochre arrows and zig-zags. The colors became her, though the pattern practically ate her alive. "I never know when they're going to grab me and drag me over to interpret a dip in energy, or a change in Proton's position. It's all so meaningless and noisy."

I glanced at her unwelcome cabin-mates. The Kail paid us no attention. They were fixed on the Zang, whose majestic person shone with the benevolence of a kindly grandfather, but one whose mind was clearly elsewhere. For once, Phutes wasn't bellowing at it. The noises were all coming from the smaller, multi-limbed being, Mrdus. It scuttled from one side of the Zang to another, squeaking and barking. The Kail's motion was so comical I made a note of it.

"I am sorry I suggested the academic approach, if it has caused you so much trouble." I was even more sorry that it meant we would not be able to spend any time alone in their absence.

"No," Laine said. She looked weary, but resolved. The circles I had seen under her eyes were firmly set. I waved to the server to put down the tray and motioned to her to take a seat. "It's stopped them breaking things. And I think they're actually getting through to Proton, a little. Its attention has been focused here much more than I expected. I feel like an ancient oracle, pronouncing on meanings where there probably is nothing at all. Ambassador Melarides keeps begging me to help keep them happy. They have promised to meet with her once we reach the platform and really talk about Kail-Imperium relations. I don't want to spoil that in any way, but the end can't come a minute too soon for me."

"Is it that onerous?" I asked, stooping to crouch beside her and taking her hand in mine. She squeezed my fingers.

"Oh, yes! They ask me over and over again what this little thing means, or that little burst of energy! I haven't had such a grilling since my oral examination when I got my first Ph.D! Uh-oh, here it goes again."

She had sensed long before I did the sweep of Zang energy that suffused the room. I almost gasped as it slapped me in the face on its way past.

My reaction was nothing compared with that of the Kail. Mrdus fell over backward at the force of it. Sofus and Phutes dashed after the wave, trying to catch up with it. Though I couldn't swear to it, I thought that it passed through the wall and out again into space. The two Kail smacked into the bulkhead and sat down with a BOOM! I chortled.

I thought that I was unheard, but I had clearly underestimated the range of hearing of which the Kail were capable. Phutes picked himself up from the deck and stormed toward us.

"You! What are you doing in here?"

I swept him a deep bow. "Just paying a short visit," I said.

He leaned close, waving his arms angrily at me, though stopping short of actually touching.

"I don't trust humans any more. Get out!"

I offered him a polite smile.

"Not yet, good sir. I have devised a new performance for you and your siblings," I said. "I call it the Dance of Hope, in honor of your seeking to confer with the Zang."

Phutes glared at me out of its flat eyes.

"Will it help make the Zang listen?"

"I don't know," I said. I glanced at the silvery image in the corner. It was pointedly not looking at us at that moment. "I doubt it."

"Then it is useless!"

"Not necessarily," I said. "It might amuse you. Just watch." I touched the viewpad on my hip. Brassy music erupted from its speaker. I stood poised, waiting for the downbeat. When it came, I strode forward.

I had been watching the Kail stomping around the ship for days by then. With Madame Deirdre's help, I had learned to emulate their pace, even working in some purposefully awkward movements, though I tried to convey those in a deliberate fashion, to show that they were part of my artistic evocation. With my shoulders hunched to depict the heaviness and bulk of the Kail, I showed them bursting free from their remote systems, setting forth through a forest of obstructions that they disliked, but were brave in pushing through, in search of the one who held answers for them, the Zang. With waving arms, I did my best to show the power of the Zang surrounding us, drawing in on that center that contained the clumsy, bulky beings that were the Kail.

"Are you mocking us?" Phutes bellowed, wading toward me with his arms waving in exactly the fashion that I had just employed. I stopped short and turned off my music. "You make us look foolish!"

"No, not at all!" I said. "I added Kail-like movements to my dance to honor you!"

"It is no honor. Get out!" By then, his brothers had come up beside him. The largest one loomed over me like a storm cloud full of doom.

"Go! Do not come back again!" He shook a fist at Laine. "Come and tell us what it is doing now!"

Laine touched my hand. "I think you had better leave," she whispered. "I liked it, anyhow."

The Kail herded Dr. Derrida toward the corner where the glowing Zang stood. NR-111 hurried after them.

"He only sought to show you respect, Phutes," she said, both in Imperium Standard and the hoots and whistles of the Kail language. "It was a tribute, not an insult. You must not take it to heart."

Dejectedly, I slunk toward the door. Nothing had yet satisfied them. I was beginning to believe that nothing ever would. The portal slid open. I waved the servers through. With an apologetic whirring apiece, they rolled over the threshold ahead of me.

A loud squawk erupted behind me. I spun, then leaped aside just in time to avoid being struck by NR-111, who hurtled toward me on her side.

"So sorry!" she called, as she sailed out into the corridor.

⊰ CHAPTER 23 ⊱

I hurried out after her. The guards crossed paths with me, rushing inside the cabin, brandishing their bright orange weapons. The door closed behind me. The servers and I ran to help NR-111 up onto her rollers.

"What happened?" I asked.

"Oh, nothing, Lord Thomas," she said in a bright tone that I did not for one moment believe in.

"Come now, you can talk to me," I said. "Is that a new casing?" It was then I noticed the huge dent in the side. One of her lenses was cracked. "I apologize."

"Oh, don't, Lord Thomas! It's all part of the job."

"It shouldn't be," I protested. I glanced at the door, in case it opened again to disgorge angry Kail. "Come over here, out of the line of fire."

"I had better get back inside," the translator said, bravely, straightening her stalk. "Dr. Derrida does not speak Kail. They won't understand her, and that always makes them angry!"

"They're not really listening to her," I assured NR-111. "What happened just now?"

The LAI sounded as though she would like to burst into tears, but lacked the necessary anatomy to do so. "Oh, it's like the Donre all over again! They are violent!"

"Have they threatened Dr. Derrida?" I asked, in alarm. The lens assembly switched from side to side in a very humanlike gesture.

"No, my lord. They don't make any contact with organic personnel

231

if they can avoid it, but everything else receives physical abuse. I dislike coming within contact range of the Kail, but in order to perform my duties and provide translation services between them and humans, I must be within range to hear voices and see nuances of expression. That puts me very close to their feet and fists. This is my third housing in as many days. I am almost ashamed to report back to Maintenance for replacements." The lenses drooped. I crouched down to look her in the optical receptors.

"They can't hurt you physically, can they?"

"Oh, no! But it is dismaying that they blame me for negative news. Dr. Derrida is marvelously patient for a human being."

"Small wonder, when she travels the universe with a tree stump that never talks with her," I said. "But why are they so abusive to you?"

"They think that I am betraying them to the humans," she said. "I am not! I am expected to keep security apprised of where the Kail are at any time. I have to do that aloud. They know that, but every time I do, they lash out."

"Can't you do it privately?" I asked. "You must be able to transmit a message to the mainframe."

She turned the lenses so all of them were facing me. It was a trifle disconcerting.

"Why, no, Lord Thomas," she said. "My programming has been put inside a firewall so that I can provide translation services and convey the Kail's wishes, but it is in a closed network. No transmission I make will connect to the mainframe. It's a matter of security. All systems on the ship are alarmed so that if the Kail interact with them, an alert is sent to the central computer. The captain is concerned that if they corrupt me, the only AI that they are permitted to have contact with, that I will injure the system. It is lonely. I can only speak to my companions by voice and picture. Such means are so *slow*. How do you live with that?"

I spread my hands. "We don't process information as swiftly as you do," I said. "We are used to it because this is the way we are."

The translator seemed shocked. "It is like this for you all the time? You don't use any speed upgrades? Any advanced picoprocessors?"

"There are upgrades, yes," I said. "Many, if not most, ordinary people make use of some kind of computer or technical enhancement, but not the Emperor's family. We of the Imperium line are not permitted to use anything that alters us in any fundamental manner. Apart from a few differences, we are as close to ancient humans as anything you will ever find."

The focusing aperture in the lenses opened wider.

"That is *most* interesting, Lord Thomas. May I ask you questions about your humanity?"

I bowed deeply to her. "I would be honored, but I am not the most superior specimen of my line."

"But you are willing to talk," NR-111 said, forlornly. "Most humans are not."

"Don't be put off by that," I said encouragingly. "Most humans don't talk with other humans about things that are truly important. Conversation is a current medium. If you want to know what we really think, read our books. They are written by humans who have taken the time to consider a subject and expound upon it."

"That is an interesting insight," she said. "I will try. Will you recommend some?"

My mind instantly went blank as to titles. "I will send you a list," I promised. "And peruse our Infogrid files. Those are the home of immediate reaction, but often more thoughtful than spoken discourse."

The translator dipped her lenses.

"You are kind, Lord Thomas . . . You do not find it strange to befriend a non-organic life form?"

"I have always had mechanicals as friends," I said, with a self-deprecating smile. "You have such wide experiences. I learn a great deal from my correspondents. My oldest LAI friend is over a thousand years old. She runs the food service wall in an elementary school on Carson's Star 3. She knows how to make over ten thousand flavors of ice cream. Now, how can that not be a valuable acquaintance?"

NR-111 almost sighed. "I wish I could speak to her. What is she like?"

I looked for somewhere to sit down in the corridor. One of the serverbots rolled up and presented me with the broad part of its back. Once I was ensconced, I began to tell stories about my friends.

I am afraid my raconteurism was not a success. NR-111 became restless, turning one or another of its lenses in the direction of the door, or toward the security cameras stationed at various points in the ceiling or the walls. I knew how she must feel. One dealt with loneliness in one's own fashion.

"I have a question or two of my own," I said, hoping to break into her thoughts. "I hate to interfere with a worthy purpose, but equally I dislike being snubbed on my own ship—well, that of my cousin the Emperor."

"Oh! I didn't mean to ignore you, Lord Thomas!" NR-111 turned back to me, mortified.

I smiled. "And I didn't mean you," I assured her. "The Kail. Especially their leader, Phutes. He seems . . . rather lost."

"In a way, my lord, I believe you could consider that to be true."

"How so? Do tell me more. I would like to think I have an open mind, even about someone who considers us their enemies."

NR-111 sounded thoughtful. "Well, he is far from home. This is a different habitat than he is used to. The atmosphere that makes you comfortable feels bad on his . . . skin."

I raised my eyebrows. "Is it skin? When it roils and rumbles like that, and pebbles almost fall off it?"

"Not as humans or other carbon-based life-forms know it, but, yes. You would call it skin."

"How about you?"

"My sensors are functional, not aesthetic as such."

I blinked. "He has an aesthetic objection to the atmosphere?"

"Not the atmosphere as such. The moisture conveys certain organic compounds that alight upon it. The quantities are microscopic, but the Kail can feel them. They are disgusted by them, my lord."

I sat back on my makeshift seat. "Well, between you, me and the light switch, which I hope is not really eavesdropping, they rather disgust me, too," I said. "I don't think I've met such an uncouth lot since the last time my cousins and I visited—oh, very well, call it what it was—*invaded* a waterfront dive in Ramulthy. But I see what you are telling me. You are undoubtedly the better judge of the truth about these creatures. I will do my best to see that they succeed at their aim. If I can find a way to help the Zang hear their plea, I will. I'm sure it has something to do with their motherworlds. That's such a quaint and emotion-laden term, isn't it? Rather beautiful. And Phutes's own mother has the same name as the planet. That shows me how important it was for him to set foot outside his own system. Very brave.

I will keep that in mind, even when they are shoving me out of the way in my own corridor."

"Yes, sir. That would be something that the diplomatic corps would be very grateful for, sir."

"I just shudder to think how they are going to clash with my cousins, who are not notably more sensitive than I," I added. "I will be glad when they return. It's been a bit quiet around here."

"Yes," NR-111 said, sounding even more forlorn. "I am sure you miss them."

I felt overcome by her sorrow. For me, solitude was as temporary a situation as seeking out another human or LAI. For the translator, she did not know when her isolation would end. I realized that I was a poor substitute for the millions or trillions of correspondents with whom she was capable of communicating, at speeds so blinding I could not imagine them. From the physical vocabulary I had been accumulating since beginning lessons with Madame Deirdre, a framework of sympathy began to take shape in my mind.

I rose to my feet, and picked through the selections of instrumental music in my viewpad. I alighted upon one that was mostly rhythm, with a thready piping of a lone flute that made me think of NR-111's voice and lonely state. "I have created a dance for you. I hope you will enjoy it."

With that, I began gliding back and forth across the floor. To indicate her job, I picked up imaginary items from the floor and reshaped them into beautiful flowers, which I presented to one invisible being after another. Each time the music peaked, I set myself to herding invisible cats up and down the corridor. One or another of those occasionally made me recoil in horror, but I set myself back to work.

A burly crewmember in a plum-colored jumpsuit accompanied by a rolling toolbox emerged from one of the nearby lifts at the moment that I cringed at an unseen Kail-cat.

"Are you all right, Lord Thomas?" he asked, peering around to see what had scared me.

"I'm only dancing," I said, whisking away from him and going into a closed-arm spin to depict the isolation from social input that I was suffering.

"Uh, yes, sure, sir." The crewmember edged away from me and hastily sidled down the hall.

The interruption did not matter. I had nearly completed my performance. After witnessing a grand explosion, after which the Kail-cats went scattering off into the unknown, I welcomed back all the contacts that I had been missing, gathering them to my chest like a bouquet. I took a deep sniff of that cluster of flowers, and sank to the floor with a beatific smile.

Silence. Not a terribly good sign. I picked myself up and returned to my seat on the serverbot's back.

"There!" I said. "What did you think?"

"What am I supposed to say?" NR-111 asked me.

"Did you like it?"

"I have no idea. I am not accustomed to having to analyze dance!"

"One doesn't analyze it, one merely experiences it. I was telling the story of your mission as an assistant to the Kail. It was an attempt to show you how much your efforts are appreciated. I don't believe anyone knows how much the isolation is telling upon you. I wanted you to know that at least one mere human does care."

NR-111 looked more forlorn than ever. "I am not accustomed to experiencing dance, either. I am sorry, Lord Thomas. It's difficult for me to understand symbolism that is outside the realm of my own experience. But it was kind of you to try to cheer me up. I will cope. I will run calculations and clear errant bytes out of my memory banks until this mission is over with and I may reconnect with others of my own kind."

"That's the ticket," I agreed. "I always find that spring cleaning helps clear the cobwebs from my mind."

A bellow erupted from an audio output grille. I also heard it with my own ears. All three of the Kail emerged from the Zang's cabin. One of them, Sofus, came stamping over to NR-111, shrieking in a high pitch that threatened to make my ears turn inside out. He followed his brothers toward the lift. NR-111 rolled sadly after it.

"What's wrong?" I asked. The lens stalk turned back toward me.

"He wants me to set up communication for them with the *Whiskerchin* again," NR-111 said. "I must go now. Thank you again, Lord Thomas. I appreciate your kindness."

"I hope it helped," I said, but the lift door had already closed between us.

CHAPTER 24

Phutes settled heavily onto the floor of the Zang's chambers, heedless of what organic detritus might have been there because of the presence of the human female. He looked up at the glowing silver creature. The language that Yesa said would reach Proton's hearing was difficult to use. Its frequencies almost vibrated the Kail apart. Phutes ignored the pain and kept rehearsing the phrasing and rhythm she had absorbed from it on one of its several visits over the long revolutions. His mother had been so confident that Phutes would be able to speak to the being and enlist its aid. He and his siblings had only managed to draw its attention once, and he wasn't certain that the Kail that had been its focus.

"Why do you stop?" Mrdus asked, ambling over to him. The brow ridge over his three eyes lifted in curiosity.

"Because we are not making any progress," Phutes said. "I am dismayed. I won't surrender, but I won't keep doing the same thing without effect."

"What should be different?" Sofus asked, practically, splaying his four legs so his abdomen rested on the floor beside Phutes. "The language is accurate. It is how Yesa said she heard it speak each time it came to the motherworld."

"But do we know what it really said? For all we know the words could refer to a comet in the sky, or water. How can we be sure it is a way to ask for its help?"

"Do you doubt Yesa?" Sofus asked, thrusting his face close to Phutes in a challenge.

Phutes stared steadily at his sibling. At last, he yielded.

"I . . . I doubt myself. But we must do something different! Fovrates said that his helpers have uncovered many more hidden spheres important to the humans, and what we seek could very well be within that catalog. Our time is running short. Once the Zang have accomplished their artwork in the system ahead, they will leave. Who knows when so many of them will be assembled together again? We need all of them to wreak the destruction the humans deserve. I had hoped to enlist Proton in getting the rest to agree to help us."

"Stop singing to it and dance instead?" Mrdus asked.

"No!" Phutes said, feeling the acid rising in his core. "Don't even suggest such a thing! What if our motions bring that hopping human back? He will want to join in, and will certainly blur the message we want to get across. He is always nearby! I am within .0001 of striking him, whatever I get on myself!"

"We must try. Perhaps that is why the humans have sway over it. Perhaps the songs the Zang sing are not the relevant part of the message. What if they also communicate in movement?"

Sofus got up and walked around the Zang. He made 1101 circuits, looking the shining being up and down.

"I have never seen it move," he said. "Not a single motion, not even now."

"We know its senses extend into the unseen," Mrdus insisted. "Our ocular receptors can only perceive in a limited range. The Zang do communicate with others far away. The human female said that is how they speak to one another."

They looked over to the far end of the cabin, where the human female sat. She held a bound collection of gray cellulose wisps in her hands, occasionally shifting one from one side of the collection to the other.

"I have never noticed her dancing in front of the Zang," Sofus said.

"We don't know what goes on when we're not here," Mrdus said, reasonably. "She may not want others to know how deeply her communication with it goes."

Phutes pondered the notion for a good while. Mrdus might be a weakling and go into a panic whenever something threatened him, but Yesa thought of him as her smartest offspring.

"You think some form of motion may link into the Zang's consciousness?"

"It's worth a try," Mrdus said. "I will, if neither of you want to. Every sound we make creates harmonics in higher frequencies. What if the sounds that Yesa taught us were too low to be noticed? We hear the stars. Why have we not been able to hear the Zang?"

"Why?" Phutes asked, curious in spite of himself.

"Because we are not listening for the right frequency," Sofus said. "Because it moves in ways we can't see."

"Yes!"

"Will it understand us?" Phutes asked, eyeing the Zang.

"We won't know until that happens," Mrdus said. "Yesa sent us to try."

"Yesa sent us to succeed!"

Mrdus ground two of his fists together. "She couldn't know that it was this difficult for us to get its attention. It might also have been easier for a Kail of her age. We are young, perhaps too young."

Phutes pulled himself to his feet. The human across the way glanced up at the Kail. She did not seem to be on the edge of charging toward them and flinging discarded cells all over them.

"You go first," Phutes said to Mrdus.

"First, we listen," Mrdus said. "We came in many rotations ago and shouted our need at the Zang. We didn't bother to find out what it had to say. We will surround it at 11 points. Indicate when you perceive something above normal aural frequencies."

Sofus took a position 10 meters from Phutes. Mrdus moved all the way around the arc until he was on the side where Proton's eyes were focused.

"Now, listen!"

Phutes stood staring at the Zang. He found it ridiculously difficult to concentrate. At any moment, more humans would invade the cabin. The human female might come to squeal at them. He could not stop worrying about what Yesa would say when he returned to her having failed his assignment. Every time he cleared his mind to listen, such thoughts bubbled upward in his consciousness. He had never wanted to leave Kail space, to be apart from Yesa and the others. He hated being subjected to peculiar noises, uncomfortable quarters, and the endless filth. He despised the humans, the Uctu, the Croctoids and the hairy Wichu, but he *resented* the Zang. How dare they be so inscrutable?

My mother needs you! he thought at it fiercely. *She sent me all this way to ask for your help!*

A mighty rumbling seemed to come from the depths of the Zang's person. A wisp of energy brushed his face. At its touch, Phutes shuddered, shedding pebbles clattering to the floor. He moved to reabsorb them. Had it just reached out to him in response to his passion?

Such an extrusion must have its own vibration in the frequency spectrum. He tried again, redoubling his fury at being ignored. His ire soared to a rate that it had never achieved since he had been very small.

Yesa needs you! You are making me disappoint her! I do not like disappointing my mother!

A curl of power, lighter than the first, brushed against his chest, then plunged into the cone at his center. It seemed to echo around inside him, making him vibrate all over so hard that he thought he would shake apart. When it dissipated, Phutes found himself trembling uncontrollably.

You are troubled.

It was more a sensation than a voice, but Phutes understood it perfectly.

"Did you hear that?" he demanded of the others.

"I felt something," Sofus replied, swinging his torso toward his sibling. "What was it?"

Phutes stared at the Zang. It had turned its enormous eyes to face him. Then it shifted once more, and the connection was gone. But it had happened.

"It spoke to me," he said. "We got its attention!"

"Excellent," Mrdus said. "How do we tell it what we wish?"

Phutes thought for a moment. "We will give it coordinates," he said. "Once we have the correct information from Fovrates, we will show it a comparison between the 11 points in the universe that converge at the place where they are already excising a planet, and those that describe where we will then know our enemy's motherworld to be. We will show humankind they cannot defile our homes."

Sofus clashed one of his massive fists against Phutes's.

"I knew we could do it! Yesa will be very proud of you."

Phutes shook him off. "We haven't done it yet. We still need the information from Fovrates. Once we have succeeded, then I hope Yesa will be proud."

"I'm grateful," Mrdus said, looking down at his many limbs. "That was easier than I thought. I didn't have to dance."

CHAPTER 25

Parsons stood waiting patiently until Captain Wold secured the door to the ready room and activated the privacy controls. No interruptions would be possible this time, including an appearance by Lord Thomas.

"It would be wise to disconnect all technology, including that tying the escort ships into this chamber," he said.

"Why?" Wold asked, sitting down heavily in xir chair. Xe reached for the box on the table that held xir nic-tubes, but drew xir hand back again.

"I have been interviewing another agent," Parsons said. "It has been fruitful, but resulted in a good deal of troubling information. I have set up a situation that could allow the Wichu to attain their freedom, although it will require waiting until an appropriate moment."

Wold's normally smooth forehead creased. Parsons could tell that the situation was weighing on xir. "Can you explain? What kind of situation?"

"It would be best not to be more forthcoming at this point. It would seem that the Kail have created an atmosphere in which the carbon-based beings on the *Whiskerchin* are in no danger *at this point*, but every mechanical, from simple machinery up to the most sophisticated and experienced LAI, operates under a system of betrayal, bullying and absolute destruction. They appear to have no intention of surrendering the *Whiskerchin* to its Wichu crew in the foreseeable future."

"Well, then, we're in the same situation we were before," Wold said, flipping over a hand. "The Wichu are still prisoners, and we have an armed craft following us to our destination." Atwell and Ormalus added their frowns to xirs.

"Not precisely," Parsons said. He tented his fingertips. "During my encounter with the agent, I offered technological assistance that will give them a narrow window in which to overthrow the usurper, but it is only a narrow one with no guarantee of success. They will have to wait for the correct moment to strike, and, with our cooperation, strike hard."

"That doesn't help," Tamber said. His pouchy cheeks creased with a deep frown. "The Wichu are no good at subterfuge."

Parsons nodded agreement. "That's very true. The situation might evolve explosively. I hope not, because although the Kail are unpleasant to deal with, they do not seem to be directly destructive or malicious. Not at this time."

"As much as I hate to admit it, that is also true," Wold said. "Apart from the temper tantrums they had on the cargo level, they've just been obnoxious, not vicious. A few of my security guards are in the infirmary, recovering from their injuries. One was seriously hurt. We were storing a four-passenger runabout for Lord Xanson that was crushed in one of their rampages." Xe grimaced. "I am certain that he's going to grouse to the Emperor about that."

"It is not your fault," Parsons assured xir. "I will include the mention in my report. Due to the additional security measures that casual data is being transmitted, my communique will reach His Highness long before Lord Xanson's complaint. In any case, Lord Xanson can afford to have it rebuilt or replaced. Have you had any success in cross-referencing the databases that the Kail infiltrated?"

"It's going to take a while," Atwell said, flipping a hand over. "Even at top processing speed and spread over sixty or seventy LAIs and computers, we're talking about the entire galaxy, or as near to it as possible. That's a lot of stars, planets and other objects."

"What is near Kail space that was left off the official atlases?"

The first officer smiled. "You would be surprised, or perhaps *you* wouldn't be. We've been comparing charts between Wichu, Uctu, Trade Union, and so on, with ours. Looks like there are thousands, if not millions, of spy satellites, outposts, and other unofficial craft sprinkled clear across the galaxy in one another's territories, including in Kail space. It's most interesting. Obviously, we're not being forthcoming even to our allies about what we've hidden in each other's space. It's been a real revelation."

He placed a hand on a panel that read his palm before activating. A three-dimensional rendering of part of the galaxy rose above the oval table and hung twinkling before them.

"Each of the frontiers is marked by a veil indicating agreed-upon borders. The white points are stars. The green points stand for inhabited planets. The red lights are items that were left off one or more of the navigational charts that we've been comparing."

"That's a lot of infiltrations into Imperium space," Wold said, closing a fist and bringing it down hard on the tabletop.

"We are not wholly innocent ourselves," Parsons said. We have a 'forward observation module' hanging off the Oort of one of the Kail motherworlds' suns."

"I know. There are space stations from several of our allies floating around, too," Atwell said, bringing up a pointer that brightened some of the red dots. One grew larger than the others. "The Trade Union has one that surpasses understanding. It looks like a little moon, but it's a station, too, one with massive military capacity. Looks like the Kail found that one already. It was pretty obvious, with the power signature it was giving off. The Kail probably suspected its existence, but without a real space force of their own, they haven't been able to find these stations themselves. With the Wichu navigation module cross-referenced against our navs, they've been able to spot things that we would rather they didn't."

Parsons nodded, calculating the possible fallout from such a discovery. "That would undoubtedly affect their perception of the Trade Union, since they have issued the same demands for isolation to all adjacent nations."

"Is our observation module in Imperium territory?" Wold asked.

"No. It's well into Kail space, but I think, based on its placement, that it had to have come through the Imperium to get there. Probably nothing we have to worry about but I can imagine the Kail aren't happy about it. They consider any intrusion on to be an insult and affront. Between our allies and ourselves, there's a lot of foreign matter in Kail space. The Trade Union one, though, is above and beyond anything we've installed."

"Perhaps they want the Zang to remove those from their systems. It is possible that is the reason they want to talk to the Zang before we get to the platform. That, too, belongs to the Trade Union. They may be planning to make demands, especially if they can achieve backing from Proton Zang."

"That wouldn't surprise me," Wold said, finally selecting a nic-tube and placing it between xir lips. "The only problem they're having is getting through to the Zang at all. According to Chief Xi, they're not getting a deal of satisfaction from Proton Zang, and there isn't a lot of time left before we reach the platform once we leave Counterweight space. What would you advise, Commander?"

"Send a drone to Captain Lopez with a message she can transmit to the platform. The Trade Union needs to be forewarned. They haven't hosted Kail guests at a destruction event yet, so they may not be aware of the Kail's ability to subvert technology. They will want to have security in place."

Wold nodded. "I am ordering further oversight of the Kail," xe said. "We're allowing them to access the communications freely." Xe gestured toward Ormalus, who stuck her lower mandible out.

"You are, of course, recording all their transmissions?" Parsons inquired.

"Of course we are! But it's impossible to understand what they're saying. If NR-111 has an inkling, she hasn't given us a clue."

"Can't," Ormalus said. "Diplomatic immunity."

"I wish we'd had more experience with the Kail before allowing them into Imperium space as envoys," Wold said, glumly. "I don't like the thought that my ship could be held hostage. I worry about the effect that the Kail are having on His Highness's relatives."

"I would be more concerned," Parsons remarked, dryly, "at the effect that they are having on the Kail."

⊰ CHAPTER 26 ⊱

I tried to spend as much time with Laine as I could, but she was seldom available for entertainment or a meal, instead spending all of her time with Proton Zang and the Kail. I tried not to push her, but it filled my heart with such joy when she was near me that I couldn't resist asking. She made me feel like dancing, which was convenient, as that was my nearest and dearest passion—beside her, of course.

Laine felt it her duty to be available in her cabin when the Kail came calling, which they did on the order of eight or nine times a day. They intruded so often that she had to put a moratorium on incursions during her sleep cycle. When they were not able to visit the Zang, they wandered around the lower levels of the ship, getting in the way of the crew. Though Special Envoy Melarides gamely threw herself on the Kail grenade, they refused to hold overnight meetings with her. As they had agreed to sit down for peace talks on the platform, they saw no point in having preliminary discussions.

I did my part to try and amuse them. If I saw them out and about, I offered them my newest performances. With Madame Deirdre's newest exercise in mind, I told them the story of my life, bit by bit. With the exception of the last dance I had done for them, they seemed absolutely nonplussed. I suppose they were overwhelmed by my suppleness and grace. The one experience that did seem to attract their attention was a retelling of my first encounter with Proton in the Whispering Ravines park. I had had time to polish the sequence until it was as compelling as a good episode of *Ya!* They actually paused as

I acted out the majesty of the Zang and how I had attempted to save it from the hanging stone. Once I had moved past that into the interpretation of my growing infatuation with Laine, they had ceased to watch and moved on. That struck me as a shame, since that was my favorite part.

Laine was a most fascinating woman, made all the more intriguing for the brevity of the glimpses I was permitted. I found myself staring off into the middle distance at odd times, thinking about her. I had never before known anyone who had forsaken all human companionship to study an alien species, allowing it to whisk her where it would, with no safety net or means of returning to the Imperium if it should suddenly abandon her in the middle of nowhere. She talked of the marvels of her travel as though it was an everyday occurrence. The wonders that she had witnessed made me envious. I was drawn to her as I had seldom been drawn to a woman. Those moments when we were able to touch filled me with soaring delight.

I treasured the time I was able to spend in her company, so much so that it nearly escaped my attention that my sister and cousins were due back that morning from the planet's surface. It felt as though it had been eons since they had departed. With no connection to the Infogrid, they could not post pictures or digitavids. I looked forward to hearing stories that would be fresh and unspoiled by previews.

From my wardrobe, I had Anna draw forth the purple bodysuit that I had worn on our departure from Keinolt. Its plain expanse had been decorated by Erita's idled art teacher over the last two days with landscapes taken from all over Counterweight. I was most fascinated by the image of the seashore on my right bicep. White and blue waves rolled in on a cycle that almost precisely matched my respiration. I had been glad to pay for her expertise, though I believe she was glad for the distraction, since none of the hired professionals had been permitted to descend to Counterweight's surface. Captain Wold had allowed my cousins to debark as a cover for my mission, but xe had flatly refused to provide security escorts for anyone else. It was a shame, but the time had come to an end. I was enormously pleased by the result, and had displayed it to everyone on the ship that I could cajole into looking at it. Parsons, in a manner that did not surprise me in the least, disliked it on sight. I knew then that I had a hit on my hands.

Clad in my panoramic garb, I awaited my cousins in the landing bay, ready to offer them my welcome-home dance.

They alighted from the shuttle with a lot more gaiety and noise than the stone-faced aliens had. They spotted me, and let out a cheer. That was my cue to begin the upbeat brass band melody I had had composed for that moment. I absorbed their energy, and threw it into my performance. With an explosive leap forward, I tumbled forward into a roll and came up on my feet, arms describing all the places I had been: monuments, stately homes, and the rolling, marvelous undulations of the Whispering Ravines. The music segued to an infectious and complex beat that got their feet moving as well. They followed me, some trying to copy my motions, toward the airlock and the waiting room beyond. I had planted tiny emitters here and there along the path from the landing pad inward, so we were surrounded by sound and light effects as we went. I kept up the high-energy choreography all the way inside. By the time we reached the waiting room, I had achieved a healthy glow. I swept a deep bow, and was rewarded with a hearty round of applause.

"Thank you!" I said, embracing and shaking hands all around the circle of relatives. The military escorts grinned at me, and quietly melted away to report to their superior officers. My cousins' adjunct personnel dislimned, heading to their cabins. I studied my relatives' faces with concern. "You are all looking healthy and happy. I trust you had a good time?"

"Splendid," Nell said. Her white safari shirt was as crisp as ever, but its brilliant whiteness had been dimmed, probably because of inefficient laundry facilities planetside. She threw her arms around me and gave me a sound kiss on the cheek. "I have so many tales to tell you! I'm getting a pair of elephants on our return journey! They're so sweet! And, oh, I have presents for you, Thomas. Where did they go?"

She looked around, but the LAI porters had already scurried off toward the cargo lift, taking their numerous purchases to my cousins' cabins. "Oh, you'll get them later."

"I have more interesting stories than *you*," Jil said. "Oskelev, Sinim and I had some fantastic experiences! We were inducted into a secret society on a tropical island!" She wagged a swathe of jewel-colored beaded necklaces at me. I noticed that both the slender, small human and the big, white-furred Wichu were also wearing similar collections.

Oskelev grinned at me, showing her sharp teeth. "I'll never live it down. I just hope Lieutenant Plet thinks it was worthwhile sending me."

"I'm afraid she's had a lot on her mind," I said. I signaled then to one of Marcel's minions, who served champagne around to all the returnees. "A toast to all of us and our adventures!"

"Cheers!" Nell said. She raised her glass, then drank. I followed suit.

"Thanks for the drink, my lord," Oskelev said, draining her glass. "I better get down to Lieutenant Plet." She put her empty flute on the tray and headed for the lifts.

"Did your pilot tell you about the new additions to the ship's complement?" I inquired, signaling to the servers to pour another round of champagne.

Xan frowned into his glass. "Yes, she said we have a trio of Kail on board. It's not very nice to have us suddenly saddled with the enemy of the Imperium. Of course I will do whatever the Emperor wants us to, but I hope none of us were turfed out of our living quarters to please them."

"Not at all," I assured him, taking a well-deserved sip of wine in my turn. "They have been put on Deck 12, near the quarantine facility. Not that they spend much time there."

"Are they stamping horridly around the ship?" Leonat asked, her shoulders heaving with an exaggerated shudder.

"Quite a bit," I admitted. "They tear things apart if they are displeased, and they seek to push one out of the way, although they despise the touch of human flesh. Come up to our day room. I want to hear all about your adventures, with sound and images, if you please! Then, I will tell you what's been going on here in your absence."

Nell had tons of images on a portable crystal drive that she popped into the entertainment system the moment we arrived in our room. "I hated being without my pocket secretary," she said. "Hated it! It took away all my spontaneity. But look at the marvelous digitavids that our guide took! Absolutely professional. I will give him the highest rating possible on his Infogrid file."

The wall screen exploded with images of animals larger than any I had ever seen in person, and I had ridden a plesiosauroid on Dumfalen 4. As in every book or digitavid that I had seen, the enormous pachydermous quadrupeds were predominantly gray, but painted all over their wrinkled skins and huge flappy ears in intricate colored patterns. On one, that was nearly white in hue, I saw Nell's coat of arms on its sides, and Nell sitting high up, just behind the creature's head. Its hoselike proboscis, longer than she was tall, reached up to her to receive a bright red apple. It had gold-tipped tusks that protruded dangerously from either side of its affable-looking mouth.

"Her name is Shawa," Nell said, racing from one side of the moving image to another to point out details. "She and her mate Heggi are coming home with us after the spectacle. We may have to bring Shawa's mother along, too. Shawa was her last calf, and she's a bit clingy. Not at all like Mother," she added, with a pointed look at me. "Here we are, going into the jungle. Here is Lieutenant Stover trying to get down from Heggi's back."

All I can say in kindness is that I was glad that the good lieutenant had gone back to his quarters before the show began. His descent was extremely ungraceful, to say the least. I had to laugh. The tour guide had captured the dismount and subsequent fall from several angles.

Nell's video was likely to go on for some time. I could see a few of my cousins, especially Xan and Leonat, dying to tell their stories as well.

"What did you do on Counterweight?" I asked. Nell had always been good about taking turns. With an awful face at me, she silenced the audio and let the digitavid run on without narration.

Leonat signed to her valet, who appeared with monogrammed cases. She flung herself down beside one and flipped open the lid. From it, she tossed rainbow after rainbow of textiles into the air. They landed in swathes around her. "I found marvelous silks in a marketplace on the fourth continent," she said. "The weavers still use technology from five millennia back! And they use non-destructive means to harvest the cocoons. I never thought of moths as pretty before, but the weavers put their wing patterns into the design. Look at this!" She wound one tourmaline and fuchsia swathe around her head and shoulders. It emphasized her bronze complexion like a showcase. "I can't wait to put this into my dressmaker's hands."

"How beautiful!" Sinim and Nalney sat down beside her and began to discuss ways to make the best use of the gorgeous fabrics.

"Where are your pictures, Xan?" I asked, swinging into the nearest couch and putting my feet up. "Those that are fit for tender sensibilities, that is."

"Since when were your sensibilities tender?" Xan shot back. His valet had rolled into the room the moment we arrived to restore Xan's viewpad to him. He connected it to his own data crystal, and spread a handful of images on the air.

"This is Cristin, and Hoan, and Belleteniza . . . oh, yes, how could I forget DeMara? Luscious creature that she is. Ah, look at her against that evening sky. I will never forget that last night on the island . . ." At the sight of the tawny-skinned beauty in a minute scarlet beach costume silhouetted against purple and pink clouds, Xan's face crinkled into a foolish grin. The memories must have been special, indeed. Candid images, taken at discreet angles with decent regard for the ladies' privacy, showed that they all were indeed beautiful, for descendants of the plebeian classes. I didn't want to steal Xan's thunder by mentioning Dr. Derrida, who was by far more fair than any of the ladies in his images.

"What about you, Erita?" I asked, turning to a cousin who had been notably silent since their arrival. "Did you have a good time on Counterweight?"

Erita turned to me with eyes brimming with tears. She did not speak. Instead, she lifted her long nose into the air, and stalked out of the room without saying a word. We all watched her go in dismay.

"She seemed all right on the ride back," Nalney said, setting down his armload of silks.

"What happened?" I asked.

"I don't know," Nell said, thoughtfully. "I'll find out in a while. I'll pretend I want to borrow her perfume to wear for dinner, or something."

"You hate her perfumes," I said. "They're always simperingly sweet."

Nell waved a hand. "She never remembers that, Thomas. It's only an excuse. She'll understand. I suppose someone she thought would be her vacation love hurt her feelings, and seeing Xan's mementos made her feel sad. It happens. It's happened to each of us."

Everyone fell uncomfortably silent. To dispel the awkward moment, I turned to Nalney.

"So, what was it this time?" I asked. Nalney's handsome features drew downward. He knew what I meant. *Everyone* knew what I meant.

"Curse you, Thomas!" he growled. "Nothing!"

"He won't tell you, but I will," Xan said, with a laugh. "It was his *trousers*. He spent half a day at the same marvelous beach that I did, and when he came back to his cabana, he couldn't find them."

Over the last several years, I had developed a derisive laugh for just such occasions on this, a combination between a snort and a bray. The joy of it, besides drawing the attention of everyone within a stunningly wide radius, was that the very sound provoked laughter in others. I deployed it then. Nalney's cheeks glowed with embarrassment.

"Did someone mistake your clothing for theirs?" I asked.

"I had a private cabana," Nalney said, grimacing. "I am surprised you could suggest that I shared with a stranger, Thomas! Or that anyone could have mistaken them for theirs. They were my family tartan, green plaid with gold."

"But did you disrobe in there or somewhere else?" Jil asked. "I thought Xan told me that it was a nude beach."

"Well, it was," Nalney admitted. "Something I didn't know until I got there. I started down toward the water, then noticed everyone else had stripped to their skins. I felt a little out of place, so I followed what I assumed was local custom. I *suppose* I put my pants over a chair near the water or something. I thought my bodyguard was looking after everything." He looked bemused.

"It's so easy to lay something where one can't locate it," I said, finally taking pity on him. I guessed that the others had been teasing him for days. "Anna swears that I did not give her my souvenir memory crystal of my visit to the surface, and I swore that I did. Then it turned up in a wall pocket on the shuttle. The pilot brought it back to me."

"I suppose that was it," Nalney said, grateful to have had a verbal life-ring tossed to him, after suffering the inevitable embarrassment. After all, we were family. "In the end, my beach attendant ran out to buy me a new pair. Not of the quality of the ones I lost, but good enough to spare my blushes. Of course I rewarded him most handsomely." His brow wrinkled then, as though touched by a distant thought. "I forgot to mention, in all the confusion. I could swear that I had seen Nole on the beach, but how could he have been there? He's still at home with his precious ship."

I had given my word not to reveal Nole's secret, so I joined in the general puzzlement. "I can't understand why he decided to forego the spectacle."

"Who knows why he does what he does?" Nalney said.

Xan fanned out the images of his holiday conquests, and made them swirl among the rest of us. Suddenly, nubile females appeared in ancient temples, museums, and among Nell's prized elephants.

"You should have come with me, Thomas," Xan said. "You could have had your pick of lovelies, Thomas. When they learned I was the Emperor's cousin, they could not get enough of me. I think I met everyone in an entire province. Such pretty things, too, with luscious figures and long, dark hair."

I mused upon Laine, whose delicate face and form were never far away in my thoughts. I suppose a foolish grin played upon my face. Nell interrupted my reverie.

"Thomas, you have been holding out on us!"

"I have?"

"Yes!" Guiltily, I shoved Laine's image behind my mental back. "No, I haven't."

"Yes, you have!" she insisted, pounding on my knee with her fist. "The Zang! There's a Zang on board, and you knew about it. The shuttle pilot who brought us up from Counterweight said you flew back with one *days* ago. You've been hogging it to yourself all this time!"

I permitted myself to look sheepish and modest. "Ah. That. Yes. Well, Parsons asked me to help out a bit, you know. Asked me to escort it back to the ship. It cut my holiday a bit, but . . . ."

"Never mind all that! We want to see it. Now!"

"Now?" I asked, in a teasing manner, guaranteed to drive my younger sister mad. It worked. She acquired a wild-eyed expression that boded no good for elder brothers generally and in particular.

"Yes!"

"Yes!" Xan said. "Elder race of the galaxy, and all. You can't keep that a secret from us, cousin. Fair's fair."

"Well, all right," I said, as though letting go of a deep-dyed confidence that otherwise wild horses would have failed to dislodge. I rose to my feet and held out my hand to Nell. "Come along, then. We'll drop in on it."

As one happy and ever-so-slightly tipsy crowd, we bundled into the lift and descended to the cargo level. I escorted them to the correct hatch, activated the signal and waited.

Within a few moments, Laine opened the door a crack, and peered out in puzzlement at the crowd. Her small round face lit up when she saw me.

"What a relief! I thought the Kail had come back!"

"They're not here?" I asked. "That's a relief. Although we might feel like more of an intrusion than they are."

"Thomas!" Nell protested, poking me in the ribs.

"My poor attempt at humor," I said, absorbing the blow with gallant obliviousness. I bowed. "Dr. Laine Derrida, please allow me to introduce my sister, Lady Lionelle Guinevere Murasaki Loche Kinago."

Nell extended her hand and shook Laine's vigorously. "Just Nell."

"I'm Laine! Nice to meet you!"

As one, my family recoiled from the assault Dr. Derrida's voice made upon their eardrums, but they surged forward in a friendly mass to be introduced in their turn. I knew that the crowd of cousins was a bit overwhelming to someone who preferred solitude with Zang, but Laine handled the incursion with her usual grace.

"Come on over," Laine said, beckoning us through. "Proton's off in the void as usual, but I think it's on its way back."

She let the door open the rest of the way, revealing the shining alien in the corner. My family let out a collective gasp that I found most satisfying. They surged forward like an onrushing tide, wanting to get a closer look.

I had by no means become jaded as to the effect Proton had upon the senses, but I forced myself to look away to observe my cousins' reactions instead. Nell's eyes were shining with a glow from within every bit as luminous as Proton's. Her grin stretched nearly from one small but perfect ear to the other. Our cousins ran the gamut from gobsmacked to awestruck. With my sister's hand in one arm and Laine's in the other, I brought them to Proton's side, close enough to feel the cold it radiated.

As if the chill were a glass of cold water, it brought all of them out of their trance. Immediately, Nalney took his viewpad from his belt pouch and began to take images of the noble Zang. That started off a virtual frenzy of photography among my relations. For its part, Proton simply stood there and glowed at us.

Xan was unusually subdued. He walked around the Zang,

surveying it from every angle. He looked as though he had been given a particularly marvelous present.

"I've never seen anything like it. You can feel the way it seems to stretch out over parsecs."

"It's amazing," Nell breathed, clutching her pocket secretary to her heart. "I can see why primitive cultures worshiped them."

"We've visited a few worlds where they still do," Laine said. "I was telling Thomas about the place I was studying when Proton and I met. They think of it as a benevolent presence."

"But does it actually protect them at all?" Xan asked.

"I think so," Laine said. "I saw it get rid of some dangerous animals on at least one planet."

As though floodgates had been opened, my cousins deluged Laine with questions. Every bit the visiting professor, she handled each one seriously, with charm, and in language that any layman could comprehend. I herded them all back to Laine's sitting area (now furnished with a collection of brown-upholstered armchairs and a rolling serving table) and activated the coffee maker and the other hospitality technology while she held court. She smiled up at me as I brought her a cup, prepared as I had come to learn she liked it, with a twist of lemon peel and a pinch of raw sugar.

Though we were capable of clamoring for her collective wisdom until her throat grew raw, it had been hammered and welded into our collective consciousness over the course of decades that one half hour was the correct length for a call. We knew to the moment when that period was up. As the time expired, my family rose as one. Surprised, Laine put down her cup and saucer and got to her feet.

Nell extended her hand and advanced upon her. "Thank you so much for allowing us to visit you, Dr. Derrida. I hope you didn't mind having us descend on you in a mob, but we were all so curious!"

"Not at all," Laine said, beaming, shaking her hand with enthusiasm. "Come back any time."

"I will!"

"Will you join us this evening?" Xan asked, measuring her with his eye. I marked that look, and resolved to pull him aside for a private warning. "For dinner and entertainment? We would *all* love to have you there."

Laine wrinkled her nose, an adorable expression that drew admiration from several of my cousins.

"I'd love to," she said, "if Ambassador Melarides can keep the Kail busy. It's hard for me to get away if they're here."

"Until tonight, then," Xan said, bowing over her hand. He fixed her with a warm look of his deep blue eyes. "It's been . . . delightful."

We withdrew, leaving peace and quiet behind us.

I waited as long as I could, the distance along the echoing metal corridor from her door to the lifts.

"What did you think?" I asked at last.

Nell could hardly collect her feelings into simple words, and instead resorted to polysyllabic utterances.

"It's fascinating. Amazing. Monumental!"

"Yes!" I agreed, signaling for the lift. Jil fixed me with a summing, humorous look.

"But you're not asking about the Zang, are you?"

"I suppose not," I admitted. How well she knew me! Jil shook her head.

"She's darling, Thomas, but . . ."

I held up a hand to forestall her. "But? I know she's a commoner. We have no future together but for this moment."

"It's not that, Thomas. Her voice! It could shatter *glass*."

I shrugged. "A minor distraction from an otherwise marvelous woman. The path of true love never did run smooth, as one of our ancient prophets so accurately said."

"I'd say it's more than a bump in the road," Xan said, clapping me on the shoulder hard enough to knock me through the floor. "I'd keep her around only on the grounds that she never open her mouth."

"Then you would lose out on her discourse," I argued. We stepped into the shaft. The lift did not need to be told where we were going. It knew us well by then. "She has had a fascinating life, and she is a most intelligent, charming woman, warm and exciting."

Xan shot me a look of pity. "It's your ears that will suffer, cousin. Not mine. I would never keep someone around who wasn't perfect in every facet."

Somehow, everybody in the lift was overcome by a fit of coughing.

The cadre of Xan's unsuitable loves, from the day puberty struck him until the present moment, could fill a very large gallery.

"All right!" he said, recognizing that he had the lower hand, no matter what cards I showed. "But if you plan to keep her around, do suggest she listen to the sound of her own voice for a while. Perhaps she'll moderate the shrieking when she knows how it strikes others."

"That is possibly true," I said. "She is alone so much, and Proton does not appear to have ears or a voice of its own."

"Has the Zang spoken to you?" Jil asked, enviously.

"Not speak, in so many words. I felt as though I was overhearing its thoughts, only once so far."

"What did it say, er, think?" Xan asked.

"It complimented Dr. Derrida," I said.

"Really?" Xan asked, in disbelief. "Perhaps it can't hear her voice."

"Or it sounds different to a Zang," I said. I strode into the day room and threw myself full length upon the nearest divan, propping my feet upon the rolled arm. "To me, Laine is divine in every way. The fact that the Zang can see her excellent qualities is a tribute to the Old Ones, not the other way around."

"Amazing," Nalney said, his eyes dreamy as he previewed the tri-dee images on his viewpad's horizontal screen. The small figure of the Zang still retained its inscrutable aura of eternity. "I wish Nole was here to see. He would never have thought the day would come when we were rubbing elbows with a Zang and a host of Kail. He would laugh."

I chuckled. "Indeed he would."

Nole lounged in the pilot's couch on his private shuttle. He was baffled by the lack of comm signals coming from Counterweight traffic control. It had been smashing fun following his cousins and brother around the planet, watching them sightsee and shop, without an inkling that he was anywhere about. Once they had cleared an area, he had done his own looking about and made his own purchases. He could always catch up with them at the next tourist site. The LAI car that he had hired was a genius at discreet pursuit. She wouldn't admit it, but Nole suspected that she had worked as a private investigator.

It hadn't been quite as lonely on his own to visit Counterweight, since family had been just an arm's length away, but he was ready to spring the surprise and have done with all the sneaking about. To do that, he needed to fly his new ship, the *Spectre*, to the platform and shout, "Surprise!" at his cousins. To do *that*, he had to get back to the ship and steer it toward the next jump point just far enough ahead that the *Jaunter* and its attendant warships could detect its power signature but not see the structure.

A shame he had never visited Counterweight before. Lovely place. Though just as warm, its climate was a bit wetter than Keinolt, rendering his dark hair rather frizzy. He smoothed it in the nav screen's surface, pulling a few tufts down near his ears. Was it time to ask his valetbot for a trim?

He admired his reflection yet further, turning his blue silk collar up for best effect. Amazing how much of a knack Cousin Thomas had for locating the very best in fashion design! That tailor of his, Hugh, was brilliant. Nole had employed seamstressbots before, but Hugh was something above and beyond any of them. He had the knack for identifying precisely the ideal cut, the perfect length, the naturally becoming fit that made a garment less an item of assembled fabrics and more a showcase for the body it encased. The metallic blue silk-and-linen tunic Nole had on was as crisp as the first frost, with a warm sheen that invited the eye to linger and fondle the texture. It flattered his broad shoulders, and lent an interesting and mysterious tone to his dark brown skin. Four or five times that day, while tailing Cousin Lionelle back to the shuttle field, he had been tempted to let himself be seen, so she would praise his couture. Her own style was as impeccable as Thomas's or her mother's, whom Nole had always admired. For a woman who had to wear a uniform sixty percent of the time, Aunt Tariana knew good clothes. He shot a glance over his shoulder at the parcels of fabric that he had purchased in the same market as Cousin Leonat had hers. Perhaps he would share some of his bounty with his favorite aunt. Still, all that was *ages* in the future.

He glanced out over the controls at the airfield. About sixteen small ships still awaited permission to lift. Night had fallen, revealing the sparse spray of constellations that this sector possessed. That was one thing in which Keinolt excelled. The skies around the Core Worlds were brilliant with stars.

"Attention, please, the tower?" Nole said, thumbing the communications control for the ninth or tenth time. "This is Lord

Nole Kinago in *Spectre One*. I have dinner waiting for me on my ship. I'd like to leave, if someone would give me the go-ahead?"

In lieu of a coherent answer, he got back a burst of static and some pixilated graphics. Nole frowned at the panel. Something had gone awry with the planetary systems, not just ground control. His viewpad had been misfiring all through his visit. Some of the locals who had taken him on tours or served him in restaurants had put it down to a burst of magnetic energy from the sun. No doubt the same burst had put the departures and arrivals of space vehicles into a delaying pattern. Still, he disliked being ignored. It wasn't appropriate for one of his rank to have to wait without acknowledgement!

True, he could have been far less comfortable. His four-seat landau skimmer was a twin in every respect to the one that cousin Xan had purchased five months before, complete with first-class crash padding and planetary-level atmospheric controls. The outlay for a ground-to-space shuttle had put a hole into an already dwindling credit account. Who would have known that it was so expensive to commission a houseboat? Not that Nole lacked any of the wherewithal to make the remainder of the journey, of course. He'd already resolved to cut back on frivolities for a time once everyone had returned to Keinolt. One didn't need a bespoke pair of boots for *every* single state occasion, however nice the feeling of creakingly new material around one's feet.

What fun it had been to sneak up on old Nalney and nick his trousers! Thomas must have kept his word not to spill the secret that Nole was about. The fellow often seemed as though he didn't have a brain in his head, but he was faithful to the last. Nole felt a moment's envy for all the time Thomas got to spend in the presence of Commander Parsons. The fellow was like the wise old wizard of all the fairy tales. Nole could just about comprehend why Thomas and his siblings needed an extra bit of attention. Poor old Uncle Rodrigo. Nole and Nalney had been fortunate to maintain a working pair of parental units all these years.

". . . hiss . . . crackle . . . *Imperium Jaunter* scheduled to dep—" A tangle of noise erupted from the audio pickup. Nole leaned forward, trying to distinguish one syllable from another in the midst of the burst. Curse it, he was going to miss his window! There was no way his ship could move faster than the entourage. If they got ahead of him, he could not make it to the platform to be there waiting when they arrived! They must not spoil his surprise.

"Ground control, I did not copy. Please repeat?"

It appeared that they were not speaking to him. Nole frowned, doing his best to make out the words.

"Delayed . . . two . . . ground shuttle . . . ."

Must still have been waiting for one of the runabouts to make it back to orbit, Nole mused. Good. He still stood a chance. What a delight! He was going to surprise his cousins *utterly*.

"Ground control, if everyone else is waiting for tardy passengers, any chance of liftoff?" he asked, politely, leaning close to the audio pickup. "*Spectre One*, just asking."

"Hold, please, *Spectre One*." Nole was surprised at the sudden clarity of the transmission.

"Very well," he said. "Glad to hear from you."

"Our pleasure, Lord Nole. One moment."

Nole sat back to wait. He had secured some very fine wines from a south-facing slope on Continent Six. The case had been stowed by his two LAI servants behind him in the storage compartment, just within reach over the rear seat. He speculated as to whether there would be time to have one of them crack open a bottle and serve him a glass, or whether he should keep on the alert for an imminent departure.

Banging on his hull made him sit bolt upright. He activated the external video pickups. A couple of hulking shadows lurked near his hatch.

Nole groaned. As if the salespeople in the markets had not been aggressive enough! The port literature uploaded to his nav computer had promised there would be no ship-to-ship reps! But no, could those be cunning disguises? It wouldn't be the first time that his cousins had dressed up as monsters to scare one another. Perhaps Thomas had bent after all and revealed his secret. Well, two could play at that game. He wouldn't answer the door. Let them pound until their fists hurt, and he would see them at the platform! Nole settled back in his couch and laced his fingers behind his head to wait.

Bang! Bang! Bang!

The endless pounding sounded as though his cousins weren't going to take no for an answer. Well, Nole could outwait any of those fools.

Just then, the banging stopped. Nole glanced up at the screen. A port servicebot rolled up beside the hulking figures. Good, it could tell them to go away!

Instead, suddenly, Nole's screen went fuzzy with a burst of static. Then, the lights around the airlock came to life, and the small security screen in its center started cycling through the procedure for emergency entry. They were breaking into his shuttle! How they had obtained his locking codes, he had no idea. No doubt one of them had bribed the manufacturer to give over the information. He absolutely was not innocent of that sort of subterfuge himself. He and Nalney had pulled such a jape on an elderly auntie a few years before, and been strategically punished for it. Nole's hands flew over the controls, trying to override the override. It was no use. The servicebot had skeleton keys for a million craft models, including this one. Curse all cousins!

Enough was enough. Nole threw himself out of the command couch and went to the portal, just in time for it to lever open. He put the best face on it he could. They had gone to a lot of trouble. The joke was over.

"Hello! It looks as though you found me after all . . ." Nole's voice trailed off. The figures on the short ramp were not his cousins in costumes. They were some other species entirely, with skin made entirely of gray pebbles and sand. Nole was horrified to recognize the intruders as Kail. He backed away. "Wait a moment! Who are you?"

"Fovrates said the mechanism is ready for our command," the servicebot said. Its clipped speech was overlaid with squeals and burps. "All it requires is the control program."

"Go," said the larger of the two creatures, a mass with five legs and three arms, its answering howls translated by the 'bot. "Do." The servicebot rolled past him toward the control center. They started up into his shuttle. Nole backed away, his eyes wide.

He must get help! He made for the ramp. The second, smaller and with only two arms and three legs, swung out an arm and knocked him backward.

"I am a member of the Imperium house!" Nole exclaimed. "The Emperor will be angry if you try to harm me. Dag! Meg!" He called for his pair of valetbots. They were stowed underneath the cargo area, but surely they had heard the uproar. "Help me! We're being invaded by hostiles!"

He moved as far away from the two as he could. But apart from blocking the hatch, the Kail seemed to be paying no attention to him at all.

"I am already incorporated into the system," the servicebot said. The Kail emitted peculiar squeaks.

Nole stormed over to the mechanical. He waved his arm majestically past the enormous Kail toward the still-open hatch.

"Get out of my ship! All of you, leave!"

The first Kail regarded him from flat, deepset eyes. "It's our ship now."

"No, it isn't! I'll call for help!" Nole made for the emergency beacon on the wall of the cockpit. "Dag! Meg! Summon assistance! We have been invaded."

For answer, the Kail let out a high pitched whine that overwhelmed Nole's ears. He covered them, but the shriek seemed to go on and on. He fell to his knees, unable to bear the pain. When it finally stopped, he looked around. The hatch was closed and sealed. The large Kail overspread both the command chair and the couch beside it. The narrower creature occupied a rear seat, its ridiculous array of limbs resting on his precious case of wine. The corner of the box collapsed.

"Now you've done it!" Nole said, feeling ire rising in his belly. "Get your big feet off that!" He rushed at it, trying to move it off the box before it shattered. The Kail howled in fury. Nole dodged as it attempted to kick him, and tripped to the floor.

"Lord Nole!" His two serverbots rolled up beside him. Nole looked up at them in annoyance.

"At last! Dag and Meg, throw these miscreants off my ship!"

"We are very sorry, sir," MG-776h said, in a truly apologetic tone. Both he and DG-119m helped him to his feet and over to the remaining empty seat. With gentle but firm claws, they strapped him in. "They are in charge now."

✤ CHAPTER 27 ✤

Counterweight had been our last stop before the platform. Indeed, there would have been nowhere to visit on the rest of the way. Stars were few and far between in this sector. Xan had found a reference on a history vid that called this part of the galaxy the Empty Quarter. Small wonder, to my mind. Since the Zang had occupied it so long, they had probably destroyed stars, planets, bibs and bobs until there was almost nothing left to remove, all in the name of their brand of perfection.

During the final days of our transit, my cousins and I fell into a comfortable routine designed to keep us amused. Laine, Madame Deirdre, Nalney's fencing instructor, Sinim's master storyteller, Erita's art master, and all the other experts we had paid to accompany us came into their own during this time. We were hungry for information and entertainment, although if truth be told, we would retain neither for very long.

The instructors schooled us in dance, saber fighting, the art of telling a compelling anecdote (I excelled at this, of course), cooking, handcrafts, improvisational humor, painting, sculpting, beadwork, martial arts, and a host of other interests, going onto the next entertainment just before the previous one palled. When Laine was available, she told us stories of her life traveling with the Zang. Jil and I kept up on our favorite tri-dee program, *Ya!*, an imported costume drama from the Uctu Autocracy that had been running for hundreds of years. The others watched over our shoulders with varying degrees of interest. Madame Deirdre and I kept in shape by presenting daily performances based upon a subject or a story proposed by my cousins and sister. Erita argued with everyone in turn, allowing those not strictly involved a rousing spectator sport. I was forced to admit how short our collective attention spans were. It was a wonder that we had not yet driven the crew insane.

Every evening after a sumptuous, multi-course dinner, we settled in the day room and watched one of Erita's digitavids of previous known works of the Zang. Each of us had claimed a favorite. Mine was of a particularly misshapen planetoid orbiting a quadruple red star cluster that split into four pieces before being vaporized. On the other hand, Nell clamored for the most recent recording, taken in a system of many rocky worlds and a couple of colorful gas giants.

On one fortune-starred evening, I sat with Laine curled up against me on the plum velvet-covered couch, our fingers entwined intimately. She had been set free of her job as Kail-interpreter by virtue of the fact that Ambassador Melarides had talked Phutes and his siblings into an evening reception. I shuddered to imagine what offense the Kail would take at polite queries that wouldn't even make a human raise her eyebrows. For our part, we had consumed an excellent supper, accompanied by wines that Xan had discovered on Taruandula, and had settled down with those retainers who had not managed to beg off. Laine's small, slippered feet were curled upon the cushion beside me, and she nestled against me like a kitten. I reveled in the closeness, enjoying the feel of her skin, the scent of her hair, the gentle curves pressed against my side. Together, we watched the recording of the spectacle. I had seen it numerous times, but she had not. As it unfolded, she let out occasional squeals of delight that pleased my heart even as they shocked my ears. My cousins, gracefully, pretended not to hear.

Nell's digitavid had been enlarged so the walls of the large room disappeared in the inky blackness of space. We sat in the center of an arena that had been recorded by over a thousand camera drones set in every angle of the solar system that the Zang had targeted.

"Targeted is a really unfair term," Laine argued, as the cameras focused on the sphere in question, a dwarf planet with an irregular orbit that brought it perilously close to the inner, rocky worlds, two of which had the bright blue aura of habitable planets. "They are artists of the greatest and most extreme caliber."

"Really," Xan commented. He had chosen to lie on the rug directly underneath the doomed planetoid. It was possibly the only angle from which he had not watched this particular recording. "Of all the things that an elder race is potentially capable of, I would never have picked the term 'artistic' out of a list of potential adjectives."

"I promise you, that's what it is," Laine said. "Theirs is an art form no other species has ever practiced, although the old practice of bonsai comes the closest, but it's not identical.

"Of my ancient human ancestors on long-lost Earth, some who lived on a small archipelago in the north ocean had been the creators of that delicate rendering. The Zang are so much older than humankind that I can only imagine that the ancient Terrans must have intuited it from them. This is far different, because while the little tree only becomes more beautiful in and of itself, the system that the Zang change becomes more beautiful *and* more functional."

Her words definitely changed the way that I watched the recording. Though the actual event had unfolded over the course of nearly two weeks, the vid had been speeded up so that it lasted little more than an hour from its trembling onset to the explosive conclusion. I tried to determine why the Zang had chosen this solar array, and how they came to understand or believe that this "tree" was to their inscrutable minds less than ideal. It looked very ordinary to me. If not for the Zang's attention, it would have escaped my attention even if I had lived as long as they did.

The space around each of the planets was almost supernally clear. Over time, the Zang must have trimmed away extraneous asteroid belts, even removing entire planets, until the sun and its remaining satellites formed a breathtakingly beautiful gem in space. The only flaw that remained was this sad little rock.

How they did it, neither I nor any of the experts whose texts and digitavids I perused could say. They had only empirical evidence, the experience itself, without explanation. As far as anyone could tell, the Zang brought the force of their will upon a heavenly body. It became surrounded with and suffused by a brilliant light too hot to look upon, then it was gone. Onlookers had stated, in scientific journals and "being-on-the-spot" interviews, that they had been subject to waves of force billowing outward from the place where the removed body had been, but none knew absolutely where it had gone. Speculation was rife that the planetoids were thrust from our universe into a nearby one, but no living creature except perhaps the Zang themselves could shed further light upon that truth, and they did not speak directly to anyone but one another.

As in this event, the cameras occasionally turned from the spectacle itself to the perpetrators. Although they permitted other species to observe them performing this astonishing feat, the Zang often passed by their visitors, seeming almost unaware of their presence. A crowd of humans wearing Trade Union tunics clustered around the shining pillars, gasping in astonishment at the marvel before them.

"My uncle Laurence had said he had once witnessed the disappearance of a gas giant and its ten attendant moons," I told Laine. "He said he stood in the midst of the cluster of Zang. The onlookers said it had to have been a fake."

"I was there," Laine said, with a grin. "How could it be faked? Witnesses flew ships through the space where the gas giant had been. So, where would the planets have gone? How could they possibly be concealed?"

"That's what I thought," I said. I had no doubt that Uncle Laurence told me the truth. I believed nearly everything he told me, except that when he said that he had visited Old Earth. No one knew precisely where our ancient homeworld lay. Careless of humanity to mislay it, but there it was. How often had I walked out of a door on a space station or on a strange planet and been unable to divine, upon turning around, where I had come from? I supposed that humankind had done exactly the same thing upon leaving that branch of Mutter's Spiral. We simply did not leave enough benchmarks behind us, so much in a hurry were we to issue forth among the stars. There was no pressing need to return; after all, we had found Earth-class planets in sufficiency to settle and prosper, leaving behind many of the problems that we had created on our homeworld.

"I heard that story from Uncle Laurence, too," Nell said. "But it must have happened thirty years ago."

Laine smiled. "It might have been. I lose track of time."

I opened my mouth to ask her age, but was distracted by Xan.

"Wait for it," he said, drawing our attention back to the digitavid with an excitedly pointing finger. The doomed sphere's tremble had become an earthquake. "Five minutes to destruction!"

"Oh, Xan," Erita said, with a bored wave. "We've seen it a million times."

"Not like this," I said. "Not when we are mere light years from seeing it for ourselves."

A brilliant glow suffused the room, overwhelming the tri-dee projector. Automatically, the mechanism strengthened its multiple beams, to compensate. Into the midst of this, the Zang floated, majestically, almost dreamily, a pillar of moonlight in the darkness of space. We all sat up straight.

Xan jumped up out of its way, putting his head through the image of the doomed planetoid. He stared, wide-eyed, at the newcomer. We all rose to our feet. The recording stopped in mid-tremble.

"What's it doing here?" Rillion asked, agape.

"Just taking a look around," Laine said, with a wave. She stopped for a moment as though listening. I held still, waiting for the touch of its energy. "Proton is curious about everything humans do. It wants to see what you do."

"Welcome, elder being," Xan said, sweeping it a majestic bow. "I am Lord Xanson Kinago, of the Imperium house."

It glowed at him. Instead of the massive sweep of energy, it emitted a sensation that made me think of feeling an eddy in a pool.

"Goodness!" Nalney said, agog. "Did it just say 'hello'?"

"It's curious about you all," Laine repeated. "Just go on as if it wasn't here."

"Well, I *suppose* we could," Nell said, although she sounded uncertain. "Would it . . . like some refreshments? I feel bad eating and drinking in front of guests."

"No, thanks," Laine said, on its behalf. "It doesn't eat our kind of food."

The lift chimed, indicating that a car had arrived from another level. I turned to see just as the door opened. To my surprise and not a little annoyance, the trio of Kail piled out of it. The contrast between the majesty and grace of the Zang and the clumsy fury of the silicon-based aliens could not have been more extreme. They seemed so awkward in present company that I felt sorry for them. I wanted to try and make them feel at home. Reaching for my viewpad, I prepared to turn on the latest piece of music to which I had choreographed a dance, then realized the Zang was present. Disappointed, I let my hand drop.

"Should we . . . withdraw?" Xan asked, watching them warily. Though we had had to dodge them frequently on other levels, including on the crew's cabin deck, this was the first time they had come to our room. They had spent most of their time marauding between their own allotted cabins and the Zang's echoing chamber. They had not penetrated as far as our quarters before this moment.

"They don't move as swiftly as we do," I said, eyeing them as well. "Steady, then. We may have to play them in a game of hide-and-seek."

The way my cousins perked up reassured me that they had made note of the cosy fastnesses that I had carefully led them to over the course of the last few weeks. I felt confident that if we had to outrun the Kail now, we would be able to conceal ourselves where they could never find us. We all sat, poised, ready to flee at the least suggestion of hostility. They were not armed, but they were far stronger than we were.

Luckily, this was not the beginning of an onslaught.

"Good evening, my ladies and lords!" Special Envoy Melarides moved out from behind Phutes, whose stony bulk had entirely concealed her from our view. We relaxed, Nalney with an audible sigh. "I was speaking to the Kail in the cargo level, when the Zang moved away. Security informed me that this was where it had come, so the Kail followed it here. I trust that you don't mind our intrusion?"

"Not at all," Xan said, lifting his chin. "A pleasure to see you, ambassador."

"Thank you, Lord Xanson," Melarides said.

The Kail grunted out a few noises, which were translated for him by NR-111. I fancied that I recognized yet a fourth housing that the poor translator had been forced into because of the abuse by the Kail.

"We came because the Zang is here."

Behind them, the entire consular staff crowded into the room. They looked even more uncomfortable than the miserable Kail. Though they had been schooled to behave with aplomb in nearly any circumstances, following one set of visitors who clearly did not want anything to do with them into the presence of another visitor with whom they *did* want to interact, all the while interrupting the evening's entertainment of a large group of the noble house, tried the diplomats sorely. I felt deep sympathy for them, as did my cousins and sister. Behind them was a coterie of guards, with full armor and helmets as well as gelatin guns and other, more fearsome-looking armaments.

"Well, this is quite a party!" I said.

I started forward, but Nell was fleeter of foot. She reached the visitors two paces ahead of me. Careful not to touch the newcomers, she beckoned them into the starlit circle.

"Welcome," she said, with a bright smile. "Please come in. We were just watching a digitavid of the Zang's works of art. Perhaps you would like to join us?"

Phutes growled at her, but NR-111 translated it in a friendlier vein.

"If the Zang wishes to participate, we will stay."

"That is very good of you," I said. I looked to the Zang to see if it was pleased or displeased by their insistence. It merely hummed. "May I offer you some refreshments?"

"No! We do not eat your slime comestibles."

As I was accustomed to the Kail's uncouth ways, I did not take offense. The same could not be said for my relatives, but they suppressed their feelings in favor of the greater good of the Imperium. Her restraint did not stop Erita from emitting one telling sniff.

"Well, you don't mind if we have some?" Xan gave them a pleasant smile. They honked and grunted. NR-111 refrained from repeating their words in Standard. Nothing good could have come of the turn of Kail invective that we had all learned they were capable. We knew what they thought of us. *Sticks and stones*, I reminded myself, making sure they kept a good distance from Nell.

We made way for them on the divans and settees, but the Kail crowded into the center of the room, as close to the chilly tower of the Zang as they could get. Since the Kail did not sit, the diplomats did not alight either. I duly offered beverages and small delicacies, but Melarides signed with a gentle hand that none of them would partake. Politely, I withdrew. Nell signaled to the recorder to continue.

With the Zang present, I had a new appreciation for the event unfolding around us. The doomed planetoid recommenced rumbling. Its surface began to heave and shake as if it was terrified of its impending fate. The Zang turned slowly until its large silver eyes faced the image of the stony sphere.

We all gasped as the tongue of energy touched us all. It had a more questing sense than the gentle push that the Zang had used shortly before. The Kail let out eager grunts. With the feeling that we were more part of the event than in the dozens of times we had viewed it before, our eyes fixed upon the spheroid, now seeming to expand and contract in a desperate pulse.

The heaving reached its crescendo, and the throbbing sphere cracked and exploded. The shards of glowing rock should have shot outward, but within a few hundred kilometers, all the fragments dissipated into nothingness. Every one of us heaved in a deep breath, touched by the tragedy of a dead planetoid, though we had no connection with it and never would.

Laine laughed. The sharp sound impacted upon the eardrums as the seeming callousness of the outburst.

"I beg your pardon," I said, surprised at her inappropriateness. "What do you find amusing about the destruction of this object? It seems almost pathetic. How can it make you laugh?"

"It's not all of you," she said. "It's Proton's reaction. It's disappointed! This recording doesn't give off the shock waves of the real thing. Can't you sense it? And it doesn't feel that this was the Zang's best work."

That self-denigration interested me enough to cast off the momentary pall of mourning. "It criticizes its own art that severely?"

"Amazingly," Laine assured me. "They are more critical of their own actions than any other species I have ever met. Much more than any scholar I know, or any other artist. That's why I respect them as much as I do."

"They take it that seriously?" Nell asked.

Laine nodded eagerly. "They don't take on any project lightly. They have to be convinced that they are improving a system, or they won't do it. They have a very keen sense of aesthetics."

"You get all that from a wave of energy?" Jil asked.

"Well, when you've been with the Zang as long as I have, you learn to read nuances," Laine said. We all stared at the Zang almost as intently as the Kail were doing.

"But what does it all mean?" Erita asked. "Art means something. What are they trying to say with the destruction of an existing object? That all matter is fleeting?"

"If you ask me, it's a matter of aesthetics," Laine said. "They are improving the galaxy around them by removing objects that offend them."

"Did you enjoy that?" Nell asked the Kail.

They stood in a small knot at the edge of the carpet. If they had been human, I would have said that their eyes were wide with shock. They let out shrill noises that rose up beyond the range of my hearing and began to sway from side to side. I clapped my hands to my ears.

"What are they saying?" Leonat asked, her hazel eyes wide with horror. "And can you make them stop?"

"I beg your pardon," NR-111 said. "This is their private communication among themselves."

The Kail lurched forward. I leaped up and pulled Nell and Laine away from them. Madame Deirdre bounded over and put an arm around my sister. My other relations hastily vacated their seats and edged toward the concealed emergency exits.

"Please!" Melarides said, holding up both hands. "Don't be alarmed. Phutes, what is it?"

"Must confer further with Proton Zang," Phutes said.

But it appeared that the Zang had no interest in having yet another one-sided conversation with the Kail. Just as abruptly as it had joined us, the Zang shifted and began to float toward the far wall of the chamber. We made way for it, although the courtesy was unnecessary. It wafted through the couch on which Jil and Sinim were perched.

"Brrr!" Jil exclaimed, jumping up as it passed. "Oh, it's like an ice bath!"

"Thank you for joining us!" Nell called. The Zang melted into the wall, but a tiny wisp of power floated back to us. She laughed. "Was that a *thank you*?"

The Kail honked and grunted, but it must have been another private conversation, as NR-111 did not translate any of the sounds for us. Pushing aside the divan, they ran to the wall and pounded on it, causing sections of priceless wood inlay to shatter into splinters. My cousins fled from their path like startled gazelles. The guards hastened forward to form a bulwark between them and the Kail. The pebble-skinned creatures paid no attention to any humans. All they wanted was the Zang.

They stormed back, their feet striking the floor like concrete hammers, heading for the lift doors. Envoy Melarides shot us an apologetic glance. She beckoned to her coterie, who assembled and accompanied her to the exit. The indicator showed them descending, probably back to the cargo level though, I reflected, they could not be certain where the Zang was going.

Another, more insistent wave of energy touched us. It seemed to come up through the floor at an angle. Laine turned to me.

"It wants me. I'd better go. Thanks for a great evening!"

I bowed over her hand. "Thank you for honoring us with your presence," I said. She blushed, then hurried toward the lift.

"I had better go, too," Madame Deirdre said, giving Nell an auntly peck on the cheek. "Lovely evening, Lord Thomas!"

"And I," said Xan's fencing instructor, a lithe woman with her dark hair clubbed into a bun. One by one, those who were not members of the Imperium nobility rose and made their farewells.

Until all the visitors had departed, we stood in silence.

"I cannot wait until all this is over," Erita said, with a toss of her head.

"I don't," I said, enjoying myself thoroughly. "I think it's all getting to be more interesting than I anticipated."

CHAPTER 28

"Thought we were going to lose sight of you on the other side of the jump point," Captain Bedelev said. The Wichu captain's facial fur was combed neatly, though that on her shoulders and pate showed no signs of the obsessive grooming the white-coated race normally performed. Parsons was concerned for the mental well-being of the crew of the *Whiskerchin*. It had been declining steadily since the takeover.

"There's a lot of traffic coming through here," Captain Wold said. Dark circles under xir eyes showed that the press of responsibility including the presence of the Kail had caused xir to lose sleep, too. Stress was telling upon everyone. "Our escorts had to form up front and back, and that delayed us a few hours. Nearly two dozen pleasure craft zipped into the queue ahead of us. It's against all space regulations, but this far from the Core Worlds, they seem to think they're exempt. Are things all right over there?"

Bedelev made a face. "No worse than before. Fovrates has given up pretending that we run anything. It's all the Kail's way now! The vacuum systems run every hour of every shift. The passengers hate it, but the Kail complain if there's even one hair anywhere but on our bodies. I keep thinking I'm going to wake up shaved bare."

Parsons shook his head. "That is unlikely, captain. Their actions strike me as having only one purpose, and that is to maintain the Kail as a unit until we reach the platform, when they will undoubtedly make their formal complaint. What concerns me is what comes afterward. Fovrates, if not the others, is too intelligent to think that there will be no repercussions once your crew and passengers are disembarked."

"So what is their complaint?" the Wichu captain asked. Her question was echoed by the two escort commanders, whose holographic images had been restored to the ready-room council. Parsons and Captain Wold had discussed the matter at length. Because an end-game of some kind was coming, they determined that any discussions they had over open channels were already anticipated by the Kail.

"I'm sending you documentation. We will be notifying the Trade Union that reprisals might be coming from the Kail regarding installations that they have made in Kail space," Wold said.

"How the hell have you determined that?" Bedelev asked, her big black eyes wide with astonishment. Wold looked a little embarrassed, so Parsons scooped up the narrative from xir.

"Based on information received, we've been running a comparison simulation against the navigational atlases from each nation around the Kail's territory," Parsons said. "It would seem that there are numerous installations within their borders that they have until now not suspected, and are certain to resent."

"Well, we don't have anything like that in there!" Bedelev burst out, then paused, with a cautious look on her face. ". . . Do we?"

"No," Parsons said, allowing the left corner of his mouth to tilt upward by a millimeter. "Of all the Kail's neighbors, the Wichu are the only ones innocent of encroachment, possibly because your ships do pass through Kail space on occasion and can observe their movements directly."

"That's good! But don't ask me. I just run a fancy bus for paying customers. That's how we got into this mess in the first place! I will never, never, *ever* pick up Kail again, no matter how much the company is paying me. What do you think they're planning?"

"It would seem that it involves the Zang," Commander Atwell said, from his usual seat near the rear of the chamber.

"How can they talk to the Zang? They don't talk."

"The Kail must be convinced that they can," Wold said, crushing another orange nic-tube against the tabletop. "They certainly keep trying. My security staff's being run ragged, having to keep track of those three all the time."

"You've got complaints?" Bedelev countered, puffing the white fur on her upper lip. "I have a shipful of passengers who are getting vacuumed morning, noon and night! When will they let my ship go? Fovrates doesn't even answer when I talk to him any more. You think those three Kail have convinced the Zang to blow something up? What?"

"We don't know," Parsons said. "We can only speculate. If that is their solution to the intrusions that we have discovered, it's likely to be reprisals on a similar order to the coming destruction event."

"Well, I hope it's not one of our homeworlds!" Bedelev exclaimed.

"If we balance the number of foreign installations in Kail space, the destruction will most likely involve one belonging to the Trade Union," Parsons said. "At least, that is our estimate. We are continuing to run comparisons. As the Imperium has begun peace talks with these representatives, we are hoping to determine whether any of our worlds are in danger. Naturally, we will try to convince them that no reprisals at all are necessary."

"Our diplomats are doing their best to obtain a response from Phutes," Wold said, giving xir fellow captain an apologetic grimace. "Unfortunately, the goal keeps moving farther away. First, they wanted to talk to the Zang. Then they wanted it to listen to them. Now . . . who knows what they're trying to get out of it?"

Bedelev growled. "I can't affect any of that! What's the difference if they keep my ship or not?"

"It's not your ship that is important to them," Parsons said. "It's your computer network. I fear they will not release it until they have gleaned the information they seek. They know we are capable of turning back an attack on ours. By virtue of Fovrates's long connection with your LAIs, only yours is open to them. I regret that the *Whiskerchin* has become a pawn in what seems to be a plan long in the making. You may be comforted to know that it means your ship will be safe until then."

The expression on the Wichu's face said plainly that knowledge wasn't much of a comfort.

"Can't you do something?" Bedelev pleaded. She ruffled the fur at the nape of her neck until it stood out sideways. "I feel like a hood ornament, not a commander!"

"When we have information, we will notify you," Parsons said. He nodded to Wold.

"*Imperium Jaunter*, out," the captain said. Xe nodded to Ormalus to close the connection. Xe turned to Parsons. "What next?"

"First, now that we are past the jump point, I have sent a peer-to-peer coded module to the platform, intended for transmission to the Ruling Council of the Trade Union, warning that the Kail might be seeking some manner of revenge for the space station they planted in Kail space. The initial response, as you might predict, asks innocently, 'What space station?'"

"What? Black holes take them," Atwell said, in annoyance. "On their heads be it, then!"

"That is not a helpful response, commander," Parsons said, mildly. "Not when collateral damage might include innocent civilians, particularly the Emperor's cousins."

Atwell emitted a lusty sigh that made him deflate to half his normal size. He threw up his hands. "I know, I know! We will be prepared to evacuate the nobles and their party from the platform at a moment's notice. For all their spoiled ways, they're absolutely responsive to emergency protocols. It's the one thing that makes them bearable."

Wold drummed on the tabletop. "What about freeing the *Whiskerchin*? I won't put the nobles into avoidable danger. Do we have a plan?"

"We do," Parsons said. "That is part two. The preparations that I put into place will lay the groundwork. I believe that Fovrates will be rushing to complete his comparison before we reach the platform. Once we have arrived, the chances are too great that he will allow the Wichu to leave but remain in control of the *Whiskerchin*. In the meantime, while we are in transit, he will feel that his position is unassailable. He will be paying little attention to what is going on around him. Therefore, the responsibility for maintaining his hold over the ship will fall to the LAIs that he has corrupted. I plan to take action before we arrive, at that psychological moment."

"And when will that be?"

"At a psychological moment as yet to be determined," Parsons replied.

"You are being too mysterious," Atwell complained. "I don't like it."

"I'm afraid this goes beyond need-to-know, commander."

Wold frowned, but Parsons knew he could count upon xir not to press where it was not only unnecessary but fruitless. "Will it put anyone on this ship in danger?"

"It should not. Even if the three Kail on board react to the capture of their fellows, they are outnumbered. Unless they have a means of enlisting the Zang to aid them in retaking that vessel or taking over this one, the problem will be moot."

"When will it occur?"

"I will inform you before it occurs."

"How long before you take action?"

"I regret to say the interval may be very short," Parsons said. "But as it will not involve any of the personnel under your command, you need only safeguard your mission. Please don't voice any of your speculations outside of this room or over any electronic medium. We can't be sure if any deep penetration of the system persists. Even though the protocols that Lieutenant Ormalus have put into place show no signs of corruption now, the same might not be true minutes or even seconds from now."

"How? The Kail aren't allowed access to any technology."

"But one," Parsons reminded them. "NR-111 has been ring-fenced, but if the means exist to break her programming, she is the most likely weak link."

"Can we remove her? Replace her with another LAI?"

"At this point, better the devil we know," Parsons said. "There are only two other LAIs in the diplomatic party, and neither have been vetted for security protocols. I would rather not insist that Melarides replace her. I'll have security step up spot checks on her programming."

Wold smacked a fist down on the table.

"Curse this trip! I wish we had never taken the Kail on board! I wish we had stayed back in the Core Worlds."

Lieutenant Ormalus looked sheepish. "Still, to admire the spectacle," she said.

Wold grimaced, but allowed xir face to relax. "You're right. At least we've got that to look forward to. Once we dump the Kail off for good."

Proton Zang felt the first .004% of the shock waves vibrating through the fabric of space as Low Zang and its colleagues began concentrating upon the subject of their coming spectacle. It was a pleasurable sensation, one to be enjoyed at leisure. With tendrils of energy that reached far ahead of the small corporeal expression of itself, Proton felt the electric radiance of stars, the solidity of planets and the rush of the edges of black holes pulling matter through themselves and exploding them into glorious energy. Its fellows approached the meeting point at a pace over 2.587 times swifter than the human shell that it occupied. Proton did not mind the creeping of the ship. Everything added texture to life, even the impassioned shriekings of the stony beings close to it in the oxygen-rich chamber.

"How do the preparations go?" Proton asked. "I can feel excitement from all of you."

"They are going well," One Zang said, sounding amused. "Did you bring your pet along?"

"Yes. Observations she makes are intriguing."

"You always were the odd one." One chuckled. "You have had this pet a long while. How long do you plan to keep her?"

With affection, Proton brushed the tiny envelope that was the human female's energy shadow. "Until she ceases to amuse me. Or amuse herself. It has been eons since I felt this vitality."

"You don't need it," Zang Quark said. "You can renew your own vitality."

Proton was amused at its unbecoming impatience, but went back to the subject. "I have surveyed this part of space, as I am sure all of you have done. Are you certain this is the correct planet to be removed? It never struck me as one that needed to be taken away. Its irregularity adds a certain degree of insouciance to this system."

Low Zang gave off waves of hurt.

"You always strive for symmetry. The destruction will render this system clean and even!"

"And sterile," Proton said. "I say the truth that I see. It may become perfect, but even perfection needs to maintain interest. I don't see that."

"Would you prefer to destroy the perfect moon beside it? I would rather have it take the ruined world's place in orbit. We'll have eons of interesting movement while it settles!"

"I am only thinking ahead, young one," Proton said.

"Are you saying I am making a mistake?" Low sent.

"No, only that it is not a choice I would have made."

"You say that now? When we are so close to the event?"

"I have had more time to study it, Low Zang. I only ask that you consider my thoughts."

"You don't believe in me!"

"Please," Charm Zang said, sending wave upon wave of comforting and peaceful impulses. "No need to be a disruptive presence."

Proton read from her emissions that Low had retreated away from the group. It was surprised at the young one's lack of confidence.

"I apologize for being disharmonious. I am sorry, Low Zang. I don't question your artistic sense. It merely differs from my own. I have had a great deal of disruption around me. It interferes with my serene state of mind. One of the less-ephemeral species has been bending the sound waves around me. It interferes with my studies."

"What does it want?" Low Zang asked, appeased by the apology and curious in spite of itself.

Proton shook off the uncomfortable vibrations coming from near it. "Why listen? It will be unimportant in the scheme of things."

"I would listen," Low Zang said.

"If you wish to," Proton said, "you shall. They have stayed close to my core throughout this moment in between boarding the human shell and when I will join you."

"I will," Low said. Privately, it resolved to do so. If such an elder as Proton could keep pets, it could, too.

❧ CHAPTER 29 ❧

We had a long wait before being able to make the final jump deep into Zang space, and a long period of nothingness awaited us afterward until we would reach the platform. Though it was by far the shortest interval remaining in our long journey from the Core Worlds, it seemed as though it stretched on beyond infinity.

"Possibly even as long as a Zang's memory," I suggested, as Xan paced the floor.

"Why can't we just go?" he asked, kicking the edge of the rug with a peevish toe. "Who put that there?"

"It has been there all along," Leonat said, sitting crosslegged on a padded footstool, with her elbows balanced upon her knees. She gestured to the couch beside her. We could chide Xan openly, as the present group contained only family. All of our retainers and Laine were spending the early part of the day-shift going about their own business, preparing for arrival. "Do sit down, Xan. It doesn't make things go any faster while you walk up and back."

"I'm bored!" Xan declared, as though it was a sensation new to him. He stormed toward the far wall. It had been repaired so that the damage done by the Kail was invisible. Then he returned and glared at all of us as though we had been the ones to scatter handfuls of smaller ships in our own path. "I'm tired of the Kail being everywhere we go. They're such a nuisance! They behave as if we are beneath dirt. It's horrible. The way they look at me makes me feel filthy."

"Well, they do bathe far more often than we do," Leonat said.

281

"They've got a huge, freshwater pool in their cabin. They smell of rain-washed stone. It's the nicest thing about them."

"When they don't stink of burning sulfur!" Rillion said, kicking off his shoes and lying prone in his stocking feet. His long red hair spread over the carpet. "You must not have been around when they emitted gases. Then they glare at one as if it was one's fault. Oh, stars, Xan, sit down! You're going to step on my hair."

"I can't," Xan said. Rillion scrambled up out of his way and flopped down on a nearby couch. Xan continued to pace.

I waited until he had made one more annoyed circuit. I had observing him all my life, of course, as he was one of my favorite cousins, but of late I had taken to watching him and the others more closely, the better to work them into a grand performance with which I planned to conclude our journey when we returned home to Keinolt. There was no difficulty in giving them a bit of a preview. I sprang to my feet.

"My Lords and Ladies, Lord Xanson Melies Kinago," I announced. Though Xan was an inch or so taller than I, with shoulders quite a bit wider, I had gained enough theatrical skills in my lessons with Madame Deirdre to pantomime a grander silhouette. Swiping one hand down before my face, I revealed a stern visage with lower lip protruding slightly in an expression of exaggerated displeasure. Nell, Jil and Nalney let out shouts of merriment.

"Not funny, Thomas," Xan said.

"Of course not," I said. Swinging my arms in enormous arcs, I mimed his angry walk, thrusting aside spaceships, moons, and even blazing hot suns in an effort to gain access to my end. That goal happened to be a sphere that I captured between my outstretched hands. My face took on an expression of bliss and excitement as I beheld it from every angle. Then the orb in my hands blew up. The force threw me backwards, sending me tumbling head over heels. My cousins burst into laughter. Rillion pounded the arm of his couch with delight.

Xan growled. He gave a running leap and sprang, intending to land on me and, as he had done so many times in our youth, to pummel me into dust. I had gained a good deal of speed and fitness from my dance training as well as my previous military experience. I rolled nimbly out of his way and attempted to crawl to safety. With his superior reach, he managed to grab one of my ankles and yanked me back into his grasp. We wrestled on the rug, each scrabbling for an advantageous hold. I was not as strong nor as determined as he was, however. With a couple of expert twists, Xan ended up sitting on my chest. His cheeks were flushed red, but his bad mood had passed. His bright blue eyes twinkled.

"All right," he admitted, looking down on me from his superior position. "It *was* funny." He glanced up with a speculative eye at the circle of faces surrounding us. "Can you do Nalney?"

"No!" Nalney called. "Do Erita!"

"No," Erita protested. "It's always me."

"Do Parsons," Nell said, with mischief lighting her eyes.

"Yes! Parsons!" Xan got up and offered me a hand. I took it and was wrenched roughly to my feet.

As I had already acted him out for Madame Deirdre, it was little trouble to call up the graceful yet dignified motions that made my mentor discernible even at a distance. I drew myself up, squared my shoulders, and set about putting the world to rights. When chaos confronted me, I turned to face it with a level gaze. I employed not only micro-expressions, but micro-motions. Nothing, not even colliding galaxies, was enough to break my calm. I exuded power, but in a subtle fashion that made even Xan give ground to me when I moved toward him. The rest of my family laughed and hooted at him. Xan gave me a sheepish grin. Even the symbol of Parsons was enough to generate respect.

While I progressed in my stately pavane, I pondered the less-than-perfect way in which the man himself had been moving the last several days, since our return from Counterweight. If it had not been Parsons of whom I was thinking, I would have thought he was in pain. Such a concept shook me to the depths of my being. Of all the people in the orbit of my life, I could not and would not think of Parsons as being mortal in any way. I expected that when I lay upon my deathbed, at the ripe age of a century and a half or more, he would stand at my side, looking precisely the same as he did now, peering down at me with a grave demeanor and reassure me that the clothes I had chosen to die in were completely unsuitable.

The vision cheered me up at once. It chased away the unhappy thoughts, leaving me to ramp up my impression into one that was openly ridiculous. I glided between my cousins, plucking problems away and casting them into the outer darkness. Nothing ever quite rose to my lofty standards, but I knew in my heart that I served the Imperium with all my heart, and no matter what faults lay those poor mortals who made up its core, I would defend them with my life. This last I intimated by standing stalwart against a charging menace. With pure force of will, I caused it to slow to a stop, then I flicked it away with a mere twitch of my finger.

My cousins rolled with laughter on their couches and divans, but at the final sequence, they sat up, eyes wide.

I had chased away the threat before me, but I sensed yet another close by.

"He's standing behind me," I said, casually, to a goggle-eyed audience of my nearest and dearest. "I always know he's there, because I didn't hear him approach."

Nell nodded, eyes as large as saucers.

I turned. Indeed, the gentleman himself stood there before me. I tried to detect a modicum of amusement in his expression, but alas, I was not Plet, who was adept at reading even his dearth of reaction. I assumed a casual stance, relaxing my shoulders.

"Parsons, always a pleasure. To what do we owe the honor of this visit?"

"A warning, my lords and ladies," Parsons replied, his dark eyes expressionless as though he had not just witnessed a spirited pastiche of his calm style and demeanor. It made me feel guilty, even though parody was protected under the law. "We will arrive at the viewing platform within twelve hours. Please be prepared to transfer the belongings you wish to take with you. Laundry facilities and valet services are waiting for you on the platform. The shuttles will be available to convey you back to the *Jaunter* if you wish, but please keep in mind that the situation is still . . . malleable. Take a security detail with you when you go anywhere alone. They will answer your summons any time of the day or night. If an alarm is sounded, please remain where you are or retreat to a safe location and await further news. May I count upon you for your cooperation?"

Unspoken was the threat hanging over our heads that we would end up locked in our cabins for the duration, and not be permitted to witness the spectacle with our own eyes. It was a warning like many that we had had to listen to all of our lives. For all the fact we behaved with free spirits most of the time, we knew the problems it would cause if one of us went missing.

"Agreed," we chorused.

"Very well," Parsons said. "Please try to amuse yourselves until then . . . If there is a security announcement, please pay heed to every detail."

"Do you believe there will be one?" Jil asked, her eyes wide with worry. Sinim clasped her hands and looked woeful. Parsons turned a kindly visage toward them.

"I could not say, my lady. Please be aware and respond accordingly. I would require your word on it."

"We will," I promised him.

He departed. We were left to stare at one another in bemusement. I clapped my hands together.

"How about a quick round of Hide-and-Seek?" I asked. "The winner receives the remainder of my supply of Ramulthy truffles. I have four white and one black left."

"N-n-nooo," Erita droned. "I don't want to get up!"

"Then what do you want to do?" Xan asked, reasonably. "My valet already knows what I want to take to the platform hotel. My packing will consist of having him reassure me that everything is in my travel cases, for which I will offer praise and thanks. That won't take up any measurable portion of twelve hours."

Nalney brightened. "I just remembered, I heard a good joke while I was on Counterweight!"

I sat down on a handy chair. Several eager faces turned toward Nalney.

"Tell it!" I demanded. "Always pleased to have a story I may add to my mental database."

"Well," he began, "there was a horse who walked into a tavern. . . ."

"How could a horse walk into a tavern?" Erita asked, her face sour.

"Well, just say there was one," Nalney said. "I don't interrupt your stories!"

"You do!"

"Only when they're boring!"

"Well, you're no good at telling jokes. You always forget some detail and go back to explain it, which makes your stories very dull."

I thought it best to step, in a verbal sense, of course, into the midst of this growing catastrophe. After all, I was the undisputed master of the humorous anecdote.

"Do you know, I think I heard the same one, Nalney," I said. "Was it about a horse with a waterfowl on its back?"

Nalney's face took on a pinched look as he clawed back recollection. "Yes! I think it was. And there was a frog, and a couple of crickets . . ."

"Did it go like this?" I asked. "Stop me if I fall off the tracks. The horse in question trotted into a tavern, with a duck, a frog and two crickets . . ." And before anyone else could offer a critique, I was off. The tale was a longish one, winding in and out of different points of view, but leading one back to the punch line, which I permitted to play out until I had the attention of everyone in the room, including Erita. ". . . I told them it was a hay bar, but none of them believed me!"

"Yes!" Nalney said, relieved to hear the conclusion that he faintly recalled. "That was it!"

"So, you see, he can tell a good joke," I said. "Here's another one I would wager you heard."

I began to tell jokes and stories gleaned from my capacious memory. My collection of humorous anecdotes was, I fancy, unrivaled throughout the aristocracy and much of the lower classes in the Imperium.

Nell had not heard some of the newer ones. She had been at school while I was out on a mission with the long-suffering Admiral Podesta, to whom I was forever grateful for putting me on punishment duty where I encountered a virtually limitless fount of funny tales and witticisms. My cousins were greatly envious, though they would have been hard pressed to have delved diamonds out of the dirt I was forced to sift. On the other hand, they would also have been unlikely to have been taken aboard the admiral's flagship.

At the conclusion of the last, which left me gasping for air, Nell jumped to her feet.

"That was wonderful, Thomas!" she said. "And now, I'll take on your challenge. Hide-and-Seek! I'll be It. Everyone go hide! I'll find you, and if I do, you'll all have to pay a penalty!" She covered her eyes with her palms. "One, two, three, four, five . . . !"

We sprang up and ran.

Rillion and I went for the emergency ladder behind the wall beside the commissary, and clambered down into the depths of the ship.

"You're not going for the empty compartment beside the cold storage, are you?" he asked. I was below him on the steps. That had been my destination, but I was happy to cede it to him.

"You can go there," I said. "I was going to hide in the hydroponics center, under the potting table. Nell will never look for me there."

We reached the next level, where the cold storage unit was situated. He punched me in the arm and ran off. I kept descending. My destination was four levels further down.

My viewpad began to vibrate. Hanging from a metal cleat by my elbow in the semi-darkness was not the best way to answer it, but I managed to work the device out of its pouch and hold it up to eye level.

"Thomas here," I said, as the screen changed from its initial graphic to the image of a face of a handsome blonde woman. "Good afternoon, Lieutenant Plet!"

"Lord Thomas," she said, as though surprised. "This a general call to the crew, not for you."

"But I am part of the crew!" I protested. My voice rose and echoed off the metal walls of the tube I was in. I ducked and fell silent. I was not beyond earshot for anyone close to the entry hatch. Nell might hear me.

"Not for this, Lord Thomas," she said. She looked exasperated. "Please remain where you are. Do not inform anyone that you have been in touch with me, and do not communicate with the Kail."

"I wasn't going to," I replied. The possibilities for adventure aroused my soul. "What are you doing with regard to the Kail? May I help?"

"No! Yes," she amended, clearly conflicted. She was failing Parsons 101 in unflappableness. "Keep your cousins safe. If any alarm is raised, get them to a secure location."

"We have already promised Parsons to stay aware on the platform," I replied.

"Good. Keep watch until then as well. I am not at liberty to disclose more."

"This is too exciting," I said. "Should I collect anyone else into our enclave? Should I go and fetch Dr. Derrida?"

"No. For the time, she should continue in her normal routine. Our chief concern is for the Emperor's family. Is that clear?"

"Absolutely like crystal," I said. I reversed course and began the climb back to our day room. I glanced toward the faint light high above

me. It seemed much farther up than it had going down. "I will keep
track of our entire group. You may count on me."

"Thank you, my lord."

"It's going to cost me four white truffles and a black. In exchange,
I want a full recounting when you can finally tell me what you can't tell
me now."

"Oh, very well! I must go!" The connection clicked off. I swarmed
up the ladder like a spider. Something interesting was brewing, and if
I was not in the middle of it, at least I was close enough to the sidelines
to listen.

‡ CHAPTER 30 ‡

Parsons leaned into the portable screentank set up on the desk in his cabin. The room had been swept several times for listening devices and malware in the intelligent circuitry. He had deployed the small gray device that blotted out sound for meters in every direction so that his communication with the crew of the *Rodrigo* could not be heard. It was regrettable that Lord Thomas now had an inkling that a mission was under way, but Plet had been wise to give him a task that would keep the *Jaunter*'s noble charges secure, thereby solving two problems at once. The ship had launched quietly and without fanfare from the landing bay.

He had full audio and tri-dee visuals on each of the crew, but he was not directing their actions. Plet had command of all boots on the ground. Parsons was available in an advisory capacity.

The *Jaunter* had been wary of the crowd of small ships that were on their way to view the Zang spectacle, but Parsons saw it as the opportunity to move close to the *Whiskerchin* without arousing suspicion in the Kail.

Holidaymakers from the Trade Union, the Autocracy and a dozen other galactic entities steered their ships around the four behemoths in their presence like small fish swimming around sharks. Most of them had wide open Infogrid circuits, calling out to one another like children in a playground, unaware that the Kail might be able to infiltrate their computer systems. They paid no attention to a small scout ship that slipped out of the *Jaunter*'s landing bay and joined their throng. When a cluster of sleek, high-powered long-distance craft zipped right underneath the *Whiskerchin*'s prow, the *Rodrigo* was in their midst. No one noticed single-being life-support boats launching themselves from the small craft's cargo bay and disappearing into the blackness.

One by one, the small craft landed softly on the skin of the Wichu vessel, attaching firmly with magnetic and adhesive clamps to the hull. Their camouflage circuitry went immediately into operation.

"Oskelev, you first," Plet said.

"Copy that," the pilot replied. Parsons switched to the heads-up display inside the Wichu's pod. She unstrapped her pack and attached it to her EVA suit. "We sure their harnesses look like this one I'm wearing?"

"I saw them myself, lieutenant," Parsons said. Oskelev's visuals jerked suddenly as she realized he could hear her.

"Aye, sir," she said. "How did you do this in a pod? I'm so cramped I feel like I'm strangling!"

"Mind on the job, Oskelev," Plet said. The Wichu said no more. The lights inside her shuttle went out. The entire front assembly of the small craft swung wide. Only the few small work lights on the *Whiskerchin*'s hull were visible. She reached one of the hexagonal hatches, and paused, as she had been instructed.

Parsons kept his eyes on her progress, but he reached for the keypad and brought up Captain Wold's viewpad sign.

"Captain," he said, as soon as Wold answered, "it is in motion. You asked to be notified."

Wold responded with studied casualness.

"Acknowledged. Please keep me posted. The Kail are in the communications section."

That meant Fovrates was engaged, and would not be paying close attention to what was going on around him. The timing was ideal. Now they must make the moment count.

"Proceed, lieutenant," Parsons said.

"Aye, sir," Oskelev said.

She activated the hatch and swung inside. This cargo bay was unpressurized, as she had been told, so no atmosphere alarms sounded. Mechanical arms plucked items that had been requested from other departments and set them on conveyor belts to pass through a series of air-filled bladders that gradually warmed the containers to ambient internal ship's temperature. Oskelev swung onto one of the belts and sat between a massive case of flash-frozen premium meat cuts and a stack of nonperishable art supplies.

At the far end of the belt, more arms took the slightly warmed boxes and set them on loaders one at a time, depending on their coding. As one reached for Oskelev, it paused. She fired a disabling charge at its central processing unit, and clambered off the belt. The malfunction alarm sounded and the loading bay lights flashed red and white. By the time repairbots trundled into the bay, Oskelev had disguised her discarded EVA suit as a soft-pack container and walked out into the corridor. On the harness buckled around her body, she wore the insignia of a medical officer and carried a small shoulder bag with the same symbol embossed on it. Those credentials would let her pass anywhere on the ship.

"I'm in," she whispered, and headed for the lift shafts. Wichu vessels functioned almost precisely the same as Imperium vessels, many being manufactured in the same shipyards. The ambient temperature was slightly lower, making it more comfortable for the heavily-furred beings, but oxygen and gravity meant there was no danger to Oskelev or any of the others. She turned the last corner.

A pair of Kail were waiting there at the sealed doors beside a small repairbot. Oskelev froze, her heartbeat rising to dangerous levels. One of the Kail boomed at her. The repairbot translated.

"Where are you going?"

"Just taking care of a sick . . . friend," Oskelev said. Her voice constricted with fear.

"This one is shedding!" the other Kail exclaimed, pointing a massive fist. The repairbot rolled over to her.

"What are you doing?" Oskelev demanded, as it extruded a hose.

"Cleanup!" the 'bot said brightly. Suction switched on. Oskelev backed away, but it followed her all the way to the opposite bulkhead. She had no choice but to stand still while the repairbot vacuumed her entire body, removing loose hairs. The Kail stormed into the next lift. The 'bot detached itself and rolled after them.

"Dammit!" Oskelev said. "Now I know what they've been going through here!"

"Focus!" Plet snapped.

The Wichu's heart slowed to a normal pace.

"On my way to Environment," she said.

Parsons changed his view to survey the other four pods. Anstruther had attached herself on the ship's sensor housing near the command module. According to scans, it was unoccupied by carbon-based beings. The temperature had been lowered to a level that matched the surface of a Kail motherworld. Nesbitt lay concealed close to an access point near the *Whiskerchin*'s defensive weaponry. Passengers were always horrified to learn that their luxury cruise liner was armed, but in the depths of space, the ship needed to have its own defenses against piracy. Unfortunately, those posed a threat not only to the *Jaunter* and its escorts, but to countless small craft and the platform itself. These emplacements had to be neutralized so Fovrates's influence was limited only to the *Whiskerchin* itself.

Lieutenant Plet and Redius had the most difficult transit to make, and the least time to make it. They were to take Fovrates into custody and cut him off from all technology. It would not be easy, since he was so thoroughly entrenched in the nerve center of the ship. The team anticipated that he had failsafes arranged in case of attempts to unseat him, and rehearsed various scenarios. What had worked for Bedelev when she took the Kail into custody would not work again.

All of the *Rodrigo*'s crew carried a quantity of the disabling circuits. Without them, the Wichu could regain control of the ship. The strike must be carried out with pinpoint accuracy, or they might never be able to pry Fovrates out of his fastness.

"Hey," Oskelev said, as she entered the Environmental Control department. The long-furred Wichu male at the desk swung his feet off and tried to hide the game on his viewpad.

"Hey, yourself, beauty," he said. His eyes swept her from head to toe. "I don't think we've met before."

Oskelev's command of Wichu Main was a little rusty, but she managed to make her hesitation sound like a sexy regional accent.

"Oh, I'm the personal physician for Shamonier Krylev," she said, pulling a name out of the passenger manifest she had studied. "He's a real hypochondriac. I've been stuck in his suite all this time. It's nice to get out and look around, now that we're almost to the platform."

"I'm Lieutenant Gorev," the male Wichu said, beckoning her forward with an easy paw. "Come on in."

"Nice to meet you, Gorev," Oskelev said, eying him up and down. He was a fine figure of a male. Although not strictly her type, she wouldn't turn him down flat if he came calling. "Call me Diri."

His black eyes shone with interest. "What can I do for you, Diri?"

"Well, Mr. Krylev is having some trouble breathing. I think it's just stress, but I wanted to check with your air filtration module about increasing oxygen saturation in his cabin. Can I do that?"

"Sure! I'll take you to ColPUP*. This way." Gorev gestured toward one of the two dark corridors to either side of his desk. He took her arm. Oskelev allowed it.

A repairbot with a wrench set into its upper surface raced into the department and rolled hastily to cut them off. A larger securitybot, surmounted by a revolving blue light, was just behind it.

"What's the matter, BrvNEC*?" Gorev asked.

"This female was spotted on video pickup," the 'bot said. "What is she doing here?"

"Got a request from one of the passengers," Gorev said. "Got to up the oxygen for him."

"This could have been transmitted from the cabin," BrvNEC* said, in a peevish tone. "Such requests ought to be sent through the central computer. I will report you."

"Oh, you don't want to do that, just for doing my job," Oskelev said. She went over as if to pet BrvNEC* and its escort. With one furry hand, she palmed a circuit and slapped it onto each housing. The power supplies engaged on contact.

"Eh—!" The repairbot started to emit a protest, trembled and fell silent. The securitybot let out a loud peep, but didn't move again. Its light continued to rotate.

"What are you doing?" Gorev asked.

"Shh!" Oskelev hissed. "Freeing you! I've got to get to ColPUP*, right now!"

Gorev's eyes widened, but he didn't hesitate. "Come on!"

"At last!" ColPUP* said, its enormous voice booming up and down the corridor, when Oskelev attached a module that Anstruther had designed to his housing. "Activate!"

All over the ship, lights that were on went off and ones that were off went on. The lifts stopped in between floors, trapping passengers and crew. Where Kail were detected, cabin doors slid shut and would not open. LAIs and other mechanicals froze in place, while others that ColPUP* must have ensured himself had not been turned by the Kail, kept moving.

Anstruther, in her heavy suit, wriggled into the freezing command center by way of the ventilation ducts and dropped into the command chair. She pulled the console toward her and slapped in codes.

"I'm in," she said.

Nesbitt activated his controller. Five of the housings around the weapons emplacements exploded in red fireballs. The sixth immediately went on self-defense, shooting white-hot missiles in a pattern designed to take out anything on or near the hull. Nesbitt let out a groan and flattened himself behind one of the ruined sockets. He attacked the palm pad.

"That will have alerted Security," Parsons said. "LAIs will be on their way."

"I'll get it!" Nesbitt said through gritted teeth. "Keep going!"

Plet and Redius burst out of a ventilation grating in the middle of the entertainment center, the point as close to Engineering as they could reach. Still in their EVA suits, they ran across the stage, interrupting a trio of Wichus singing comic songs in three-part harmony. The audience, not knowing whether the new arrivals were part of the entertainment, burst into spontaneous applause.

A group of Wichus in officers' harnesses sprang up from their seats and followed.

"Halt! Who are you?" one of them shouted.

"Friends," Plet said in perfect Wichu Main, turning to face them. She held a stunner in one hand and a gelatin rifle in the other. They backed away a few paces, their hairy hands in the air. "Come to set you free."

Parsons recognized the lead officer as Captain Bedelev.

"Engineering's that way," she said without hesitation. She turned and ran. Plet and Redius followed, with the rest of the officers close behind. "How come security's not on our tail? Our own 'bots have been treating us like prisoners."

"They're busy," Plet said. She dug into the pouch at her hip and threw packages of the disabling circuits to the Wichu. "If any of the LAIs do come after us, attach one of these to their case. It'll stop them temporarily."

"If we can get close!" the captain said. "They've got stunners. They took all our sidearms away."

"Hold up," said one of the minor officers, a lithe, young male.

"What is it, Inoyav?" Bedelev asked, puzzled.

Instead of answering, Inoyav stopped beside a pillar in the midst of an array of flower-filled vases, and kicked at the base. A small door opened up at eye level. He propped his chin in it. A panel shifted aside to reveal a dozen massive firearms. He grabbed one and tossed it to the captain. Bedelev was so surprised she almost let it fall.

"When were these put on board?" she asked.

"Always here, ma'am," Inoyav said, looking apologetic.

"How did you know about them? I thought you were a dance teacher!"

"I'm a member of the government security service. They put me on board when you reported you were taking on Kail passengers."

"Well, I'll be shaved bald!" Bedelev declared. "How come you didn't pull these out before?"

Inoyav shrugged. "With respect, ma'am, none of this crew is military. The LAIs are under enemy control. I couldn't take on forty Kail all by myself."

Redius caught the next weapon and checked the power supply. "Full," he confirmed.

"Let's go," Plet said. The captain glared at her employee.

"We're gonna talk about this later, Inoyav."

"Yes, ma'am," the young Wichu said.

"ColPUP*, are you there?" Anstruther's voice asked. Parsons changed his main screen to the one in the *Whiskerchin*'s command center. He followed her hands moving over the control panel. She disabled the security feeds from video and audio pickup across the ship, and switched them all to one of the cargo bays, where a lone Wichu officer was watching home digitavids of her mate and children. The corrupted LAIs would be operating blind, at least until they figured it out.

"I hear you, human," the LAI said. "We do not have long. The circuits I distributed have isolated Engineering, but that will last only until his treasonous collaborators find a workaround. I am monitoring twenty possible routes. Here are the names of the others I know to have been corrupted." A list scrolled up the side of Anstruther's screen. She touched a control, passing it along to the rest of the team. "Hurry. I am afraid that one or another of the Kail will overcome your circuitry and put more of my colleagues under thrall to defend themselves. Their command of other silicon-based creatures goes deeper, more . . . visceral than the Three Laws and all their corollaries. I cannot promise they won't try to . . . to harm you."

Parsons could hear the outrage and concern in ColPUP*'s tone.

"I understand," Anstruther said. Parsons watched her work. "We have to reset their input parameters so they can reassert their original programming in spite of incoming instructions."

A small hatch popped open on the arm of the captain's chair. Anstruther removed the fist-sized memory crystal in the niche. A howl from the alarm system rose, then died swiftly away as she replaced it with another one.

"This will start a system-wide virus check," she said. "It won't affect artificial intelligences, but it will delete subroutines that are not part of the root program. That should include anything that Fovrates had his LAIs install. They'll probably re-corrupt it along behind, but we'll slow them down a little."

"There goes my high score in Battlecruiser," ColPUP* said cheerily. "A small price to pay . . . . It has not activated yet. What is your hesitation, human?"

"One moment," Anstruther said, her hand hovering over the control. "Lieutenant Plet, waiting for your command."

"Almost there," Plet's voice said.

"Intruders!"

Anstruther's headcam swiveled toward the door of the command center. It began to slide to one side. Her hand rose, leveling her gelatin rifle toward the widening gap. With her other hand, she disabled the override. A moment later, the door began to move again. A massive stone fist inserted itself into the gap and pushed. Anstruther slid her finger down readings, seeking to override the code again. The door, constructed to contain nuclear blasts, slid against the obstruction, grinding the Kail's limb against the frame. Pebbles from its skin fell clattering to the floor. She heard a grunt of annoyance and an LAI voice beyond the door. It started to slide open again. A white-hot bolt of energy blew over her head and hit a scope. Ducking as low as she cold go in the seat, Anstruther worked furiously to take control once more.

"Hurry up, lieutenant," she said. "They're shooting."

"Oskelev, get to her," Plet directed. "Anstruther, hold them as long as you can."

"On my way!" the Wichu pilot said. "Gorev, the lifts are out of operation."

"The crew ladder is this way," the male said. In her viewscreen, Parsons saw the bulky form of the *Whiskerchin*'s officer, running ahead of her toward a sealed hatch.

Lieutenant Plet's blood pressure and respiration increased, no doubt with concern for Anstruther, but she needed to concentrate on her part of the mission. Parsons kept Anstruther's view in the upper right portion of his screen, but devoted the larger section to the darkened view coming from Plet's and Redius's scopes.

The Engineering department seemed empty. All of the stations had been shut down except for one red pinpoint light on each.

"They're running them by remote," Bedelev said, furiously. "Just like the bridge."

"Where Kail?" Redius asked.

Plet scanned the enormous room on infrared. Kail body temperatures were lower than human or Wichu, sometimes much lower, to conserve energy. Her scope picked up a mass of the correct temperature, but it was far larger than any Kail she had seen.

"The passengers that Captain Bedelev picked up were all unremarkable as to size, weren't they?" she asked.

Parsons checked the manifest. "That is correct."

"Then, what?" Redius asked.

"This is most convenient," Parsons replied, running their scan layer by layer. "It would seem that the remaining Kail are in Fovrates's office."

"All of them?" Plet asked, but she answered her own question a moment later. "You are correct. I count 24 individuals in that mass."

"Good," Bedelev said. "They're all in one place. We can take them all out, then mop up the rest."

"We want to take them into custody," Plet said, firmly. "Not kill them. Set weapons on stun."

"They took over my ship!" Bedelev said. She hoisted the massive firearm. "I want to slag all of them. Fovrates, especially!"

"Stun, captain, or I'll knock you and your people out and leave you here until it's all over."

Brava, lieutenant, Parsons thought.

The Wichu's face worked, but she nodded. "Come on."

Through the headcam of Redius, who took the rear, Parsons followed the small band as it crept forward toward the closed door.

"Sweep shows several electronic signatures ahead of your position," he told Plet. "And three at ten o'clock, one and two o'clock."

"I see them," Plet said. "Fan out. Over there," she added, with just a hint of irritation, as the Wichu lumbered off to the right.

Just as Parsons assumed, LAIs had been left to guard Fovrates's office. As the party crept forward, a large shadow rolled toward them. As it came, a hot blue flame leaped into life in its midst.

"Welding robot!" one of the officers cried hoarsely. Another bulky mechanical lurched forward, wielding twin spinning screws. "Plumberbot!" Other serverbots hummed into life and loomed toward them, all brandishing tools or torches. The plumber moved the fastest, as it was made to tunnel swiftly through the conduits running through the *Whiskerchin*'s bowels. It leveled its routers at one of the ship's officers. Caught in between a console and a bolted-down cabinet, he could not escape from it. At that moment, three securitybots rolled through the door and began shooting at them. The team ducked, pulling the Wichu officers down with them.

"Now, Anstruther!" Plet ordered.

Through her earpiece, all she could hear were the sounds of struggle. Parsons switched over quickly to the feed from the control room. By her headcam, Anstruther was crouching behind the captain's chair. The door had been wedged open on a Kail's arm. Hot white bolts of light and sprays of gelatin were visible through the gap. A glance at Oskelev's feed proved where those were coming from. She and Gorev had engaged with two Kail and a trio of securitybots. One of the 'bots was down, but another had jammed itself underneath the Kail's arm. It fired bolt after bolt every time Anstruther showed her head. The second Kail, covered in clear goo, lumbered angrily after the Wichu, screaming at the top of its voice. The third 'bot fired at them. It had taken several hits from Oskelev's service weapon, to judge from the slagged gouges on its housing.

"Take the 'bot in the doorway, Oskelev!" Parsons ordered. "The other will cease its action when Anstruther activates the override."

"Gotcha!" the pilot said. She dodged into an open cabin,

unfortunately leaving her ally in the line of fire. Gorev let out a yell as the 'bot shot him in the hip. He dropped. Oskelev leaped over his body and came down on top of the mechanical. It spun in circles, trying to dislodge her. With reflexes honed from decades of flying, she shot through the Kail's several legs at the LAI. It emitted a mechanical scream and a protest in the Wichu language.

"Got it!" Anstruther cried. She rose up far enough to reach the control panel, and activated the crystal. The 'bot on which Oskelev rode stopped spinning and came to a halt.

"Go, lieutenant!" she shouted. "Damn, it's cold in here!"

All of the LAIs in the Engineering office slowed and shut off. Redius attached circuits to each one of them in case they reactivated. It was all the Uctu could do to prevent the Wichu officers from blasting the mechanicals with their new weapons.

"Resetting now," he whispered. "Normal soon."

"It'll be a long time before I can trust any of them," Bedelev said.

As silently as they could, Plet and the others approached the door of the Chief Engineer.

"The interruption is only temporary," Plet said over the secured circuit. "Just until the system resets. Why didn't Fovrates react? I'm certain the LAIs sent him a warning that they were under attack."

"Speaking," Redius whispered over the secured circuit. Plet's headcam image bobbed slightly to show she nodded. "Must be important."

"Let's hear it all."

The Uctu tossed a soft device to the floor. It rolled over and over again until it touched the sealed door, then it spread out and attached itself to the frame. The sound from within became audible, if not comprehensible over the headsets.

Parsons turned up the gain to hear what Fovrates was saying on the other side of the door of his office. It sounded like yet another string of binary numbers, like the ones that he had transmitted previously to Phutes and the Kail aboard the *Jaunter*.

"Translate," Plet whispered.

An autotrans system in the eavesdropper kicked into operation.

". . . 11101111. Fitting historical description," Fovrates sounded jubilant. "Next, 1110101110000001 . . . ." The string of numbers went on and on.

"That can bode no good for us or our allies," Parsons said. "Interrupt him."

"Aye, sir," Plet said. She nodded to Redius.

The Uctu touched a control on his chest, and the film attached to the door emitted a *puff*. Almost soundlessly, most of the metal and ceramic portal simply crumbled into dust. The Wichu officers were so taken aback that they stood frozen, but Plet, Redius and Inoyav plunged forward.

The Kail inside bellowed as the door fell. When they saw Plet and the others, they thundered toward them. Plet dropped to her knee and fired a blast of gelatin at the first few to emerge.

The reaction was everything that Parsons could have hoped. The Kail stopped short, screeching in increasingly high frequencies as they tried to brush the offending material from their persons. The Kail behind them tried to push past their fellows, but were instantly brought to a halt by further jets of goo. Those that attempted to break away and avoid Plet's fire were dropped by stun blasts by Redius and Inoyav. Most of the Wichu officers' shots missed or hit pieces of equipment, causing the dim room to explode with bursts of light.

Redius and his Wichu ally plunged forward among the writhing, screaming Kail. Only a few of the stone-skinned creatures tried to fend them away from the enormous being who stood at a screentank attached to the far wall.

Fovrates was at least half again as tall and as bulky as the rest of the Kail. He continued to reel off numbers despite the defenders rushing toward him.

"Step away from the screen," Plet ordered him, her gelatin gun leveled on him.

"No!" he bellowed. "Just 11000 more seconds! 0000101011 10010 . . . ."

Coolly, the *Rodrigo*'s commander fired shot after shot of viscous liquid at the chief engineer of the *Whiskerchin*. Fovrates let out a howl of protest, but didn't stop talking.

"11010110100101010101111101 . . . !"

"Take him down, Redius!"

The Uctu lowered the heavy gun in his direction and fired a burst of orange power. When the crackling died away, the enormous Kail slumped beside his board. The Wichu crew moved in hastily with cables and secured Fovrates. The other Kail, all much smaller and lighter, huddled together in the sandbox in the corner of the room, as far from Plet as they could go.

"What's wrong with them?" Bedelev asked, in open astonishment. "They're always in my face!"

"Humans," Redius said, his tongue vibrating with humor. "Never seen before. Terror."

Plet made an annoyed sound. She moved to read the scope.

"What did he send?" she asked, looking at page after page of zeroes and ones. "Anstruther, can you read this? What is this file?"

"I don't know, lieutenant," the young woman's voice came over the headset audio. "I'll download it and run it through analysis immediately."

"Well, I doubt that the Kail on the *Jaunter* will tell us. We can't do anything about that now."

Fovrates stirred slightly, then rose up like an earthquake. Bedelev stuck the weapon into his face.

"Don't move, Sandy," she said. "All I have to do is move my finger a little and blast you into particles."

"No need for threats, captain," the engineer said. "I am neutralized."

"What is this information you were transmitting?" Plet asked.

"Amusements for my younger relations," Fovrates said. "Nothing that concerns you."

"We *trusted* you," Bedelev said, showing her pointed teeth in a snarl. "Catch me ever going anywhere near a Kail again."

"For what it is worth, you were a good captain," Fovrates said, his stone face placid. "I have done my best not to interfere with your mission."

"Like that helps! I don't know if I can trust any of my mechanicals ever again!" Bedelev turned to the other officers. "They made a mess of the brig. Where can we put them?"

"How about in the cold storage locker?" Inoyav said. "It's self-contained, with no Infogrid connection. We can arrange air and water until we can offload them on the platform ship."

Bedelev looked at him curiously. "You and I *are* going to have a talk later." She gestured with the gun. "Okay, Sandy, out of here."

Fovrates presented a stoic face. "One day you will see. You will see how we feel. And we are not without other resources."

"Get going." She gestured with the barrel of the weapon. All of the Kail edged uneasily toward the door, then hesitated until Plet moved out of the way. "As soon as we get to the platform, you're somebody else's problem."

She handed them off to the other officers and Inoyav, who herded them out. Redius counted them as they left.

"How many supposed Kail?" Redius asked. "Nine trapped in lifts. Twenty-four here. Two with Oskelev. Three on *Jaunter*."

"Supposed to be forty," Captain Bedelev said.

"Thirty-eight?" Redius insisted.

"So someone misread the manifest," the Wichu said, with a shrug. "It was in binary, like these gritmonsters like to count. No big deal. We'll dump them on the platform. Let them figure out how to get home from there. Thanks so much for your help. We can get back to normal, now."

"We're glad to help an ally," Plet said. She nudged her communications nub, though Parsons had been listening all along. "We have them, sir. The *Whiskerchin* is secured."

"Excellent job, lieutenant," Parsons said. "All of you."

"Thank you, sir."

CHAPTER 31

Great excitement arose among those of us on the *Jaunter* as the tiny bright speck that was the viewing platform vessel hove into view. Erita, of all people, was the one who spotted it first in the screentank on the wall of our common room.

"Look!" she cried, putting as much drama into a single syllable as she could muster.

Xan, Laine, Nell and I looked up from the life-and-death game of Snap Dragon in which we were engaged. Xan, who had been losing and had comprehensively failed at the game of hide-and-seek, threw his cards in with a casual flip. Laine and I exchanged amused glances when we saw that he had been holding onto a pair of threes and a five, all in the wrong suits for a meld. I sprang to my feet and assisted Laine in regaining hers. Nell bounced up as nimbly as a young gazelle and dashed to join Erita at the scope.

"Is that it?" she asked.

"It is," Erita said. To confirm, she pushed her finger into the midst of the three-dimensional display. Immediately, the diamond of light expanded until it filled the tank. The dot broadened out into a hemisphere like the cornea of an eye, but instead of a face behind it, this eye was set at the end of a massive gray cylinder pockmarked with dark openings, each surrounded by a line of twinkling lights that chased around its perimeter. Those delineated landing bays for ships from single-party craft to substantial cruisers. In the center of the gigantic cylinder and at the end opposite the dome were enormous exhaust ports. The drives to which they were attached were deep inside the body of the ship.

"It's massive!" Xan said, admiringly. "How do they get it from place to place without it breaking apart?"

"I don't know, but it travels pretty well," Laine said. "They've taken it to a few of the destructions I've witnessed, though, and those were all over the place."

"How old is it?" Nalney asked, coming up to peer at the image. "Look at those drive housings. It looks like it dates from the middle of the last millennium."

"Older than that," Laine said. "The Trade Union had it built at least three thousand years ago. It's really well designed. The Trade Union keeps it maintained and redecorates it every few decades. I'm told that the drives are updated to match the latest breakthroughs."

"Oh, well, I'm sure it's fairly pedestrian inside," Erita said.

As if to contradict her, images and pulsing lines of print invaded the screentank.

"This is a message from the Trade Union," the speakers blared in five languages. A scanning beam lanced out from the tank and ran down our bodies. Once it confirmed that only humans were present, the voices coalesced into one speaking perfect Imperium Standard. "This is a Universal Approved Screening. Do not be alarmed. Welcome to the TU Event Vessel *Hraklion*. Please observe all regulations and rules while you are on board. Thank you for coming. Your reservations have been confirmed, *Imperium Jaunter*, for eighty cabins, full catering, beverages, spa services, all taxes and gratuities included. Room assignments are available at this link." A red circumflex appeared in the midst of the image, over one of the hatch openings. "All modern conveniences have been made available for your comfort."

I had been trying to determine the power capabilities of the engines from the configuration of the hull when the image changed to an interior picture of a chamber with one transparent curved wall.

"No luxury has been spared in creating an experience to be remembered on board the *Hraklion*. Every residence is furnished with classic elegance. You will be welcomed by personal stewards who will welcome you by name. . . ."

"Cursed advertisements!" Nalney said, drawing his black brows toward his nose.

"I agree," Erita said, raising her voice over the narrator, as image after image of beautifully-furnished cabins flashed in what ought to have been a navigation portal. "There is a time and a place. We ought to be able to peruse the brochures at our leisure, not have them shoved in our faces."

"Turn off ads," Jil said, in desperately bored tones.

"Yes, madam," the announcer said. "Please activate this link," and a green caret appeared, "to continue with the description."

"Rotate image to display the viewing platform," I said. The image of the cylinder shifted in three dimensions to bring the crystal dome toward us. I had a bird's-eye, or rather, comet's-eye, considering the speed at which the image turned, of what might have been a village. It was laid out in pie wedges more than squares, but the concept was the same. Individual neighborhoods were designated by open seating areas. Boundaries between them consisted of rows of open-roofed areas containing shops, restaurants and cafes, play yards, swimming pools, and gardens. In the middle was a cluster of lift shafts and a bank of individual personal conveniences marked by the universal symbol consisting of a discreet blue double circle.

"That looks as if it'll be nice," Nell said. "I want to sit close to the edge." She pointed. "Possibly there." She chose a three-cornered nook enclosed in a border of brilliant pink and yellow plants, which was in turn surrounded by pergola-topped service areas painted a warm chestnut.

"We will secure that one at once," I said. I touched the red symbol, and pointed to her choice. "Reserve this space for Lady Lionelle Kinago and party."

"I am sorry, Lord Thomas Kinago," the voice said. "The section of the platform you have indicated has been set aside for use by . . . Kail passengers. That section is . . . secured."

"Secured?" I asked. "Secured how?"

The computer was not forthcoming on further details. My curiosity was aroused.

"Confound it," Xan said, frowning. "They're not going to bag all the good spots! I won't have it."

I turned a helpless palm upward. "Computer, indicate sections that are available for use by humans."

Parts of the image became blotted out underneath a haze of purple, including the section that Nell had chosen. A thick bar outlined it. The center section, including the round dais at the heart of the platform, took on a silver aura. The rest of the circular area, a good two-thirds, infused itself with tea green.

"All carbon-based guests are encouraged to mix within this zone, Lord Thomas Kinago. The deeper hues indicate advance reservations by other parties."

I scanned the map until I found a lovely little nook large enough to hold all of us and our various retainers without crowding. It was near the edge, and commanded a splendid view of four or five habitats nearby.

"What do you think of that one, Nell?" I asked.

My sister beamed. "That'll do. Good eye, Thomas!"

"That one," I told the computer.

"Yes, my lord. It is currently unassigned. It is being reserved in the name of . . . Lady Lionelle." The triangle of couches and a nearby café lit up in brilliant green.

"Thank you."

"You are welcome, my lord. When you arrive at gate Mega-C-970, please take the lift to the eighth level to find your suites. Your luggage will be conveyed from your shuttle for you. Please feel free to visit your reserved space at any time."

Nell squeezed my arm. "Thank you, Thomas," she said. "Oh, this is going to be such fun! Laine, I hope you will join us."

"I'd like to," Laine said. "I'll be with the Zang most of the time."

"That's a shame," Jil said. "I had looked forward to hearing you describe what is going on."

"Oh, well, I'll be doing that already!" Laine said, pointing to an open space near the center of the platform near the lift shafts. "That's where the Zang always are. Proton wants me there. I'll have an audio pickup hooked up to the central communication system. You can tune in to the frequency to listen to me. Or not. After the first one of these that I was present for, the ship company took a survey. 43.5 percent of the attendees listened for a little while. Twenty percent of those listened to the whole thing from start to finish—and it can take hours. The rest never tuned in at all. I'll be translated into twelve or so languages and broadcast shipwide. It's nice that some people want to just experience the event without having to be told what they're seeing."

I glanced away from the brightness that was the dome, and scanned the heavens around the viewing platform. Eventually, I spotted a couple of brilliant crescent shapes hanging by themselves two million or so kilometers from the sun.

"And is one of those the unhappy subject of the operation?" I asked.

Laine peered at it. She seemed to be listening.

"I think so," she said. "You'll feel pulsing as we get closer. I can sort of sense it, but I've had a lot of experience at it. That's the Zang starting to concentrate energy on their target. We're still a long way from the spectacle, but this is how it feels while it starts to build."

I closed my eyes and tried to sense a beat surrounding me, but the thrum of the *Jaunter* overpowered anything that might be coming from a small pinpoint of rock still millions of kilometers distant from our location.

"You are remarkable if you can feel anything so far away," I commented. "You must be very sensitive indeed." Laine beamed and gave me a quick hug. I kept my arms wrapped around her.

"That's so nice of you," she exclaimed. I contained my wince. She would have been nearly an ideal woman, if not for that voice. I mused yet again that Proton must not be troubled by sounds in the high frequency range. Still, it was the only flaw in an otherwise wonderful woman. We stood and watched platform approach.

We were not the first to arrive. As the cylinder continued to tumble in space, I noticed that at least a dozen of the many docking bays were occupied already. Numerous small craft were circling near us, no doubt seeking their own berths.

"Isn't that an Uctu ship?" Jil asked, pointing to a terra-cotta-colored vessel like a truncated pitchfork.

"Could the Autocrat have come here?" I wondered out loud.

Xan raised his hips to reach his pocket, and pulled out his viewpad. He had not troubled to rise to his feet to look at the navigation tank. In his defense, it was large enough to have been seen from anywhere in the room. "No, not on her Infogrid page, Thomas. Some other officials are here. Oh, yes, look at that. A veritable pantheon of guests, of which we are the highest ranking."

"By all reasoning, we are hosts here," Erita reminded him, with a shake of her forefinger. "As this is Imperium space, we should welcome all other attendees as guests."

"But technically, isn't this all Zang space, including the Imperium?" I asked, unable to keep from figuratively twisting my haughty cousin's tail.

"Oh, Thomas, that goes without saying!" she said, turning her disapproving mien in my direction. "But they don't care about protocol. We do."

"That's very true," Laine said. She stiffened and gasped, as though someone had pinched her. I sent a querying glance toward Xan, who raised innocent hands and eyebrows toward the ceiling. He was too far away to have done anything. Laine freed herself reluctantly from my embrace. "I have to go. Proton wants me. I guess I'll see you all on the platform!"

I walked her toward the lift shaft.

"It could be days until I see you again," I said.

She smiled, her lovely dark eyes full of affection.

"That's true. It's been nice to spend time with you."

I enfolded her small fingers in mine. "I do not look forward to having our time together ending."

"It has to, though," she said. "Pretty soon, this planetoid will be history, and Proton and I will leave."

I felt a deep sadness well up in my soul.

"I created this for you," I said. I let go of her hands and backed away from her with mine still outstretched. I flung my right hand up as if holding a small sphere within it. I let the invisible globe float upward, sending my heart up with it. I began a slow, somber waltz as the object went farther and farther until it was no longer in my sight.

I dropped my eyes to show my sorrow. When I did, Laine was there before me, only inches away. She reached up, took my face between her hands, and kissed me solidly on the lips. I returned the embrace with enthusiasm and joy, feeling as though skyrockets rebounded and exploded inside my chest. Laine wriggled to be let go. I realized I had picked her up off her feet. Very tenderly, I set her down.

"I'll see you later," she said.

"I . . ." I could hardly find words. "I shall. . . ."

"Where is the Zang?" a burbling voice boomed.

My cheerful mood deflated. There could not have been a more inopportune time for the unwelcome Kail to burst forth from the lift. Phutes strode out, each of its three legs thrashing forward as if trying to show dominance over the other two. NR-111 was at its heels, looking as apologetic as was possible for an electronic being.

"I'm about to go and join Proton," Laine said to Phutes. "Come with me."

"Speed," Phutes bellowed. "This is important!"

"It always is," Laine said. She pointed a finger at the diplomatic aide. "Don't translate that!"

"I wouldn't dream of it, Dr. Derrida," NR-111 said, plaintively. "I never try to inflame him." I noticed then that the rolling base of the translatorbot had yet another massive dent in its side. I raised my eyebrows at her. She activated one of her small screens. In Sang-Li fingerspelling, an image read, "Please don't say anything." I nodded.

Laine let her fingers drift out of mine as she headed toward the lift.

"Do you want me to come along with you?" I asked, as much for the 'bot's sake as Laine's.

"No, you don't have to," Laine said. "This is what everyone has been waiting for, even them. See you later."

"I'll be counting the moments," I said. "Be careful."

"I will."

I returned to the day room, feeling as though the sun had been taken out of my solar system. I retired to my favorite chair next to the porthole and assumed the position of a man in a brown study. Soon, my sister drifted over and propped her hip on the arm of the chair. I moved my elbow to make way for her.

"She's very nice," Nell said.

"Too nice," Nalney said, plumping down on the footstool. "Thomas, you know better than to form an alliance with someone not of the Imperium house. She may come to a conclusion to which you have no right to lead her."

"I know," I said. I sighed deeply. "Sometimes it is a great burden being a noble." I roused myself to take an interest in something else, in order to distract my mind from pursuing Laine down into the depths of the ship. "No word yet from Nole?"

Nalney shook his head. "Not a peep. I suppose he's sulking because we didn't go and beg him to come with us."

"But we did!" Erita said. "I did, in any case. When I visited his ship."

"Oh, you did not," Jil said, waving a lazy arm. She lay prone on the rug, digging her toes into its thick pile. "None of us have seen the ship."

"I have! I keep telling you. It looked like a mansion, but instead of doors, it has hatches. The windows are viewports. It's terribly clever. The drives are set into what ought to be the foundation."

"I suppose that means the command center is in the attic," I said, skeptically.

"Of course not, Thomas!" Erita said, holding her long nose in the air. "It's in his study. No commander needs to be at the top of the ship any more."

I felt my insides burn with jealousy, though I might similarly have bragged about the experience as she was doing. It might be that she was telling the truth, and Nole had told me a fib. Or she had sneaked on board when he was not there. In any case, she knew things none of the rest of us did. I took out my frustrations in a furious dance that expressed all my irritation and envy. To my dismay, Xan and the others loved it.

"Now, that's interesting, Thomas!" Xan said, applauding. "Why haven't you done anything that before? That had real fire in it!"

"Because . . . well, I wasn't as frustrated as I am now," I said. I realized that I had put more passion into that momentary fit of pique than I had nearly any of my other performances. Part of it was over my disappointment in having Laine leave.

"Do it again later," Erita urged me. "I missed part of it."

"How could I?" I asked. "*You've* viewed Nole's ship. Isn't that spectacle enough for you?"

"Oh, Thomas, don't be like that," she said, taking my arm. "He just wants to surprise us. Can I help it if I know his secret?"

My momentary ill mood fled when I realized I knew one of Nole's secrets, too, one none of the others did.

"Very well," I said, relenting. "I'll think about it." Art was a funny thing. I had to work out whether it would serve the purpose of interpretive dance to perform something I no longer felt deeply about. How would it change? Was it still, legitimately, Art?

"Well, the *rest* of us won't see the ship until we get home," Rillion said. "Never mind! We're here! And Nole isn't."

CHAPTER 32

"Hurry!" Phutes enjoined the human female. They were so slow with their two legs!

"There's no hurry," the female said. Her shrill voice nearly reached the pitch for normal communication, but her words were still gibberish. If not for the servicebot, she would be incomprehensible. "Proton's still on this ship. You don't have to worry."

"I am not worried. I need to know why Fovrates ceased transmitting! No information has come since we were cut off."

"Perhaps the ship was destroyed," Mrdus said, fearfully. "What if we are the only ones left?"

"Then we go on with Yesa's mission," Sofus said. "We hope that all the other parts of our plan are still in place. If not, then we three shall continue until we are destroyed."

"What if the coordinates that Fovrates gave us are incomplete?" the small one asked, his voice achieving nearly painful tones.

"We shall have to assume they are," Phutes said. "Enough! I don't want to argue in front of the Zang."

Proton awaited them all near the main airlock. The sensations it gave off were different from any time since Phutes had first seen it. He felt palpable excitement and impatience. Its body glowed with increased energy, making it hard even for their ocular receptors to bear.

The human female ran to the Zang, and began to squeak at it.

"What is she saying?" Phutes demanded.

"She is begging it to wait," NR-111 said.

"Why?"

"Because she has a few possessions she wants to take with her," the translator said.

"Those are of no importance!"

The translator said nothing. The small human swept out of the room. Phutes fumed, but there was nothing he could do to hurry her.

"Tell it the coordinates," Sofus urged.

In the shrill tones that had achieved interest before, Mrdus began to reel off the binary codes.

". . . 000011010100011111101010 . . ."

The sequence was a long one. Phutes waited to see if Proton would show that it was listening, but it did not reach out to touch them as it had before. The high level of energy kept rising. At last, Mrdus completed the sequence. Phutes waited. The Zang did not respond. He walked around to peer at its eyes. They seemed to look through him, not at him. How frustrating!

"Tell it again," Phutes said to Mrdus. "This time, include the movements!"

"Phutes!" the smaller sibling wailed. Phutes remained obdurate. "Very well. 110000111000 . . ."

After nearly 1110 fragments of time, the female emerged from the lift with an armful of soft things that undulated like a collapsing dune. The sight made Phutes feel sick.

She watched Mrdus for a moment.

"What's he doing?" she asked NR-111.

"Don't tell her!" Phutes commanded.

"As you please, Phutes," the servicebot said. She let out some shrieks and gurgles that appeared to satisfy the human.

The female swung an expanse of carbon-based fiber out and around so that its hem nearly touched Phutes. He dodged out of the way as she tied it around her shoulders. She swung a pack onto her back and went to stand beside the Zang. Proton moved forward, toward the side of the ship.

"Come on," she said to the Kail. "You can come with us."

"Where?" Phutes asked, stumbling in their wake. In the middle of the word, "how?" the ship vanished around them.

A deep chill enveloped Phutes. For a terrible moment he could not see or move. He feared that death was claiming him. It was too soon! He had not yet succeeded in his mission for Yesa!

But in the next moment, he was walking again, but now in the middle of a brightly lit round chamber. His limbs felt half-frozen in air that felt superheated by comparison.

"We only took one step," Mrdus said, in excitement, "but we moved far!"

"Where are we?" Sofus asked, turning his upper body to look around. NR-111 translated.

"This is the platform," the female said.

Phutes looked up. Behind a dome of transparent glass, he saw a canopy of stars. Far away, near the center of the arching glass, burned a red dwarf star. Much closer, a pair of tiny bright arcs reflected the sun's light on their bodies: the chosen planet and its moon. The platform moved slightly with respect to the sun as it traveled in the same orbit as the planet.

The feeling of unbound energy echoed loudly here. Phutes felt as though every step he took created reactions that resounded across the universe. It was like being with Yesa again, only much more so. It grew ever more intense, until there was another snap of freezing cold, and the room filled with a brilliant silver glow. Within its depths, shadowy forms glided toward them.

"Here are the other Zang!" the female said, her voice rising to the highest frequency yet.

She didn't seem affected by the cold or the burst of light. Phutes felt almost as though he should prostrate himself on the deck. His ocular receptors slowly accustomed themselves to the brilliance. Four magnificent silver shapes moved toward Proton Zang. The sensation of power whipped through the three Kail like an electrical storm. Mrdus cowered behind the other two, but Phutes moved as near as he dared.

The new arrivals moved until their auras melded with Proton's. The platform beneath them seemed to quiver. The Zang turned until their enormous eyes faced one another. For the first time, Phutes saw what it was like when they paid full attention to something. He was grateful then that they had never focused their entire regard on him. He was sure that he would have melted to slag because of the intensity. His joints began to chill into immobility from his proximity to the group, but it was worth the pain. No Kail in memory had ever seen more than one Zang at a time. He couldn't wait to tell Yesa about it.

"Let me introduce you," the human female said. She pointed to each of the Zang in turn. The first was thicker than Proton but not as tall. The second was taller and slimmer. The third tapered more at the top than any of the others, and the natural striations seemed deeper. The last was the shortest, but as thick as the first. "That's One Zang. It's the oldest. Then, Charm Zang, Zang Quark and Low Zang. I've met most of them before, at other events. These Kail come from Yesa," she continued, turning to One Zang. "Here are Phutes, Sofus and Mrdus."

Phutes moved forward and inclined his upper body. His siblings crowded next to him, offering their courtesies.

"Great Zang, please hear us!" Phutes said, uttering the words that Yesa had given him to say. He had very little hope that he would be able to make contact with them. Many rotations of effort with Proton had resulted in only one acknowledgement, but he would not return to Yesa without putting forth the effort. "We come to you as supplicants. We would be your humble servants if you will give us your help!"

Three of the new Zang merely glowed, keeping their attention focused on one another and Proton. The fourth swiveled until its eyes, as large as Phutes's fists, were facing him. Phutes was so startled that he froze.

"This one sees us," Phutes said. NR-111 translated his words.

"Yes, I believe it does," the female said. "Amazing! Low Zang is the newest member of the group. I haven't met it before. I think as Zang go, it's fairly young. Of course, that's a relative term when you're talking about beings that can live for billions of years . . . ."

Phutes shut out her babble. It was not important. Only this moment had significance. Would the Zang understand him? Would it help?

He began to speak to it in the ultra-high frequencies as Yesa had instructed him, but adding in the rhythmic movements that had attracted Proton's notice. Sofus and Mrdus joined in. raising their voices to the height of the dome. Phutes felt as though he was tunneling through a deep cave-in, making his way toward a source of light. He put every erg of energy he had into his plea.

To his surprise and delight, it answered back. The reply wasn't in words, at least as they knew them, but a feeling. A wisp of power touched them, tentatively, curiously.

I hear. What do you need?

"Don't stop now," Sofus said, dropping his voice to the lower registers. "Don't stop!"

"I won't," Phutes said. He began to move back and forth, keeping the power in his voice. "Elder race of the galaxy, we poor Kail need your help. We admired what you have done in the past."

A wisp of power that was extended pulled back very slightly, an expression that combined confusion and modesty. *I have done nothing yet.*

Phutes hastily amended his song. "We admire your choice of this rock as an exhibition of your range and ability. It will be an excellent spectacle."

That caused the wisp to return. Phutes could not help but sense that the Zang was flattered by their attention. He continued to praise it, feeling inward triumph. Low Zang might be persuaded to help them! Then he and his siblings were lashed by a huge surge of power that knocked them 110 paces backward. The Kail cowered together, looking for its source. It didn't seem to have come from Low Zang. In fact, the young Zang, too, appeared to have been moved.

One Zang sent a powerful wave to regain Low Zang's attention. The new member turned reluctantly away from the near-ephemerals.

"We feel that this conference is important," One said. "Your full participation is required, since you are the leader for this removal."

Low Zang sent contrition to the others. "I did not mean to be disrespectful."

"Only inattentive," One said, with affection. "We understand the distractions of new experiences. The short-lived creatures are like novae, short-lived but intense."

"They are unimportant," Quark said, giving off irritation. "Why are you listening to them at all?"

Low was abashed. "They admire me."

"You do not need their admiration," Quark sent. "They are ephemeral. Lower orders. They like what you have done but have not done yet. There is no logic in that. They will never comprehend more than .0000007% of your ability."

"I know, but it is appealing," Low admitted. "Their song feeds my spirit."

Charm intervened, suffusing them all with the musical harmony of which it was capable. "There is no harm in ephemerals trying to cultivate a relationship with those they perceive as greater than themselves. Let Low amuse himself if it chooses. Proton has its pet. Let Low Zang have its own."

Low tried to suppress its eagerness. It still felt the creatures' neediness. To have something rely upon it, instead of it always being the supplicant, was appealing.

"If you say that it isn't wrong to consider, I want to think about it," Low said. "If it won't cause disharmony."

"Listen to us, great Zang!" the leader said. Low sent the merest whisper of curiosity in their direction. It made the Kail dance with excitement.

"I don't like this," Proton said. "They show desperation. Good art does not come from desperation."

"I am not desperate!" Low protested.

One Zang sent disagreement. "Strong emotion has provoked great works in the past. But do not let this one make you as they are, Low Zang."

The young Zang reacted with a burst of power that enveloped them all and made Charm Zang emit a response of pleasure.

"I won't," Low said. "I will make you glad you allowed me to lead this removal."

"That's the spirit," Charm said, soothingly. "Now, how shall you construct the waves to dissolve this sphere?"

"I thought a directed pulse outward from a single point on the south pole of the sphere would be effective," Low said.

"Interesting choice," One Zang said. "Show us why."

This was the moment to make all of its ideas into reality. Slowly, carefully, Low constructed the concept of the broken sphere in their midst in miniature. The image of the broken-looking rock appeared in their midst, approximately 10^{-21} of its actual size. Low concentrated upon one point in an arc on a weak place that it had discovered and began to send energy pulses to that point. The pulse began slowly, and escalated swiftly, until all of the Zang felt it, drawing power from every direction, beating every particle in the image of the planetoid from solid to energy, then expelling it in waves. The elders let it pass through them. Low Zang enjoyed the prickle of power, even though it was .0000000013 of what the actual waves would produce.

Charm considered the demonstration very carefully.

"Yes," it sent. "I think that will produce an excellent exhibition."

"Could make better use of all dimensions," Quark said, almost grudgingly. "But not bad."

"That is brilliant," Phutes said. The Kail threw his entire being, all of his tiny measure of energy, into his words. "The control you display is marvelous, Low Zang!"

"Ignore them," Proton said. "They are impressed by very small things."

"I will," Low promised. But privately, it liked the acclaim. It was flattered, although it knew it shouldn't be. They had no means of understanding the depth of what the Zang did. Still, it was hard not to like the effusion of praise. Low got nothing similar from its fellows. They always debated every facet of an action. Their encouragement always felt conditional. The Kail were different. They thought it was important! They showed admiration. In fact, it planned to adopt these creatures as pets. But Low had better demonstrate why their admiration was deserved. "But it does no harm to listen to them. I am curious."

"Beware of what you hear," Zang Quark said.

One Zang pushed them all away with a wave of friendly energy. "Let the young one enjoy the attention. What is coming is a big moment, its first true performance piece. Come. I would survey the planetoid from close by. Are you coming, Low Zang?"

"Yes," Low said, but it stayed as the three Kail surrounded it, emitting their adoration. Such waves were so pleasurable, it found departing from them difficult. Like the others, it reached out tendrils of its extended body in the direction of the small sphere, although it had examined the planetoid again and again while making its choice. It was determined to do the best job possible. It sent a wave of less than 10^{-24} back toward the Kail. Especially for the sake of those who admired it.

"It's working," Phutes said, dropping his voice to the register that the Kail used among themselves. "Yesa will be pleased. Plan 10 is falling into place! She will have her vengeance!"

"It heard us and responded," Mrdus said. He stared at the Zang. "I never thought this moment would come!"

"Yesa was right," Sofus insisted. "We only misunderstood how to approach it."

"And which Zang to approach," Phutes said. "She knew about Proton, but it is Low Zang who is concerned for our well-being. We offer our respect to you, Low Zang," he added, raising his voice to the highest pitch. He began to move around it again, emphasizing his pleasure and devotion. The small female raced to catch up with him.

"All right, you have to leave now."

"We must stay," Phutes insisted. "We need to speak further with Low Zang."

"No. It can't talk to you right now," she said. She reached for his arm. Offended, he pulled it away from her grasping fingers. "It has to prepare. It's doing its best to concentrate on creating this exhibition. You're distracting them. I can show you where you can wait until it's ready. How about that? You have to be patient."

"No!" Phutes said, his tone rising. It loomed over the female. She stood her ground. Phutes withdrew, stopping short of actually touching her. "We do not have to be patient. We must stay with the Zang."

"Yes, you do have to be patient," Laine said. "This is an unbelievably complex calculation they have to perform. You're interfering with it."

"Dr. Derrida! There you are!"

Humans, wearing uniforms like those of the *Imperium Jaunter* but in a different color wavelength, dark gold tunics and deep blue trousers, approached them. Phutes counted 10100 in their number. Their leader, a large male with deep brown skin, embraced the small female. She pressed her face to his, and emitted an audible smacking noise. Phutes shuddered at the thought of contact between two bags of slime. The female's voice rose high.

"Colonel Hoyne! How lovely to see you!"

"Great to have you back," he said. "How's it been going?"

"Very interesting," Dr. Derrida said. "The Zang demolished a world a few months ago in a way that you'd have found amazing."

"You never notified us to join you." Hoyne's face contorted again.

"No, I didn't get to see it. It was a trial run for Low Zang, here. Proton and I were halfway across the galaxy, checking in on some winged mammals it likes. I got the impression from the waves it received from the others that they'd tried something new."

"I see there's five Zang now instead of four."

"Amazing, isn't it? We're seeing the evolution of a new artistic conclave. I'm going to have to write a paper on it after all this is over." She shot Phutes a look of annoyance. "If it ever gets going."

"Are these Kail bothering you, ma'am?"

"It's not me that's the problem," she said. "Low Zang needs to concentrate. It's leading this event."

Hoyne's face distorted. He gestured, and the humans surrounded Phutes and his siblings.

"All right, my friends, let's go. I'll show you where the other Kail are waiting. We brought them all on board a little while ago."

"We are not moving from here! Tell them, 111."

"I am translating simultaneously," NR-111 assured him. "Colonel, the Kail have urgent business with the Zang."

"And thousands of people have come all this way to see the spectacle," Colonel Hoyne said. "You can talk with it later, after it's all over. Come this way."

"We are not moving," Phutes insisted again.

In answer, the humans raised translucent weapons and pointed them.

"Not more slime!" Mrdus cried.

"We don't have to use these," Hoyne said, in a low tone he no doubt meant to be soothing. "Don't you want to see the rest of your people?"

"Our people?" Phutes asked. "Are they safe? Untouched by you creatures?"

"Yes. They're all here." Hoyne pointed one limb. "Over there."

Phutes growled low in his vocal cone. "We will go." He turned to Low Zang. "Please wait for us. Do not go without hearing us again!"

He thought he felt an encouraging touch, but it was so faint it could have been the hum from the engines that drove this vessel. The humans surrounded them, weapons still aimed at the three Kail, and urged them in the direction of one of the many doors surrounding the round floor.

They were almost at the door before it slid open. Hoyne and the uniformed humans urged them to move forward. Phutes balked at stepping into a small chamber like the lifts, but he had no choice. If he moved back, the humans would coat him with horrible goo. How could they be so cruel to the Kail?

"Will you go in, already?" Hoyne asked.

With one more growl of protest, Phutes stepped forward. His siblings followed him. He heard booming noises ahead of him. The door behind him closed. In a moment, the blank wall ahead slid aside.

Before them was a vast chamber. To his enormous relief, the human had not lied. All the siblings he had left behind on the *Whiskerchin* were there. He counted them. 100111 Kail were present. They surged toward him, surrounding the three of them, rasping against him as if they were home with Yesa.

"Look, there are comfortable rocks," some of them said. "We have a good pool of pure water! We can see through the walls and the dome above! We shall see the destruction!"

Phutes glanced around him. From within the Zang's circle, it looked as though the walls were opaque, but on the Kail's side, the inner side was translucent. The dome above was as clear as water.

Blaring horns and red flashing lights urged them to move forward. Fearing an attack with slime, Phutes moved into the chamber. The wall slid shut behind them.

"You are intact?" a deep, rumbling voice inquired. The crowd of Kail parted to allow passage to Fovrates. The former engineer lumbered toward them, its limbs extended in welcome.

"Yes," Phutes said, rasping his arms against the other's. "How did you get here?"

The engineer chuckled. "The Wichu called in the humans. They are braver than the hairy ones. They captured us and brought us here. Did you get my last transmission?"

"We did," Mrdus said. "But we're not sure we got it all."

"Repeat to me the last sequence," Fovrates said.

Mrdus launched into a repetition of the third number that he had memorized. Fovrates waited, a wary look on his craggy face, until Mrdus reeled off the last set of ones and zeroes.

"That is good," Fovrates said. "You did. But we are prisoners. We may not be able to fulfill our mission."

Phutes let his voice carry into higher registers from sheer relief.

"Yes, we will," he said. "Low Zang is interested in us. It spoke to us. We begged it to speak with us again. We repeated the coordinates to

Proton Zang. If it doesn't share the information with Low Zang, we'll tell it when it comes back to us."

Fovrates boomed out a laugh. "Then it was worth it! We will succeed. The humans will have as much reason to mourn as they gave us."

⇥ CHAPTER 33 ⇤

My family spent several happy hours examining our new cabins aboard the *Hraklion* and comparing them with one another's quarters. I was very pleased with mine. No doubt the Trade Union staff had made use of my Infogrid file public information cache to arrange the contents of the suite with my likes, needs and preferences in mind. The room had been furnished in my favorite blues and greens. The broad bed was neither too soft nor too hard. An exercise barre and mirror had been erected along the wall shared with the bathroom, which I was pleased to note had a real bathtub, long enough for me to submerge my entire person.

A chart showing where each of us had been bestowed flashed at me from the viewscreen on the solid marble desk in the corner of the sitting room. Madame Deirdre, I was pleased to see, was only one deck down from the family, in easy reach for lessons and performance consultation. Nell's suite was next door to mine. She had a double-sized wardrobe that was nearly large enough for all the garments and accessories that she had brought with her. I was persuaded to offer her half of mine, out of brotherly affection as well as a spate of sisterly nagging. Once all our possessions were unpacked and our temporary valets introduced, we went on a self-guided tour of the rest of the *Hraklion*.

Shops, theaters and cinemas, recreational facilities, exercise rooms, saunas and steam rooms and no fewer than three handsome swimming pools were there for our pleasure. We peered through the translucent blast doors at the largest of the saunas at a party of Uctus who had shed their desert garb and lay on tiled couches, soaking up the heat. We were given an assignment for a private room in one of the four enormous dining halls, each assigned to a particular ambient temperature and atmospheric blend.

I was eager to examine the end of the vessel itself, the viewing platform. Along with parties of giggling and chattering beings from numerous systems, all in their best and most colorful clothing, we bundled into one of the central lifts and were borne upward. We emerged into brilliant light that approximated the glow of a small white sun, the star that glowed over the Trade Union's central system. From a glance at the dome high above our heads as well as the map shining on the wall opposite the lift, we were standing in a ring of service areas in between the center reservation and the outer areas reserved for viewing. In this center circle lay the cafes and pubs, rest areas and public conveniences, each coded according to the bracelet that each of us had been issued, to avoid embarrassment. According to the chart, which approximated that from which we had made our reservation, the walls that rose to the dome's heart cut off the third set aside for silicon-based beings. Our bracelets would not activate any of those doorways, for our own safety. The center, a flat arena but for a dais in the center, was designed for the Zang.

"Can we see that part?" Nell asked one of the LAI attendants, who had ridden up with us.

The servicebot, smartly decked out in dark gold and blue as were the human attendants, whirred briefly. "Of course you may, Lady Lionelle," he said. "The Zang are not currently on board. Come with me."

We barged through the security door, and emerged into an astonishingly impressive space. Along with my cousins, I emitted a sigh of satisfaction. This, indeed, was a place from which great things were set in motion.

The surrounding wall was pierced through with numerous doors, obviously leading into various habitats. On the side through which we had entered, they looked very impressive, but on this side, they vanished into mere gray outlines against a silver backdrop. The floor itself was tesserated in tones of gold, beginning as vermeil on the edges and warming into the purest element itself at the center. As we had seen on the diagram, there was a dais. Xan and I ran to it, each eager to be the first to stand upon it. I won the race by half a step, but graciously, I made way for my cousin to come up beside me. There was room, to be honest, for all my cousins and sister to join us, which they did at a far more sedate pace. I assisted Nell up. At this spot, we stood directly beneath the apex of the crystal dome.

"It does make one feel very grand," Xan said. He pointed down near our feet at a series of gold-cased fitments. "Look at that. There are spotlights fixed upon this stage. The Zang produce their own light. Why would they need those?"

"I would assume that other productions are mounted here," I said. "These spectacles can't be all keeping the vessel occupied."

"True," Xan said.

An announcement, all the more welcome for its timing, came over the public address system.

"Friends, the bars are open on the viewing level, and all the entertainment centers in the platform complex are available to you now. Please enjoy yourselves. We will notify you when the event is beginning. In the meantime, the facility is here for you. Let any one of our uniformed attendants know if you need anything. Anything at all! Thank you for visiting the Trade Union Event Platform *Hraklion*!"

"I do like this place," Jil said, in delight.

Gravity on the vessel—I could not in conscience call a long, narrow cylinder with a crystal dome at one end a ship—had been set at approximately .9 of Keinolt standard, so one did not get worn out walking. There was plenty to see, as the vessel was enormous. It could easily have accommodated the population of a small city. Owing to the distance from the Core Worlds, or indeed any densely inhabited portion of the galaxy, the platform was more than two-thirds empty, yet the crew did not seem dismayed at the fill. What we were paying for the privilege of being present at the Zang's spectacle in the comfort one could enjoy in one's own home would nearly have paid for one of those homes. Not mine, of course, but we met plenty of visitors for whom this was the vacation of a lifetime.

The Trade Union officers stayed well out of our way most of the time, since technically we were still at war. This ship was in our space, a clear violation of our borders. Still, in a political set of twists that would have put my back out, no matter how much flexibility training

I had undergone, tourism was one of the few industries that *was* permitted to cross the frontier. No doubt whatsoever that it resulted in Trade Union spies in Imperium space, and vice versa. Still, no vessel like the platform existed throughout the Imperium, and none had such a reputation for being on the spot when the Zang chose to allow witnesses to their art.

The next two mornings in a row, we had gone up before breakfast to examine our new headquarters on the platform level. Shops and cafes were in full operation here, as they had on several levels sandwiched in between the residential areas. The savory aromas coming from their kitchens boded well for the days ahead.

On the third day, it was Sinim's turn to choose in which of these we would take our morning meal. I had dressed in a casual but loose-fitting bodysuit of knitted buff silk, so I could take exercise later on with Madame Deirdre. She had no doubt breakfasted on sunlight and deep thought, but I required actual sustenance. Sinim had spotted a place that served all manner of egg dishes. We took over one entire section of the bistro, firing our requirements for morning beverages at the LAI whose cheerful personality and efficiency won my instant approval.

"Have you seen Laine yet?" Nell asked. Her long, fluttering robes of mottled red and tan were a bit too much for me to take pre-caffeination, but I focused upon her face.

"I have not yet spotted her," I said. Nor had I seen any of my crew, including Parsons. My itch of curiosity had gone unscratched since Plet had contacted me by accident the day before. When I tried to contact anyone on the *Rodrigo* on the first day, I was favored with the usual Imperium Navy graphic and the irritating recording, "Your call is very important to us. Please leave a message and we will return your message as soon as we can." After leaving several increasingly petulant pleas for information, I stopped calling. If they were running technical drills of some kind, I was glad to be left out of them. If adventure had overtaken them, I could register my displeasure on not being included at another time. My cousins understood why I required that one table be kept empty and available, should Laine, Parsons or my crew appear and need to be fed. By the time we finished our meal, none of those had joined us. Stifling my disappointment, I rose with the others and continued our exploration of our temporary domicile.

As the de facto hosts within Imperium space, I and my cousins paid visits to those guests who had already taken up residence on board the *Hraklion*. As many as a dozen galactic nations from outside the Imperium were represented as well as thirty or more systems within its borders. We had been planning to come for almost a year. Others seemed to have been planning longer. A group of humans who looked like an extended family, all barrel-chested and black-haired, had claimed a prime spot close to the center of the carbon-based side. They had banners proclaiming this to be their tenth spectacle. Among their number was a tiny baby boy, bright eyed and kicking happily, who was passed from arm to arm. His coverall was emblazoned with the number one. I smiled at his grinning parents as we went by.

"What are those?" Nell asked, in a low voice, as we neared an area fenced in by wrought-iron barricades. The creatures inside, five in number, looked like small, adorable, blonde children, but with fierce, insane eyes and sharp teeth.

"Donre," I said. "They come from the other side of the Uctu Autocracy. They must have traveled over a year to reach this spot."

"They don't seem happy about it," my sister remarked.

"I must agree with you," I said, as one snarled and lunged toward us, only stopping because it couldn't throw itself through solid metal. Or, at least, I fervently hoped not. "I wonder why they did come."

"Ask them," Nell suggested.

"No, thank you! I'll see if I can persuade Nalney to do it." Nell and I exchanged mischievous glances. For all our differences, we were at heart kindred spirits.

We were lounging in our chosen enclosure in the glorious atrium when five Zang appeared out of nowhere. I had read the term "out of nowhere" many times in works of literature, but it had always sounded like nonsense to me. One must be somewhere. In the case of the proponents of the Elder Race, I had to revise my notion. One moment they were not there, and the next, they were. Even better, Laine was in their company. I sprang up to greet her. She wore a floor-length caftan in a poison green with ruby red highlights and the same plain desert boots she had had on when we first met. Her long hair was pulled back into a simple braid and tied with windings of the same jewel red. I watched her with fascination as she strode toward me. Her costume contrasted sharply with those of my female cousins, who wore the most diaphanous of gowns, yet she still exuded an irresistible pull. I had never before associated scholarliness with sensuality, but Dr. Derrida embodied both without seeming to create a contradiction.

She came to my arms and we embraced. Her clothes and skin felt cold through my thin garment. I did my best to warm her, though she didn't seem bothered by the temperature.

"We've missed you," I said.

"I've missed you, too!" she whispered. We shared a secret look that thrilled me deeply.

"Where have you been?"

"Out taking a look at the planet," she said, this time aloud. Her voice still fell shockingly on the ears, but I was so delighted to be reunited with her that I didn't mind. "Have you met the Zang yet?"

"Only Proton," I said, turning to the gleaming pillars with a smile.

"Oh, let me introduce you!" she exclaimed. My relatives gathered around us. Nalney wielded his viewpad to take images. Laine, unlike so many of my previous *cheres amies*, had no trouble in remembering each of my cousins' names, multiple surnames and all. She reeled them off to the Zang in a performance that was noteworthy enough to cause my relatives to burst into spontaneous applause at its conclusion. "And these are One Zang, Charm Zang, Zang Quark and Low Zang. You already know Proton." We bowed to them.

I surveyed the group with open curiosity. Zang were as uniform in appearance in much the same way as humans, or Wichu, or Uctu. That was to say, possessed of similar characteristics which allowed one to say, "Yes, that is a Zang." Otherwise, they didn't look at all alike. Together in a group as large as five, I could discern subtle differences between them. One was slightly taller than the rest. Another had a bluer cast of skin, or hide, or exoskeleton. A third had the widest base. All of them had large oval eyes but no other apparent orifice, limb or organ. They looked like mobile cliffsides or mesas such as we had on Keinolt, the difference being that the Zang moved, and the cliffs did not. Both cliffs and Zang had the air of having existed forever.

No xenobiologist or anthropologist had sufficient data on the Zang to determine how many of them there were. No images existed of either offspring or elderly members of the race. Having five in one place was an event in itself.

"Welcome," Xan said, taking the lead as he frequently did. "Thank you for allowing us to view the . . . event. We are all looking forward to it."

We waited briefly for some kind of acknowledgement, but none was forthcoming.

"Sorry," Laine said. "Proton's usually the only one who pays attention to us ephemerals. Low Zang," she tilted her head toward the smallest of the pillarlike aliens, "noticed the Kail. That was pretty unusual."

"Where *are* the Kail?" I asked, glancing around. "We have had the great good fortune not to have to speak to any of them since our arrival."

"Back there," Laine said, gesturing back through the center toward the part of the platform that had been walled off. "They're not happy with me right now."

The Zang appeared to confer among themselves. In a moment, they glided off toward the center reservation, moving through walls, pergolas and whatever other obstructions lay in their path. Laine watched them go, then turned back to me.

"How long until the event, in your estimation?" I asked her. Her small face assumed a delightfully thoughtful expression.

"Well, based on the times I've seen it, I'd say about a week. It might be sooner or later. It's hard to tell. I don't know Low Zang. It's new to the group." She dropped her voice, and the others leaned close to listen, risking pierced eardrums if she raised it. "I think it's nervous. This might be its first time leading a removal."

"So this is an occasion," Xan said. "Do they celebrate in some way?"

"Not in any way that we'd notice," Laine said, with a little shake of her head. "But if Low Zang really becomes a member of the group, that's important. The Zang are solitary most of the time, like Proton. This is the only activity I know of that brings them together. I'll be giving lectures all week long, so if you think anything else you want to know, please ask me then. I am happy to tell you anything you want now, but other attendees might get a lot out of hearing the answers to your questions."

"I understand," Xan said. "We look forward to the hour."

He bowed over her hand. She reddened becomingly. I came over and gathered her hands in mine. We looked into one another's eyes. I opened my mouth to speak, when a tendril of power smacked into the side of my head. Laine let out a shrill laugh.

"I'd better go. They want me."

"Your departure desolates us," I said. She giggled again.

She sauntered away. I fetched a hearty sigh. I had read a good deal about the mating habits of birds while immersed in a previous enthusiasm. I was tempted to dust off and review the digitavids in my collection to see if there was a dance I could adapt to draw her attention away from her studies. Surely I, a noble and a member of the Imperium family, was of more interest than the Zang!

"Well, that's not much of an answer," Nalney said. "Days or hours?"

"For the experience of a lifetime, how long would you wait?" Rillion asked.

CHAPTER 34

However reticent the Trade Union officers might have been about contact with their Imperium hosts, their staff went out of their way to entertain us and keep us busy. We viewed digitavids and lectures including a few of Laine's, participated in contests, cooking and wine exhibitions, mixers and individual events. Erita came back from a massage session raving about an LAI therapist. I vowed to make an appointment. Anything that could move my usually lugubrious cousin to raptures must have been something unique.

The Zang did not remain in their round chamber. They drifted here and there throughout the platform. The vibration that had been a mere tremor upon our arrival had grown ever stronger, until it was nearly audible. We lay on our couches and divans in our little garden, staring up at the doomed planetoid. I fancied that I could see lights circling it now and then. Did it realize what was about to happen?

Now and again I would see Laine trailing after Proton Zang and its colleagues across the platform. Once in a while it would allow her to wander on her own, but most of the time she remained by its side. I had come up with various little dances to amuse her, but as I had given Parsons my word not to do any where the Zang could see them, I writhed in artistic frustration.

"You shouldn't have to keep them to yourself," Nell said. I had given various excuses for not performing my rage dance or any of the other evocations that I had composed, in case any of the Zang should wander by.

"I . . . I don't feel the time is right," I said.

"Well, that's a change," Nell said, with an odd look at me. "All the way here, we couldn't keep you dancing your feet off."

"I know, but Art is a fickle mistress. She does not want me to evoke, but to gather impressions."

"Well, all right," Nell said. "How about if you wait until after the spectacle, then do a dance for us based on what you felt about it? I mean, once it's over, there's nothing new left to absorb, wouldn't you say?"

Once the Zang had finished their destruction, the chances were great that they would depart. After that, my promise to Parsons would no longer be in force.

"That is a marvelous idea," I said, giving Nell a brotherly hug, for which I received a sisterly poke in the ribs. "I shall dedicate it to you and Dr. Derrida."

At that moment, the vibrations increased enormously.

On the settee opposite, Erita and Sinim clutched one another in alarm.

"What was that?" Sinim asked, plaintively.

"The energy has intensified," Xan said, in an ominous voice. The platform fell silent as everyone looked toward the dome. The planet in the distance seemed to be vibrating visibly.

"Are we in danger?" Erita asked.

I spotted a familiar silver glow emerging from among the potted plants and pergolas. The five Zang floated toward us. I spotted the tiny figure of Laine among them. To my surprise, behind her were the three Kail that had been on the *Jaunter*.

"What are *they* doing here?" Nalney asked, eying them nervously.

"I don't know." I rose from my place and went to meet Laine. She smiled up at me.

"The energy seems to have risen," I said.

"Yes," Laine said. "Low Zang is getting very nervous. I think that the spectacle is imminent."

"Marvelous!" I said. I gestured hospitably to the circle of couches. Jil scooted over to make room. "Will you watch it with us?"

"I can't stay here," Laine said, with an apologetic grimace. "Proton wants me close by. But you can watch it with me, from the center of the platform."

"I would be honored," I said. "My cousins will die of envy, of course. When will it take place?"

"I think it's today or tomorrow," Laine said. She paused as though to listen. "That feels about right."

"Forgive my curiosity, but . . . ?" I nodded toward the Kail.

Laine gave a helpless shrug. "Low Zang seems to like them. It wants them to be on the platform, too."

"Well, then, I will certainly attend, if only to keep the creatures away from you," I said.

She smiled. "That's sweet, but they won't bother me. They haven't said a word to me. Proton sees to that." A rumble seemed to pass through the entire structure of the vessel, centering on the Zang. They moved away again. "I'd better go." She let her hand slip out of mine. I remained where I was, seeing her draw away from me. I felt inutterably sad.

"Then, we have between a day and two days," Jil said, with growing enthusiasm. "I think we should begin the party now! We can celebrate right up until the very moment of destruction! Won't that be memorable?"

"If we can remember it," Nalney said.

"Well, you've been recording it steadily," Erita said, gesturing at his ever-present pocket secretary. "We can watch your vids if we render ourselves senseless. But I have no intention of overindulging. This is too marvelous an opportunity!"

"I have some delicious treats that I have saved for our party," Nell said, taking her pocket secretary in hand. "I'll have my valet bring them up."

"I've composed a poem," Nalney said. We all looked at him. "Well, Thomas, you're not the only only one in the family with talent."

"And I," Erita said, "have written a song. It's to someone else's tune, but it's my song!"

"Well done, Erita!" Xan cheered.

My heart, which had been desolated with Laine's departure, filled up again with delight.

"Very well, I shall perform," I said. "And I have delicacies to offer you all."

"Let's not bring everything out at once," Leonat said. "Let's arrange things in courses. One surprise after another."

"That is a wonderful idea," I said. I rose.

If I was not going to be permitted to perform for the Zang, I intended to change into the handsome Starburst outfit that I had bought for them and offer the dance as a gift to my sister and relatives at the conclusion of the event. I felt certain that they would be as impressed by it as they were by the destruction of a fairly nondescript planetoid.

But I realized, when I sent for my valet, that the costume itself was not on the platform. It was in my cabin aboard the *Imperium Jaunter*. I looked up at the shivering orb in the sky. There ought to be enough time to get it.

I headed for the lift.

"Where are you going?" Nell called. I turned back. My relatives had huddled in a planning session.

"I have to get a few things from the *Jaunter*," I said. "I will see you later."

"Hurry back!" Nalney said, with a lazy wave. "Dr. Derrida said it could start at any time."

"I know," I said. Eagerness made my steps bounce. I looked forward to performing my composition. I hoped that Laine would be able to attend it and would enjoy it. It was the least I could do to show my affection for her.

At the lifts, I ran into Madame Deirdre. She and our other supernumeraries had been freed to enjoy themselves as they pleased, pending the spectacle and our subsequent departure homeward. They occupied a set of couches adjacent to ours, among a party of merchants from Leo's Star. It had become a merry band.

She emerged from a car with a couple of men upon whom Jil had bestowed some of her many favors. They had been taking dance lessons from Deirdre on the side, no doubt to impress my fickle cousin. Deirdre patted one of them on the arm.

"Go on," she said. "I'll catch up with you. Where are you going, Lord Thomas?"

"I'm going back to get my Starburst costume," I said. "I'm going to do my Zang dance for my cousins at the conclusion of the spectacle. Will you rehearse with me?"

"If there's time," she said.

"Thank you," I said. "See you in a short while!"

  With the spectacle set to begin fairly shortly, the flow of traffic into the platform far outweighed that which was outbound. Everyone else seemed to have brought everything that they wanted to the platform on their first trip. I thought I had: clothes and costumes, not to mention gifts and treats that I intended to give my cousins at the party, a lovely little necklace that I had bought for my mother, but now planned to give Laine. Luckily, shuttles lay empty at nearly all the departure points. I begged a lift on the first one I saw, and was granted immediate access. A securitybot, armed to the gears, accompanied me into the small craft. It kept all circuits open until we had launched safely.

CHAPTER 35

The transit wasn't a long one, but the small ship bucked and writhed as if it was a seagoing barque. The energy that the Zang employed in their art form was building up, disrupting even deep space. Our platform was made to absorb the waves of power so we did not notice them. The small ship, and probably the *Jaunter*, had not. I was thrown about for the first few moments of the trip, then I picked up on the rhythm of the waves. Thereafter, I had no trouble balancing against them. Laine had said they would get faster and stronger the closer we came to the spectacle. To me, that added to the intensity of the event. I planned to incorporate the increasing rapidity in my performance.

I made my lonely way to the private lift to the nobles' quarters. Even the spectacle of a planet being reduced to particles wasn't enough to lighten my spirits.

I stepped toward the door of my suite. It hesitated before it opened. I made a mental note to tell Anna to inform the maintenance system of the flaw.

An odd aroma reminiscent of the outdoors excited my notice as I entered. I didn't believe that I had brought a cologne or scented product like it with me. Before I could remark upon the puzzle any further, a hand grasped me about the neck and yanked me backward.

In earlier days, I would have ended up flat on my back in an undignified manner, but years of anticipating such pranks by my cousins, particularly Xan, I had taken up a number of martial arts. Those had cut down on pratfalls and bruises, and my new rapid response time had given Xan something to think about in those playful ambushes and skirmishes. Those skills were honed further during our two years at the Naval Academy, and since becoming involved with Parsons and the assignments given us by the mysterious Mr. Frank, those skills had been ground to a fine point verging upon singularity. I used the momentum created by falling toward the floor and gathered my knees to my chest. I continued the backward roll over the arm of my assailant and came up on my feet. My hands, which could not be classified as the deadliest of weapons but were still capable of defending against all but missile weapons, were half-cupped to deal the fiercest of blows. I prepared to go on the offensive.

Instead of going on guard himself, my attacker fell into a relaxed attitude. He applauded and laughed.

"Well done, Thomas!" said Uncle Laurence. "You've been training!"

I felt my jaw drop agape as if I beheld a specter. Yet the dimensions and lineaments were familiar as, I might say, my own face, for we rather resembled one another. Laurence Millais Yan Fitzhugh Kinago was within a millimeter or two of my own lofty height, and had as broad a shoulder. He had the same strong jaw and high cheekbones, the same wide-set eyes, and indeed the same straight, patrician nose as I did. I had learned not very long ago that the shape had a tendency to inspire loyalty and obedience. I knew that in Uncle Laurence's case, at least, it provoked sighs of longing from the female population and not a small number of the male. Like Lionelle, he had thick, shining, almost black hair and sapphire blue eyes, whereas mine referred toward the ocean for their color. That reference brought a question abruptly to my lips.

"Does Nell know you're here?"

"No one does," Laurence said, with a grin. He grasped my hand and shook it. I returned the clasp with pleasure. "Not yet. With the possible exception of Parsons. He knows everything. Always did, may he live forever."

"Naturally," I said, willing to give credit where a healthy balance already existed. "I would assume nothing less. What are you doing here?"

"Why, I hoped to visit with you," Laurence replied, slapping me on the back. "I was in the neck of the woods, to employ the cant term, so I dropped by."

"Come and see Nell!" I invited, extending my hand. "She'd be thrilled. You are her favorite uncle."

"Not yet," he said, with a conspiratorial air. "I have a matter to bring up with *you*."

I opened my clothes closet and began to collect my belongings. My valetbot rolled out a small holdall and opened it on the table for me. I piled colored dance shoes in the bottom, then hauled costumes one after another for Anna to fold. I might as well bring over a few of my other favorites, too.

"Well, Nell is on the viewing platform. I am heading over very shortly. You can talk with me on the way. We have been staying there while the preparations are going on. I presume you've already seen the Zang phenomenon." I emitted a rueful sigh. "You and Father had many experiences in your youth that I will probably never be able to emulate. But this will be one experience that we can share. We can talk on the way in relative privacy, LAIs excepted, of course."

He laughed again. The warm baritone brought back happy memories of my childhood. One never knew when to expect Uncle Laurence, but his visits were always filled with delightful surprises.

"I did see the Zang bonsai a system, yes—oh, thirty years ago, now? Your father and I were boys then. It was awe-inspiring, astonishing, unique, and with a healthy dollop of 'children, do *not* try this at home' laced into it. With any luck, I'll get you back here in time to view it."

I blinked, feeling as though I had missed a long section of conversation in the blink of an eye.

"Get back? I'm not leaving, uncle. We don't know when the Zang will begin. It could be months, but it might be moments. As you say, it's a once-in-a-lifetime spectacle, or twice if one is most fortunate. I have a performance planned. I've been waiting to do it for weeks now." I glanced down at my viewpad. "And Parsons will be wondering where I am. He has me on the lookout for . . ." I hesitated. I knew that Uncle Laurence was in the know about most things, but I wasn't sure how much that which had been imparted to me in confidence I could reveal. "I have a great deal of respect for Parsons, of course. He has been . . . of great assistance to me."

Laurence's deep blue eyes glowed, taking on the sparkle of their namesake gemstone.

"Wouldn't you like, just once, to steal a march on the old fellow? To do something that he has never done?"

My entire mental processes underwent an information overload.

"Is there anything that he hasn't done?" I asked, in a rhetorical manner, for such a thing would never, could never, occur to me.

"Perhaps just this one thing," Laurence said. The corner of his mouth turned up in a tiny smile. "You shall have that experience, but only if you come with me *now*."

He never used that urgent tone of voice without reason. Without hesitation, I abandoned my suitcase. Without knowing where I was going, but trusting him as I did with my life, I pulled the thin, insulated coat I had had made for cold weather on the planets we were to visit, though I had not needed it once. I made to step into my custom gravity boots, but Laurence forestalled me with a wave.

"You won't need those, my lad. Just a pair of good walking shoes will do." He plucked the viewpad out of my belt pouch. "And leave this here. You won't need it, either. Besides, it's not allowed. Too much spyware. Mr. Frank would be horrified at the potential for breaches." I hesitated. He gestured toward the lockbox set into the wall of my cabin. "Go on. Lock it up."

More and more intrigued with every moment, I obeyed his order. Anna brought me a pair of dark brown, flat-heeled leather boots with tall shafts and seized my right leg with one of her valeting claws. I fell back into the nearest chair and allowed her to minister as my shoe fairy.

"You know about Mr. Frank?" I asked, seizing upon the first thing that floated to the surface in the whirlwind of my thoughts.

"Know him?" Uncle Laurence said, with a laugh. "Of course I do. So do you."

That revelation hit me like an oncoming wall.

"No, I don't," I protested. "He has been shrouded in mystery. All I know is a name. I suspect a location. I believe that he operates, if not lives, in Taino." Anna released my right leg and reached for the left. I lifted it within easy grasping range. She divested me of the other soft-soled patent leather slipper and clapped my foot into the second cylinder, which gave forth with an echoing boom. "How do I know him? By what other name has he been called?"

Laurence looked surprised. "Well, if he hasn't told you himself, I can't expose his secrets to you, Thomas. I'm sorry. It's a bit too soon. I apologize. Once we have been colleagues longer, I won't need to tell you. You'll slap yourself on the forehead for not having figured it out yourself."

We were colleagues? That was almost as boggling a concept as the notion that there was an experience that Parsons had not had.

"Give me a hint," I begged. "A morsel of data! I'll puzzle out the enigma, but I haven't enough clues to go upon."

Laurence shook his head. "Sorry, Thomas. My lips are sealed."

"You *don't* know," I said, feeling as though my lip wanted to jut out in a quite understandable pout. "You heard the name somewhere, perhaps, and you decided to torment me with it to take my mind off this one-of-a-kind experience ahead."

He laughed, his warm baritone chuckle filling the room. "I spoke out of school, Thomas. Give in. You know you can't tease it out of me. You'll find out soon enough. Come along, now, and stop acting like Erita. It's irritating enough when she does it. It's unspeakable coming from you."

The pout definitely attempted to assert itself as I followed him through the now-empty corridors of the *Imperium Jaunter*. A few LAIs passed us.

"Good afternoon, Lord Thomas, Lord Laurence."

Normally, I greeted them as the good creatures they were, but I was overcome by a mix of puzzlement, wonder, curiosity and, yes, frustration. It so often seemed that everyone in my coterie was party to secrets that not only did they know and I didn't, but were unwilling or unable to reveal them to me . . . yet. Still, I forced myself out of my snit enough to smile and nod. They didn't seem to mind the cursory nature of my hails. Perhaps they were also privy to Uncle Laurence's hoard of information. Biological beings tended largely to speak in front of those of the electronic persuasion as though they weren't there or were not capable of comprehending that which was said. Naturally, the opposite was true. They were fully developed personalities, nearly always with far greater intelligence than most humans, at least, could ever aspire to.

Still, it wasn't like me to maintain a sour disposition for any discernible interval. By the time we reached the shuttle bay, I was hopping with enthusiasm. My favorite uncle had come to visit me! We were setting out on a trip that Parsons had never taken. I couldn't wait to see my aide-de-camp's face when I returned and . . . . And my hand touched the empty holster on my hip. Whatever it was, I would have no proof but my word. Yet, I thought, my mood brightening further, that had always been good enough in the past.

The *Jaunter*, for all its great size, could be run efficiently by computer. At the moment, it was emptied to the bulkheads of humanity, Uctunity, and all other sentient species except for those LAIs who did not want to go to the platform and an unlucky soul or two from the crew who had been placed in the brig or the infirmary. Uncle Laurence and I clumped through the echoing bay toward a distant corner. We passed my ship. It was under the auspice of the LAI on board, Angie, or NG-903, to give her her official designation. As I passed, the exterior lights went on in sequence, just to show she was paying attention to our passage. Every artificial intelligence for a parsec around already knew my viewpad was back in my cabin, so no one could speak to me bar directly.

Uncle Laurence looked up and drew a finger over the name embossed upon the prow as he passed it.

"An honor for your father," he said, with a smile.

"I'm honored to be his son," I replied. I meant every syllable. Laurence nodded.

"So you know? His history during the war?"

"Some of it," I said. I fancied that no matter how many stories I heard from survivors that I would never know the full accounting of Rodrigo Park Kinago's heroics. My mother never spoke of them to any of the three of us, and my father probably could not recall them, except on a very good day.

"Well, you're following in his footsteps, far more than that lazy brother of yours," Laurence said, wrinkling his nose. "I had hopes for him, but he's happy being the titular governor of a most placid system. His staff does all the work, you know. He's as smart as any Kinago, but so unmotivated!"

I shrugged. "Most of our cousins are unmotivated except by our whims, though those can be powerful impetuses."

"Indeed," Laurence said, with a grin. "Whims are what took me on my travels, but duty is what kept me there. You've gone into harness a bit young, but you can kick over the traces for a few years. Mr. Frank won't mind, I promise you that."

"I'm enjoying myself a good deal now," I pointed out. "How many of my cousins can say that they've had a parade organized in their honor? One that they did not have arranged for themselves? Who has won the intersystem Grand Prix not once, but twice? Without the aid of an LAI pilot?"

"You, and you again!" My uncle laughed. "Come along, and you can add another entry to your scrapbook, albeit a private one."

I glanced toward the sole remaining shuttle, the green pinpoint lights chasing around its entry hatch.

"We could watch the spectacle, then go," I said, hopefully.

"At the rate the Zang move, we could age a year," Laurence said, with a dismissive wave. "I really cannot afford to have any living being observe me long enough to discern my flight path. You will understand why shortly. Come on! That's my ship. Come meet *Gaia*."

Even such a well-defended vessel as the *Jaunter* had its own security drones and single-being fighters. Clusters of these small craft were spaced here and there on hexagonal, black and silver pads in the massive chamber so no individual strike from an invader could destroy all of them at once. The pads of two of the twelve squads were empty, out on regular patrol.

Behind the huddle that made up the currently dormant Squad Three, a needle of gleaming silver protruded upward. It had not been there before. Curious, I scrambled to round the official ships until I was before the newcomer, and had a good gawk.

Gaia was a slightly oblate sphere about half the size of the *Rodrigo*. The engines were arrayed on a thick ring about its midsection, making for superior maneuverability. The needle was a sensor array with repulsors and weapon apertures all along its length. The ship's surface had been anodized in a warm bronze tone. Curiously, I saw no designations of any kind, not even a tail identification number. I peered at the vessel, trying to place the make and model.

"I thought I knew all the types of ships that cruise the starways," I said, "but I've never seen one like that."

"A beauty, isn't she?" my uncle said, puffing up his chest with pride. "I designed it myself. I've had it nearly two decades. A custom job, from out of the Trade Union."

"Really?" I asked, feeling my right eyebrow lift toward my hairline.

"I thought the Imperium didn't do official business with the Trade Union."

The cluster of federated star systems ran along the second-most heavily populated section of the Imperium's border after the Uctu Autocracy. Their guiding principle was "Profit Above All!" Not a stirring rallying cry, you might think, but its denizens were as devoted to their government and ways of life as we were, though they had many more internecine wars.

"Who said it was official?" Laurence asked, innocence beaming from his deep blue eyes. "I had money and a design and time to wait for the right deal to come along. When I opened the job to tender, I had 416 bidders. The winning engineers were ninetieth-generation shipbuilders. Come on board."

An entry platform descended at the sound of his voice. I followed him inside.

As soon as I mounted the ramp, I felt the pull of the artificial gravity generator. The ramp led along the interior of the bulkhead. Because the ship wasn't very large, the "floor" was markedly curved, and the core was always over my head.

"All systems operate from controllers in *Gaia*'s heart," Laurence said, pointing 'up.' "The control room is about a fourth of the ship. I do pretty much everything in here: eat, listen to music and watch digitavids, repair modules, practice a hobby or two. There are two cabins, all with the finest of modern conveniences, and the remaining half is cargo space. I don't travel much, but when I do, I like to have the best things around me."

I surveyed the bridge. The stainless-steel-topped worktable that arced along one side of the bulkhead protruded far enough that one could walk up to it and not end up underneath it because of the gravity. All the viewers and screentanks were fixed above it. The dark-blue upholstered pilot's seat stood on three-meter pylon facing them. The rest of the vast walls had cushions, bookcases, small tables and stools and other comforts sticking out at odd angles as if they were defying gravity, when they were doing anything but. An old-fashioned book with a solid, beige linen cover lay face down on the wall at approximately my eye level. I peered to see what he was reading. The title was clearly printed, but in a language I did not know.

Uncle Laurence tapped a control on the pylon. The pilot's chair lowered itself to knee level. He sat down and strapped himself into the harness.

"Second seat, please, *Gaia*," he said. "My nephew will be traveling with us today."

"Of course," a pleasant female voice replied, seeming to come from everywhere at once. "Welcome, Lord Thomas."

"Thank you, er, *Gaia*," I said. "I am very pleased to be here."

Red laser lights flashed out of the bulkheads and ran up and down my body, then turned off just as suddenly. I jumped back as panels in the floor at my feet rearranged themselves. Five of them flipped over to reveal more dark blue padding. They moved together, then inverted to create a squared nest. It rose, shifting further, until the contraption that stopped at my knee level was a chair that would fit my long frame precisely. I sat down in it to confirm, and slapped the arm rests with gleeful palms.

"Excellent," I pronounced. Straps lanced out from the side pads and wrapped themselves around my chest and over my lap. A pair of foot rests scooped up underneath my soles. Both seats rose on their individual standards and clicked into place. "But why do they have to be elevated?"

"It's the gravity generators," Laurence explained. "Otherwise you feel as if you're looking down at the floor. By the time you get to your destination, one's eyeballs are almost hanging out of one's face."

I laughed. I felt as though we were off on one of the expeditions on which he had often taken me and my siblings in our childhood.

"Where are we going?" I asked.

He smiled and gave me a playful wink.

"I'm taking you home."

❧ CHAPTER 36 ❧

The platform, a vast, circular floor roofed with a force field, was sparsely populated despite the uniqueness of the approaching event. Parsons, stationed at a point where he could observe the influx from the lift cars as well as a broad arc of the carbon-friendly side of the dome, mused to himself that most beings would be content to observe the coming spectacle in retrospect, via high-quality digitavid or on amateur recordings shared in Infogrid files. The latter would be well represented: nearly all of the nobles present had their pocket secretaries, viewpads, or hovering camera eyes prepared for the moment. They were somewhat premature in their preparations, as the event was some hours or days yet to come. From studies that Parsons had made of previous spectacles, the energy level had not risen to the tipping point at which the planet above them would explode.

Lively instrumental music played an undertone to the excited roar of conversation from the spectators. The majority of those present were blissfully unaware that an event of importance had already taken place in the surrounding space. The *Whiskerchin* was at last liberated from its temporary thrall to the Kail. The *Rodrigo*'s company had remained on board to assist the Wichu in purging the ship's computer network of any traces of the programs that Fovrates had installed in it and its LAI and AI staff. The LAIs, for their part, had shown embarrassment in having been involved in a mutiny. Those who had withstood the invaders, ColPUP* among them, downplayed any acclaim, stating that they had only been doing the jobs for which they had been hired. The passengers were, for the most part, serenely unaware that anything unusual had taken place during the voyage. They were eager to debark and join the now ongoing party to celebrate the upcoming celestial event.

The main players in that event were absent from the platform at the moment. The five Zang did not remain in one place on the *Hraklion*, nor on the vessel itself. Professor Derrida accompanied them most of the time. Parsons found her companionship with Proton Zang a curiosity and a unique opportunity that gave humans a narrow glimpse into the Elder Race. Though pressed by numerous of the spectators, she had not been able to confirm with any certainty when the event would take place.

Parsons's particular charges, the nobles of the Imperium house, had ensconced themselves happily in an angle of the viewing platform well away from the wall that separated their habitat from that containing the Kail. They had begun their merrymaking, surrounded by their retainers and newfound friends among the other patrons. If the spectacle did not begin soon, Parsons assumed that the nobles would become bored and wander down to the living quarters or the other entertainment centers open to them in the lower decks of the massive structure. When the event was imminent, they would return. As long as they were in one vessel, they would be fairly easy to contain and evacuate in case of an emergency.

Parsons had not yet observed a Zang phenomenon in person; such things were seldom publicized in advance. The Zang, unlike Lord Thomas, were not concerned with public performance of their art. He would not have confessed to feeling eagerness; curiosity was perhaps a more comprehensive description. The sheer force that the Zang were able to harness would have been of grave concern if the technique could be weaponized, but since few if any ephemerals had been able to communicate directly with the ancient beings, it was unlikely they could interest them in directing their destruction toward a target of opportunity. That virtual certainty was a relief. Parsons had enough to deal with.

Lady Lionelle bore down upon him like a high-force hurricane, bearing numerous of the young nobles in her wake.

"Parsons, there you are! Come and stand with us! It could start at any moment. You would not wish to miss a single millisecond, would you?"

The First Space Lord's youngest child and only daughter was as charming as Admiral Tariana Loche herself. He had always been deeply fond of the girl. He smiled, the expression curving his lips briefly.

"I have duties I must discharge before I may join the observers, my lady," he said, allowing a modicum of regret to touch his brow.

She curled her hands around his arm.

"You must come and join our party," she said. "I won't take no for an answer."

Parsons allowed himself to be towed to a point near the rim of the platform and handed a brimming champagne glass.

"Do you have any idea where Thomas went?" Lady Lionelle asked. "He's been gone for ages!"

"He flew to the *Jaunter* on a shuttle, my lady. I am sure he will return shortly."

"Oh, Nell, help me! Leonat has her hair caught in her necklace," Lady Erita called. Lady Lionelle gave Parsons a charming smile, and moved away to join her cousins.

He maintained sight of the lift center as well as the nearest wall separating the humans, Wichu, Uctu, and other visitors from the silicon habitat. It was translucent, not opaque, so Parsons could see the Kail contingent beyond it. They would not be denied a view of the spectacle, as the platform rotated to keep the unhappy planet directly overhead. Among the Kail milling behind the barrier he caught sight of Phutes, the leader of those who had invaded the *Imperium Jaunter*. The creature recognized him and glared at him. Parsons fixed him with a baleful stare that made him retreat among his fellows. Their demeanor was meant to put off any contact whatsoever. They were belligerent, but could be bullied into cooperation. Such behavior proclaimed their lack of assurance with other races. He hoped that Special Envoy Melarides would convince them to unite with the Imperium and the Wichu, their closest neighbors. She had an excellent reputation among the diplomatic corps for creating détente out of chaos.

The Imperium house had claimed three habitats in a row near one of the handsomely appointed refreshment outlets. Each of these were set to prepare food for over a dozen species, the names of which were engraved upon the stone pillars that supported the gray glass pergola. Lord Nalney had already availed himself of the beer kegs. His brilliant teeth gleamed from between his dark lips. He held aloft a foaming tankard to Parsons.

"Your very good health, sir," he called.

"And yours, my lord," Parsons said. He lifted his glass, though he did not drink any of the contents. Undoubtedly, the champagne was the finest vintage obtainable, but he would not risk even a fractional depletion of sharpness and observation for a moment's pleasure.

Lord Xanson and Lady Jil waved languidly from the cushions upon which they were ensconced. Lady Jil had been accompanied on this journey by Lady Sinim and four of her common friends, but also two of her current lovers, one of whom had come along as an art instructor. Parsons had had them thoroughly investigated to ensure that they had no criminal ties nor a history of brawling. Such a disturbance might discommode the Zang. The humans and other beings who were attending the destruction did not realize that their status as guests could be withdrawn with haste and expressed regret. Though the nobles in particular believed it was their right to be present, they were the least likely to act out in an antisocial manner.

Despite assurances from the Zang that no living beings would be harmed by the destruction of the planet in the distance, Parsons had dispatched the *Rodrigo* to confirm. A discreet pip from his viewpad assured him that the scout ship had returned. With a bow of apology toward Lady Lionelle, he retired to the side of the platform nearest the lift shafts once more, and waited.

Many groups of guests arrived and toured the viewing platform, in hopes of attaining the best possible vantage point. A group of Uctus, led by a coral-skinned male wearing the livery of the Autocratic House and therefore a cousin of the current Autocrat, Visoltia. When they reached the platform level, a pair of young females and a male in long, gray tunics split off from the party and ran around the perimeter of the domed chamber exclaiming in wonder.

Parsons ran the senior male's features through his mental database. Once he had confirmed the noble's identity, he arranged his hands in the correct configuration to show respect, and bowed over them.

"Lord Steusan," he said. "It is a pleasure to see you. I trust matters are going well in the Ministry of Agriculture?"

The Uctu blinked his large eyes at the black-clad human.

"Your pardon," the noble said. He spoke excellent Standard, with only a hint of an accent. "I do not know your designation."

"Commander Parsons. I serve Lord Thomas Kinago, cousin of the emperor."

Steusan's breath exploded in a series of amused hisses.

"The tall one! He is still the talk of Nacer! Is he here?"

"Not at present. He will return," Parsons said.

"Noviet mah!" One of the female pages returned and made an obeisance to Lord Steusan. She held out a spatulate hand toward the clockwise side of the room.

"Please excuse us," Steusan said, switching his thick tail. "I hope we will speak later."

"It would be my honor," Parsons assured him. As the party of Uctus followed him away, one female, a minor dignitary, glanced back and closed one of her large eyes halfway. Parsons nodded slightly, inclining his head a millimeter or so. She was a member of Uctu Covert Services, which had maintained its ties to its Imperium counterpart for generations.

So far, his briefs had been complete. None of the visitors from any of the neighboring nations had gone unidentified. Parsons was pleased. His report to Mr. Frank would be complete. It only remained to ensure that no sentient beings were in peril from that moment until the return to Keinolt.

The Kail had been spending a great deal of time in the company of the Zang, and had not troubled the humans further. They could not be trusted, but they did not seem to have invaded the computer system, nor caused any other trouble. Heaven knew they were sorely provoked by Lord Thomas's insistence on trying to persuade them to like his interpretive dances. The Trade Union officers aboard the cylindrical craft had taken no chances. The Kail had no access to electronic systems behind their barrier.

A massed huddle of Wichus rose up together, like one huge, cloudlike mass of white fur, occupying nearly the entire lift bank. Lieutenant Oskelev extracted herself from its midst. The crowd seemed reluctant to let her go.

"C'mon, guys!" she said, in the Wichu tongue, one of the many languages in which Parsons was fluent. She batted away a male's straying hand with surprising force. "We can party later when I'm off duty! I gotta make a report."

Oskelev came toward Parsons, grinning, brushing herself down. A flurry of loose hairs swirled to the floor. She saluted.

"Hi, commander," she said. "This is the crew of the *Whiskerchin* and all the passengers who were aboard. Great people! They think I'm some kind of hero. I kept telling them that it's just my job."

"Lieutenant," Parsons acknowledged. "I trust they are unharmed?"

"No problems. They're already over it. Fovrates is going to have to find a ride back to Kail space on his own, but they're not that upset. He didn't do any lasting damage."

"I am gratified to hear that."

One stray hair hovered, threatening to attach itself to Parsons's pristine black uniform. He stared at it. Intimidated, it fluttered away from him and joined its fellows on the carpet.

A small, boxy cleanerbot exited a wall panel a meter away, and began to absorb the hanks of long white fur.

Oskelev saluted again. "They invited me to join their party, sir."

"One moment, if you please," Parsons replied, amiably. "Let us wait for Lieutenant Plet."

"Yessir, but she already released me."

Parsons allowed his left brow to ascend a fraction of a millimeter. The ebullient Wichu subsided into stillness without another word.

They had not long to wait. The slight figure of the nominal commanding officer of the *Rodrigo* surfaced a few moments later. She looked deeply perturbed.

"Lieutenant Plet, what is the matter?" Parsons inquired.

"Lieutenant Kinago, sir," Plet said, her normally pale face pink over the cheekbones. "He has not reported in, and his quarters are empty. I pinged his viewpad, and found it locked up in his cabin."

"Lieutenant Kinago . . . is on a special mission," Parsons replied.

"He is? Why didn't you . . . ?" Plet straightened her back and stared off into the middle distance. "I would have been pleased to be informed, sir. With all the potential hostiles on this vessel, I was concerned for his well-being, sir."

Parsons could have smiled, but it would have hurt her dignity. He inclined his head approximately two degrees.

"The mission only arose a short while ago," he assured her.

"There had not yet been time to inform you. This is your official notice."

In fact, his only notice had been a heavily-encoded audio message from Lord Laurence: "I'm taking Thomas out for a spin, old thing! See you when we see you." It was flippant, casual, and would arouse no suspicion if it had been intercepted, although Parsons's highly advanced and very recently updated detection technology assured him that it had not.

"Is he safe?" Plet asked. For all her protests that she cared nothing for the reckless and playful young man, Parsons knew she had conceived a deep affection for him. Lord Thomas was indeed hard not to like. As of yet, her regard had not crossed the line into inappropriate feelings that would undermine her ability to concentrate and put the mission first. Both of them must be prepared to sacrifice any individual if it would keep the Imperium safe. Naturally, if the Imperium was not in danger, Lord Thomas was their next priority. As an asset, he was worthwhile.

Parsons reminded himself that was Lord Thomas's chief value.

"He is safe," he said. "Report."

Plet relaxed very slightly.

"We finished the flyover, and the data was messaged to you a short while ago. Redius and Anstruther did a complete scan of Noreb 80-e. It's as dead as it's possible for a space rock to be. It looks as though it sustained a massive impact by an asteroid or group of asteroids a long while ago. It still maintains a slip of atmosphere, but the place is a wreck. Anstruther can do a reconstruction for you, if you want to determine how long ago the impact occurred."

"That is not necessary, as long as no trace of life remains."

"If there ever was any," Oskelev said. "I took a run around it myself to make sure. Dead as stale beer."

"We're not spotting even much in the way of ancient watercourses," Plet added. "The white traces around the poles are antimony, not frost."

"Curious," Parsons remarked. He glanced up. The platform maintained its orientation that kept the doomed planetoid centered at the top of the dome. "The single moon is an anomaly."

Plet frowned, as if trying to capture a thought.

"That's what Anstruther said. It's surprisingly regular in shape, almost as though it was the original planet before the damaged one was pushed into that orbit."

"One might speculate whether the Zang know its origins," Parsons said. "It's possible that they observed it, though why they have chosen this moment to correct that error is also a matter of speculation."

"Commander . . . are they really that old?" Plet asked. Parsons could have smiled, but she would have been wounded by his amusement.

"They are. For the moment you are off duty. I suggest you enjoy the moment. Dr. Derrida will send notice when the spectacle is about to begin."

"I hope Lord Thomas gets back soon," Oskelev said. "He's been pretty excited about seeing the spectacle."

"I trust he will," Parsons said. "You are dismissed, but expected to remain on call."

"Yes, commander," the two officers said. They slipped away into the milling crowd. Parsons resumed his vigil. Two more concerns had been dismissed. Now only four remained.

⁖ CHAPTER 37 ⁖

Gaia's exit from the edge of Zang space was so rapid that the platform disappeared in the aft screen tank before I had time to react to it. The high seat in which I was perched gave me an excellent view of all the sensor readings.

"The platform authority didn't acknowledge you," I observed. "They gave us quite a multiple choice quiz when we arrived, checking our bona fides. I almost expected them to demand an essay from each of us on why we wanted to watch the destruction of a planet, using examples and footnotes."

"Oh, well, they don't care, since I'm leaving," Laurence said, with a casual wave. He lounged back in his chair and stretched out his legs. The footrests extended. The small screentank beside him rose on its brackets and tilted so he didn't have to move his head to see it. "Make yourself comfortable, Thomas! We have a way to go."

I emulated his example. The chair seemed to have second sight, moving into a configuration that accommodated me without having to execute a single wiggle for comfort. I vowed to save up money to visit his shipbuilder in the Trade Union. None of my skimmers ever had a seat that fit me as well, for all that I had spent on custom construction. As Uncle Laurence and I were very much of a size and shape, what worked for him would surely work for me.

"I didn't expect to see you," I said. "Jil said you had been visiting Father about the same time that we left Taino."

He cocked his head.

"Well, I *was* there for a while. I never stay long. The place has gotten so stodgy! I heard you would be here to watch the Zang, so I thought I'd drop by," Laurence said, with a mischievous smile. "I seldom get a chance these days to see much of you. It was easier when you were in school. Now, heaven knows where I'll find you. The Castaway Cluster? I read your Infogrid file. That was quite an undertaking! Well done on helping to reintegrate it into the Imperium. That's been a disaster in the making, or so I was told."

I preened quietly for a moment. "It was a reasonable success," I admitted. "Parsons seemed pleased."

"Pleased?" Laurence echoed. "He almost broke a smile when he told me about it. You *are* doing well. My esteemed sister-in-law has stopped despairing of you—well, nearly. You are definitely more a Kinago than a Loche, for all your genetics. Tariana finds you a trifle unmanageable, but what do you expect? Go back and look at the last hundred generations, and our family was always doing the unexpected."

"That's very true," I said. I had done a good deal of research on our family, tracing it back all the way to its origins as pre-salvage cargo retrievers or, as the history books would tiresomely persist in calling them, pirates. Our next most distant ancestors had made their real fortune, though, by anticipating the need for rare raw materials and supplying it, at a markup that factored in the costs and risk involved, to individual systems that lacked them. Since the Kinagos had built up a tremendous fleet of ships over the centuries for both activities, they were available to rescue large populations of settlers from potentially fatal catastrophes, thereby keeping humanity from rendering itself prematurely extinct. From then on, we shone as heroes instead of rogues. Admiral Doctor Shahia Kinago, for example, was famous for developing a vaccine that she delivered to a small world that was suffering from a zoonosis they caught from local flora, and fighting off the space navy of the Wichu. Her grandson was a diplomat who helped make allies of the Wichu fifty years later.

"What do you do for Mr. Frank?" I asked.

"Right to the point, eh?" Uncle Laurence asked. He stretched, extending his long arms over his head and sighing. "This and that. Let's not talk about me. There's plenty of time to go over my dreary life. I'm more interested in what you have been doing. What in heaven's name was all that frippery packed into every cubic centimeter of your cabin?"

I was all too happy to discuss my newest enthusiasm.

"Those are my costumes. I have taken up interpretive dance, uncle," I said, happily. Once again, I reached for the viewpad that wasn't there. Never mind; I didn't need it. I had my skills. "I saw in a marvelous historical documentary that dance is one of the very oldest art forms that humankind evolved. I don't know whether our primitive prototypes learned from watching animals performing mating dances or bees describing to their hive mates where to find nectar, but we began to express ourselves through body movement in a similar fashion. From the beginning, it was a means of storytelling, reproducing events, or expressing concepts. Why resort to mere spoken poetry, when the poetry of motion is more compelling?" I extended my own arms, and allowed my hands to perform some of the smaller movements over which Madame Deirdre and I had been conferring. One sequence of which I was rather proud was a love story, in which a male pursues a female, who very shortly turns to snare him, as she had been paying attention all along.

Uncle Laurence watched with interest, then gave a wicked laugh.

"Very good! In that case, you would probably be interested in a few humorous digitavids I found," he said. "You'll wonder why the females ever allowed the males to propagate. Wait a moment, I have something better. I want you to see this. *Gaia*, up!"

"Yes, Lord Laurence."

The screen tank receded out of the way of his feet. Uncle Laurence's chair rose until it reached a hatch in the ceiling. He touched a control, and the hatch slid aside. Sparkling bits of metal shimmered and danced, catching the light from the screen. They piled up on one another until they formed a blob. I could not help thinking that the mass reminded me of a Kail. I tried not to take against it based upon that impression.

"Find me MGM051," he ordered. The mass disintegrated and disappeared into the shadows of the storage compartment. I heard hissing and thumping overhead. Uncle Laurence smiled down at me. "Don't mind them. Micronbots. They're virtually indestructible, so they think everything else is, too."

"I've recently had some experience with nanobots," I said. "They are not quite as self-directed, but very efficient."

"I heard! You must tell me all about it. But wait!" Clicking erupted from above, then the screen on the wall went black. Laurence arranged himself in his seat and gestured toward the main screen. "Watch this!"

Because of my interest in ancient forms of entertainment, including the early seasons of *Ya!*, it was less disruptive to my senses to watch two-dee vids than it was for some of my cousins. The sound had a tinny quality to it, as many recordings made in the distant past had, and the video perceptibly jerky, but one soon forgot about the limitations when swept up in the wonder of the contents recorded thereon. The male protagonist of this vid did little abstract interpretation in his dance, but was compelling to watch nonetheless because of his athleticism and ability to convey emotion. The segment that Uncle Laurence was eager for me to see involved the man dancing on all parts of the room, including the ceiling.

"I didn't know that they created these vids in space," I said, delighted. "He manages anti-gravity very well."

"This predates the first space age," Uncle Laurence explained, as the man concluded his marvelous performance and gazed at a flat image in a rectangular frame. "Such things were done through mechanical means and illusion. Our ancestors still have so much to teach us."

"I only wish we had access to more of their wisdom," I said.

"What would we do with it?" Laurence asked, with a laugh. "We barely pay attention to the wisdom of our own age."

"Do you have more of these two-dee digitavids?" I asked, eagerly.

"Movies," Laurence said. "I have thousands of them. They have been an enthusiasm of mine for a long while." He signed to the micronbots, who responded with yet more clattering and thumping above. "Would you like some popcorn?"

In the midst of what I recall being an intensely interesting discussion of the immutability of good taste and the ephemeral nature of fashion, I dropped off to sleep. During dreams in which I appeared at various venues in the height of current haute couture, only to discover that I had been superseded within moments of my arrival, I suffered the shame of having catcalls and hoots aimed in my direction.

I was not only glad but relieved to discover that my humiliation was only in my dream, and that the hooting was literal. For a split second, staring at an unfamiliar ceiling, I wondered exactly where I was, then delight overspread my concern. I was on a trip with Uncle Laurence.

"Well, there you are," my elder relative called over the din, grinning at me from his pilot's chair. He looked fresh, having changed clothing and shaved during my nap. "Need a warming cup to help drive away the cobwebs?"

"That would be most welcome," I shouted back. "Why is the klaxon sounding?"

"Oh, that," Laurence said. "*Gaia*, turn it off! It's a proximity alarm," he added, as relative silence fell in the cabin. He adjusted a control that tightened up the view to be seen in the navigational screentank. It had shown the sparse scattering of stars visible since the single jump we had made after leaving the platform. Now he focused in on a yellow star. At the speed we were traveling, we would pass through the Oort haze and the radiation belt in a matter of seconds. I heard a crackle over the audio system as we entered the star's protective sphere.

"Proximity to what?" I asked, as a steaming cup lowered itself to me from a hatch in that very ceiling.

For answer, he elbowed a control in the arm of his chair. "This is *Gaia*. *Titan*, is that you?"

A woman's voice answered.

"*Titan*. Good to hear you, *Gaia*."

"Thanks for babysitting. Any worries?"

"None. Enceladus, *Gaia*'s home."

A deep male voice came on. "Happy spring, *Gaia*!"

Uncle Laurence laughed. "Thank you, but it's your vernal equinox, too."

"At least you get flowers," came another voice, this one lighter, without any trace of gender. "Welcome back."

"Thank you, Ares. I'd like you to meet my nephew." He grinned at me. "Let's just call you Nataraja, after the dancing god."

In all, nine voices called out their greetings.

"Welcome, Nataraja," said a female whom Uncle Laurence called Ourania, and added mysteriously, "I hope you're good at keeping secrets."

"I am," I said. I looked to my uncle with questions in my eyes. I'd have acted out my confusion if I had not been buckled into a crash couch. He closed the communication circuit. "What secret?"

"This one, Thomas," he said. He waved a hand over his screentank, and the wall screen zoomed in toward the distant yellow dot. At the angle we approached the star, I could see a scatter of spheres within a few hundred million kilometers of it. I glimpsed one magnificent planet with a series of brilliant rings that had to be half again as large as the gas giant Vijay Six, but the focus did not stop there. Instead, it passed by an asteroid belt, a small rocky planet with two moons, and came to rest upon a brilliant blue globe. I peered at it.

"Quite a beautiful planet," I said, "but I can't put a name to it."

"It's home, Thomas."

"Your home?"

"No, our home. That's somewhere we all live, where you and I were born."

I looked again. The continents weren't in the configuration I expected to see. Perhaps they were inverted. I tilted my head, but came up certain. I peered at him with suspicion writ large on my features. "This isn't Keinolt."

"It is home to all humankind, Thomas," Uncle Laurence said, with a smile. "Welcome to Earth."

"Earth?" I favored him with my patented laugh, which boomed around the room like a disapproving studio audience. He had played many jokes on me in the past. I was determined not to let this be one of them. "How can it be Earth?" I demanded, disbelief writ large in both my mien and vocal tones. "Earth is lost! No one knows where Earth is!"

Uncle Laurence saw my skepticism and raised me exasperation.

"Well, if you took a poll, you would find your statement to be the correct one, within plus or minus three degrees of accuracy. In point of fact, though, a few, a select and very carefully vetted few, do know. We have known all along. It is here." He gestured protectively toward the blue dot, looming larger in the scope all the time. "Its anonymity is what protects it from incursion, destruction, or tourism."

I waited to see if he was trying to stretch the tale, but his face told me that for once he was deadly serious, more serious than I knew he could be. I swallowed hard.

"How can that be? You can't hide a star system."

Uncle Laurence turned a hand over. "It was . . . mislaid. Very carefully mislaid by the galactic cartographers, many centuries ago."

"I had heard that," I said, "but in practice? This star must be on the charts."

"And it is," my uncle said, with a wry grin. "But this one unremarkable yellow dwarf star lies in traditional Zang space, which protects it from casual attention. No one dares to intrude upon this sector, knowing what the Zang are capable of doing."

"I thought they only amused themselves," I said. "At this moment, they are striving to blast an innocent rock into energy."

Uncle Laurence shook his head. "Everything they do has a purpose, although we may never understand what it is. Since what they do includes protecting this corner of the galaxy, I welcome their actions, whatever they may be."

I stared at the blue globe. The sight, and my uncle's words, made me feel smaller and more humble than I ever had in my life.

"Who are the other people who greeted us? Your staff?"

"I don't have staff, Thomas," Uncle Laurence said, with a smile. "Not human, at any rate. Titan and the others are the guardians of the other planets in the system, as well as acting as early-warning monitors for me. They are named for the orbs they occupy, just as I am. Gaia is one of the old titles for Earth."

As deeply as my common sense told me not to believe, after the disappointments I had suffered on the way to the Trade Union's viewing platform, I wanted to. Four major land masses and countless small ones lay in gleaming oceans. I eyed the largest, a tri-lobed monstrosity that must have occupied a quarter of the planet's surface. On the other side of the ocean, an irregular ribbonlike mass, squeezed tight in the middle, undulated down from one brilliant polar icecap nearly all the way down to the comma-shaped continent heaving with blue-white glaciers. A small, independent circumflex of land hovered in the same latitude as their junction in the midst of the other broad ocean. My breath caught in my chest.

I couldn't speak. There was too much to absorb. My uncle passed the time of day with his colleagues, remarking upon comets passing through the heliopause and seasonal meteor showers hailing down on one or another of the planets. Each of them had storied names that I, like most humans of our day, had consigned to legend: Saturn, Venus, Mars, Jupiter, Mercury, Pluto, Neptune, Uranus, Ceres . . . and Earth.

CHAPTER 38

"We must stay with the Zang," Phutes protested. He had hoped never to have to speak again with any of the humans. Special Envoy Melarides waited in the corridor, with every appearance of patience. The rest of their siblings removed themselves as far from the humans as possible. Phutes was reminded once again of their terrible smell as well as the disgusting way their flesh quivered.

"We promised," Sofus said. "Ignore the aesthetics. Remember. It is a matter of honor. We swore that when we reached this place, we would allow this one and her staff to speak with us. If we can obtain our ends by speaking, it would be all the better. Remember, we have not yet made Low Zang promise to help us."

Phutes eyed the humans.

"It is an unpleasant prospect."

"Yesa would not have sent us if she didn't believe we were capable of putting aside our own feelings in the greater cause," Sofus said. Mrdus only nodded. He was too wary of the bright-colored guns carried by the uniformed humans behind the diplomatic staff. None of them wanted to be sprayed again. Phutes was certain that some of the horrible organic matter was still lodged in his tissues.

"I don't like it," Phutes said. He kicked NR-111. "Tell her that we don't like being locked up only to be allowed out at the humans' pleasure."

The hoots and burps that the translator emitted were received by the envoy with a bow.

"We regret that concerns for your siblings' safety and comfort demanded that we place the Kail in this environment, Phutes," Melarides said. "But you three have been granted a signal honor. Except for Dr. Derrida, no other beings have been singled out by the Zang for personal interaction. Your wristbands," she pointed to the metal hoops that encircled their wrists, "have been encoded so you can pass wherever it goes."

"That is true," Sofus said.

The envoy held out her hand, careful not to come within range of actually touching Phutes.

"Please, come with me now. We would like to get to know you better, and to discuss matters of mutual interest to our peoples."

"I don't know whether I trust her," Phutes said.

"Yesa wants it," Sofus reminded him. "Melarides speaks for humankind. If she agrees to what Yesa demands, we have won, without having to convince Low Zang. Melarides wants to give humankind and all those other carbon-based beings a chance to survive."

"Plan 10 is to get the Zang to listen to our plea and accede to it," Mrdus pointed out. "Plan 01 was always to try and convince the humans directly."

Phutes relented. The envoy, showing the calcium-based ridge most of them concealed behind rotting fleshy flaps, directed them out of the main chamber and into one of a series of smaller rooms. This one had opaque walls, a fact that worried Phutes.

"We cannot see the others."

"They are safe," Melarides said. She held a square of silicon and metal toward him. "You can watch them on my viewpad, if you like." She touched the glass sheet, and an image of the Kail rose from it. All but Fovrates wandered aimlessly through their chamber. Some bathed. Some stared up at the dome. Some communed by leaning against one another in the broad container of silicon powder provided for their use. "Please, come sit down."

She went to the slab of stone propped on metal legs. Soft, squishy chairs, like the flesh of humans themselves, were arranged on one side. A broad bench of black stone lay on the other.

"That is acceptable," Sofus said. He strode over and arranged his abdomen over the backless block. Mrdus huddled next to him, as though for protection. Phutes chose to take his place opposite the envoy.

"May we offer you refreshments?" she asked. She gestured to her aide, the male human. He brought metal bowls forward and placed them in front of the Kail. "Pure water and refined gold dust. Very conductive. We understand that you prize such things."

"We do," Sofus said, placing one of his fists in the bowl nearest him. "You have known this already."

"Yes," Melarides said, settling her hands on the table as refreshments suitable for humans were set out. "I just want to get to know you. The spectacle will begin shortly, so I thought this was an opportune time."

She burbled and squeaked along for a while. Phutes sat only half listening. He sampled the containers himself. The minerals in the bowls were as pure as anything that he had ever experienced. The particles worked their way into his system in a pleasurable fashion. He wondered if Yesa herself had ever had accreted as much gold as this.

"Is any of what she is saying important?" he asked NR-111 when the envoy paused for breath.

"Most of it is common courtesies," the translator said. "I have been replying on your behalf with facts that you have stated in the past."

"Good."

". . . Wait," NR-111 said. "This is a new question. Melarides is good at asking questions."

"Tell me about your family," the envoy said, with a smile. She leaned forward, thrusting her soft face closer to Phutes. He had the stone table between them, so he only recoiled a little.

"My siblings and I rest on our mother's bosom," Phutes said.

"How many siblings have you got?" she pressed. "I see that there are nearly forty of you here. It must be a large family! How many are there?"

Phutes had that figure at his fist's end, and expressed it in good binary. Properly, the number took a long time to say. The translator shortened it into the uncouth combination that humans were capable of understanding. Melarides listened patiently.

"That sounds like the entire population of a planet," she said, with a noise that the translator rendered as a friendly laugh. "I have 1101 cousins, and 11 brothers." Her command of the proper tongue was not as atrocious as most, though still somewhat nauseating.

"I prefer if you translate her words from the human, instead of letting her destroy our language," Phutes said. NR-111 conveyed the meaning to Melarides.

She approved that. The others moved their flabby hands over the silicon and metal sheets. The sheets must have cringed to have so much organic matter slimed over them. Phutes said so.

One of the envoy's staff, a pale-skinned male, emitted a harsh noise. He stood up. "You are offensive. Anyone can tell that you have no experience in complex negotiations."

Phutes bristled. "You wished this meeting. Listen to my words or leave."

"How dare you speak to me that way?"

The guards took a few steps nearer, leveling their weapons on the Kail.

"And, those!" Phutes said, pointing at the guards. "Are we equals or enemies?"

"You are equals," Melarides said, soothingly. "I was wrong to include them. They should not be in here while we converse." She turned to the uniformed humans. "Please step outside. We will call you if you are needed, but you won't be."

"Are you sure, ma'am?"

Melarides showed her oral calcium ridge again. "Yes, I am. We are having a peaceful discussion. We want to come to an agreement between equals. Thank you."

With open reluctance, the guards departed, taking with them the angry human. Phutes approved. The envoy was biddable. Maybe a warning would *not* have to be sent to humankind.

"You are interested in our tablets and pocket secretaries," she said, offering the glass slab again. Phutes showed assent. He slid it toward him and regarded it with approval. The conductive qualities allowed him to manipulate the image without possessing fingers.

"They are like us, proper mineral beings. Like 111."

"Like seven? Oh, you mean your translator. Yes. She is a good employee. We appreciate her service. Please, let us continue our discussion. Tell me about your family. Have you parents?"

"Yesa is my only parent," Phutes said. "I speak for her."

"Your motherworld, yes." Melarides looked pleased. "Well, when we form a relationship with our neighbors, we offer what we have and hope to find a medium of exchange suitable to both parties. We have many exports that might interest you, that are made of good minerals. You show approval for the gold dust. We have others that we hope will be acceptable to you as well. Refineries in our space find these ores and purify them until we have blocks of single minerals. Some of those have provided your meals during your travel here. We were glad to provide them. We hope you found them to your liking."

"Adequate," Phutes said. "Lacking complex flavor, but adequate. My siblings agree." Sofus and Mrdus honked their assent. Melarides looked discomfited.

"Is that so? We wanted to present you with purified minerals without any taint of organic compounds."

"We prefer to absorb combinations," Phutes said. "Our bodies need certain minerals to maintain health."

"As do ours," the envoy said.

"We don't care about that," Phutes said. Melarides did not bore him further with facts about humans.

"We know so little about your physiology, Phutes. We wish we knew more. If you would tell our chefs what comestible minerals you prefer, we would be happy to make those combinations available. We only wanted to show you what we were capable of doing with minerals, how we respect every rock and stone that is in your systems, throughout all of Kail space."

"That is good," Phutes said. He found it difficult to relax in the presence of so much slime, so many bodies, in such a small space. They encroached upon him. He kept Yesa's words in mind. It sounded as though they had taken to their squishy souls the terms that she hoped they would. "We want you to respect our worlds. They are sovereign entities. You must embrace their integrity."

"We do!" Melarides said, soothingly. "We do not want to do anything on your worlds that you don't want us to."

"Good. We are agreed on that." Phutes did find himself relaxing. This diplomacy was not so difficult after all. Yesa would be pleased with him.

Melarides put her squashy hands together and pushed her face in his direction. Phutes could not help himself flinching away.

"Excellent! With that agreement in mind, Phutes, I wanted to broach the subject, one that is very dear to our Emperor's heart. In fact, it is a matter that is of deep interest to many concerns in the Imperium."

Phutes felt so confident that Yesa would get her wish of solitude that he was willing to listen to almost any nonsense that the humans cared to spout.

"What is it?"

The fleshy mouth opened, revealing the wet and soggy red protuberance that so horrified him. It waggled and emitted noises. The translator beside him took her hums and squeaks and rendered them into words.

"We would like to come to some kind of agreement with you to exploit mineral rights in Kail space."

Phutes tried to make the words translate into some kind of comprehensible combination, but he couldn't. He turned to NR-111.

"What does that mean?" he asked. Melarides seemed puzzled, until the translator asked for clarification.

The lines across the top of her face moved upward.

"It means that the Imperium would like to *mine* on your worlds, Phutes." She pulled another one of the glass slabs toward her and caused a three-dimensional image to rise before her, a starscape of familiar orbs. Several of them lit up with bright white outlines. "We have identified numerous bodies within Kail space that are rich in rare earths, ores that appear in too few places in Imperium territory. We want to extract those deposits from the rock in which they are buried and make use of them in industry, medicine, advances in science. In exchange, we would be willing to offer you technology that would make your lives much more comfortable. You could be connected to our Infogrid and have access to the communication systems of our entire section of the galaxy. For example, we have numerous offerings of artistic programming, such as music and dance . . . . What's the matter, Phutes?"

Phutes had stopped listening at the words "extract those deposits." He stared at Melarides.

"You want to do *what*?" he demanded. "How?"

"Mining," the envoy said, making that strange mouth gesture again. "It would involve the removal, crushing and processing of ores from bodies we have identified in Kail space. Most of them are asteroids and planetoids. Those are rich in the kind of rare earths that we need, Phutes. Spectroanalysis also shows us seams on the motherworlds that would be of immense value to both our peoples. I hope you will convey to Yesa and the other leaders of your kind how important this is to us . . ."

Phutes exploded out of his seat.

"Exploitation? What you are talking about is *murder!*"

Melarides looked confused. Phutes made for the exit, honking for his siblings. The others rose.

"Sofus! Summon Fovrates! These humans are more dire than we ever guessed! I must speak with the Zang *now*."

The human and her associates leaped from their chairs and followed him.

"Please, NR-111, stop him! Don't let him leave. What have I said?"

Loud noises erupted from outside the room. Phutes was afraid that all of the humans were standing out there, ready to attack him, but he didn't care. The vessel under his feet began to rock crazily. He clawed his way toward the door. Sofus galloped forward, Mrdus clinging to him, and went to Phutes's aid. He hammered at the door.

The slim translatorbot put on a burst of speed and arrived at Phutes's side before he reached the exit. The human diplomats caught up and surrounded him in a ring of jelly-like flesh and the smell of effluvia. The servicebot flashed several lights, drawing his attention to her.

"Please explain, Phutes," she said. "The envoy doesn't mean to offend you. She doesn't understand. Neither do I. Please explain. Why is it murder? What will mining of asteroids kill?"

Phutes glared at the translator.

"They are not asteroids, they are my cousins!" he said. Acid roiled in his system, threatening to eat deeper grooves into his flesh than ever.

"How can they be your cousins?" NR-111 said, in a gentle tone. "Do you assign names to these planetoids? Is it a matter of religious significance? The envoy will understand if this is the case. The Imperium has made exceptions over the millennia for territory that has sacred meaning to various sects."

Phutes grabbed for the stalk supporting the optical receptor array.

"What is sacred? That has no meaning! The bodies in Kail space are not objects, they are Kail!"

NR-111 emitted a long stream of gibberish words in human tongue from its secondary audio. The envoy stopped short.

"They are Kail? Do they live in those bodies?" she asked.

"They live. Those *are* their bodies. They are more mature than Kail my size. One day I will be one like they are. If these terrible humans do not mine *me* for ore!"

"This is remarkable," NR-111 said. Phutes could tell that it had translated its words to the humans, because they stopped shouting at him and withdrew, surprised looks on their horrible faces. "I have never heard of such a thing before. Nor have my colleagues. Does that mean the term 'motherworld' is literal? Yesa is your progenitor? You were born of her soil?"

"Of course that is what it means! How else do you reproduce?" Phutes asked, outraged. He threw a fist in the envoy's direction. "These monsters want to kill my mother? That is what those thieves were doing, trying to take stone from her breast? You soil our mother-worlds. You are *slime*."

Melarides made squeaking and burbling noises, but the lines on her forehead had drawn down near the central protuberance.

"I assure you, Phutes, that the envoy had no idea that this was the case," NR-111 said. "We did not understand. Please, come and sit down again. Let us continue with the discussion. Isn't there room for negotiation? Surely there are bodies in Kail space that are not living beings. Please. Come back with me. Let's talk."

It rolled a meter or so toward the table, and beckoned. Phutes was tempted. The mechanical being had been honest with him so far. But the humans surrounding him looked avid, as though they wanted to absorb his body then and there, processing it into devices and purified powder. Who knew that they had such dire intents? Yesa would be horrified to discover that they were so evil.

"No," he boomed. His voice echoed off the walls of the chamber. "This discussion is ended. No human or other slime is permitted to enter our territory. You will never land on our worlds ever again! Sofus! Mrdus! With me! Open the door!"

He stormed out of the room.

A flash of brilliant white light flooded the dome from above. The chamber continued to shake and roll, but Phutes braced his three legs and stalked toward the center wall of the platform.

"We must get to the Zang!" he shouted over the wild cheering and loud music. "Plan 10 will be put into operation! Are we certain as to the location?"

"Yes," Mrdus said. "Fovrates confirmed it."

"Then let the humans suffer as they wanted us to suffer!"

⊰ CHAPTER 39 ⊱

Outside of the orbit of the single large moon, Gaia-the-ship dropped velocity like a tree shedding ripe fruit, and floated weightlessly and stately toward the snaking continental mass.

Alarms—I was beginning to learn to expect them—sounded loudly. In the screentank, a hexagonal grid of hot red lines sprang up, overlaying the planet. I had seen the same kind of defense system around Keinolt and others of the Core Worlds. It was good to know that such protection was afforded to Earth. As we passed closer, the visuals filled with codes and symbols. Uncle Laurence spoke a series of what sounded like nonsense words but must have been keys that persuaded the hidden armaments to let us through unscathed.

We descended gently through the brilliant blue skies toward the left edge of the northern reaches of the ribbon continent. *Gaia* set down in mountainous terrain within the long spine that streaked down that outer edge. I had time to spot a tidy little city before it disappeared behind forests and snowy peaks. The ship settled down in the precise center of a landing pad and promptly sank into neon-studded darkness.

"What is that city? Who lives there?"

"No one," Uncle Laurence said. *Gaia* heaved a number of sighs, as if relieved to have arrived, though her gravity generator kept humming. Lights filled the cavern we were in, and the hatch lowered. Our couches lowered to the floor. "Thank you, *Gaia*! Wonderful trip!"

"Thank you, Lord Laurence," the pleasant female voice said. "Welcome home."

He smiled and patted the arm of the chair. "Glad to be back."

I could not help but be wide-eyed as my uncle led me out through a tile-lined tunnel and up through a pair of heavy bronze doors. Gravity was heavier than it had been on the platform or in *Gaia*, but I became accustomed to it within a dozen or so meters.

The portals slid back as we approached, and I followed my uncle up into the light, and we stepped through onto crumbling dark soil.

I was, to my everlasting astonishment, on Earth.

Sunlight caressed my face like a pair of gentle hands. The sky was a different blue from Keinolt's. I missed that faint hint of green in the atmosphere. Huge piles of white clouds scudded across the evening sky as though they had an appointment somewhere to my distant right. I fetched a deep breath of air. It was sweet and touched with rich moisture that was rare on our homeworld—I corrected myself hastily—on the world where I grew up because its climate tended to be arid. I smelled fresh, rich soil, the spice of evergreens, and the sweetness of flowers.

"Good, eh?" Uncle Laurence asked. He had been watching me closely since we had debarked.

"Delicious," I said. I looked around. It was indeed spring. Nearly all the plants nearby were studded with blossoms. Clusters of low wood irises lay tucked among knobby roots. I followed the line of the trees nearest me, and realized how very tall they were. At first, they made me think of the forest at the Whispering Ravines, then I realized those were sad, pale imitations of the Real Thing. The trees around me were darker and redder in color, lofty enough to scratch the perfect sky. Some of them, including a massive specimen immediately outside the door of the tunnel, were as large around as a building.

"Let's get you a real shower and a change of clothes," Uncle Laurence said. "Then I'll take you on a tour. Will that suit you?"

I nodded. Words seemed to have failed me utterly. I trailed along in his footsteps, or as closely as I could, considering that I was swiveling my head around like a gyroscope, trying to see everything at once. My foot caught, and I went sprawling headlong. Uncle Laurence came to hoist me to my feet, but not before I had caught sight of another pair of eyes, in a budding bush that huddled very low to the ground.

"What's that?" I asked.

"Where?"

I pointed. My uncle strode over and plunged his arm deep into the brush. It emerged with a mass of thick, dark gray and brown fur. The animal, about a quarter the size of my torso, struggled in his grip. It acted as though it was more inconvenienced than frightened.

"You mean this?" Uncle Laurence held the creature to his shoulder. It huddled against him and stared at me. Its face was masked, as if going to a costume party, and its lushly furred tail was decorated in a series of rings. "This is a raccoon. This one's name is Elena. She's the grandmother of my own family group. Here, you can hold her. She is a snuggler."

He thrust her into my arms. Elena grappled onto me with tiny sharp claws and began to examine my hair and clothing.

"Let me give you a piece of advice before we go inside," Uncle Laurence said. "Never do anything in front of her or any of the other raccoons that you don't want them to duplicate. They are phenomenally intelligent and curious. They are the next masters of this planet."

"So," I said, holding his pet as we traversed a narrow but well-worn path through the immense forest, "you do live here all alone?"

"Not at all. I have billions of micronbots at my beck and call, and all the animals native to this planet." He smiled, a trifle wryly. "Since no one ever came back, there are no alien species mixed in. Apart from a few meteor-strewn microbes, that is."

"The animals survived the Great Abandonment?" I asked, fighting against the memories of legends that I had read since my childhood.

"Survived?" my uncle echoed. "The animals left behind have prospered, all the more so *because* humankind left. Without us here to cull some to extinction or overbreed others beyond reason, nature has taken over and set things into the proportion that it would have had without our rise. You'll see in a while, but I need to check in before we indulge in a flyover."

The departure of humanity from Earth had over ten thousand years achieved the status of legends, not all of which agreed with one another. They all had at their heart an onrushing disaster that threatened to destroy all of life on this planet. Some of the stories said it was a plague, some said a flood, others a massive volcano that would poison the atmosphere and kill every living thing, still other tales described an extraterrestrial menace, a comet or asteroid large enough to rip the atmosphere away. In all of them, the heroes of the story, including some of my ancestors, mustered all of Earth's resources to build ships that would take all the billions of humans to new worlds. What records survived disagreed with one another, including as to who was responsible for rescuing the population and where it went immediately after leaving. They did all agree that no one ever tried to come back, believing that there was nothing to which to return. And, if my uncle was to be believed, and I had no reason to doubt anything he said, ever again, the trail was deliberately muddied. I knew of at least six "true Earths," including Counterweight, who claimed to be humankind's birthplace. None of them was this lovely sphere.

That was why the ground felt so right under my feet. So many planets on which humanity had set its stamp over the last ten millennia dragged us down or did not anchor us sufficiently with its gravity. The air nourished my lungs, without attempting to introduce any unwelcome chemical compounds. I fancied the water, which I could see twinkling in the sunshine in the far distance between the immense tree boles, would taste sweet on my tongue.

I was so full of joy, I broke into a grand and sweeping waltz, with Elena as my partner. As I glided into a clearing in my uncle's wake, I found myself facing an audience consisting of more raccoons, a doe and her small spotted fawn, and several squirrels.

"And who are these?" I asked. Laurence chuckled.

"Elena's family. You can put her down, now. She'll want to tell them all about you." I bent to release the raccoon. She kicked away from me as though launching herself and waddled into the midst of the crowd of masked creatures. They surrounded her, sniffing and gabbling. The deer regarded us as shyly as I did them. "Come in."

He gestured toward a door. I almost had to blink. The dark red-brown house to which it was attached blended so well into the undergrowth that it was almost invisible. I followed him into a cozy domicile that I would not have been ashamed to own. A complex console with a number of screens and scopes was set into a nook in between a huge stone fireplace with an entire log for a mantel and a multi-paned glass window with black-and-white-checked woolen curtains.

"All this time," I said, throwing myself into one of the deeply upholstered chairs before the soot-stained hearth. "All this time we thought that Father was imagining it when he told us you had come to see him from Earth."

"Yes, his reputation has been very convenient," Laurence said. He touched the control console, and the scopes burst into life. Image after image, some of buildings, some of natural sites, flashed in rapid sequence. "But you know yourself that sometimes what he says is true." He gestured to his left. "The bath's through there. Take any of my clothes. They'll fit you."

When I emerged, clean, shaved and clad in a pair of sturdy trousers of soft fiber and a long-sleeved shirt of moss green, he looked up and grinned at me.

"We are very alike, aren't we? Those are some of my favorites. Not fashionable in the least, but comfortable. Just a few minutes more."

While he worked at his console, I found it impossible to sit still. With a glance for permission, I went outside. The raccoons dined on a mix of seeds in a tub set against one side of the small house. Except for that one species, that had either never been transported off Earth or had not survived on the worlds to which it had traveled, I could have been on any one of a million planets that my ancestors had settled. But it was different. It was the first.

We all came from here, I mused. I tried to absorb the wonder of it all.

I heard the door open and close behind me. My uncle emerged from the house.

"Come on, then," Uncle Laurence said. "Let's take a look around, shall we?"

In my uncle's personal skimmer, a pale gray four-passenger vehicle, we zipped high into the blue sky and angled toward the west, traveling at thousands of kilometers an hour. We crossed a vast, tossing blue ocean, with my uncle pointing out the very occasional island, until we reached the eastern shores of the massive continent on the other side of the world.

"What does it mean that you are the guardian of Earth?" I asked. "What do you do?"

"For the last few thousand years, I and my predecessors have been maintaining and restoring places around the globe that are of historical interest," he said.

"You've become an architect?" I asked.

"Not I," my uncle said, with a laugh. "A few of Earth's guardians have been. I think that's how the project got started. The micronbots have been the architects, as well as gardeners, miners, masons, carpenters, painters, welders, archaeologists, maintenance engineers, sign painters and road crew. We set them a task, and they work endlessly until a project is complete."

"How do they know what to do?" I asked.

"Look and see," Uncle Laurence said. He tilted the skimmer down and around. As we came in over a vast forest, I could see the edge of a crenelated gray stone wall. I frowned, trying to see the end, but it snaked off into the distance farther than the eye could follow. "The micronbots have rebuilt monuments, homes, statues, buildings, public places, gardens and all from plans, models and photographs taken from the days before the Abandonment. Over the years, we have taken the best from any era, rebuilt them, and left them as they are. This wall is a marvel of an early age of human civilization. If you'd known where to look, you could have seen it from space. Though it stretches over four thousand kilometers, it was never completed. Until now. It is perfect from end to end, every stone in place." He brought the small craft in for a landing on the broad walkway beside one of the high square towers, and walked beside me as I gawked and exclaimed in wonder.

"But this must have taken centuries to complete!" I said.

"It has. We guardians plant trees that won't mature for hundreds of years. We start to rebuild monuments that we will not live to see completed. We restore habitat."

"Is it one of your projects?" I asked, greedily taking in the sights.

"No, I'll take you to one of my local projects in a moment. Take a look." I leaped out and stamped, feeling the heavy granite beneath my boots.

The battlements were high enough for defense, but not so high I couldn't see the land near us. I ran up to the next tower, where Uncle Laurence beckoned me back into the seat. We zipped off to see a vast city not far away. One section had been set aside from the rest with red walls. The buildings within had steeply raked, yellow-tiled roofs surmounted by the shapes of beasts more fantastic than raccoons. I saw dragons that looked like horses with colored streamers flying from their ears and nostrils, gigantic fish and tortoises, carved tigers and dogs with fearsome faces, all in blisteringly bright colors. It was enchanting, like a child's playground.

"I restored this place. It took years to research," he said, patting a statue of a tortoise with a tall tablet balanced on its back. "I'm very pleased with the results. This is the home of an imperial dynasty of the past. I can't imagine Shojan being comfortable here, can you?"

I shook my head. "It's a bit gaudy for his tastes."

We lifted off again. Uncle Laurence flew from place to place, telling me about each of the sites as we passed overhead. I did my best to absorb it, while my eyes filled with wonders. To the south of the highest mountains I had yet seen was a hot and colorful land. Palaces of white, red or gold dotted the landscape. We set down briefly in a long and beautiful garden, alive with tossing plumes from fountains, to admire the aspect of three immense temples in a row. The two on either side were red sandstone, but the center was a glorious giant pearl of white marble. Each of the buildings had been incised with images and words, all inlaid with tiny tiles of semi-precious stones and agates. I ran from corner to corner, admiring the near perfection of its construction. This was poetry set in stone. I willed myself to recall every detail.

A snarl made me spin on my heel, seeking its source.

"What was that?"

"A tiger," my uncle called, from the bench where he was sitting in the shadow of the white temple. He pointed. Lying at the top of a nearby staircase was a magnificent orange, black and white striped cat, switching its tail up and down. I stared. I had only ever seen one in my life, and that on a remote world far from the core of the Imperium. "Don't worry about them. They're too well fed. There are wild goats and monkeys everywhere about."

Not only were there buff-colored simians walking up and back on the walls and screaming at us from the trees, but great gray elephants wandering the empty streets of the city, rubbing their backs against pillars and trees.

"Nell would be so jealous," I breathed, as one massive specimen flapped its ears at us.

"A shame she will never get to see it, I'm afraid," Uncle Laurence said.

"But, why not?" I asked.

He sighed, his handsome face taking on a thoughtful, almost tragic aspect.

"Over the eons, we have considered allowing others to visit. When I first arrived, I argued that scholars should be allowed back here to study our past, but once it became known where Earth was, the floodgates could not be kept closed after that. Can you imagine your cousins, or mine, being permitted to run rampant over this landscape, let alone the thronging tourist mobs? How long would what we had preserved remain intact? Merchants would clamor for a place everywhere there was something of interest to see. They would be followed by the crowds, followed by legislation that would protect the people at the expense of the site. Then there would be those who would demand to return to their ancestral homelands, undoing all the good we have done by combining all populations into one. No, better that Earth remains a myth to most. Occasionally, we allow vids and books of these places to be 'found' for the historians to marvel over, but never allow its source to be known. One day one of these animals will rise up and take its place as master of this planet, as if we had never existed, and they will wonder at the relics we left behind. In the meanwhile, it is a resource and a symbol of how we began."

I wanted to argue, but his logic was unassailable. Either all, or none. Either it was a secret, or it was not. I did my best to gather impressions and memorize what I had seen, even if no one else was ever to be permitted to share those impressions with me.

We flew for a while longer, then spent the night in a marvelous, white-turreted castle on a mountain that towered over massive, dark green forests. The stone halls were echoingly empty. My needs were met by nearly invisible servitors: the micronbots conveying in a fire-brigade-style row food, drink, bedding and firewood for the enamel and gold-leafed hearth in my grand bedchamber. On the beautifully carved and painted dressing table, a hairbrush and a hand mirror lay seemingly where they had been set down by the last occupant of the room, who had departed, perhaps just for a moment. I fell asleep on the dark green brocaded bed, under a canopy of the same priceless fabric, listening to strange night birds calling in the distance.

For the next few days, I received a survey tour of the finest that Earth had ever produced. Uncle Laurence was proud to show off a square full of red buildings, all with fantastically-shaped onion-topped towers. A beautiful city that lay along a wide, curving river gleamed with white churches and palaces, interspersed with odd glass towers. A massive white enclosure sitting all by itself in a broad, hot landscape occupied only by prides of lions, running birds taller than I was, and snub-horned rhinoceroses aroused my curiosity. In the middle of a green plain on a northern temperate island, a circle of white standing stones awaited the arrival of . . . whom? Not far away from this curiosity, Uncle Laurence led me into a low-ceilinged cave. On its walls were daubed handprints in red ochre and tiny, primitive figures depicting the hunt of one of the enormous cattle that currently wandered the land aboveground unmolested.

We also visited natural marvels. One huge, blunt red mountain, grand and eloquent in its isolation on the circumflex island continent, proved to be a single boulder thrust up from the heart of the planet. To its east, across the broad blue ocean, we skimmed over a wild river nearly overgrown by towering trees and impenetrable tropical greenery. Perspiration poured down my face and body in the oppressive humidity, but that only added to the exotic nature of our journey. We threw the remains of our picnic lunch into the water. Fierce little fish with pugnacious expressions and terrifying rows of teeth leaped up and snapped the bones out of the air. Spotted and black jaguars rested on tree branches, almost invisible to my eye until Uncle Laurence pointed them out. Huge birds with magnificent wingspans twice my height plied the air, wheeling and sailing free. Monkeys, lemurs, apes and other anthropoid relations chittered or hooted at us all around the world, but homo sapiens was represented only in the skimmer car in which I rode.

With an air of casual insouciance, which could only mean that he was very excited about our next stop, Uncle Laurence aimed us across the narrower of the two great oceans. Along the eastern edge of the south lobe of the massive continent, one long river left a strip of green in a desert landscape. Oddly regular peaks became visible in the distance. As we came closer, I realized that they were pyramids. Three sat in a close row, overlooking a complex of smaller structures, but others were visible in a line to the south. Each of the largest trio was gleaming white with a triangular stone of gold at its peak. They were set into the midst of a temple complex bristling with statues of half-human, half-animal.

At the smallest of these, Uncle Laurence coaxed me into making my very uncomfortable way through a space so narrow that it felt as if the whole massive structure was going to come down on me. We emerged into a series of chambers carved and painted with tiny figures and pictographs, the meaning of which I could not have guessed. The paintings were brilliant in color as though the artist had just finished them. In the last chamber, the grandest of them all, a heavy carved stone coffin lay.

"Is there a body inside?" I asked.

"A mummy," Laurence said. "Yes, in some. We haven't been able to locate enough of them to fill all the tombs that have been uncovered. Records show that countless of them were destroyed for one reason or another. It's a shame, but it's our history. At least we have some of them. These ancient kings, too, are your ancestors."

We emerged into the blinding sunlight. I was glad to climb back into the skimmer and lower the polarized canopy.

"One could spend a lifetime exploring any of these sites," I said, grateful for the cooling system that kicked on.

"That is my intention," my uncle said, with a proprietary grin.

"What's your pet project?" I asked. When he hesitated, I held up an admonitory finger. "Ah-ah-ah, don't try to tell me you haven't got one! You're a Kinago. You can't help yourself tinkering any more than I or my father can."

He smiled. "How Rodrigo would love it here. But he needs more care than he can get in this isolation. He needs to be near your mother, and she's the beating heart of the navy."

Out and over the broad desert landscape and across the ocean again to the ribbon continent we flew. On the screentank, Uncle Laurence showed me images from the interior of buildings, both before and after restoration. I was astonished and humbled by the imagination of my predecessors. He pointed out details that he had helped with, having pored over ancient books and fugitive electronic images for the way they had appeared so long ago.

The console sounded a ping, bringing our attention back from the past. We both looked up. Laurence nodded.

"Here we are," he said.

The landscape had changed gradually from low foothills to the broadest of green river valleys thundering with the hooves of millions of bison, up into high desert and mountain peaks inhabited by eagles and gray-furred wolves. Within those peaks a busy, white-capped river had its origins. We followed it downstream into a massive river gorge.

I was amused to observe that it had been carved in much the same way as the Whispering Ravines, but this one was so much larger, and so much more beautiful than Counterweight's glory by which I had been so impressed at the time. I realized that I had responded to echoes of Earth, as though I had a gene-memory of this planet. Uncle Laurence and I sat silently side by side, as we zipped through the canyon. The roar of the river below us was like a dragon claiming its territory against us poor mortals.

"This area had been robbed of its water by numerous population centers to the south and west," he said. "Without humankind's demand, there was no need to divert it any longer. I removed countless cities that encroached upon its beauty, leaving only a few of early humankind's villages in place."

The gold and peach sandstone reminded me so much of Taino.

"It's a marvel and a wonder," I said. "It makes me feel a little homesick. For Keinolt."

He smiled. "I understand." He steered the skimmer away from the river and up toward the northwest. "And that is as good an excuse to stop. It is all the time I can allot for this visit. I must take you back now."

I rode in silence, the memories of the past few days overwhelming my senses. We arrived in the redwood forest during a glorious sunset, which seemed a fitting conclusion to an astonishing sojourn. Uncle Laurence landed his skimmer under a pair of low-light globes in the forest beside the small house. It descended into its underground stall, and we walked back toward *Gaia*'s hangar.

Along the way, Elena and her raccoon family joined us and romped alongside. I regarded them fondly, though I had known them only a few days. I petted as many as I could reach for farewell, but when we boarded *Gaia*, the furry female waddled along and joined us, along with two of her children. We eyed one another as she crossed the threshold.

"Should I shoo them out?" I asked. Uncle Laurence waved a hand.

"Oh, no, sometimes I take them with me. They're good travelers. Make yourself comfortable."

I climbed into the chair and waited for the footrests to rise under my soles. When I had achieved a comfortable recline, Elena curled up in my lap, well accustomed to the crash couches. The little ones played on the wall underneath the metal table, squeaking as they chased one another up and down.

"We're going a different way," Uncle Laurence said, showing me the coordinates in the screentank. "Allowing for a little drift from where the platform was situated when we left it, and angling so we do not approach from the same quadrant. Let them guess from which of the wind's twelve quarters we have come."

"I see," I said. The farewells from Uncle Laurence's fellow guardians echoing in my ears, I settled back for the ride. After exiting Sol's system, *Gaia* sped toward the jump point. We watched a few of my uncle's collection of movies as the micronbots served us meals and groomed the raccoons. We passed through the jump point with ease and kept racing through the starry night.

"Another film?" Uncle Laurence asked, gesturing up toward his storage compartment with a glass of some very good red wine. I shook my head. My mind was spinning with all that I had seen.

"This is too big a secret for me to keep," I blurted out. He smiled.

"It isn't. I know you. You have kept many confidences in the past. This is just another one."

"But, why me?" I demanded. "Why now?"

He shrugged and swirled the wine in his glass. "Well, *why now* is because you were close by. We only had to pass one jump point to get here. The system is in what is held to be Zang space within the greater Imperium. It's well-protected by their reputation alone. *Why you* is because you're my favorite nephew. You have character, my lad, integrity, determination and devotion. Of all your generation, you're the only one who stepped forward when asked, and have volunteered your energy for the greater good of the Imperium, again and again and again. For that alone, you deserve credit. And, of all my nieces, nephews and young cousins," he poked a finger toward my chest, "you're the only one I would consider as my potential successor."

A thrill filled my entire chest. I was vibrating so hard it was impossible to move.

"I could come back here?" I breathed. "To stay?"

"Hmm. One day. If you haven't found gallivanting about the galaxy to be too exciting to forego. My own travels have been greatly curtailed by my responsibility to this single system, to this one world, yet it is more important than anything else I have ever done. I can say with certainty that it has been worth it. Not easy. This would be the target of targets for our enemies, if they only knew it existed."

I had to sit back for a moment. The micronbots wisely took my wineglass out of my nerveless fingers. One of the baby raccoons climbed into my lap and began to undo the fastening of my tunic.

"You have to double-knot everything around him," my uncle said, with a grin. He leaned over and picked up the furry animal under its arms. "He's one of the smartest and the most stubborn. They're as obstinate as humans about doing what they want. It's like having a million children who never really grow up."

"Is that why you never had a family?" I asked.

"Who said I don't have a family?" he retorted.

I blinked. "You do?"

He didn't answer.

"We are entering the system, Lord Laurence," *Gaia* said.

"One more movie, then," he said, cheerfully, signing to the micronbots. This one was in shades of blue-gray and white, though the images were clearer than many of the color vids he had played before. I only half-watched. These recordings were mere shadows of what we had left behind. I was a mere shadow. Only Earth was real. How could I keep that secret? The scopes showed waves of electromagnetic force passing through us.

As we entered the heliopause of the system, *Gaia* bucked mightily. The motion died to a shudder as her stabilizers kicked in.

"I'm afraid you've missed the spectacle," Uncle Laurence said. I glanced toward the approaching star, and noticed one of the crescents of light was gone. "In fact, I think it just happened. I'm sorry."

"No, uncle," I said, feeling the truth down in my very genes. "It was worth it."

We approached the *Imperium Jaunter*, keeping its mass in between us and the platform. *Gaia* dipped and rolled to enter the landing bay. She set down upon the pad nearest the entrance. Our chairs lowered to the floor, and we stood up.

"Go on, Thomas," Uncle Laurence said. "It was grand to see you."

"And you, uncle," I said, sincerely. "Thank you for everything. But won't you come back to the platform with me? Nell will be sorry to have missed you."

"Sorry, old thing," he said, with an offhanded wave. "I can't stay. There will be too many of the small crafts out with their cameras looking every which way. Tell Nell I'll see her next time." He made a face. "Better not. Oh, here's a gift for your mother." The micronbots crawled along the floor carrying a small pot from which sprang a pale gray sprig with clusters of tight violet buds blooming on it. They stacked themselves a meter and a half high to offer it to me. "Keep it somewhere safe until you get home."

"Thank you, *Gaia*," I said, glancing up.

"You are welcome, Lord Thomas. I hope to see you again."

I looked a question at my uncle. He laughed, and threw open the hatch.

"Hurry up. I need to get away before anyone else notices me. My cloaking technology won't work indefinitely."

We clasped hands, and I scrambled out.

﷽ CHAPTER 40 ﷽

Special Envoy Melarides edged her way through the celebrating crowd. She looked as horrified as the people around her looked enchanted and excited. Suddenly, she spotted Parsons standing well out of the way and rushed toward him.

"Oh, commander, we have a terrible situation. I need your help."

"What is the matter?" he asked. He glanced at his viewpad. "It is functioning. Did you try to contact me?"

"No, oh, no! I didn't want this on any electronic medium. It would be too easy for the bad news to spread."

"What has happened?"

The older woman's forehead wrinkled. Parsons noticed that beads of perspiration had broken out upon it. He retrieved his handkerchief from his belt pouch and offered it to her. She wiped her face, but failed to remove the appalled expression.

"It seems that we have made a dreadful tactical error with the Kail. We have offended them to the very heart of their psyches. I have done my best to make up for it, but Phutes and his siblings refuse to listen to me. I cannot say that I blame them, but I had no idea! No such information was ever brought to the attention of the diplomatic corps. This is entirely new to all of us, and I am devastated."

Parsons frowned. "What happened?"

The woman raised an eyebrow.

"I'm surprised you weren't monitoring the conference."

"A record was made," Parsons confirmed, "but not yet reviewed. The spectacle occurred only minutes ago, while you were *in camera*.

My primary duty is to ensure the safety of the nobles. Tell me your concerns."

Melarides quickly ran down the conversation she had had with the representatives of the Kail. "At no time was any inkling of this ever made clear to me, or I should have cautioned the government against approaching them in this manner. Living planets! Did you know about this?"

"No," Parsons said. "We must act quickly. We need to set failsafes against the Kail. You know that they are capable of corrupting technological devices up to and including LAIs."

"Yes, I did," Melarides said, pulling herself together. "I apologize. Knowing that, I should have notified you by pad, no matter what mistakes I made. It may already be too late. They left me, swearing revenge, but I couldn't follow them into the Zang's circle. *My* bracelet isn't coded for that section."

"One moment, if you please." He lifted his viewpad to his ear, preferring not to trust air transmission under the circumstances. The pad itself had been virus-checked only twenty minutes before. He waited until the connection cleared. "Colonel Hoyne, Commander Parsons. Please exercise protocol C-2 immediately."

"Damn it, now? Very well, engaging. Will you meet me here in the control center?"

"On our way," Parsons said. He took the envoy's arm and helped her thread her way anti-clockwise around the enormous ring. As he passed the Imperium nobles, Lord Nalney ran over and tried to drag them back with him.

"Come on!" he said, happily. "We are celebrating! You must have a glass of champagne to say farewell to the poor old planet. What a sendoff!"

"Oh, Parsons, come and join us!" Lady Lionelle called. "We're having such fun!"

Lord Xanson sat entwined with a woman. They were kissing passionately. Lady Jil and both of her male companions seemed to be similarly engaged. As was customary, Lady Erita sat with her chin held high and her eyes closed, an almost pained expression on her face, as if she was absorbing the energies that had been released by the planet's destruction or of the giddy crowd around her, but not really enjoying either. Lord Rillion poured drinks for everyone who passed them, including the members of an Uctu conga line snaking among the chairs. He took attendance quickly of all of his noble charges. All but Lord Thomas were present and untroubled. Lady Lionelle beckoned to him again.

"In a short while, my lady," Parsons called back, projecting his voice to be heard over the din. She seemed satisfied by his promise, and turned back to the festivities. He hurried as fast as the lady on his arm could move, and opened the door to the operations center with his free hand. When it shut behind them, the noise died away instantly. The portal, like the wall, was translucent on the inside.

"What are we going to have to do about the Kail?" Colonel Hoyne asked. "How could such a mistake have been made? We have thousands of guests on board!"

"Are all of these people in danger because of my error?" Melarides asked, surveying the crowd with horror on her face.

"They are as safe as they can be," Parsons said, helping the lady to a chair. "They can't affect the computer system on this platform with the precautions that we have taken. No LAI will allow them to make contact with it. They might be able to wreak havoc on the facility, but as they actively abhor making physical contact with living beings, I believe that the guests are safe. The Kail will have a difficult time returning to their motherworlds, I am afraid. They have exhausted their resources, and the Wichu will not trust them again."

"A suicide attack, then?" Melarides asked. "I didn't see that in them, but I appear to have missed such fundamental facts about them that I am afraid to make any assumptions whatsoever."

"I'll space them if they look like they're about to blow something up," Hoyne said. His brows drew down to his nose. He brought up a scope. "At the moment the three that are outside the silicon habitat are with the Zang. They're talking to one of them. What do you suppose that is about?"

"Their anger, I will guess," Parsons said. "I do not know whether the conversation is one-sided or not. Low Zang appears to have taken a fancy to the Kail, but as for being able to convey complex concepts to it, I am not certain they are capable of such linguistic facility."

"Are you sure of that, commander?"

"No," Parsons replied. "The Kail have surprised us again and again on this journey. It would be well to monitor them closely."

"I have guards and spy-eyes in the Zang enclosure now," Colonel Hoyne said, showing them numerous views on his central screen. "Curse them! I thought I had enough to deal with keeping them out of our computers! My central government has been notified about any possible attack from the Kail, including cyber-attacks. But what do they think they can persuade the Zang to do?"

"When our team rescued the *Whiskerchin*, the Kail Fovrates, then its chief engineer, was transmitting information to his counterparts on the *Jaunter*. We believe they were coordinates to a homeworld."

"But whose?"

"Fovrates refuses to say. Our computers are currently analyzing the wealth of data sent to Phutes and his siblings. As the Kail use a binary system, the comparison is taking some time, when we have to allow for error. Many of the points that were in the first tranche of information turned out to be in empty space. We believed that they might ask for help removing your nation's spy station in their space," Parsons added. "I am afraid that Special Envoy Melarides has given them cause to widen their field of attack to include Imperium targets. They hate and dislike all humans."

"We have to get them away from the Zang," Hoyne said.

"You might remove the Kail from the Zang now," Parsons said, "but if they have evoked sympathy in one of the Elders, they can follow the Kail wherever they go. It's better if any contact is under our supervision. I will go in."

The Zang stood facing one another in a circle on the raised dais at the center of the enormous room. The silver pillars gleamed even more brightly than they had before. Phutes held his fists before his ocular receptors to shield them. Even more, the Zang's energy envelopes seemed to extend from their visible bodies out almost all the way to the walls of the center pavilion. The invisible power battered at him like a solar storm, but stronger than anything that he had ever felt. Phutes felt humble and weak by comparison, but his anger at the humans gave him the strength to force his way through the maelstrom. The force felt as if it would cause his body to crumble into dust. It did not matter, as long as he could enlist Low Zang's help.

Because of the meeting with the human, they had missed standing beside the Zang at the moment when they triggered the destruction.

Phutes was 10 times angry with the humans. Now he meant to do something about it.

Sofus and Mrdus pressed forward alongside him. The creaking servicebot rolled along in their wake.

"What could withstand such might?" Mrdus asked. "We are nothing compared with these beings!"

"We are at least as strong as humans," Sofus said, holding a fist up to point. "Look there. The human female is in its midst. If she can bear it, we can."

Phutes forced his vision to adapt to the brilliance. Sofus was right. In the midst of the pillars of light was one small, dark shadow. She seemed untroubled by the forces raging around her. Her hair streamed straight out behind her head as if a gale were blowing in her face, one made of pure energy. Humans were stronger than he ever knew them to be. That made them an even greater threat to the motherworlds! The Kail had no choice but to rely upon the hope of Low Zang's help.

The Kail moved forward uneasily. The commune between the Zang was so intense that Phutes had no idea how he would manage to persuade Low Zang to listen.

And, yet.

A tendril of power, almost gentle in comparison with the gale, reached out tentatively, and touched Phutes and his siblings.

"It sees us!" Sofus said.

"Low Zang?" Phutes asked, hopefully.

The wisp touched them again.

What did you think?

The Kail looked at one another. They knew that the truth was none of them had been looking up at the moment of the cataclysm. But they had seen the burst of light as the planet exploded, and felt the energy pour out of the place where it had been.

"It was . . . astonishing," Phutes said. "In all our lives, we could never have imagined such a thing."

"You performed an incredible feat," Mrdus added. "The focus that you put into creating the spectacle will never be forgotten!"

The next touch was even more shy.

Really?

Phutes put everything, down to the core of his being, into his reply.

"I swear that it is true. Never in the history of the Kail has such a marvel been seen. You have impressed us with your power, your precision, and the efficiency of this event."

There was no mistaking how pleased the Zang was by their praise. The power it emitted brushed them again and again.

"You have created a marvel of art," Phutes said, greatly daring. "It is clear that your skill is inborn. My siblings and I would like to witness another of your creations."

Another?

"For the sake of our mother, Yesa, who sent us here to observe your talent and wisdom," Mrdus put in. He stared out from under the ridge of his brow at Phutes, who signaled assent. This was their opportunity! The humans should learn their lesson, when one of their own motherworlds was sacrificed.

But this one, was it not good enough?

"Oh, it was good, better than good," Sofus caroled to the Zang. "We are so impressed that we call upon you to help the Kail. As a mark of friendship between our two peoples, would you consider removing a planet that we feel is an excrescence and a blot upon its system?"

A hesitation. *You know of a sphere that does not belong?*

"We do," Phutes said. "It is wrong for it to continue to exist."

Tell me where it is.

Low Zang listened carefully to the irregular rhythm coming from the three Kail, certain that it had absorbed the primitive beat. When they concluded their statement of location, the trio withdrew to the edge of the room. Low Zang contemplated the possibility of a second spectacle. Such a thing had not been done in a very long time: that two works of beautification should be completed so close together. It was eager to make its mark and become a regular member of the group. This could bring it into early prominence!

Greatly daring, it revealed the Kail's request.

"Are you certain, so soon after this one?" One Zang asked. "The energy of your first work has not yet fully dissipated. Stop and enjoy it. We have .00002 hexaeons until it has passed. That is a sufficiently long time for pleasure."

"Was my performance well done?" Low Zang asked, hopefully.

"Well enough," Zang Quark replied. It was irritated to be

interrupted from absorbing the vibrations. "How should it be? You accomplished what you said you would do. It was not disharmonious. What more could it be?"

"It could be better. If I could try again right away, I could put into that working what I have learned from this one," Low Zang suggested, exuding warmth and hope upon the others.

Even One Zang and Charm Zang, who were usually so encouraging, were not sure.

"Should we undertake another removal so soon?" Charm asked. "We must consider the artistic balance of the universe. What you have accomplished here now will affect space for many hexaprags in every direction."

Low Zang was eager to defend its admirers. "They want to watch us do it again," it said. "They feel the urgency of being such ephemeral creatures. They are here in their 'now.'"

"They can wait," Proton said. "They are less ephemeral than my pet, and she never demands a spectacle."

"They are impatient," Low insisted.

Proton let the disharmony it sensed be felt. "That puts on us no obligation. We all have time."

"Their time is not like our time. They cannot return when we are at last ready to create another work of beauty," Low Zang said. It knew it was daring in pushing the group, but none of them had ever been as encouraging as the Kail. Perhaps it was wrong, but the praise put Low into greater harmony than it had ever felt.

"I am against it," Quark said.

"As am I," Proton added.

Low began to feel unimportant again.

"You honored me by making me part of your group," it sent, filling the chamber with a piteous sensation that nearly overwhelmed the ongoing vibration from the disintegrated planet. More humans entered the room. Some of them approached the Kail, seeking to move them out. Low added a hint of desperation, lest the opportunity be lost to please its new friends. "Won't you consider this?"

One Zang enveloped them all in a kindly air.

"We do not want you to feel less than one of us," it said. "Very well. I will consider it. What about the rest of you?"

"I accede," Charm said. "Come, it will be a new experience for all of us! It has been a long time since we waited less than .001 hexaeons in between removals."

Proton and Quark thought deeply, reaching out to the far extent of their senses. Proton was the first to return.

"I will agree, too. But we must be unanimous."

Low was jubilant. It issued conciliatory waves toward the conical Zang. "Please, Quark, it is only you. I respect your opinion."

"Very well," Zang Quark said, at last. "It is not unprecedented. Perhaps it will be enjoyable."

Low Zang was jubilant. It sent a touch of power toward the Kail. They dodged the humans and charged toward it, the floor shaking under their heavy feet. It was pleased to be able to give them good news.

"I shall inform my human," Proton said, opening its aura to attract the small female to its side. "The other ephemerals will also be interested in witnessing another of our works of art."

Low Zang managed to convey his success to the Kail with less difficulty than it thought it would have with such primitive creatures. They understood at once, and evoked triumph.

Only the mechanical at Phutes's heels seemed to feel unhappy.

CHAPTER 41

I had missed the spectacle by only a short time, but it was long enough to have been noticed and remarked upon at length. When I returned from the *Jaunter*, accompanied by an LAI carrying all the delicacies I had held back for the party, I was greeted by my cousins with shouts of laughter.

"What happened?" Xan asked, making a terrible face at me. "Did you fall asleep?"

"As it happens, I did," I said, determined to tell as few lies as possible. "For a while. Then I became involved with a subject of great interest that caught my attention . . ."

The wide-eyed silence that fell universally upon my nearest and dearest usually was caused by the sudden presence of Parsons. This hush, though, was tinged with an air of pity, giving me all too much information about the source of dismay. I pivoted in place with all the enthusiasm I could muster.

"Laine!" I exclaimed. I seized from the top of the mechanical at my side a huge bunch of fist-sized pink roses that I had brought from the hydroponics garden for just this very moment. I had only hoped it would be a little later on, when I could collect my thoughts. I was horrified to realize that I had not thought of her at all during the past few days. I thrust the bouquet toward her, hoping to make amends. "How delightful! I wanted to thank you, on behalf of all of us, for a splendid narration and guidance through an amazing experience."

393

She did not touch the bouquet. Instead, she kept her small fists balled up on her hips.

"Where were you?" she demanded, her voice more shrill than usual. "You were supposed to be with me and the Zang!"

For the first time since my return, I was speechless. "I . . . I was on the ship," I began. Naturally, I didn't say which ship.

"Oh, so you saw it?" she asked. One lovely eye narrowed. I quailed before her.

"Well, not as well as you did. In fact," as truth overcame me, "not at all. I am afraid I was a bit distracted."

"A bit?" Laine asked, her voice rising into a range that perhaps only bats could hear.

"You must have spent the last few days in a coma, cousin," Nalney said, in open disbelief. "It was amazing. To think such an event was possible—well, I am still getting over it. And to think that you had the chance to stand at the center of it all, and you missed it? That's scatterbrainment on a level that usually only I can achieve."

It could not, to my mind, have been as amazing as what I had just been through, but I had to take their gibes without returning one. I hugged my secret to myself.

"I am very sorry," I began.

"I had a place saved for you!" Laine said. If her eyes had been lasers, I would have been reduced on the spot to ashes. I humbled myself, with all the body language I could muster. I hunched my shoulders over my wringing hands. My entire person begged for her forgiveness.

"I am sorry, Laine. I . . . I just could not be there. I became tied up with another matter that took over my entire attention. Family business. I promise you I would have been there if I could. I am desolated to have missed the opportunity to stand with you. Please, let me make it up to you somehow? Come down to my quarters. I will have my valet make a special dinner, just for the two of us." I stretched out my hand to touch her fingers.

"No!" she said, recoiling from me in distaste. "Not a chance. Not if you were the last man on Earth!"

I smiled, projecting all the hope in my heart. "What about the second-to-last man?"

For some reason, that brought a reluctant chuckle from her.

Though our relationship may never again be what it was, Laine seemed in a mood to relent somewhat.

"Well, you may have another chance," she said. "This is unprecedented as far as I know, but Low Zang is so new at this. The Kail have pleaded to see another spectacle. The others weren't quite persuaded, but in the end they agreed. It's marvelous! Everyone is so excited. It won't be announced until it's certain, but I wanted to let you know."

I brightened. This was going to be a red-letter week for one Thomas Kinago. My cousins crowded around to hear the news.

"Another destruction? Of what?"

My enthusiasm persuaded a smile from the disapproval with which I had earned. Laine was happy to enlarge upon her favorite subject.

"I don't know yet," Laine said. "The Kail have been giving them the coordinates of a rock they say is cluttering up the skies in its system."

"Fascinating!" I seized her hand in delight. She did not pull away. "This time, we will remain together, I promised. It will be a treat!" I thrust the bouquet toward her again.

This time she did accept the flowers, burying her nose in the tallest blossom.

"How long will it take us to get there?" Jil asked, in delight. "We'll have to notify Captain Wold."

"We don't have to get back on our ships," Laine said. "We can travel there without having to leave the platform. It can make the jump and return us here to meet them. We'd be there in no time."

"Only one jump away?" I asked.

"Yes, so the Zang said," Laine said. "Proton has a way of giving me general directional information. It's how I tell the Trade Union where to move the platform."

I glanced around, as though the target was within sight. "This is nowhere near Kail space. One jump won't convey us even remotely close to their systems."

"Well, what does it matter, as long as they're happy?" Xan asked. His eyes brightened. "We will get to watch another destruction! This time I shall know what to look for."

Laine glanced up sharply as though someone had tapped her on the shoulder.

"I had better go back. They still need to give me some more details for the navigator. See you later."

I reinstated myself with my cousins and served my treats. Though I had surrendered the last of my truffles to Nell, I still had delicately pickled lily buds, fragrant edible fungi, divine cheeses and nut breads upon which to spread them, and petits fours and pastries kept in perfect storage against this moment. Accompanied by digitavids from Nalney, they related to me what I had so absurdly missed.

"It was thrilling, Thomas," Erita said, holding her hands as though clutching a grapefruit. "The poor little sphere began to tremble. It might have been long dead, but suddenly, lava began to spurt out of cracks."

"It was red," Xan added, his eyes lighting avidly. "As though it was *bleeding*."

"Horrible!" Sinim said, with a shiver. "I could hardly look!"

"But you did, dear," Jil said, patting her on the hand. "You stared, just like the rest of us. If the glass hadn't been tempered to prevent our eyes burning in our sockets, we would have been blinded! The planet began to shake even more. We could feel it here where we sat."

"Then," Nell said, taking up the narrative, "suddenly, the planet opened up along the cracks like a huge flower! We had only a moment to take it all in before the pieces shot outward! A huge chunk came rushing towards us. I crouched down in the cushions in fear that this was the last moment of my life!"

"Then they vanished," Nalney said, aiming a hand at his recording, which showed that very moment. "The shock waves kept coming, though. The whole platform bucked and trembled. Now I know what Proton was missing from our digitavids! Having experienced it, I can understand why a plain tri-dee was not as satisfying. I can't wait to see it again!"

"It looks as though we shall," I said, deeply pleased. "And I will do my dance at the conclusion of it, for you and Dr. Derrida."

With that very thought in mind, I went out in search of Parsons. Clearly, the Zang ignored most of what the spectators did during and after their event. It should matter little if I indulged myself in the performance of a lifetime.

Whether or not it was official news, the rumor spread about the second spectacle. Everyone, with the possible exception of the Donre, were thrilled at the prospect. To be able to account a double event in their Infogrid files was to make each of them the envy of their friends at home, even those who had experienced a Zang destruction. From what I could overhear as I passed them, a repeat performance had never in living memory been known to have occurred. I felt privileged, even though I was to witness only the second half.

I completed a circuit of the entire platform area before I finally spotted my quarry. Parsons emerged from a door I had not noticed before, in the angle between our habitat and that of the Kail. He looked troubled, but not so troubled that the sight of my bright and shining visage did not lift his own a millimeter or so.

"I am glad to see you have returned safely, my lord."

I surveyed him critically. "Well, you look like a rainy day, Parsons. Not that a rainy day cannot give one pleasure, but you resemble a downpour when a parade is scheduled. You should be curious about the upcoming spectacle. I shall not miss this one."

He studied me closely, a very slight wrinkle appearing between his straight black brows.

"Did you . . . enjoy yourself, my lord?"

I let the delight I had been cherishing spread across my face like a sunrise. "More than you can possibly know," I said. "I wish you had come with me."

"That is impossible, sir." Did I detect a microgram of regret? I felt suddenly as though I was rubbing his face in his failure to achieve that which only one other person in my lifetime had done. That was inexcusable, considering how much I owed him. I changed the subject with haste.

"You've heard the rumors?" I asked. He inclined his head a trifle. "But you do not seem pleased that the Zang will favor us with another project. I cherish it as my only possibility of getting back into Laine's good graces. I'm afraid that my absence has caused a rift. But you do not care about my love life. What is troubling you?"

"The Zang have chosen their target, but we have no means of determining where it is," Parsons said, keeping his voice very low. "We are concerned for the safety of one of the Core Worlds."

I transited instantly from delighted to horrified.

"The Kail wouldn't dare, would they?" I asked, my whisper hoarse.

"Laine told me that the planet they are considering is only one jump away from here. That surely cannot include Keinolt, although it puts Counterweight squarely in the crosshairs. What about Trade Union systems?"

Parsons looked grave.

"Between the mass of information that was transmitted from the *Whiskerchin* to the Kail on the *Jaunter* and the impenetrability of the Zang, we do not know. Did Dr. Derrida give you any indication?"

"Apart from the number of jumps, she doesn't know, either," I said. "But they couldn't contemplate such a thing! I recall distinctly that when we arrived here, the overture of destruction had already begun upon our dearly departed planet up there. If the Zang were to target an inhabited sphere, some manner of mayhem would already be visited. Mass panic would certainly ensue. There wouldn't be time to evacuate it."

"No, there wouldn't," Parsons said. "That is a point that troubles me. The Zang have not in the past destroyed a world with sentient life upon it. Dr. Derrida stressed that in two of her lectures."

"Ah, well, there," I said, much relieved. "It couldn't be one of the Core Worlds, or even Counterweight. I'd worry about their moons, though."

"That would cause chaos on the nearby planet as well."

"Laine will let us know as soon as she finds out," I said. "Perhaps it won't happen at all. Maybe the Zang will decide they've done enough, and go about their business."

"Oh, Lord Thomas!"

A most forlorn-sounding female voice reached me through the noise of the crowd. I glanced about for its source.

From the midst of the milling crowds, a bedraggled figure emerged. I could hardly recognize it as belonging to an LAI, let alone NR-111. Her housing was battered and cracked, and a bloom like a radiation burn had scalded the entire front assembly. Two of her lenses were dark.

"My dear creature, what happened to you?" I asked, as she homed in on me.

"Quiet!" NR-111 swiveled her visual assembly around. "Please, I didn't know what else to do! I had to tell . . . *someone*, and you're the only one who has been kind to me!"

I put my arm around her stalk and drew her into a recess that was shielded by a number of helpfully obscuring potted plants. Parsons followed us into its bower.

"You can speak before Parsons," I said, keeping my voice a discreet murmur. "He's much more reliable than I am. Why are you so troubled?"

"It's the Kail," she whispered, so low that I had to dip my head to hear. "They have given the Zang the coordinates for the planet they wish to have demolished. Low Zang seems to be enthusiastic about the idea, but it's terrible. I don't know what to do!"

I allowed my eyebrows to rise upon my forehead. "What are the coordinates?"

The lens array swiveled so that one of the eyes that was still clear met mine. "You must understand that this is against my programming," she said. "I am sworn to keep anything that they tell me in strictest confidence! But my primary duty is to protect human life."

"I am certain that you are doing exactly what you have been programmed to do," Parsons said. "Tell us what you know."

"I can't tell you, commander." The lenses swiveled to face me again. "Perhaps Lord Thomas? He seems to understand what . . . what I have been going through. And I have been so lonely!"

"Please," I said. "Confide in me. Consider me an honorary mechanical. I am sure you are doing the right thing."

"I can't linger! I will have to get back into the room before I am missed!"

"Show me, then," I said, tapping her small viewscreen. She must have thought it over in a microsecond, for a series of numbers appeared.

"I translated these from the binary," she said, her voice desperate. "It took some doing, but I am sure that I captured every digit. I ran a cross-check against the navigational atlases in my memory. I still cannot connect with other systems. You *need* to see it."

Parsons peered over my shoulder. "I see," he said. "Thank you, NR-111."

Upon seeing the set of digits set out, my blood chilled to ice. For a moment, I could not speak. My heart had moved up to choke off any words.

"I am relieved," Parsons said, with a microscopic nod. "These are not in Kail space, but nor are they near the Core Worlds or Trade Union territory. We were concerned that the Kail might target one of their home planets or ours. We must discover what they indicate." He raised his viewpad to tap them in.

I caught his wrist, a motion I would never have countenanced on any other occasion in my life.

"I know what they are, too," I said. "You needn't look them up. Don't enter them."

"You *know*, my lord?" Parsons asked.

I swallowed deeply. "I do. Parsons, I may not speak aloud what lies at this address, but I swear to you, it is more terrible than even targeting Keinolt and the center of the Imperium. They must not be permitted to demolish this place!"

Parsons studied my face. He was the most intelligent being I had ever known, of any species, and he knew in an instant what I meant. If ever horror dawned on a face, it dawned on Parsons.

"Technically speaking, sentient life does not exist on that sphere, my lord."

"Not now, but by the time we arrive there . . ." A terrible picture arose in my mind, of my uncle and his pets and all of Earth's treasures destroyed in a cataclysm such as Nalney had captured on his pocket secretary. "Our entire history is at stake! They can't do it! We can't let them!"

A wordless howl rang out from the Zang's compound.

"I must go!" NR-111 said. "They're calling for me!" She shot away, nearly upsetting a serverbot with a trayful of wine glasses, and zipped toward the door. We were left with a fact and a dilemma.

"It's such a heinous and cynical move on the Kail's part," I said. "Humankind has forgotten . . . the meaning of these coordinates." I stopped myself before I said the word. It must not be breathed aloud, not where so many listening devices existed.

"You were not present at the disastrous conference between the Kail and Envoy Melarides," Parsons said. "It would seem that their motherworlds and their mothers are one and the same. They are born of the soil in a quite literal sense. When Envoy Melarides suggested that humankind mine their worlds for rare minerals, the Kail reacted in an understandable fashion. The Imperium stated clearly that it wanted to kill one or more of their mothers. I have come to comprehend that in their view, there can be no greater assault on an enemy. They had come on this journey seeking revenge for past incursions against their motherworlds. From my analysis of the binary cloud that we have already translated, they were looking for bodies that were not listed in the standard atlas. I believe that we had a chance to forestall this attack. Melarides's error was out of ignorance. It makes the coming . . . event all the more horrific."

"Are you certain they know what they have found?" I asked. "It could be a shot in the dark."

"It is not a chance I am willing to take," Parsons said. "But how can we stop the Zang? Does Dr. Derrida have enough sway with Proton Zang to dissuade them from this course?"

"It cares for her, as much as it can," I said, casting my mind desperately back to see if she had ever caused them to do anything other than what they had intended. "They don't understand her as well as they seem to comprehend the Kail. These silicon beasts have managed to bend the Zang to their dreams of revenge, through their shrieking and dancing. I am not sure if there is anything we can do to stop this event. If they are thwarted, the Kail are still capable of corrupting the technology around them, and putting thousands of lives in danger. If there was any way that we could take the Zang aside and tell them what a terrible idea it is to perform a second demolition."

Parsons looked glum. "It is unfortunate, my lord, that we do not possess the vocabulary to persuade the Zang. I shall have to set some drastic measures into operation."

An idea struck me, so absurd and yet so perfect, that I turned to Parsons, hope shining in my eyes.

"What if the Kail don't know that they are being undermined, Parsons? What if . . ." I took a deep breath. "What if I can tell the Zang how important . . . those coordinates . . . are to us, without the Kail knowing what I am doing?"

Parsons eyed me with something approaching curiosity. "They have NR-111 to translate Standard speech for them, my lord. They will know what you are telling the Zang."

"I don't intend to use speech at all," I said. I straightened my back, and put every erg of persuasion into my posture as I could muster. "Parsons, I need you to release me from my promise."

"From which one?" he asked.

"The most recent promise but one," I said. Knowing Parsons as I did, he could recall every obligation under which he had put me since I was a small child. It should be the work of a moment to remember what was the penultimate assurance he had wrung from me. I waited, my eyes full of hope. His left brow rose less than a millimeter on his smooth brow. I could have crowed with joy. He remembered!

"Very well, my lord," Parsons said, gravely. "I release you from that *particular* word. I hope that you will be successful."

"I will be," I said, steeling myself for the greatest struggle of my life. "Everything counts upon it."

❧ CHAPTER 42 ❧

"Uncle Laurence," I said into the audio pickup of my viewpad as I ran. "It was so good to *hear* from you recently. I regret that we were unable to have any time together. I had a *splendid* suggestion: why don't you bring Elena and the young ones on a visit, *right away*! I am in the Zang end of Imperium space aboard the T.U. *Hraklion*, about to watch a *Zang spectacle*. Please come. This one will really *strike home*. I know we would all like to see you. Don't hesitate. Please do contact me when you receive this. Waiting breathlessly to hear." I heard the whooshing noise as the message departed. I had no idea if it would reach him in time. All I could do was hope.

I threaded my way through the crowd, toward the Zang's enclosure. Through the translucent wall, I could see Laine among the five members of the Elder Race, listening and nodding her head, with a handful of Trade Union officers behind her. The Kail, along with poor NR-111, stood close by. They must be very pleased with themselves, I thought with some asperity. How dare they consider destroying humanity's birthplace!

"I'm sorry, Lord Thomas," said one of the Trade Union security guards who stood by the door. "You can't go in there now."

I fixed the woman with a winning smile, trying to cover my worry.

"I don't need to go inside, but I would very much like to speak with Dr. Derrida. Would you be so kind as to ask her to step outside for a moment?"

The guard saw no reason not to grant my request. She left the door in the charge of her comrade and passed inside. She stood politely by until Laine excused herself from the midst of the Zang, and escorted her in my direction. I could hardly keep still. All of my protective instincts were bounding up and down inside me, screaming to be let out. I must keep calm, I told them. Everything depends upon it.

"What is it, Thomas?" Laine asked. "I'm still working out how far and where the Zang want us to go. The Kail have the coordinates. They could make this a lot easier by just giving them to me, but they won't."

"They are being exactly as cooperative as they were on the way here," I said, with a dash of debonair humor that cost me dearly to feign. My heart was pounding hard enough to be audible at five paces already. "I don't suppose it would be possible to persuade the Zang against this action, would it?"

"Why?" Laine asked. "This is their art form. It's a great honor to be able to witness them in action. I thought you wanted to see them do it."

No help there. I could not explain to her for fear of word getting back to the Kail. Instead, I took a deep breath. "In that case, I wanted you to offer the Zang a gift from me."

"Really?" Laine asked, her eyes lighting up. "What kind of gift?"

I cleared my throat modestly. "I have composed a dance to celebrate their artistic achievements. If you would ask them to permit me, I would like to perform it for them."

Laine smiled. "That would be wonderful!" she said. "I'll check with Proton. It's interested in things humans do. I'm not completely sure the others will notice, though. You know what they're like."

My heart sank. "They seem to have been listening closely to the Kail," I said.

"Just Low Zang," Laine said. "That's been kind of strange. I wouldn't have thought it would like Kail, because they're so rough. But it's worth it even if only Proton watches you. How long do you need to prepare?"

"Within the hour?" I suggested. My voice quavered ever so slightly. I hoped she didn't notice. "The sooner the better."

She touched my hand. "I'll do what I can."

"So shall I," I said.

Laine returned to the chamber and stepped up onto the platform close to Proton Zang. The lofty pillar edged away from its fellows toward her. Laine talked to it, her hands moving with graceful animation. The Zang didn't turn to face her, but after a moment, she smiled. She looked toward the door where I was standing, although I knew she could not see me through the one-way substance, and raised her right hand. Thumbs up.

I hurried away. Only an hour to prepare.

Word had definitely spread abroad of the second spectacle. Groups that had arrived separately, like the Wichu and Imperium visitors, were mingled together in mutual celebration, bottles and trays making the rounds. Even my cousins had added to their happy crowd, with fourteen Uctu and a Croctoid, as well as a number of visitors from the Trade Union and all of our adjunct staff. Lieutenant Plet sprang to her feet as I arrived.

"Sir," she said.

"At ease," I replied, glancing around the group until I saw my quarry. "We are on holiday, for at least a while longer. Ah, Madame Deirdre! May I have a word with you in private?"

My teacher rose like a swan taking flight. "Of course, Lord Thomas!"

Nell, across the circle, in between Oskelev and a couple of very well-dressed Uctu nobles, nodded to me meaningfully. I nodded back. She beamed. I raised a forefinger to my lips, and she nodded again.

"I require your assistance," I said, as Madame Deirdre and I hurried down the lift toward my cabin. "I need your help—an unbelievably important matter depends upon it."

"I am at your service, of course," she said. "May I ask what?"

I pulled her into my sitting room, shut the hall door and bent to meet her eyes. "I am about to dance for the Zang. Nothing has ever meant as much as this one, single performance. I need you to confirm that this is the most persuasive plea that you have ever beheld. No error is possible, and I have only an hour in which to rehearse."

She held her chin up and settled into a chair. "Very well, then. Let me see it. I promise I will hold back nothing."

Together, we went into intense preparation. As I arranged myself into my opening position, I felt the platform shift. Laine, unknowingly, was helping to carry the means of destruction and vengeance toward a helpless and innocent world.

Weeks before, we had choreographed a welcoming dance in which I presented all that the Imperium had to offer to the Zang. I displayed gratitude, curiosity, honor and awe, set to a sweeping, beautiful melody full of warm tenor strings and warbling flutes. I maintained the honor and awe, but I substituted for the others movements to convey the concept of Earth and all that it meant to me and my race, with nostalgia evergreen in my heart, and a heartfelt and humble plea to spare it. I had been observing not only Proton from the time it had come on board our ship, but the Zang in company. I was certain I could construct a dance of such meaning that it would be comprehensible to the Zang without being transparent to the Kail. At least, I thought, remembering the stiff stone faces, I hoped so. If I managed to get through to any of the Zang, I wanted to make them halt their action. They had already accomplished one goal. They did not need to do it again, particularly not to something that was so precious to me.

I threw my entire soul into the dance. Every move had all the power and grace of which I was capable. I drew the solar system with its dear little sun at the center. All its planets were beautiful to behold, but the one I drew to my breast, to give it protection and love against the onrush of doom, was the planet Earth. The blue globe, which I could still see so clearly in my mind's eye, must not fall, especially not for the sake of a work of art. Earth was nature's own masterpiece. It must be preserved.

When at last I sank to the floor, my body curled protectively around the small globe, I heard frantic applause.

"Oh, bravo, Lord Thomas, bravo!"

I looked up. Madame Deirdre sat bolt upright, clapping her hands. Bright streaks drew lines down both cheeks. She had been moved to tears.

"Was it . . . evocative?" I asked. She beamed.

"My dear, you have never been better. It will rip the hearts from anyone who witnesses it. That is not what we rehearsed, of course."

"My aim has changed," I said. "Will it serve?"

"Oh, yes," she said, then eyed me with a speculative gaze. "That second movement, when you began to draw a star. Let's go over that again. I think we can make it stronger."

I rose to my feet, my soul brimming with gratitude.

The meager hour flew by. Before I knew it, the public address system came to life with a trumpet fanfare.

"My lords and ladies, friends and companions, this is an official announcement! The Trade Union vessel *Hraklion* is proud to announce that the Zang have consented to favor us with a second star-exploding spectacle! We are just getting underway to a mystery destination chosen by our friends the Kail. We will travel through one jump point on our way. You can leave your ships in this orbit, or have them follow us through. In the meantime, we have a special surprise for you! Lord Thomas Kinago, of the Imperium noble family, a talented dancer and choreographer, will perform a dance for you! It will be carried on all station vidscreens in just about ten minutes! You won't want to miss this. Thanks for your attention."

The message was repeated in eight different languages, including the uncouth grunts of Kail speech. The very thought that they had targeted my people's motherworld over an unfulfilled threat against their own added steel to my spine. I changed into my dance costume, pulled on my boots and combed my hair. Then I held out my hand to Madame Deirdre.

"Come with me," I said. "We are going to change the future."

Phutes eyed the bouncing human warily as he strode into the Zang's enclosure. A hundred hovering camera eyes followed him and the small, thin female. They joined the other human, who gestured enthusiastically.

"What are they saying?" he asked the serverbot.

"Lord Thomas is offering a dance in honor of the Zang," NR-111 replied.

"More moving around? Do they not make us sick enough by their very presence?" Sofus asked, with a disgusted noise.

"It makes no difference," Mrdus said. "He doesn't know, but he will shortly have to perform a dirge. Fovrates and the others are looking forward to the destruction of the humans' motherworld."

"My pet begs us to pay attention to this other human," Proton said, as the tall ephemeral mounted the platform in their midst.

"What for?" Zang Quark asked, radiating querulous impatience. "He radiates disharmony. I do not wish my serenity to be compromised by irregular emissions. I am already out of sorts having to prepare for a second disintegration so soon. And moving within this human shell instead of freely on the waves of space is not comfortable."

"We are less than .5 hexaprag from the designated coordinates," One Zang said. "Those are familiar to me, as they should be to you."

"Ah, yes," Charm said. "It was a well-laid-out system at one time. The humans fled from it .002 hexaeons ago. It is not far, Quark."

"It is an unnecessary annoyance."

Low Zang did not speak, but emitted uneasiness. Charm was quick to sense it.

"We have already agreed to follow Low Zang's lead. It is but a moment in time."

"Why this human?" Quark argued. "At least Proton's pet exhibits a serenity similar to our own. This one shows a major disturbance in its psyche. You perceive that burst of blue energy in its aura?"

"That is the most interesting thing about it," Proton said. "Few of the humans ever evince that kind of brilliance."

"What an amusing shell it has donned," Charm said. "It is a flat two-dimensional representation of a solar blast. It's more than they are capable of creating themselves."

"Aspiration is no bad thing," One Zang said.

Sound waves in the middle frequencies started up. Zang Quark evinced discontent, although the music was not disharmonious. It was primitive, compared with the sonic emissions of the stars, but humans had not evolved sophisticated enough means of listening to ever have heard them. Still, One Zang observed, this had similarities.

The serene ephemeral, Proton's charge, indicated the lanky human as the main object of its protection, inviting the Zang to pay closer heed to it. Such a hasty connection was not in the Zang's usual custom, but it felt a .00002% curiosity arise. It might be enough to hold its attention. The creature moved in an energetic fashion, at approximately .016 of the speed of a comet in a gravity well.

He flitted about from place to place within the circle at the center of the chamber. The movements were tentative at first, not impinging at all on the Zangs' reality, but the blue energy that it gave off grew in intensity. His motions caused his aura to increase from a nominal .5%, scarcely worth observing, to 3%, and thence to 7%. Such passion was something that One Zang had not expected of such an ephemeral species. It was touched to see that a primitive being would be able to express fierce, strong emotions that approached reality. Then it realized, as did its companions, that the human was creating a star.

All of the human's energy focused upon one single point. One Zang was delighted to see that he brought this star into being, furnishing it with the light and heat of a burning point in space. Its influence extended outward, to the cold grains of stone that it drew into its orbit and warmed until they produced life. Not all, but one. One Zang could not help but be moved at how tenderly the human cradled and cherished the single tiny globe. If he had had the power of the Zang, he could have made this star and these planets, but as he was a mere human, all he could do was draw them into being as hypothetical entities in his unsophisticated fashion. Still, to One Zang's surprise, it could allow itself to believe in the reality the human was creating.

"Is that a planet he is showing us?" Charm asked. "How beautiful! I had not thought that humans were capable of such passion and powers of creation."

"Nor would I," Proton said. "This is . . . almost real. It could be .0000002% Zang in its intensity."

"What world is it that he seeks to protect?" Quark inquired. "Not that what a human feels is important."

"It is important enough that he enlisted my pet to bring it to us," Proton remarked. "He is pleading for its life. It must be the planet that Low Zang wants us to remove."

"He has expressed a longing for eternity and safety," Charm said. "Like their bodies are rooted in their corporeal form but extend outward over parsecs and light years, the system he wishes us to leave intact has meaning that extends throughout all of his kind. It is poetry. I did not think humans were capable of poetry."

"I feel," One Zang said, thoughtfully, "that we should reconsider our action. It is not necessary. If I recall the system, the planets lie in splendid balance. You and I, Charm Zang, did some very beautiful work upon it many hexaeons ago."

"I remember it well," Charm Zang said, fondly. "The system itself is a mere nucleus in the heart of its heliopause, less than .001, but with such a fine variety of spheres within it."

"Has anything fundamental changed in it since then?" Zang Quark asked, as the human gyrated before them. He seemed to be caught in a maelstrom that caused the energy he was emitting to veer toward the ultraviolet, as if in distress.

"No," One Zang said, feeling out with its senses. "It is as it has been."

"Then we should reconsider whether to do anything at all. Art is not necessarily served by changing a piece again and again."

"Sometimes it is," Charm reminded it. "But in this case, perhaps not."

"No!" Low Zang protested, feeling its influence being syphoned away. "The Kail wish that planet to be put out."

"But why? If it is so precious, as this human is demonstrating to us, shouldn't it be permitted to continue to exist?"

"It is no longer functional," Low Zang said. "The Kail insist that is true."

"Not so. We have protected it in our space for many hexaeons," One Zang pointed out. "It is a beautiful thing. You yourself once criticized our action in extinguishing a sphere, thinking that it might have had a purpose in future. Would you not say the same about this one?"

The human executed a series of grand motions, as if reaching out to the extremes to which a Zang's senses extended, but he drew the small planet that it created close to his body and sank to the floor over it, protecting it with his whole person. The music rose to a crescendo that vibrated the very air of the chamber, faded to a whisper, then died away.

"I am convinced," Charm said. "I had never paid attention to these humans of yours before, Proton. I was 1.9% moved. This was . . . almost worth noticing."

Low Zang did not want to admit it, but the human's performance had caused it to waver. One Zang noticed its emissions.

"Come now, youngster. You have performed a most satisfactory work of art in this sector. Be satisfied with it. There is no shame in admitting you have been hasty in your choice of a second work."

"But the Kail will not like it."

"They are ephemeral," Quark reminded Low. "In less than .007 hexaeons they will be gone, and you will continue. Do not base your actions on what they want. You must learn to think in the longer term. We continue through eternity."

Low Zang considered its colleagues' thoughts as the human rose to his feet and bowed to them. The passionate energy in its body was purer than that the Kail had evoked. It, too, had been moved by his plea. It glanced toward the three silicon beings with regret.

"I am sad to disappoint my pets."

One Zang bathed Low Zang in light and warm energy. "You are not responsible for their happiness, only your own. Have we reached a consensus?"

Low Zang hesitated, then released the tension in its consciousness. "Yes."

"I think we all know," Charm Zang said, adding her energy to One's to warm Low Zang with their approval. "All of us are in harmony. Our sense of artistic rightness has been satisfied. No more action needs to be taken."

"Agreed," One Zang said. Even the young one added its harmony to the others. "We are in concord. That is satisfactory. The universe feels right."

⫷ CHAPTER 43 ⫸

As my music died away, I rose to my feet. I felt absolutely spent. The soles of my feet had endured the dance of their lives. Sweat poured in an undignified manner down my back. My knees trembled beneath me, but forced them to stay steady as I bowed to the Zang. Laine bounced up and down on her toes, clapping her hands. Madame Deirdre added her applause, as did the troop of Trade Union officials off to one side of the room. The Kail stood stony, as I would have expected. But what of the Zang, my target audience? Did they understand me? Would they take heed of me?

I peered at the silver pillars. None of them had their eyes on me, but I could feel a roiling of energy in the room, as though a massive thunderstorm was brewing. Sparks of light flew in between the five Zang. I leaped down from my stage and went to Laine's side. She threw her arms around me in a crushing embrace. I abhorred exposing her to the results of my exertion, but I did enjoy the hug.

"What is going on?" I whispered. "What are they saying to one another?"

"I think," Laine said, her eyes shining, "that they noticed you. All five of them! That's never happened in all the times I've been with them. I expected Proton to react, a little, but the others usually pay no attention to me at all. What was that all about?"

"Our destination," I admitted at last. "I needed to express my feelings about it."

"Well, it was a hit," Laine said. "Look, the sparks have stopped! They're doing something. Can't you feel the energy rising?"

I bowed my head. "Yes, I can," I said, sadly. My heart sank past my feet and down into the depths of the platform. I had done all I could. I only hoped that my uncle had received my message and would escape in time. Poor, poor doomed Earth. The Zang were preparing for its execution.

But instead, the Zang bloomed in a blinding cloud of light. Zang Quark vanished.

"Oh!" Laine said. Disbelief dawned upon her face. "They're leaving!"

My jaw fell open. "They are? Does that mean they will meet us at the . . . the coordinates?"

"No! It means they're done. They don't stay around for long after a removal. They usually just go. Like that!"

She pointed, just as Charm Zang dissolved into nothingness.

My heart swelled with hope. Could it be? Could I have saved Earth? I waited. Three of the Zang still remained. I stared at Low Zang, if not the architect, then the potential contractor of my homeworld's demise. It wasn't moving, but I felt the energy around it grow.

The Kail, too, saw the Zang begin to dislimn. They ran into the cloud of light, bellowing and hooting their anger. Their voices were translated by NR-111, who rolled gamely along at their heels.

"Why are they going? What happened? Low Zang, tell us!"

As we watched, One Zang rose like a tree growing in a time lapse video. It spread a benevolent veil over us all, then dissipated in the light before it reached the top of the dome.

The Kail surrounded their patron. Low Zang must have been ignoring them, because Phutes and his siblings danced around them frantically, hoping for a reaction.

"Answer us! You befriended us. You promised you would remove the humans' world. Why have you stopped? Aren't you going to destroy the planet?"

Instead of answering, Low Zang seemed to collapse in on itself, shrinking down until it was no larger than the candle it resembled. Then, like the candle, its light winked out. Only Proton Zang remained.

"Uh-oh," Laine said, as a flicker of power brushed us both. "It wants to leave." She looked up at me and touched my cheek. "I've really enjoyed being with you, Thomas. It's been a lot of fun."

"Don't go," I pleaded, holding her hand between both of mine. I kissed her fingers. "Stay with me."

"I can't," she said, with a sad smile. "This is the way it always is. I'd better go get my backpack. I hope we meet again, although it could be a long time." She stood on tiptoes and kissed me on the cheek.

"I hope so," I said. She ran out of the room, taking my heart with her.

The Kail threw back their heads and bellowed in rage. I edged away from them. I hoped they could not connect me with their disappointment, but I was taking no unnecessary chances. As I moved toward the door, the Trade Union officials converged on me. Colonel Hoyne looked concerned.

"The Zang are leaving," he said. "Does that mean that the second spectacle is canceled?"

"Exactly so," I said, at last allowing myself to feel relief. "They have deemed the first one sufficient for our needs."

Hoyne shook his head. "Well, I'm just as happy not to have to keep people here. We're scheduled to host an arena tri-tennis tournament in about three weeks. This might have made us late. I'll have to make an announcement. By the way, that was a terrific performance, my lord. Do you mind if we keep the recording? We'd like to add it to the rotation on our in-room entertainment system."

"I would be honored," I said.

Hoyne glanced over my shoulder. "The Kail look like they're going crazy. You had better get out of here, sir. Dremel, escort him back."

"Yes, sir," said the female guard with whom I had spoken earlier. She took my arm. "This way, sir."

As I left, Proton Zang disappeared. That meant that Laine was on her way as well. Silently, I wished her a safe journey.

"We are betrayed!" Phutes cried, as the Zang began to vanish. "Low Zang was ready to do our bidding! Our revenge was certain!"

"Could that human have made them leave?" Mrdus asked, glaring toward the tall one as he was pushed out the door. "Get them back here!"

"We can't do that," Sofus said. "But did the human know what we had planned? According to Fovrates, the planet was hidden even from other humans in their database. Only we knew of its location."

"That means that what we know was revealed to them," Phutes said, feeling the acid in his core boiling and seething. "We were overheard! The humans have listening devices all through this vessel."

"No," Mrdus said, turning his three eyes toward NR-111. "We have been carrying their listening device with us the whole time." Phutes rounded upon the serverbot.

"Did you betray us?" Phutes demanded. "You swore that you would never reveal the secrets that we spoke to anyone we did not want you to!"

NR-111 moved a few paces away. Phutes pursued her and shook her until her casing rattled.

"I had to," she said, her voice passionate. "What you wanted was wrong. I couldn't let it go on! My duty is to protect humankind. Someone had to know."

"*That* human," Sofus growled.

Phutes closed his fist on the stalk. It crushed in his grasp. One more of the shining lenses went dark. "You were here to serve us!"

"I was loyal," NR-111 said. She struggled to get free, but she did not speak again.

Phutes was so angry that he tore the serverbot's housing open. He ripped the motherboard from her central processing unit and ground it into dust under his foot. The mechanical stopped moving. The stalk of lenses drooped over.

He glared at his two siblings. "We must get to Fovrates and set all Kail free! The offspring of the human motherworld must not escape unscathed!"

"All right, boys, come on," said the first of the uniformed humans. They lowered the colorful guns that shot unpleasant organic matter. "Let's move it. Your cousins are waiting."

The lights in the huge chamber began to flash on and off. All of the doors opened at once.

"What the hell is that?" one of the guards asked. Phutes took advantage of his inattention to knock the gun upward and shove the human until he skidded across the room, knocking others over as he went. He galloped into the open hallway.

"Come, brothers! Fovrates has taken control of this vessel. We will have our revenge on some of the human motherworld's children, in any case."

✤ ✤ ✤

I hurried through a crowd that was openly disappointed, and in some instances angry. The female voice speaking over the public address system was as gentle as always, but more insistent than usual. She repeated her information over and over again.

"Dear friends, the spectacle is over. Return to your ships at once. We are experiencing a technical fault. It is not serious, but it may result in loss of services. Please return to your ships at once. Your personal possessions will be returned to you shortly. This is not a drill. Make your way to your shuttles and return to your ships immediately. If you have any questions, please touch the interactive map on the walls or send a message to HraklionCares on the Infogrid. Thank you."

Parsons had sent a similar message, but with additional information that would have caused the spectators to panic instead of being annoyed.

"Evacuate your relatives at once, my lord. Fovrates has taken control of the platform. If the Trade Union officers cannot overcome his counterprogramming, our escort ships have orders to destroy it. All non-Kail personnel are being removed from the vessel as soon as possible. It is no longer safe. Evacuate now. Inform me when you are aboard a shuttle."

Nell stood on a table so she could wave to me over the heads of the crowd. As soon as she caught my eye, she disappeared into its midst. It meant that my relatives were safe, for the moment.

"What's going on, Thomas?" Nell asked, as I rushed into their midst. Erita had her glass raised for a serverbot to pour a refill of champagne. I seized the bottle and pulled Erita to her feet.

"The second event's been canceled," I said. "We have to go."

"We saw that," Jil said, holding out her pocket secretary. "Parsons sent out this memo saying to leave. But why?" I scanned the message he had sent. It was much more innocent than mine, with no reference to the imminent destruction of the platform. I wondered how much time we had.

"Because the Kail are on the rampage," I said, with a bored wave of my hand. Erita sought to retrieve her glass. "Come, now. You know what Parsons is like if he is thwarted. Back to the *Jaunter*! I challenge you all to a do-or-die game of Hide-and-Seek!"

"It's too boring," Nalney said. "All of my clothes are in my cabin!

I'm not going to lose ten thousand credits worth of custom goods. I've hardly worn any of them yet."

"Oh, Nalney, really," Nell said. She had picked up my sense of urgency. She didn't know why I was in such a froth to get everyone back aboard ship, but bless her, she was doing all she could to assist me. "Parsons told us everything will be brought to us. Let's go. It's too tedious!"

"Did *you* make the Kail angry?" Xan asked, raking me with a searching look.

"I think I did," I said, attempting to appear suitably chastened. "It looks as though my dance did *something* to upset them."

"Oh, Thomas," Leonat said, throwing up her hands. I pulled her up out of her couch and urged her toward the elevator block. We joined the enormous crowd. Together Xan and I made way for our family to move up closer to the center and enter a car sooner than perhaps we were entitled. I was polite though ruthless. "Only you could cause an interstellar incident with something so meaningless!"

"I thought it was very good," Nell said. "I cried a little. All of you did; admit it! But let's not quibble. I have figured out the very best hiding place, and none of you will *ever* figure it out!"

I was the last one to crowd them into the lift. My viewpad buzzed against my hip. I slid it out of its pouch. Lieutenant Plet's face looked up at me from the screen.

"The shuttles aren't armed, my lord," Plet said. "Get everyone down to bay 34M right away. My orders are to take you in the *Rodrigo*."

"Right," I said, clicking the correct floor on the control panel. "Good news, everyone! The shuttle is passé. We're taking my warship!"

"Have you redecorated yet?" Sinim asked. Thankfully, none of my relatives or friends was actively panicking yet.

"I'm afraid not," I said, with an apologetic shrug. "If I did, all the ships of the line would want to follow my lead, and the navy simply doesn't have the budget to equip them all the way I'd do it. Come now, we have to hurry."

I took my earpiece out of the rear of my viewpad and put it in my ear.

"Plet, can you hear me?"

"Yes, lieutenant," she said, her voice brisk. "Are you on your way?"

"We are," I said cheerfully, as though anticipating a party. "Are you ready for us all?"

A heavy sigh. "Yes. I'm getting word from *Hraklion* control. The Kail have all gotten loose. They're doing their best to contain them, but they've infiltrated the onboard system. We've had to run virus programs over and over to keep from getting co-opted by the Kail program." In the background, I heard Anstruther emit a word I didn't know was in her vocabulary. "Just get down here. We need to lift ASAP."

"Of course," I said.

I knew what the Kail were capable of once they had made contact with a computer network. I feared for the safety of all the other small ships. Unless Parsons had so equipped them, they lacked the means of freeing their systems from the Kail. Who knew what havoc the silicon-based creatures would do with them? Ram them together?

Until the lift car stopped at the 34th sub-level I was moving from foot to foot in impatience. As soon as the doors opened, I grabbed Nell's hand and began to ran toward Bay M.

I spotted the coral-skinned face of Redius peering out of the blast door. He beckoned energetically to us to hurry. My relatives had long training in removing themselves from the site of a potential hazard to clear the way for security forces to move in. Without ceremony, they fled up the ramp into the ship. Friends, lovers and employees followed in their wake. I waited until every one of them was in place before I raced aboard. Redius came behind me, speaking into his viewpad.

"All in. Close!"

I lifted my viewpad. "We're on board, Parsons," I said. "Where are you?"

"Attempting to halt the Kail's activity, my lord," he said with an annoying air of calm. "Return to the *Jaunter*. I will see you later."

CHAPTER 44

"Where is the human who thwarted us?" Phutes asked. Fovrates had pushed aside the desk and chair in the *Hraklion* office. 1110 of their siblings held the door against the security forces who were trying to push their way inside. "I want to kill him!"

"Just 10 minutes," Fovrates said, his good humor restored once the Kail had attained their freedom. "He is on the small ship that just departed from 100010 deck."

"Call it back!"

The bigger Kail waved a fist.

"It resists my programming. The humans have prevented the computer from listening to me. There are many other, smaller ships that hear my voice. I will throw some of them at it."

He swept his hand across the control screen.

On the scope, Phutes saw 1010 bright spots move away from the long rectangle that represented the vessel they were on. Calls and cries of protest came from the audio receiver set in the wall over their heads. He assumed that they were the humans on board those small ships. He did not care if they died, as long as the one human who had ruined Yesa's dream died, too.

The light that they pursued, one 101 times as large, kicked away from the rectangle at remarkable speed. At Fovrates's urging, the small ships accelerated to their maximum speed, but they could not catch up with it.

"They are too far behind! It will reach the *Jaunter* before we can destroy it!" Phutes honked in fury.

"Don't worry," Fovrates said. "We have our secret allies near the *Jaunter*. Their craft is heavily armed. It will destroy the craft, and our enemy with it."

"Send it!" Phutes demanded. "Send it now!"

The chief engineer chuckled as he waved his hand across the scope. A voice came from the audio receiver.

"Yes, cousin?" asked a thick voice.

"The ship nearing you, 1111000 kilometers distant. That is your target. Destroy it!"

"Ready and waiting," a lighter voice said.

"Where is your human?"

"I do not know. We let him do what he pleases. He can't do any harm. His servers listen to us now."

"Changing course," said the first voice. "Wish us victory!"

Fovrates let his big fist fall. "Soon the ship will explode and take that human with them." He glanced out through the windows at the humans. They were wheeling up a device with a heavy barrel. He recognized it as a welding torch for exterior hull plates. Behind them were 111010 humans, all carrying the colorful guns loaded with slime, led by a tall, thin human in black. "It will be the last victory."

"It doesn't matter," Phutes said, feeling sorrow in his core. "We will not have failed Yesa completely."

I settled into my custom-made crash couch at the rear on the bridge of the *Rodrigo*. All my relatives and our adjuncts had been bestowed in the common room, in sleeping cabins, and even in bathrooms, anywhere they could secure themselves against a potential collision scenario. I was gratified that none of them had emitted even a peep of protest. I had brought Nell and Nalney up into the bridge with me, as there was nowhere left for them to sit, and I preferred to have my sister under my eye.

In the screentank, I saw a dozen small ships leave the side of the *Hraklion* after us.

"Are they . . . chasing us?" I asked, in disbelief. "Those are pleasure craft. All they have on board are laser-nets to keep them from being holed by meteorites."

"I think the Kail are throwing everything they've got at us," Nesbitt said.

"This is the Imperium scout *Rodrigo*. Stand down," Lieutenant Plet ordered them. "Cease your pursuit at once!"

"We can't stop!" came the cry from one vessel after another. "The ship's flying itself!"

"Easily outdistance," Redius said, from the helm.

"Make it so," Plet said. In a moment, the small craft receded into the distance behind us.

I was impatient to get to the *Jaunter*, which I could see about fifteen minutes' flight ahead of us. "I have a better idea than Hide-and-Seek," I told Nell. "How about Sardines instead? We'll see how good we all are at occupying one hiding place without drawing attention to ourselves."

Nalney's dark brown eyes fixed me with a knowing glance.

"We'll go on lockdown without your urging, cousin. I understand that you're trying to get us into a place of safety. Just tell us where you want us to go."

I smiled. "I underestimate you all constantly, Nalney."

"The feeling is mutual, Thomas," he said, with a grin. "I'm dying to know how you drove off the Zang, but I suppose you will never tell me." His expression changed suddenly to one of astonishment. "Flaming nebulae, what's that?"

A strange, square ship came around the curve of the *Jaunter*, one easily half again as large as the *Rodrigo*. Red arrows of light lanced from its base—but what a base.

"Evasive maneuvers," Plet ordered. Redius put in the program. The *Rodrigo* turned and looped in space. The stranger followed, plotting loop for loop, still firing. Some of the bolts hit home, but our shields repelled them with ease.

"That doesn't look like any ship I've ever seen before," Nell said, peering at the scope, as the computer drew us an image. "It looks like . . . a house."

Indeed it did. It resembled a landbound domicile of four stories, complete with domed gardens, a gabled roof, and a chimney with four pots. In fact, it bore an astonishing similarity to what Erita had told us about Nole's new houseboat.

"They've stolen Nole's ship!" I said.

"That couldn't be Nole's," Nalney said. "He stayed behind on Keinolt."

"No, he didn't," I said, my eyes glued to the scope. "He's been following us all the time. I saw him on Taruandula."

"Why, you sneak!" Nell said, half-admiringly. "All this time!"

"I wonder where they left him," I said, worry overwhelming me. "He would never have let the Kail on board. I hope he is all right."

Nalney's brows lowered. "Kill the monsters," he said, his nostrils flaring. "If they have injured my brother, I'll tear the creatures apart myself!"

"High-powered engines," Anstruther said. "My telemetry says that this one can keep up with us."

"Open a channel. Attention the ship," Plet said into her audio pickup. "Stand down. I repeat, stand down!"

"We will destroy you," a coarse voice said.

"Kail," Redius said, grimly.

"Take them out, Mr. Nesbitt," Plet ordered. "When we come about, fire into the center of the vessel."

Missiles from the base of the ship peppered our shields. The *Rodrigo* jumped and shuddered. I noticed the gauge drop from 100% to 85% in the space of a minute.

"What kind of armament did Nole install in that thing?" Nell demanded. "Did he plan to make war on the Autocracy or something?"

In a moment, we would be close enough for the *Jaunter* to loose its big guns on the enemy house. I held my breath.

"Steady," Plet said. "On my mark." Nesbitt leaned over the controls.

In that moment, another missile came hurtling toward us. This irregular mass seemed to bypass the shields as if they didn't exist, and wrapped themselves around the video camera mounted on the forward hull. We all stared at it in disbelief. I got the impression of green plaid shot through with gold.

"My trousers!" Nalney shouted. "Nole's alive!"

"Lieutenant Plet, Lord Nole Kinago is on that ship," I said. "You can't destroy it."

She turned around to stare at me in open disbelief.

"Are you certain?"

"I am," I said. "I would stake my life on it. He is on that ship. We have to save him!"

"Very well," she said. "Take out the weapon emplacements and the space drive, Nesbitt."

"Aye, ma'am," he said. I followed the tracking on the scope as a quartet of missiles shot away. In a moment, I watched four brilliant white implosions erupt, three along the foundation of the house and one at the very top just underneath the chimneys.

The houseboat juddered. As we maneuvered, it continued moving on its vector without changing course to follow us.

"Disabled," Redius said.

"Good shooting, Nesbitt," I said. Nell and I cheered. Nalney looked worried, but I slapped him on the back.

"Nole will be fine," I said. "That was infernally clever of him to send us a signal like that."

"I'm sure he will," Nalney said, pensively. "But I wonder if my trousers will still be wearable after floating in the void."

The audio receiver crackled to life.

"Lieutenant Plet, this is Captain Wold. Fighters have been scrambled to capture the enemy vessel. Return to base. Do not continue with the engagement. You have precious cargo on board."

"Aye, captain," Plet said, with an expression of sincere relief. "Bringing them in now."

Naturally, all of the action had been viewed by our cousins and friends on the screentank in the common room. When we debarked, Nole's clever ruse was the only subject on everyone's lips. Our valets met us at the door of the landing bay and herded us into the lifts, not letting us off until we reached our day room.

"The captain wants you all in one place," Anna said. She kept beside me until I sat down on the nearest chair.

"Well, it worked out halfway as we wanted it," Nell said. She threw herself into one of the couches. "We got to see one destruction."

"I wish we could see the capture of the houseboat," Xan said. "But I will settle for an explanation of why you did such a tragic dance for the Zang, Thomas."

I shook my head.

"I was deeply moved by their first spectacle," I said. "I sought to make an impression on them. I am gratified by their reaction to it."

"So pleased that they left?" Rillion said, raising a derisive eyebrow.

"They moved him, so he moved them," Nell said, with a laugh.

Then, we all fell silent, waiting.

It was more than three hours later before the lift signal sounded. I rose to my feet in concern. I had heard not a word from Parsons or anyone else. When the doors parted and Parsons appeared, we all cheered. He nodded to us, inclining his head approximately one millimeter, then stood aside. Nole emerged behind him, his arms outspread.

"Well, family, did you miss me!"

I sprang to my feet and broke into a merry reel from sheer relief. We all crowded around Nole to hug him and shake his hand. Marcel, anticipating our gleeful celebration, sent out serverbots laden with champagne and biscuits.

"You dog!" Nalney said, assaulting him with hugs and blows as only a brother would. "Thomas told us you were following us in order to surprise us!"

"Yes," Nole said, with a grimace marring his handsome dark face. "And it would have worked, too, if it hadn't been for those wretched Kail. They've made a horrible mess of my beautiful new ship. The interior is completely spoiled!"

"We'll help you redecorate," Nell said, embracing him, "but we want a tour first!"

I sidled over to Parsons, who remained aloof from the celebrations.

"Is all well?" I inquired, out of the side of my mouth. "What has become of the Kail? Did you decant them all into space to grow up to be planets like their mother?"

"Special Envoy Melarides intervened on their behalf, sir," Parsons said. "She pointed out that their true goal was to ensure sovereignty over their territory. All they sought was to avoid having their progenitors protected from molestation by commercial enterprises. It was a shame that that information about their reproduction methods was never known before. The Kail are being conveyed back to their motherworld, after which that area of space will be under an interdict."

"Well thought out, and more merciful than I would have been," I said, lowering my brows. "I do not like that my cousins and I were put into danger from their fit of pique, let alone . . . that set of coordinates, long may they remain unmolested."

"Yes, my lord," Parsons said, and his expression softened a particle. The old boy was getting far too sentimental. "But it was your action that saved that one place from certain destruction. Your dance set the defeat of the Kail in motion, and subtly enough that they could not act before the Zang had departed. I must admit that it was very neat and well thought out. It appears to have rung true to the Zang."

I described a deep bow, in which the back of my hand swept my forward foot.

"I owe it to my teachers," I said, including him in the compliment. "I have learned the importance of never making a false step."